HIDD

AN ASH PARK NOVEL

MEGHAN O'FLYNN

PYGMALION

HIDDEN

Copyright 2017

This is a work of fiction. Names, characters, businesses, places, events and incidents are either the products of the author's imagination or used fictitiously. Any resemblance to actual persons, living or dead, or actual events is purely coincidental. Opinions expressed are those of the characters and do not necessarily reflect those of the author even though a day completely hidden from people and responsibilities doesn't sound all that terrible. That weapon-wielding psycho thing though … she's cool without that.

No part of this book may be reproduced, stored in a retrieval system, scanned, or transmitted or distributed in any form or by any means electronic, mechanical, photocopied, recorded or otherwise without written consent of the author. Just pretend she has a machete.

All rights reserved, and protected by medieval weapons and an enormous dog.

Distributed by Pygmalion Publishing, LLC

IBSN electronic: 978-0-9974651-8-1

For my children,
whose awesomeness inspires me to be a better,
stronger, more patient version of myself.
I love you to infinity and beyond, to the moon and back,
and even the boundless expanse of space
cannot contain my adoration.
Even if you prank me.
Maybe especially then.

Now put the book down, boys.
Come back when you turn twenty-eight.
Trust me.

OTHER WORKS BY BESTSELLING AUTHOR
MEGHAN O'FLYNN

The Ask Park Series:

Famished

Conviction

Repressed

Hidden

Redemption

"Alien Landscape: A Short Story"

"Crimson Snow: A Short Story"

DON'T MISS ANOTHER RELEASE!
SIGN UP FOR THE NEWSLETTER AT
MEGHANOFLYNN.COM

PROLOGUE

I ONCE CONCEALED my dominance beneath a cloak of leather. But I no longer need the mask.

I pull my body up, down, up, my shirt plastered to my back, the fabric sticky like blood. Every time I release my body below the bar and catch a glimpse of my arms, rippling with exertion, I can practically see my rise to supremacy in every taut muscle— each of them once so weak, now hard as rock. Even the lamp-light, staining the walls with yellow haze seems to shimmer off my glistening skin, not daring to touch me.

It was not always so.

I used to think my fate was predetermined—set in stone. Father told me as much. I threw like a girl. I was soft-spoken. Hesitant. No one saw me and trembled.

That is the mark of a real man, is it not?

A bead of sweat carves a wet path down my nose and I stare at the drip until it falls, then push harder, growling against the sting in my agitated triceps as perspiration trails down my cheeks like tears. But real men don't cry. Men play football and fight battles and work honest jobs that eat at their knuckles— construction, janitorial, even truck driving. I no longer detest the memory of my father's hands around my throat. A real man is an imposing force, one whose mere voice inspires terror, and now the rasp from my own damaged vocal cords is a testament to his brutality, the ultimate measure of manly affection. Father made me more respectable. He did his job well.

Outside a car honks and I feel it in my gut, one sharp prick of agitation. But it passes just as quickly, because the bastard driving clearly has no way to assuage his irritation at his own inadequacy but to pound on some blasted horn. He cannot do what I do. Creating is savage, requiring more slashing and tearing and stabbing than any macho job one might have—my work is the epitome of power. Of dominance. Unlike some stupid horn.

Those who cower behind their car horns, protected by cold steel doors and windows of glass, could never understand what this hot, raw power feels like, or what it has granted me. A woman who gave her love to an undeserving man, to some joke of a football player, deserves to suffer. A woman who looks at me and winces does not deserve pity—she deserves to be broken. A woman who availed herself of my friendship but withheld the devotion she was meant to give has little recourse when I show her my blade.

I was owed their affections. I was owed their adoration.

I was denied.

I drop from the bar and the floor shudders with the force of it, the very light wavering, as if the room itself is trembling within my presence. And it should. Because I know better now. Though I may have been rebuffed in years past, I'll never again let anything best me. I'll never again accept a whore passing me over for some shmuck, some jock spending his daddy's money, each fancy car an extension of the bastard's ego, a symbol of his power. Most men are of this type. Overt, free, undisguised, their authority always assumed and accepted because of the nature of their appearance—perhaps even because of their birth. In years past, women ignored me in favor of "better men." I was no more significant than the dirt upon their high heels. And in the midst of every denial, my father whispered in my ears that I needed to get up, stand up, put them in their place.

I needed to be a man.

And so I became one. I took back the women's affections from those self-proclaimed masters of the universe. Those men were more like mild-mannered shepherds tending their flocks, relaxed as they surveyed their domains, knowing the sheep were theirs to be slaughtered at will.

But they were fools.

I no longer have need to take; they follow me willingly, thankful to be in the presence of such power, grateful to me for showing them what a real man looks like. The lucky few that I've chosen will never again need to tolerate the affections of lesser men—now I have them for all time. Subservient. Silent.

Hidden.

1

EDWARD PETROSKY FELT it before he opened his eyes that Thursday morning: the pressure. Some days, it was more a tugging in his chest, like a motivated but sloppy panhandler snatching at his lapels. Today, an elephant was crushing his sternum. Tomorrow it might squash him completely.

He hacked once, twice, then swallowed the slime and watched the pre-dawn light spread slowly over the ceiling, trickling down the walls like dirty water dripping into a catch pan under a roof leak. *Drip, drip, drip.* Already the day was trying to make him insane.

The light reached the boy band poster on the wall above the bed, illuminating each gelled specimen with its frozen smile, and his heart seized, as always—but he'd never remove the picture. He welcomed that pain like an old, devoted friend. Other than the poster, Julie's room had been scrubbed of her, though her clothes were still boxed in his bedroom closet. He imagined her sifting through the slouchy socks and fuzzy headbands when she hit thirty, "Can you believe I used to wear that?" And she would have laughed. But now there would be no sighs of remembrance —all that was left were the clothes.

And that fucking poster.

A knock at the front door pulled him from thoughts of the

clothes Julie would never outgrow, but Petrosky didn't move. The knock came again. He rotated his ankles, trying to release the stiffness and the swelling. Maybe his chest would explode, the light would suddenly fade to black, and it would be done. But the light kept coming with the persistence of a leaky pipe—like that knock, begging to be acknowledged, when all he wanted to do was go back to bed and forget he was drowning under the crushing pressure of another day.

The knock came a third time, more insistent, each rap sending a stabbing pain through his skull. Petrosky grunted and pushed himself to sitting, the tattered comforter sliding from his leg to the carpet. The woman beside him stirred—maybe because of the sudden loss of the blanket, maybe because of the pounding from the kitchen—and shifted her weight toward the wall. She had taken her heels off, but still wore her miniskirt under one of his T-shirts.

His stomach gave a liquid lurch. He swallowed hard to keep the sour awful from creeping up his gullet and shot an agitated glance at the empty bottle of Jack Daniels on the end table. And the needle beside it–empty now too. Empty for two years, the length of time it'd been since he'd allowed himself to partake. Four months since he'd set the Jack aside. He still kept both sitting on that end table, a constant reminder of the night he'd overdosed, and the morning after when his partner Morrison had found him unconscious on the living room floor in a puddle of vomit. The horrified look on Shannon's face, staring down at him when he'd awoken in the hospital. And the cost—he was still paying that off. Morrison had taken him to a private hospital to hide his sickness from the department. The kid didn't know when to give up.

He punched the Jack off the table and watched it teeter on one square side then tip onto the floor where it was saved by the comforter. Jack was one smug bastard. And rightly so—no matter how many times Petrosky tried to walk away, Jack stuck like an infection too deep to heal.

Petrosky staggered into the kitchen, not quite limping but favoring his left leg though he couldn't recall doing anything to injure it. He coughed again, phlegmy, gelatinous, and spat into the sink. The foam appeared angry, a mass of slime tinted pink by the night-light on the wall.

"Hang on!" he yelled at the door. If they wanted to come this early, they could wait.

Petrosky grabbed a slice of two-day-old pizza from the open box on the counter and chewed off a stale corner while he poured grounds into the world's most unreliable coffee pot— though maybe it'd actually work today. His wife had gotten the good coffee pot in the divorce, along with the good half of everything else. The coffee pot spluttered like she had when he refused to sign the divorce papers, and then it gave up—like he had.

He threw the front door open before the knocking could blast another round of pain through his temples.

"What the fuck is wrong with you?" Shannon's blue eyes flashed venom— his partner's wife, always the instigator. Stray snowflakes clung to one blond tendril that had come loose from her bun in the blustery wind, and her jacket billowed around her pin-striped suit despite her crossed arms. Her car was still running in the driveway. The kids were probably asleep inside, on their way to the sitter so she could head to work at the prosecutor's office.

"Did you bring coffee?" he said.

"I'm not my fucking husband. And if you disappear like that again I swear I'll slap the shit out of you."

"Well good morning to you too."

"I'm not kidding, Petrosky. Morrison's worried sick. Says you dropped him at the precinct last night and took off. He's been calling you all morning."

"All morning? Where's he at?"

"At work. Like you should be."

A toilet flushed, and Shannon frowned as her gaze darted to the room behind him. "You have a working girl in here again?"

He raised one shoulder and took another bite of his pizza.

"Goddammit, Petrosky. You're going to lose your job."

But Shannon wasn't going to turn him in. Petrosky was the

only one who knew about the man she'd killed. Not that he'd use it against her—Frank Griffen had deserved to die, would have in short order anyway because of the tumor in his brain. "So what if I do lose my job?" he said. "Without me handcuffing your husband to this city, you'd get a free pass to move wherever you want." *Away from that asshole ex-husband of yours.* Roger McFadden was the head prosecutor in Ash Park. How Shannon still worked with that twat was beyond him, as was the fact that his partner didn't seem the least bit concerned about Roger's obvious desire to make Shannon his again.

She clenched her jaw and the needle scars around her mouth puckered—remnants from two years ago when a psychopath had sewn her lips shut. Still felt like yesterday, a sentiment his partner shared if Morrison's posse of guard dogs was any indication.

Shannon put her fingers to her temples as if the conversation was giving her a headache, too. "Listen, just ... forget it okay? You want to lose your job, that's on you. Just don't act like an asshole and make the kids ... worry about you." She dropped her arms. "How about dinner tomorrow?"

"Soon."

She rolled her eyes and turned toward the car.

"Taylor, wait."

She reeled back to him. "I married Morrison years ago, you can stop calling me by my maiden name."

"Some feminist you are." Petrosky stepped back into the house and grabbed a box from the floor of the closet: a remote control car that sang the ABCs when you drove it.

He thrust the package at her. "For Evie. And Henry, should he seem interested. Tell them Papa Ed will see them soon."

"You better make good on that, Petrosky." She stared at the gift like she thought it would be the last thing he'd ever give her. It just might be.

As soon as the door shut behind her, Petrosky grabbed another slice of pizza, watched three drops of sludge hit the bottom of the coffee pot, and then retreated to his bedroom, purposefully ignoring the pink princess night-light that cast a rosy glow on the countertop.

His blue button-down shirt seemed unnecessarily optimistic somehow, like he was anticipating lunch with the fucking queen. He hauled it on anyway, covering the tattoo of Julie's face that he'd had inked on his shoulder. The wound had stopped bleeding since he'd gotten it last year—but it would never heal. The buttons strained over his spare tire, hell who was he kidding, this was no doughnut, but the real deal, earned honestly through fast-food and booze. He could barely tuck his shirts in these days. He resisted the urge to kick the Jack bottle and heaved on jeans, gray sneakers, and his shoulder holster.

Petrosky turned abruptly when the phone rang, and followed the peal of "Surfin' USA" to the kitchen, scowling at the irritating-as-shit ringtone his partner had put on his cell, knowing he had no idea how to turn it off. *Fucking surfers.* He snatched the cell from behind the coffee pot—last place he would have looked if it hadn't been ringing. "What's up, Kid?"

"Hey, Boss. We've got a situation over on Pearlman, off Martin Luther King. Woman hacked up on her front lawn. Texting you the address."

"You know I hate tex—"

"Too bad, you old fart. I'm bringing you coffee too, so turn that ancient machine off."

Petrosky side-eyed the coffee maker, which was still belching steam into the air. There were three drops in the pot, same as when he'd left the room. *Son of a bitch.* He opened his mouth to give Morrison a snarky comeback, but the line clicked.

"Everything okay, baby?" The girl smiled shyly, like a little kid, but she wasn't a child. Old eyes stared at him from beneath mascara-clumped lashes, her frown lines caked with makeup. She'd removed his T-shirt to reveal a halter top and a skirt that wouldn't have been warm enough in May let alone in the dead of winter.

"I have to run." He pulled his wallet from the pocket of his coat and peeled off four hundreds.

Her eyes widened. She took the money. "You don't want me to ... do anything for it?"

"Buy a coat."

She stared at him, open-mouthed.

9

"Come on, I'll drop you back where I picked you up." He pocketed the phone, glowered at the empty coffee pot, and hauled on his jacket. Another day, another girl, another drive to leave her on the corner just as cold as he'd found her. Maybe today would be the day some perp finally put him out of his misery for good.

2

_____

THE UNDERCARRIAGE of his car groaned as Petrosky maneuvered over rutted side streets and fought a skid on a rogue patch of last night's sleet, now hardened to ice. The houses on Ash Park's east side were packed closely together, some with little more than squeeze room between one person's detached garage and the neighboring home. Most of the drives had been cleared of snow, the ice already melting on salted walks. Clean. Friendly, almost like those who lived here were inviting you up into their houses. The windows were the only sign of insecurity—most had bars. Clean up all you want, you couldn't prevent the destitute surrounding area from encroaching.

Desperation knew no bounds.

Neighborhoods like this had four kinds of people. Squatters who kept to themselves. Kids with college aspirations who'd probably end up working at McDonalds—not because they were dumb, but because they didn't have time for school when they were helping their parents with the basics. The third type was the old folks who'd moved into the hood back when Detroit was a thriving metropolis. They stuck to their guns—literally and figuratively—told stories about the good old days, and clucked their tongues when the squatters failed to take care of their yards. Sometimes the old bastards even called the authorities, like the cops had nothing better to do than settle disputes over fucking grass.

He turned onto Pearlman and frowned as the flashing red-and-blue lights from a parked police car irritated his eyes. Then there was the fourth type: the criminals. Burglars, dope fiends, the odd rapist. And of course, the killers.

The street milled with brass, most of them stringing yellow crime tape or barking orders. Asshole flatfoots who had no idea what they were doing. Around the perimeter of the barricades, people clustered in knots of three or four, appraising the bustling crime scene with shifty eyes. Almost all were over sixty —figured. Maybe their perp was among them, but more likely these fuckers were just busybody jerk-wads with nothing to do.

Petrosky parked across the street behind Morrison's ride, a Fusion that the kid insisted would save the world because it was electric. Though Morrison also said the car was blue when it was really a washed-out gray—a kind of pewter, like halfhearted thunderheads.

Petrosky couldn't see the lawn past the patrol car in the driveway, its lights flashing like a beacon for the lookie-loos, its tires probably destroying critical evidence. But what did he know? He was only a fucking detective.

He squinted through the windshield at a group of older males, one of them laughing at something the other said, steam escaping his mouth below a knit hat. Far too much fucking glee for the situation. When he felt eyes on him, Petrosky noticed the group of old hens standing at the curb behind his car, and glowered at a woman in boots and a housecoat until she looked away.

None of the other cops were watching the watchers. *Idiots.* They needed to pay attention; many killers liked to come back and admire their handiwork. Probably wasn't that type of situation—a front lawn stabbing was likely a robbery gone bad, maybe with a rape since they'd called him—but he'd been extra paranoid since the Adam Norton case.

It had been two years since Norton had kidnapped Shannon and her daughter, Evie. That he'd gotten away still chapped Petrosky's ass. And the house where Norton had tortured his victims was less than two miles from the frigid bit of loathsome tundra he was sitting on now.

Petrosky exited the car and started toward the driveway, but paused in the middle of the road to assess a pair of black streaks on the asphalt—tire tracks. From their perp, or some other assface peeling out? Someone better have gotten samples before the spectators showed up.

He glanced up at the sound of approaching footsteps, and here came Surfer Boy, a head above anyone else on the force and with teeth big enough to take a bite out of you if he wasn't always grinning like a pothead who'd just found out grass was legal. Though these days, the circles under Morrison's eyes were darker, the hollows deeper. The job—it got to you. Life fucking got to you. At least the kid still dressed well; the collar of his suit jacket poked above his wool coat. A buttoned-up Hulk Hogan but without the fancy-ass yellow sweatband.

He should get Morrison a sweatband. Kid would love that shit.

"They check this here?" Petrosky snapped, gesturing to the street.

"Morning, Boss. And yes, they got samples off the treads already. Pictures, the works." Petrosky could almost smell the animal on Morrison's leather-clad hands as he passed Petrosky a stainless steel mug. No Styrofoam. Save the damn planet, and all. *But screw the cows—leather gloves are warm.*

Morrison sipped his own coffee out of another steel mug with a peace sign emblazoned on the side in an aqua far too bright for any self-respecting officer. Same one every day, like the kid needed a reminder to be zen.

Morrison gestured to Petrosky's coat. "That the one Shannon and I got you?"

"That's right, Nancy. You make the best style choices."

"I'll tell Shannon."

Petrosky shrugged. It really did have a good gun pocket. Way better than the department issue jackets.

"You catch the Lions last night?" Morrison smiled.

Petrosky cleared his throat and narrowed his eyes.

"I called you twice," Morrison said. "Figured maybe you were … watching a game or something."

No, you wanted to know if I was plastered. Petrosky resisted the urge to slap the knowing look off Morrison's face. "I was just busy, Kid." He took a sip from the mug—Morrison's brew was far better than what his coffee maker produced on its best day. "Go brush your fucking hair. You look like you just went down on a donkey."

Morrison ran his hand over his haircut: short on the sides, thick and wavy and way too long on the top. The kid called it the "Marky Mark"… whatever that meant. "Speaking of hair, you should consider that Rogaine stuff. With a little spit and polish you'd be a hit with the ladies."

"Fuck you, California." He might have been irritable, but at least he was sincere.

"I grabbed you a granola bar too," Morrison said as they started up the drive toward the detached garage. "It's in the car."

"Next time, save yourself the trouble and hit the doughnut shop. What kind of cop are you, anyway?"

"Think outside the box, Boss."

"Just because *you* have a fancy English degree and more hobbies than James Franco doesn't mean the rest of us are evolved. Some of us are still talking monkeys."

Morrison raised an eyebrow. "What do you know about James Franco?"

Petrosky didn't have time to answer. Past the police cars, the lawn came into view, a knot of cops and techs in the middle blocking what was, presumably, the body. They stopped beside a kneeling crime scene tech in a hooded black jacket, and the man's gloved hands paused above the dead grass.

"What do you have?" Petrosky asked him.

"Small prints, big prints, some holes in the ground." The guy kept his gaze on the dirt, his face hidden in the black hole of his hood.

"Small prints, huh?" Frigid wind stung Petrosky's nose. That's why they'd called him. Sex crimes dealt with special cases: prostitution, domestic violence, child abuse, and the like. With a kid involved, this wasn't a standard homicide or home invasion.

"Yeah." The tech still didn't grace them with a glance. "The smaller prints go all the way up to the house, but they seem to start out here, on the lawn. Could have gotten here over the pavers in the back, though. Probably made by a child either way." He gestured to the street. "I'm thinking your killer came from the front, had the kid with him, maybe had the kid knock on the door to lure our victim out. But you'll be able tell more after they powder the door—the prints aren't my job today."

Speculation isn't your fucking job either. Petrosky squinted at the ground where dirt bubbled up through the dead grass like someone had tried to slice open the earth. "Let me know when you have something conclusive from forensics instead of bullshit suppositions."

The guy finally raised his head long enough to grimace as Petrosky headed to the sidewalk in front of the house, scanning for anything out of the ordinary—well, anything besides the dead woman on the lawn. The drive was still iced over from the early morning sleet. Glassy and slick, no indication that anyone had disturbed it since the storm, but precipitation could hide evidence or wash it away altogether—they'd check underneath the ice to make sure they weren't missing something. Beside the drive, the disturbance was more obvious; muddy divots marred the lawn as if someone had used the business end of a baseball bat to assault the ground. What the hell would make a print like that? A pole? But no, the marks were too big for that—softball sized. And ... the footprints. Some small, some larger, but none particularly deep in the frozen earth. Nothing on the walk, save a smudge that might have been a child's heel. And what looked like a sock print on the porch.

He leaned closer. Tiny pink threads were embedded in the mud on the ball and heel of the foot in uniform rows like treads. Slipper socks. Julie'd had a few pairs of those. From the color of the fuzz, the child was probably a girl.

A kid without shoes in the middle of winter was definitely a bad sign. Maybe she was running from the perp and had knocked on the door for help—which made the victim on the lawn collateral damage instead of the target. Without knowing the intended victim, their case would be even more of a pain in the ass to solve, and they still had a child in trouble. Somewhere.

"Victim's Elmira Salomon," Morrison said as Petrosky sipped his coffee—annoyingly delicious, as always. "Sixty-eight, slashed to death with some kind of large knife, maybe a machete. I'm going to head around back, check out the footprints on the side of the house." He tapped the folder under his arm. Since Shannon had been kidnapped, Morrison's paperwork had only gotten more specific. Must be the nerves. Maybe the guilt. Petrosky understood that all too well.

"Got a classified folder going already?" He asked, using his partner's weird name for the case file's subsections. "Thinner folders are easier to walk around with" Morrison had told him, though they tossed it all into the main case file at the end of the day anyway.

"Always have the classifieds." Morrison turned to leave, already opening the folder to check whatever notes he had on the footprints. "Got one for the scene notes too, and another one for canvassing in case we need to split up."

"Sounds like a waste of a tree," Petrosky called after him, then swung his gaze to the victim and the two crime scene techs on the ground by her body. She lay facedown in the grass just off the front stoop, her robe splayed out around her as if she were being smothered by a snow angel. Stiff gray curls coiled from her head like springs, save the ones that were matted flat with blood—blood, and what might have been brain matter. The stains on her back were wide, the gore a frozen burgundy under the dim yellow glare of the porch light—her heart was still beating when she'd bled through the robe. But the robe itself hadn't been slashed open. *Interesting.* Though she was on her front now, she must have been lying on her back when she'd been assaulted for that much blood to soak into the back of her clothing. And her legs stuck straight out as if she'd simply fallen forward and landed facedown in the grass. She'd been *arranged*.

Petrosky squinted at the ice around the body, then the exposed earth near her legs. There were a few footprints, but not the disturbance you'd expect with a major struggle. She hadn't had time to fight.

He stepped over to the techs. "You guys flip her?"

"No sir," one said. "This is how we found her. And the ME was already here, so if you want a look before we bag her ..."

Petrosky was already kneeling on the ground. "Help me out, tech."

The guy scowled but cooperated, and they gingerly flipped what was left of Salomon. The tech retreated as soon as her body flopped back against the earth.

Aw, fuck. A gaping incision bisected her throat, angry and jagged. The side of her head had been hit hard enough with a blade that white and gray brain matter, tie-dyed with blood, was visible beneath the gouge. On her chest and abdomen, half a dozen slashes—most deep enough to have caused death on their own—crosshatched her ribs, belly, breasts. Gaping wounds, gelatinous and wet, black with congealing or frozen gore. One rib poked through the surface of her skin like a sword made of bone. Surely her killer hadn't tried to rip the bone from her chest. Had whatever he stabbed her with gotten stuck? Probably the latter—the attack was vicious, but the killer'd had no time to remove bones or anything else. They were on the front lawn in a quiet, but populated, neighborhood; anyone could have shown up.

Petrosky glanced to his right, peering into the house which was not more than five good-sized steps away. The exterior doors stood open, a tattered piece of screen flapping in the January air. Another crime tech was prying something from the molding around the door, his pea-soup down jacket blocking Petrosky's line of sight.

Petrosky's boots thwacked against the walk and he tried to ignore the difference in size between his own prints and the tiny feet that had made the others. *Just a kid.* How much had the kid seen? Was the child still alive?

The tech at the door turned, a new guy with a crooked smile and eyes narrowed by the wind and some brand of Asian genetics. "Detective."

"What'd you find?"

"Stabbing, wounds to the chest and head. Bled out."

"I can see that, genius. I mean what are you doing up here?"

The kid reddened. "Oh, okay. Uh, we found some marks here on the molding. Pretty deep—had some power behind them. Like someone swinging an axe, but this was sharper. Thinner. And the pattern ..." He gestured to the doorframe and Petrosky leaned in to squint at the marks. Some were small—a few inches tops, the size of a standard knife—but each one had obliterated a chunk of the molding on one side. The other marks were long, much wider than an axe, the edges straight and uniform around the splintered wood.

"Two different weapons?"

"Looks like it." The tech nodded at the door. "And one of the weapons has a barb, like a hook. It yanked off sections of the molding when he pulled it out. Hopefully we'll get more when I take the molding itself apart." He shook his head. "Never seen anything like it."

A hook. That explained the rib. Petrosky locked his gaze on the lower gouges. Darker than the others, but not because of the depth of the slashes. *Blood.* Some of the carnage had splattered around the doorframe as if the killer had swung the already soiled weapon and missed, or like the blade had hit Salomon and then continued its trajectory toward the house and embedded in the doorframe. Had to be the same weapon used on the vic, but what the fuck would leave different-sized gashes like that? Had the killer really been swinging two different weapons?

"Definitely not the work of a seasoned pro," Morrison said behind him, and Petrosky turned. How long had that sneaky hippie been standing there? "He didn't just come here to kill her, or he would have planned better, kept it clean. Not your usual robbery either."

So why did someone come here and hack her apart? Petrosky stepped back onto the lawn and examined the front of her robe instead of looking at the bloody mess that had been her torso. The terrycloth was speckled with tiny bits of dead grass. "Was she on her back when you got here?"

Morrison shook his head.

Odd that they'd have killed her, let her bleed out, then flipped her onto her belly. Maybe the murderer hadn't wanted to see her face. Was watching her dead eyes judging him too much? Even Petrosky didn't want to meet her vacant stare.

"The neighbor flipped her." Behind Morrison, Officer Norman Krowly, the son of the chief of police, marched up the walk. Thick neck, wide shoulders, and the same fresh-faced look they all had before the job sucked the life out of them. Petrosky might have been bitter about working with Krowly if he hadn't suspected the chief would have no issue booting her own flesh and blood off the force if he fucked up. Just a few years back she'd fired her right-hand man for hiding an illicit affair. The chief had no time for bullshit. Petrosky liked that about her— except when she was on his case for screwing up.

"Neighbor was coming home from working the night shift." Krowly pointed to the house across the street. "He thought he could help her, picked her up to take her inside, but dropped her —that's why she was on her stomach. He moved her legs too because he said it wasn't right for her to be lying spread-eagled, like how she landed. I told him you'd be over in a little bit."

"So it's fine if she's on her fucking face in the dirt?"

"He feels shitty about it," Krowly said.

"He should. He fucked up a crime scene." Petrosky turned to the Asian who was wrapping the last piece of molding he'd pried from the house. "Get over to the neighbor's and take tissue samples. Blood, skin, hair, under his fingernails, the works."

"You trying to rule him out?" Krowly asked.

"Or arrest him if he killed her."

The Asian passed his bags to another tech and started across the lawn.

"Don't be afraid to hurt him a little," Petrosky called after him. The tech practically ran down the walk.

"I give him three weeks," Krowly said. "One if he has to spend another hour working with you."

"He'll be gone by tomorrow if he keeps telling me shit I already know."

Krowly turned to the crowd, which was growing by the minute. Petrosky scanned the faces: curious, sad, scared, but no one who looked excited because they'd just wielded a machete against their elderly neighbor.

"Off to finish the grunge work," Krowly said, eyes still on the crowd. "I'll have a list of names and addresses within the hour if you're still here."

"Fine."

"Thanks," Morrison said, and Petrosky startled. He'd forgotten the kid was there. Morrison jerked his head toward the house, eyebrow raised, and Petrosky nodded.

At least inside it'd be warmer. Morrison's fucking hippie coffee was the only reason his hands weren't already frostbitten.

3

THE TATTERED SCREEN LOOKED OMINOUS, but the front door itself was intact. No slashes in the metal frame. A tiny wooden entry table topped with lace sat on spindle legs just inside the door, a knick-knacky ceramic vase on top. The lace whipped around with the chill draft from outside like it wanted to fly away.

Petrosky squeezed past two techs into the kitchen. A pot rack over the sink held four saucepans, the handles all facing the same way. He ran his finger along the top of the fridge—clean. This was the job—looking, examining, pausing to take in every detail, seeing what others couldn't. But it took time, and there was a kid out there somewhere, probably terrified. The thought hooked a spot in Petrosky's gut, though surely that hook was smaller than whatever this psycho had used on Ms. Salomon.

Kneeling on the spotless kitchen floor, a twenty-something woman with jet black hair was powdering the lower cabinet drawers while a pimple-faced ginger peered at Petrosky and Morrison from behind owlish glasses. What was he, twelve?

"Thought there were rules against child labor," Petrosky muttered to Morrison.

"There should be laws against working the elderly, but then you'd be out of a job."

Petrosky snorted then asked the kitchen: "Anything yet?"

The black-haired girl turned. She looked ready to spit at him, so they'd probably worked together before, but he always remembered the idiots—she must be competent. *Good.* "Looks like normal patterns so far," she said, "no signs of an intruder, but we'll get everything down to forensics to make sure." She drew a breath through flared nostrils and brushed at the next cabinet.

Petrosky turned to the entryway. Freckle-face had disappeared.

Morrison put a hand on Petrosky's arm and the weight of that paw was so unexpected that Petrosky stared at it until Morrison let go. "Drink your coffee, then we'll check the bedrooms for signs of disturbance. Single woman, that's where I'd keep valuables. Jewelry anyway."

"You ordering me around, Surfer Boy?"

"No, sir." Morrison gave him a mock salute. "Just suggesting that the elderly need more breaks."

There was a snort from the floor. Petrosky decided he didn't like the black-haired spitfire after all. He watched Morrison go, sipped his coffee, wishing it wasn't so fucking good, and eyeballed a door at the back of the kitchen. Probably the garage. But ... the garage was detached. Had to be the basement. He tried the handle, but it held fast, and above the knob gleamed a newer model deadbolt—no way to jimmy that one with his Swiss army knife. He could break the door down, but—

"I haven't found anything yet, sir." The ginger had miraculously reappeared, freckles now redder than his hair. "But I'll make sure everything gets to the lab."

Evidently it was repeat-obvious-bullshit day. If only Petrosky had gotten the memo. "Got a key to this door?"

The tech's face fell. He shook his head and Petrosky pushed past him. They'd worry about it later.

The living room was immaculate. Unblemished floors. Couch cushions in a floral velour fabric, no stains, no evidence of sagging, unlike his own lazy bastard of a sofa. The two potted plants near the bay window didn't even have dirt on their leaves, not a smudge of grime beneath the pots. Nothing disturbed, no evidence of breaking and entering, no dust mites, even. Just their mess in the foyer: fingerprint dust, and the occasional leaf skittering around in the icy breeze from outside. Oh, and that hacked-up doorframe. If there was such thing as an afterlife, Ms. Salomon was looking down, royally pissed.

He headed upstairs. The guest bed was made so tight you could bounce one of the crime techs off it. Through a Jack and Jill door in the bleach-scented bathroom, Petrosky entered the master bedroom. The closet door was open, one neat row of clothes visible inside, but a wooden hanger sat lonely on a carpet where he could still see vacuum tracks. The bed was unmade, the comforter crumpled at the foot of the bed. Messy enough to be an anomaly.

"Looks like she heard something, grabbed her robe, and ran downstairs," Morrison said from his spot by the window, scribbling on a sheet inside his manila file folder like the notes would matter later—and they probably would. That was why the kid was in charge of the paperwork.

"Think she caught our guy trying to break in?" Morrison asked.

Who brings a kid on a robbery mission? But then again ... people did weird shit. And they had to rule out all possibilities or they weren't doing their job. "She heard something unusual, that's for sure. But that weapon ... a gun's far easier for robbery or even for a murder mission if he wanted her dead." Petrosky scanned the bedroom, disheveled by this woman's standards, exceptionally neat by his own. "I can't imagine he planned to come here and hack her up on the lawn. If theft was the motive, maybe she spooked him, and he grabbed the weapon from his car."

"Or she."

"What?"

"A female killer with an axe would have gotten enough power behind her swing to do ... that." Morrison abandoned his notes and pulled one curtain panel back to gesture out the window. "Hopefully forensics will get something off the tire tracks."

"Any signs of disturbance besides what Salomon did herself trying to get downstairs?"

"Not in here. But there were some other footprints out back

and around the side of the house. And the basement window—glass was broken with a rock."

"The door to the basement's locked," Petrosky said slowly. Too much of a coincidence that the one place someone smashed a window was the one place that was locked up. Either the killer was trying to get in or the kid was searching for a place to hide. "Maybe this psycho was looking for something—it could still be down there." He crossed to the dresser. A silver-handled hairbrush sat on top—fancy, not that cheap plastic shit he always bought—along with a pincushion and a paperback novel.

"The killer wasn't trying to get into the basement, Boss. The prints around the side of the house next to the window were the child's." Morrison went on to describe a larger set of running prints they'd found closer to the drive, a man's boot, sized eleven or twelve. Same as the larger prints out front. Morrison's expression was pained as he said, "I'm guessing the kid was running from the suspect and tried to crawl through the window to hide, but the opening was too small. The window breaking was probably what woke Ms. Salomon."

So the kid had tried to get into the basement and failed. If she'd escaped into another house, someone would have alerted them by now. And if the killer had simply been ambushed by a child there'd be another body on the lawn. A killer caught hacking up a woman wouldn't have hesitated to hack up a witness, child or not. So what were they dealing with?

A headache was taking root in Petrosky's temples, and the muscles in his neck twitched as if little electric currents were trying to jolt their way down his spine. "We'll check the basement anyway." Petrosky rubbed at his neck, trying to loosen the cramp. "Want to make sure Ms. Salomon doesn't have some huge coke stash down there."

"She doesn't seem like the type," Morrison said. "Though I guess they rarely—"

"Sure they do. Almost always."

"That's just because you're suspicious of absolutely everyone."

"Like you should be." Petrosky knelt to look under the bed but saw nothing, not even a single dust bunny like the ones that overran his place. "There's got to be more here than we're seeing." This guy had swung his weapon hard enough to lodge it in the wall, at least six times—way more force than was necessary to incapacitate an old lady. He hadn't just wanted to make sure she was dead. He'd wanted to tear her apart.

Raised voices from somewhere downstairs cut through Petrosky's thoughts—a female, yelling. He and Morrison looked at one another and hit the stairs.

"No, this is my mother's house," a female voice was pleading. "I have to talk to someone in charge."

Just what we fucking need. Petrosky's legs were leaden—his shoes felt tight. He needed a freaking nap already and it wasn't even lunchtime.

At the bottom of the stairs, Krowly stood with a pale, blond woman in heeled boots, pajama bottoms, and a poufy jacket that all but swallowed her thin frame.

"No family in my crime scene," Petrosky barked.

"Please, I—"

"What's your name?"

"Courtney. Courtney Konstantinov."

He cut his eyes at Morrison and Cali whipped out his pad to make a note. "I'll speak with you at the station," Petrosky said.

Her face was streaked with tears. "I just want—"

"Since you're here, we'll need a key for the basement door."

"I ... don't have one on me, but—"

Petrosky turned to Krowly. "Break it down."

"No, please, I'll get the key! It's around here somewhere!"

"We don't have time for a blind search."

"I just lost my mother, dammit!" Her voice had become shrill. "She loved this house, just—"

"We don't have time for a search," Petrosky repeated more softly. "There might be something in the basement of relevance to this case. I'm trying to catch your mother's killer, not play housekeeper."

Morrison put a hand on his elbow. Petrosky shook him off, but moved aside so Morrison could have a word with Salomon's daughter. The kid was better at that grief shit.

"Why is the door locked, ma'am?" Morrison's voice was so

slow and calm Petrosky could have believed he'd just smoked a fucking joint.

The woman's shoulders relaxed and she took a deep breath. "I know it's weird, locking the basement like that, but it made her feel safe."

Safe. Maybe Ms. Salomon had a reason to be afraid ... but a lock on the basement door wasn't going to keep anyone from hurting her. Hadn't kept her from bleeding out on the lawn. What was she hiding? Petrosky stepped forward. "Was someone after your mother? Did she keep something special down there?"

"Oh, no, nothing like that." The woman shook her head. "Mom kept it locked because she has bats living down there; bats and mice and maybe rats too—she was always freaked about disease or whatever. She never could get rid of them no matter what she did, and she is such a clean freak ... *was* such a clean freak ..." Her eyes filled with tears. "Please don't break it down. Please. I'll get you the key."

Petrosky stared past her into the kitchen where the basement door called to him like a siren, practically begging him to find a way inside. But the woman's sniffling, the beginnings of grief or maybe denial ... she was trying to hang onto something, anything she could control. Sometimes it was the little things that gave you comfort. Like a dead daughter's rose-pink night-light above the kitchen sink. And unbroken doors.

"There's no evidence that the killer even tried to get into the house," Morrison whispered behind him. "Just the kid. And the opening in the window is definitely too small for the child who made those prints to have squeezed through. I'll show you in a minute."

Mellow Mushroom was right. With the scene out front—the deep prints in the mud, the blood spatter—they'd have evidence if the killer'd broken in to snatch something in the basement. But ... they still had to look. Not like they could ignore potential clues.

"I can break it down." The ginger was staring at him expectantly, and Petrosky's blood pressure rose, pulse pounding in his temples. Who the fuck did this kid think he was?

"We can search the basement tomorrow," Morrison said. The

kid seemed keen to save Salomon's door, perhaps as a consolation prize for her grieving daughter. "We'll station someone outside in the meantime, in case the killer comes back."

True, that would preserve the evidence until tomorrow. Everybody wins. Well, except the carved-up lady on her way to the morgue.

Morrison squeezed past Petrosky into the foyer to address Courtney something-or-another, asking her about any valuables. Nothing expensive but a hundred and fifty dollar pearl necklace that she kept in a safe deposit box at the bank. Petrosky kept his eyes on the basement door.

"What about personal files?" Morrison continued. "Insurance papers, tax forms, bank account information?" The kid knew what he was doing. They didn't need tax forms; they needed access to the bank box in case there was any evidence that Salomon'd had an enemy—and with a crime this brutal, someone with a grudge was a definite possibility. A safe deposit box could hide a blackmail note. Unlikely ... but missing the smallest detail could spell a cold case.

Petrosky left them in the foyer and headed for the kitchen. *Mice. Rats. Bats.* He put his ear against the basement door. Nothing.

From the foyer, Courtney said, "Not here. She kept everything at the bank. Her accountant takes care of her taxes, or has since Dad died."

"What about passwords to her accounts?" Morrison said. Petrosky's head throbbed with a dizzying ache, but the chill wood of the doorframe calmed the heat in his temple.

Courtney sniffed. "Never wrote them down." Her voice shook. "She'd just tap her head and tell me her brain was a steel trap. I was worried she'd get old and senile, you know? And we wouldn't be able to manage her money. Now old and senile sounds ... wonderful." Her voice cracked on the last word and something in Petrosky broke. Every morning, Julie's princess night-light reminded him why he still worked the beat. Why he still bothered with anything. No child should die in a field alone, raped and burned and with her throat slit the way his baby girl had. And this woman's mother shouldn't have died on an icy lawn, a murderer standing over her, watching her bleed. *A hook for fuck's sake.*

"What about a boyfriend?"

Courtney snorted. "Absolutely not. She said my dad was her one and only."

Might be true. Might also just be what she'd told her daughter.

"Did your mother mention seeing or hearing anything strange in the neighborhood? Conflicts? Anyone who seemed sketchy?" Morrison asked.

"No, she really liked it here. I tried to get her to move over to Rochester Hills once I had the kids, but she wouldn't leave. 'Born and raised in Detroit,' she'd say." She wiped her eyes with the back of her hand. "I just can't believe this."

"She go to church?"

"Not since they got this new Pope. She says he's making a mockery of Catholicism." She blew her nose. "I really like him." She pressed her lips together and their silence stretched, the only sounds the crime techs scratching at cabinet doors and rustling evidence bags and some imbecile out front humming "Welcome to the Jungle" like a fucking tool.

Petrosky headed back to the foyer and her tearful gaze met his —not only sad, but afraid, a nervous twitch at the corner of her eye. Because of him? Or did she know more than she was saying?

"Any idea where that basement key might be?" Petrosky asked. Unless forensics came across it, locating a key would take time—time their missing kid probably didn't have.

She sniffed and looked back at Morrison, the safer one—or at least the more stable one. "I have copies of all her keys at my house. And I'll call pest control and have them meet us here tomorrow, just in case Mom was ... right." Her voice cracked again and she covered her face with her hands.

Grieving. In shock. She'd surely seen the bloody lawn, even if they'd already taken the body away. Petrosky peered past her toward the front door, then dropped his eyes before she noticed.

The yard was where the action was—not the basement. "You can call pest control, but don't let them down there until we've checked it out," Petrosky said. "Why don't you go home and let us finish up here. Bring the key in the morning and we'll look downstairs." He was a fucking sucker.

No, not a sucker. Their priority needed to be finding this little kid with the pink socks. Courtney was in the way, and Ms. Salomon was already beyond help—whatever was in the basement could wait. The child was the one in danger.

Morrison showed her to the door to make sure that she didn't touch shit, jotting down a list of things she needed to bring tomorrow. When she was gone, Morrison turned to Petrosky. "We'll have the car keys tomorrow too—no sign of disturbance out there anyway. For now, you want to check out the prints?"

Petrosky followed Morrison out the front door to the driveway and then up the drive to the side of the home. In the mud next to the house, one small set of stockinged prints led from the front lawn to the side basement window. They were covered with dust and what might have been that clay the techs used for casting indentations. The jagged remains of the window were gray too—the break itself no more than eight inches wide, marred with fingerprint powder and grime. Apparently Ms. Salomon's cleanliness did not extend to the exterior windows of a rat-infested basement.

"They take the rock she used to break the window?"

"Bagged in evidence."

Petrosky knelt beside the prints outside the window. *Small.* "Maybe six years old?" he said. "Seven? But they're wider than I'd expect."

"Might be the socks themselves, or the kid was wearing more than one pair," Morrison said. "But with the treads—looks like these bulky slipper-sock things Shannon bought Evie and Henry."

"Your son can't even walk yet."

"He's learning, though." Morrison beamed. "And Shannon wants to be ready. He misses you by the way. And Evie keeps asking about Papa Ed."

Shannon must not have told her husband that she'd visited

Petrosky two hours ago to tell him the same. "I'll come by this week."

"You said that last week."

"I mean it this week." He glanced into the backyard where the earth was hidden beneath a sea of cement pavers. No bare ground anywhere. "Looks like Salomon didn't even want dirt outside," Petrosky muttered.

"Nope. And they didn't find much back there with the sleet last night. Hard to tell where the kid came from. But at least the prints in the grass are intact."

Petrosky gestured to the divots in the earth, sporadic indentations beside the prints. "I was thinking he had a baseball bat or something to threaten the kid or even Salomon with, but the way these are smeared … looks like knees, maybe. Like the kid was running and fell." But there were so *many*, as if the child had fallen over and over. Drugged? Or just scared, tripping, constantly checking behind her? He could almost see the girl, face still round with baby fat, panting and scrambling across the frozen ground, her screams lost on the howling wind. Her pursuer was brutal, and surely angry after chasing her. They needed to find the girl *now* or they'd be picking up her corpse.

Morrison nodded. "I thought knees too, but I was hoping"— he dropped his gaze—"for anything besides a kid sliding and collapsing while running from a killer in the middle of the night."

"There's no room for hope in this job, California," Petrosky said. He could almost hear the little girl's screams.

"I've got you to keep me grounded, Boss."

"You won't always."

"You'll be around for a good long time yet."

"There you go again with the optimism. You need to think darker."

"Maybe I'll balance you out."

"Don't count on it, Kid." Petrosky touched the basement window and leaned down to get a closer look. Too dark to see anything, but he could hear a subtle rustle like tiny claws, then a tinny squeak that stopped abruptly when he shifted at the opening. Maybe a feral cat, but probably not. A cat would have made more noise if it took off across the floor. *Rats*. Probably had fucking rabies. No wonder the old woman was paranoid.

"You hear that, Cali?"

"Hear what?"

"The rodents down there—scratching." Petrosky scooted closer to the window, planting his knee against the brick. "Hello?" he called into the opening, half certain a bat would come flying out and slap him in the fucking face, all wings and claws and fangs. "Police ... anyone in there?" Of course there was no response save the keening of the wind and the distant prattle of the officers out front. Stupid idea—the opening was far too small for a child to climb through. He pulled his head from the window. "Glad the pest guys are coming out tomorrow. I'm allergic to varmints. All varmints. Rats and bats and cats."

"You're not allergic to my cat."

"I'm allergic to the idea of cats. Those antisocial assholes would eat your face off in ten minutes if you died of a heart attack in your living room."

"So would you."

"Yeah, but I smell better."

"That's debatable."

Fucking surfers. Petrosky started for the driveway. "Let's go talk to the neighbors and see what Krowly missed."

4

"WHERE EXACTLY WAS she when you found her, Mr. Frazier?"
Petrosky eased back onto the floral sofa, Morrison beside him
with his notepad at the ready. Though neat and tidy, this home
felt remarkably different than the one they'd just come from—
here, life went on, while even the air at Salomon's felt heavy and
still with death.

Derrious Frazier, the neighbor who'd found Elmira Salomon,
sat across from them on a green La-Z-Boy, wearing a threadbare
blue robe, red striped pajama pants, and the shell-shocked look
of a combat pilot. He'd taken a shower, and his wet salt-and-
pepper hair released the occasional drip into his bulging brown
eyes. He blinked, once. Twice.

"She was right near where I left her, only face up." It rang
true—the marks in the doorframe indicated she'd been killed
just outside the door, almost exactly where Frazier had dropped
her.

Frazier had been driving home from the factory, he told
them, just like every other night. When he'd passed the house,
he'd seen the open door and a crumpled body in the yard.
Petrosky furrowed his brows, watching the set of Frazier's
shoulders, the twitchy little movements of his mouth. This guy
was nervous as hell. Not that he shouldn't be after finding a dead
neighbor and fucking up a crime scene, but still.

"So then you ... what? Decided to pick up a woman who'd had her throat slit?"

Frazier retched, choked, got control of himself. "I ..." His hard-bottomed slippers clacked against the edge of wood around the thin rug that looked like wool but was probably cotton. "I shook her. But she didn't move, and that's when I saw the slashes down below and the front of her robe ... it was all cut up. Before I thought it was just the pattern in it, you know? Like maybe she'd come outside having a heart attack."

"You didn't notice the slices in her robe before?"

"I just ... I never would have thought ... and it was kinda dark, I guess."

Petrosky thought back to the scene. She'd been found right outside the house, and with the porch light on, it wouldn't have been "kinda dark" at all. "You're telling me that you couldn't see she was—"

"My eyes aren't what they used to be, okay? I thought that if I moved her inside where the light was better I could ... help somehow." *Clack, clack, clack* went the slippers. Somewhere a grandfather clock chimed—twelve o'clock. The longer the child was missing, the less likely they'd find her alive.

"So you picked Salomon up and then what?"

"I slipped. And she fell ... I dropped her." He looked at his hands. "I used to be much stronger." He said the last like he was trying to convince Petrosky, or maybe reassure himself, that this was true. "And then I called you." Frazier squeezed his own thumb, maybe testing his own strength, maybe punishing the digit for failing him.

"Did you see anyone when you pulled down the street initially? Other cars, other people, kids?"

Frazier jerked his head from side to side in a movement that was more like a shudder.

"Did you hear the squeal of tires?"

Again a head shake. "Why?"

"Got some marks outside the house."

"That's just neighborhood kids. Don't know any of them, but they always ..." His eyes widened. "You think one of them ..."

Nope. Not with the brutality, the fury, at the scene. Unless one of them was a psycho with a kid sister who followed him out on a killing spree. "Covering all the bases, sir. Now did you see anything at all out of the ordinary? Unusual lights anywhere nearby?"

"Nothing."

"When you got out of the car and approached the body, did you notice any strange sounds? Someone moving away or heading around the side of the house?"

"I ... I was just looking at her and it was all I was seeing." Frazier straightened at the sound of the front door opening. A gust of bitter air blew into the room, and a spry woman in cream slacks, a red turtleneck, and faux leather rain boots rushed around the corner, her unbuttoned black overcoat streaming behind her. But her black hair seemed impervious to rain and wind—piled high on her head in stiff curls.

"Derrious? Der—" She knelt beside his chair, gaze flicking from Petrosky to Morrison to Frazier. Frazier put his hand over hers and held it against his still rollicking knee.

She looked at Petrosky. "Is it true? About ..." Her eyes filled.

Petrosky nodded.

"Oh, dear God." She sat on the floor. "I ... not Elmira. She was a good woman. Never had a bad thing to say about anyone."

"That's not true," Mr. Frazier said, and Morrison stiffened. Someone was fucking lying, and it was probably the person trying to paint life all rose-colored. Real life was a shitshow.

"Don't you speak ill of the dead, now," Frazier's wife said.

"I'm not, Trina. She didn't like no one."

"She liked me fine."

Petrosky cleared his throat, adding enough impatience to the sound that both Fraziers turned. "Ma'am, what can you tell me about Ms. Salomon's character? It might be important for the case." Especially if she was enough of an asshole to have made a few enemies.

"She was a good woman. A good, good woman."

Mr. Frazier pursed his lips like he wholeheartedly disagreed.

"I don't care how good she was, ma'am," Petrosky said. "I need to know if she ever mentioned anything, did anything, that might have made someone else angry. What about a boyfriend?"

"No, no boyfriend. No other friends even." Mrs. Frazier stared at him, tears drying on her cheeks in the breeze from the door. She stood and backtracked to the foyer, out of sight for a moment, and the wind disappeared with a sound like an airlock closing.

"Ma'am?"

Mrs. Frazier reappeared, her face drawn. She swallowed hard. "Well, she didn't like her neighbors, you know. The ones on the left. They had parties sometimes that kept her up. And they didn't take out their trash every week, so sometimes it stank back there. 'Lazy fools' she called them."

"To their faces?"

She nodded.

"Anyone else she didn't like?"

"Well ..." Mrs. Frazier looked at her husband as she sat on the arm of his La-Z-Boy. "Her son-in-law, I guess. Called him a hoity-toity good-for-nothing. Though I seen her daughter—she looked happy. Well taken care of, too." Mrs. Frazier glanced from the floor to a candelabra on the end table and back to Petrosky. "She didn't talk to anyone else, really. Just me because I did her hair. I own the salon on Fifth." Her spine straightened —proud.

"Ironic that your husband would be the one to find her seeing as how you're her only friend."

Her eyes clouded, but like her now-silent husband, she didn't respond.

"Anything seem out of the ordinary lately? Maybe Elmira seemed off or mentioned something that distressed her?"

"Nothing I can think of."

Petrosky met Mr. Frazier's eyes. The man shook his head.

"I'll be in touch." Petrosky stood and handed Mrs. Frazier his card; Mr. Frazier's hands were too busy trying to squeeze the blood out of one another. "Call me if you think of anything at all, or if you see something out of the ordinary around the house over the next few days."

Mrs. Frazier leapt to her feet. "Around the house? You think whoever did this might ... come back?"

"I doubt he'll come back, ma'am. Just being cautious." Though

Petrosky hoped the killer would return to the scene. It was their best chance of finding the missing child alive.

THE HOUSE immediately next door to Salomon's had an unplowed walk and peeling paint on the porch rail. A blond girl who appeared to be around nineteen answered the door with a rat dog under her arm. She informed them that her ex-boyfriend rented the house and that they could take up rent issues with him when he came back from upstate.

Must be the party house—maybe the people squealing their tires. He'd have the techs grab a sample off her car and anyone else's ride they could. "Detective Petrosky with the Ash Park PD." Petrosky flashed his badge. "See or hear anything unusual last night?"

In the background a child squalled. The woman stared at them, sucking her teeth and ignoring the cries.

"Did you know Ms. Salomon?"

"Nope. But she yelled at me once, about Sugar." She lifted the dog higher, like they couldn't see that rat-fucking bastard already. "Said she barks too much."

The child's wailing grew louder.

"What about last night? Did you hear anything out of the ordinary?"

"No. I sleep like a rock."

"Did the dog bark?"

The child was still crying. The girl glanced into the house, back at Petrosky. "Nah, Sugar's a lover, not a fighter."

"Probably because she'd lose any fight she picked."

The girl glared at him. The baby wailed.

Beside him, Morrison squared his shoulders. "We'll wait while you go get your baby, ma'am," he said. "Perhaps we can come in, take a look around?"

That was one way to avoid getting a warrant. *Hey, can we check out your place, see if you're hiding a terrified kid in there? Maybe a murderer?*

She stared at Morrison, mouth agape. "I … it's not real clean right now. It's not a good time."

"Just go get the baby then," Morrison said. "We'll wait here."

She scowled—"Fine."—and slammed the door in their faces.

Petrosky turned on him. "What the fuck was that?"

"Kids aren't supposed to cry like that. It's not good for their brains."

"You read about that in *Good Housekeeping?*"

Morrison kept his eyes on his notes. Since becoming a daddy twice over, California'd become a real pushover. Though to be fair, Petrosky had no idea what his own wife had done when Julie was a baby—he'd always been out chasing perps. And he hadn't collared the one that mattered. Hopefully he'd do better finding the child who'd spent last night running for her life.

The girl returned with a runny-nosed infant wrapped in a blanket. Morrison took her information while Petrosky headed down to the sidewalk and lit a cigarette. Dark clouds hung in the distance, probably dumping more slush on the west side of Ash Park. A beat-up green truck meandered past, backfiring like a gunshot, the old man at the wheel goggling at the police tape as his tires crunched over the salted street. *Nosy motherfucker.* Petrosky squinted at the man through the haze of cigarette smoke until he disappeared up the road.

The door behind him slammed—Morrison, scribbling in his folder.

"Still messing around with your bullshit play-by-play?"

Morrison glanced at his wristwatch, jotted some more. "Just trying to be thorough, Boss." He pulled his phone from his pocket and snapped a photo of the Salomon house from the walk.

Petrosky blew a cloud of smoke into the frozen sky, violently, like it could melt the cold from the morning if he did it hard enough. "How's that going to help us?"

"Probably won't. But if I need to know what the crime scene looks like from this angle—"

"You won't."

Morrison balanced the phone on the page and made a note without looking up.

"If you want to write a fucking book, do that. But stop cluttering up my pages with useless shit."

Morrison flipped the notebook closed and shoved it under his arm as they headed up the walk. "If I *do* miss something, I won't have to come back. Plus, with photos you can get lots of close-up details you might miss with your eyes." He turned the screen to Petrosky. "See the ice on the evergreen hedges? You'd miss that just looking."

"Put that thing away before it freezes."

"My thing's just fine," Morrison said, but he slid the phone back in his pocket. "Really though, Boss, it's better to have notes. What if you forget something?"

"I don't forget." Petrosky tapped his temple. "Like a steel trap."

"It's hard as steel, that's for sure."

———

THEY CHECKED out a few more homes, a few other residents refused entry, and no one had shit to tell them. Petrosky left Morrison to finish canvassing the area and walked down the street to his car. His left foot skidded on a patch of ice, and his arms pinwheeled until he managed to right himself on his hood. After three hours of bullshit, his head felt like a drum that some jerk-hole kid had been pounding on.

Morrison had left granola bars on his windshield. Petrosky glared at them as he climbed into the car, then flipped on the windshield wipers and watched the bars slide off the hood and into a puddle of icy slush.

5

THE PRECINCT WAS BUZZING with activity when Petrosky arrived, the air clamorous with the tapping of computer keyboards, the flipping of manila folders, and the agitated hum of unsolved cases. He walked down the center of the L-shaped bullpen, past the six or so desks on either side. A few cops glanced up as he passed. No one acknowledged him.

Petrosky's desk was near the corner of the bullpen, a few feet from the large pillar that supported the roof and blocked his view of the rest of the detectives. Suited him fine. Morrison's desk off to Petrosky's right was at the corner of the L, so Surfer Boy had a view of his buddies from homicide, like Decantor, who loved to girl talk it up when Petrosky wasn't around—and sometimes when he was. Just last week Decantor'd actually had the gall to ask Petrosky what he thought of the Golden Globes, lamenting whatever jackass had won. He'd pretended to be deaf until Decantor rolled his eyes and sauntered away.

Petrosky shrugged off his jacket and tossed it on the back of his chair, then headed around the pillar and to the left where a hallway led to the conference room. Every doughnut box was empty but one, and thank the sugar gods, half a lemon jelly doughnut filled the void in his gut. *Lunch.* Morrison's protein bars were probably still lying in the slush by the side of the road, and for good reason—that hippie granola shit tasted like it was made out of crickets, cardboard, and broken dreams.

Back at his desk, Petrosky slumped into his chair with a new cup of joe, the precinct stuff, with the oily texture he was used to. It burned his throat with an acrid awfulness that relieved his self-loathing for liking Morrison's frilly coffee. And it was still better than crickets. He was raising the cup to his lips again when he noticed the sign— someone had taped a bad photocopy of a cat with the caption "Hang in There!" to the side of his PC. *Dammit, California.* He tore the sheet from the monitor and tossed it in the trash.

"Hanging in there" wouldn't do him a lick of good. He needed to get pissed. He needed to be as savage as the guy he was seeking.

So why the hell had their perp killed Salomon? He hadn't gone inside, so he wasn't after something within the house. And the footprints looked like he was chasing a kid; a kid who kept slipping and falling until he finally caught her. Then what?

The child. The child was the key. And she was in danger if she wasn't already dead.

The keyboard clicked under his fingertips as he pulled file after file from the police database. Background checks on Frazier, the man who'd found Elmira Salomon, and every other neighbor whose name he had. Most were nice old folks without a blemish on their record, but a few neighbors had misdemeanors, and others had surely flown under the radar—squatters and the like. He'd come back to them.

Abandoning the neighbors, he called up home invasions and robberies with fatalities, just in case, though he was fairly certain Ms. Salomon had simply been caught in the crossfire between a frightened child and her abuser—or maybe a child abduction gone wrong. But they'd already canvassed for children within a two block radius—no kids who looked particularly beat-up, and no one nearby with either a record of abuse or neglect charges or run-ins with Child Protective Services. Most of the neighbors didn't even have children in the home. A neighborhood full of elderly folks and the occasional caregiver narrowed the kidnapping pool.

And then there was the weapon. Searches for similar cases came up blank; the closest he got was a kid who'd killed his Sunday school teacher with an axe after years of molestation. Petrosky didn't blame him. A few standard stabbings, nothing close to a machete. A couple people had been killed in their yards over the last few years, one lured out and stabbed by an ex-lover, but he doubted this was an issue at the Salomon house, what with her pristine floors and her rabid mice. She was an elderly woman whom no one had ever seen with a companion and with the child's footprints ... not like some booty call was going to show up with his grandkids in the middle of the night.

Deductive reasoning. It was why they paid him the big bucks.

He made a few notes in the file anyway for Morrison's sake, then slapped the file closed and jerked open his desk drawer. A photo of Julie stared back at him, eyes laughing, dark brown hair cascading over her fourteen-year-old shoulders. Frozen in time. His rib cage constricted around his heart so tightly that he gasped, and his chest only squeezed harder when the phone on his desk jangled at him like a disgruntled Salvation Army Santa.

Petrosky pulled the cigarettes from the drawer next to Julie's photo, tossed them on the desk, and slammed the drawer with enough force to jar the phone from its cradle.

He snatched the receiver to his ear. "Petrosky."

"Hey, Detective, it's Brandon, down in the basement." Their lead forensics tech had the effeminate voice of a *Queer Eye for the Straight Guy* star which earned him quite a lot of ribbing. Petrosky liked him. He did a first-rate job, and did it quickly without a whiff of bullshit.

"Talk to me, Brandon."

"I haven't finished with everything, but I knew you'd want this now. The blood on the ground around your Ms. Salomon? It belonged to more than one person. Two different blood types."

They had their killer matched up already? Maybe. Petrosky thought back to the crime scene, the slash marks, the prints from that idiot Mr. Frazier, who had thrown around the body of his dead neighbor like she was a rag doll. "You compare Frazier?"

"Yep. Not his. Not male, either; the blood is definitely female and there are no matches in the database."

Probably not the killer—the child was injured. *Fuck.*

"Still have a lot of evidence to go through here, but the larger prints—your killer—looks like we're dealing with someone short, less than six feet, five-nine, five-ten, but stocky. Maybe creeping up on a hundred and ninety pounds. And the smaller prints are strange. Made by a person heavier than you'd expect for a kid with feet that size, so she might have been carrying something … a heavy backpack, maybe? The tire tracks were inconclusive, too common to mean much, though I can match the embedded soil if you get me a sample for comparison."

According to the neighbors, kids squealing the tires was a normal occurrence, and so far no one had mentioned hearing tires last night. But the loss of the potential lead still stung.

"Got tons of trace from the basement window," Brandon continued. "And the walkways too; I still have to run that. I'll keep you informed." The phone clicked and he was gone.

Petrosky liked him better all the time.

A folder hit his desk and Morrison's meaty palm landed beside it as Surfer Boy lowered himself into a chair. "The ME had a field day with this one," he said.

Petrosky flipped open the folder. "What's the deal?"

"Salomon was slashed open; wounds like what you'd expect from an axe or machete, which we already knew. First wound to the jugular killed her, but then he kept going, hit her half a dozen times afterward. The one that hooked her rib was done after she was on the ground—he brought it down with so much force that it drove the bone clear to her back before he tried to pull the weapon out." *Ouch.* Morrison grimaced. "There's a picture in the file of the weapon we believe was used. Took the substitute ME an hour to find something that might match. Bet he's excited to be filling in on this one while Thompson's out."

Brian Thompson was their usual medical examiner, and he was the only one Petrosky trusted to do shit right. "Who the fuck we got?"

"Woolverton, on loan from the east side. Knows what he's doing, but he's kinda weird."

That spindly little prick? "They're all weird." Petrosky squinted at the image: a tall wooden pole like a spear, but instead of an arrowhead on top, a long blade like that of a machete curved along one side. Opposite the blade gleamed a wicked-looking hook.

"It's called a billhook. They were more popular in medieval times, originally for farming and later used as weapons."

"Looks like he's opting for the latter." Odd, though, the weapon—brutal, sure to cause blood loss, yet not as efficient as a gun, and not useful for any purpose but to cause suffering. No one would have that by chance. Not like you could walk around with something so conspicuous, either—the killer had to have hidden it in a vehicle, maybe a van. Still, if he ever got pulled over, a weapon like that wouldn't bode well for him … he probably didn't store it there. He'd brought it to Salomon's deliberately for the purpose of inflicting pain.

And with the length of the pole, there went another lead—the killer needn't have been close enough for Salomon to score trace evidence under her fingernails. She wouldn't have been able to scratch him while he was whaling on her from five feet away. *Fucking coward.*

Petrosky grabbed his Styrofoam coffee cup and slugged back the dregs, a few drops landing on his shirt. He glared at them much the same way Morrison was glaring at the less-than-eco-friendly cup, but Petrosky made no effort to wipe the stain. "I still can't believe no one heard anything. Even the weapon striking the house would have made a sound."

Morrison shook his head. "So the girl shows up at Salomon's door. The kid's asking for help, maybe, but Salomon doesn't hear the bell. So the kid runs around the side and smashes the basement window. And before the guy can grab the kid, Salomon comes outside, maybe just to see what's going on, maybe trying to help, and he goes after her. Had to have had the weapon with him already—maybe he was swinging it at the kid."

Which explained the second blood type at the scene. Petrosky rotated his ankles which felt suddenly stiff. "Kidnapping or abuse then, since there wouldn't be a kid just wandering around in the middle of the night waiting for some fruit loop to grab them. She had to have a reason to run. And he had the weapon with him—it wasn't a crime of opportunity."

"Agreed. Oh, and I talked to the—"

"Morrison!" Isaac Valentine's toothy grin glowed against his dark skin as he approached the front of the desk. He clapped Morrison on the shoulder. "I hear the girls are taking the kids ice skating today." His smile faded when he met Petrosky's glare. He nodded. "Detective."

Kids and ice skating. *For shit's sake.* "Don't you have some work to do, Valentine?" Between Valentine and Decantor this place was turning into a middle school dance without the strobe lights and the fucking glitter.

Valentine's jaw hardened. "Catch you later," he said to Morrison, then retreated around the desks to the other side of the bullpen.

"You'd like him if you—"

"Fuck that. What'd you really come here to tell me? Besides the info on the weapon."

"Oh, just that I talked to the funeral home Courtney Konstantinov chose and secured everything for transfer after the autopsy."

"That's above and beyond, Cali." Like his big blond ass didn't have enough shit to take care of. Speaking of … maybe Morrison just came over to check on him. Petrosky narrowed his eyes.

"She just lost her mother." Morrison dropped his eyes to the files, refusing to meet Petrosky's gaze. "Did Brandon call?"

"He did. Was that your handiwork?"

"I was at the gym with him when I got the call about the case. He said he'd clear some time to look over whatever the techs brought back."

"Lucky us." Petrosky fingered his cigarettes. "I'm surprised your boyfriend didn't call you first."

Morrison shrugged and finally looked up from the files. "I haven't been to my desk yet. Maybe he likes you better." He winked.

"I figured he'd have your home number. Or catch you on your fancy-ass cell while you're *hanging in there* at the printer making bullshit signs."

Morrison's gaze flicked to the monitor and the empty space where the kitten picture had been. Petrosky pulled the cigarettes to him and tore the plastic from the outside. It wasn't even dinnertime and he'd already gone through a whole pack. "Brandon's still sifting through everything they brought back. But I'm concerned about what he found so far." He filled Morrison in on the blood at the scene, their tiny, injured kidnapping victim, and their stocky, uninjured perp. "And with the larger prints on the ground, and the height and weight, we're definitely not dealing with a female killer. This was one angry dude."

"Dude?"

Dammit. "You know what I mean. Our killer hurt a child who was trying to escape from him—and he was furious. Salomon saw it and he killed her." But he hadn't just killed her—he'd butchered her. And the child was hurt too, bleeding. Maybe dead already.

Petrosky pictured his daughter's face, smiling from the drawer, and then the image taken weeks after that, the one where she was lying on a slab in the morgue, eyes closed forever, a gouge below her chin black with crusted blood. The rest of her body was covered so he couldn't see, so he'd never have to know everything. But Thompson had told him more than enough—those words still echoed in his brain some nights. Severed jugular. Raped. Burned flesh. He'd forced it all from his head on the advice of Dr. McCallum, the department shrink who'd told him to ignore those little voices before they drove him insane. But ignoring them hadn't helped bring Julie back, and his sanity remained questionable.

Morrison's usually jolly face had darkened. "The little girl could be dead now. And if she isn't … well, if we believe the statistics, it's doubtful she'll make it out alive."

Morrison's own daughter had beat those odds, but it looked like Petrosky would bring him over to the dark side after all. Light was elusive. And in this line of work, it often seemed you were already in hell.

6

FRIDAY MORNING, Petrosky met Morrison at the precinct and they rode to Salomon's house together, the weight of the gray sky pressing down on every inch of the car like a dirty blanket. Morrison had his usual hippie peace sign cup and had brought Petrosky another stainless steel mug since Petrosky had misplaced yesterday's. It wasn't the first time. It wouldn't be the last.

Petrosky took a slug, saw Morrison watching him, and grimaced for good measure. Morrison snorted, turning to the window as Petrosky's cell rang.

"Petrosky."

"There's a pest control truck outside Elmira's house! She'd never—"

He set the coffee mug in the cupholder. "Who is this?"

"Mrs. Frazier. You said to call you if—"

"A pest control vehicle strikes you as unusual?"

"Oh, yes, Elmira wouldn't use those chemicals. Said they gave her a headache. And she was bothered by the poisons they give mice too. Cats could get into them."

No wonder Salomon hadn't called anyone in for the basement. OCD cleaning meets OCD chemical avoidance. He glanced at Morrison's mug. Or hippie-eco-obsession. Shunning rat poison in favor of varmints and black plague. Who wouldn't love that?

"Her daughter ordered the truck," Petrosky said. "It's under control." He pocketed the phone and Morrison raised an eyebrow. "Step on it. Pest control's already there."

True to Frazier's word, there was a Speedy Kill Pest Control truck outside the Salomon house when they arrived, along with a black Mercedes that had to be Courtney's. Inside, they found Courtney sitting at the kitchen table with a man in green coveralls. Olive skin, bushy eyebrows, hairy as a gorilla. A knee-high plastic tank with a long snake of tubing ending in a nozzle sat at his feet next to a set of three metal cages—empty, for now. Courtney and the pest control man stood when Petrosky and Morrison entered, the man's eyes darting everywhere but at them.

"You didn't go downstairs yet, did you?" Petrosky asked him. The guy shook his head and gazed at the floor, fingering the nozzle on his tank.

"No, we were waiting for you," Courtney said. "I thought I'd have him check out the rest of the house first. Spray. Need to do it for resale anyway."

She was wasting no time with her dead mother's estate— moving suspiciously quick. But he wasn't getting that psycho vibe from her, and how depraved would a daughter have to be to tear apart her mother, then go after some kid? "The key to the basement?" Petrosky asked, narrowing his eyes at the freshly mopped floor.

Courtney held up a yellow key ring, five keys dangling like miniature knives: two small and metal, perhaps for the safe deposit boxes or a shed, two larger metal door keys, and one with the top sheathed in black plastic, probably for the car.

"We're going to check the car too." That'd take five minutes, and if Petrosky was honest, he was in no hurry to creep downstairs and mingle with a bunch of rodents. "Keys to anything else here on that ring? A safe here in the house? A shed?"

She pursed her lips. "No. One of them is to the safe deposit box at the bank. Once I have the death certificate and her will I'm sure I can get in."

"We can make it happen sooner if we need to," Petrosky said, trying to ignore the way the pest control man kept looking at his watch. *Murder infringing on your screwing around?* He'd make the twitchy asshole wait.

Petrosky extended his hand and she thrust the key ring at him, probably angry at the intrusion—or else it was the grief. He knew as well as anyone how the anger bubbled up to keep the sorrow from eating your goddamn heart.

"I'm making coffee," she said. "I'm not going back out in the cold."

Thank fucking god. Petrosky turned to the pest dude who was shuffling his feet like a bored little kid. "And Mister—"

"Spiros." He met Petrosky's eyes finally—his whites were bloodshot like he was stoned out of his gourd. His hands worked the chemical tubing. *Fucking high-on.* Figured. Not that Petrosky had the time—or desire—to arrest some jerk-off for possession, but shit.

"Mr. Spiros, feel free to take care of the rest of the house. When you're done, wait here." Petrosky ignored the dazed look in Spiros's eyes and led Morrison out the front door to the driveway. "She didn't even offer us coffee. Rude."

Petrosky coughed, like his lungs were angry at the icy air in his throat, and unlocked the door to the old Bonneville. The door hinges squealed. "Someone doesn't like WD-40." Consistent with her not liking chemicals, at least.

He slid into the driver's seat, banged his knee on the wheel, and cursed. "Get in here, Kid."

Morrison went around the passenger side and climbed in, popping the glove box as Petrosky opened the center console.

"Damn, she's organized." Morrison flipped through what looked like a small leather checkbook. "Insurance papers and tag information, even the receipt from the Secretary of State. She's a street cop's dream."

Petrosky turned and looked into the backseat where the blue cloth actually bore vacuum tracks. Tracks like that would stay for a long time if no one sat back there—and likely, no one had. Most of the neighbors described her as a homebody. Didn't go out. Even her hairstylist came to her.

Petrosky exited the car and headed for the back. The trunk contained a roadside kit that included jumper cables, flares, and fuses, all still in sealed packages. Nothing else. Not a single speck of lint. But beneath the backseat he found one lone dime. She wasn't perfect after all, and this was oddly comforting.

Petrosky was reaching to open the compartment for the spare tire when he heard a scream from inside the house. Courtney. He jolted upright and smashed the back of his head against the inside of the trunk. "Jesus fucking Christ."

Morrison was already running, and Petrosky hauled after him up the walk and through the front door. Courtney was standing at the opening to the basement, eyes wide with terror.

"What the—" Petrosky began, but the scream came again, high and long. Not Courtney—from the basement. Mister we-kill-all-the-fucking-bugs.

Goddammit all to hell.

Morrison ran down the stairs, nearly busting his forehead on the ceiling in the narrow descent. Petrosky huffed after him, hand on the railing as if it would help ease the tightness around his heart, and watched Morrison hit the bottom stair like a fucking gymnast. And here came their screamer. Spiros ran smack into Morrison's barrel chest, bounced off like a rubber ball, and landed on his ass on the cement floor. He bounced up just as fast.

"Oh lord Jesus, oh lord Jesus."

Morrison put a hand on the man's shoulder. "Mr. Spiros, you're going to have to calm down and tell us—"

Spiros's gaze flicked up the stairs, then back to the dark bowels of the basement. "Let me out—"

"What seems to be the—"

"Jesus, let me out of here!" Spiros wheezed. He tried to escape up the stairs, Morrison's hand falling from his shoulder.

Petrosky grabbed Spiros by the shirt and slammed him against the wall at the foot of the stairs, his forearm and elbow across the guy's throat. *Deaf prick.* "What part of 'wait for us to go down' did you not fucking understand?"

"I forgot, okay? I forgot. Please—"

"You ignored the police. I should take you in."

"No, I forgot, I really—"

"You high, asshole?" Petrosky put his face close enough to Spiros's that he could smell his coffee breath and the fear radiating off him. And the hint of musty pot smoke beneath his breakfast. "Thought you'd get stoned before you showed up to work?"

"I have a bad back and—"

Petrosky pulled him off the wall and slammed him back hard enough that the fucker's head hit the cement.

Spiros made the sign of the cross and choked back a sob. "I'm sorry, I'm so sorry, please, just let me go upstairs."

Petrosky felt pressure on his arm as Morrison grabbed him. *All right, Kid, all right.* He loosened his grip and the exterminator fled up the stairs, tripping twice before he disappeared through the door into the kitchen. "Go find out what the fuck happened, Surfer Boy, and make sure he doesn't leave." Spiros was probably just paranoid—wouldn't be the first time bad weed made someone freak out.

Unless Salomon really had been hiding something down here.

Morrison lurched after Spiros. Their footsteps made it up the stairs, through the kitchen, and stopped near the front door. Low murmuring from Morrison, Spiros, and Courtney. Someone retched and then softer footfalls out the front door as if Morrison was walking them outside.

The sudden silence was eerie but welcome. Petrosky steeled himself and surveyed the basement, hand resting on his gun. The dim light from a single overhead bulb cast stark shadows along the wall and the neatly swept cement floor. For a room supposedly locked away due to vermin, the basement was surprisingly clean—all items placed in orderly piles. Not the kind of place you'd expect to have rodents, but halfway through a long Michigan winter, those bastards would sleep anywhere warm.

The broken window he'd listened at yesterday was at the far end of the basement. He approached the back wall. Beneath the window, four stacks of boxes sat in a tidy row, all labeled. Two bookcases stood to his right, the books individually wrapped in brown paper to protect the covers, and labeled with a label maker, like anyone needed to spend hours typing when you could buy a fucking Sharpie. As he got closer to the back, he noticed that the piles of boxes weren't perfect. Two stacks just beneath the window had been moved out, though they were still close enough to the wall that he wasn't going to find the body of some ex-boyfriend or Courtney's husband hidden behind them. Just ... *askew*. From the severe order of the rest of the place, the ramshackle stacks must be where Spiros had been moving things around looking for rodents when he freaked out and contaminated the scene.

Petrosky drew his eyes to the wall above the boxes where the window gaped, one side dingy but intact, the other sporting jagged glass like teeth, the frigid air huffing through the hole like the breath of a Yeti. But even as the cold sliced through Petrosky's thinning hair and chilled his scalp, it didn't cut the stale dank in the basement. Though the heavy air might have been a reflection of the utter lack of life as opposed to an actual smell.

Then—

Scratch, scratch.

Petrosky jerked around, his gun drawn on reflex, searching for the source of the sound. A mouse ran from an old bookcase to take refuge in the corner adjacent to the shattered window. He lowered his gun, heart hammering. Fucking high-on exterminator had him antsy too.

He turned back to the stacks along the far wall, frowning as he peered through the crack between the brown boxes. The shadows on the ground behind the stacks were deep but ... there was definitely something back there. Small. Probably a nest. What kind of exterminator was Spiros anyway? Not like a family of mice could hurt you—way better to have mice than rats.

But why would mice build a nest under the one place there would surely have been a draft? He stepped back to examine the row again. All the boxes were positioned at least a foot from the cement exterior, presumably to avoid the dewy walls of an unfinished Michigan basement. But below the window, those two crooked stacks were pulled out a few inches farther … .Spiros? Or was Salomon actually hiding something in the dark behind the cardboard?

He forced his fingers around a middle box and pulled, shifting the top three toward him, and peered into the dim space. The nest seemed … rounder, at least on one side—*was* it a nest? Maybe the little girl had used another rock to smash the glass and it had landed on the rodents' home. Good news—they might get some prints. If Spiros hadn't fucked it up.

Petrosky bent to the floor, gripped the bottom container and tried to shift the entire stack of boxes farther from the wall, but nothing moved. Too heavy. He jerked the top box from the pile and set it on the floor behind him. Then the next, so light it surprised him until he spied cloth—blankets—through a slit in the cardboard. He jumped again as something made a sound, a tiny squeak.

Goddamn, he hated mice.

He grabbed another box and heaved it aside, one more, and —*finally*—leaned over the remaining waist-high stack. He froze. Not a rodent's nest. Not a rock.

Fucking hell.

He tossed the next box onto the floor behind him. It toppled over, and a wrapped teacup rolled free of the paper and shattered on the cement. His stomach knotted as he shoved the last box aside so he could get to the mound on the floor.

The infant was nude, its bottom half covered in what looked like black tar but was probably newborn poop. The kid's shriveled skin was purplish like a bruise in some places, grayish in others, and coated in waxy white stuff. A crusty umbilical cord curled against its abdomen. He peered closer. *Her* abdomen. Shit. Far too young to have survived on her own. And her left arm was cocked at an unnatural angle, U-shaped, broken. The boxes might have eased her fall but not nearly enough—she'd suffered before she died. He eyed the window above. No blood apparent on the windowsill, but with the state of the body, the feces, no wonder the rodents were climbing back here—she'd be good eating.

Petrosky thumped one meaty fist against his chest where

ribbons of sharp pain were radiating into his shoulder. "Fuck," he whispered.

Morrison's footsteps echoed on the stairs. "Spiros is at the table. He said he was shoving things around to spray the perimeter and saw a—" He stopped behind Petrosky. "Holy shit."

Morrison pulled his cell as Petrosky knelt beside the child, touching her cheek. *Cold.* Then her skin lit up abruptly, the beam shaking so much it appeared like a roving spotlight against her flesh. Morrison's flashlight app. Petrosky listened to Morrison's sharp intake of breath and the light stilled.

Marks on her belly. Her arms. Tiny punctures surrounded by bruising—like little needle pricks. Not from the fall. Had someone drugged her to keep her quiet? But there was no reason to shoot a tranquilizer into a kid's belly. And a doc sure as hell didn't give newborn vaccinations in the chest or the groin.

"That's why the girl broke the window," Morrison said. "She wanted to hide the baby."

Hide her. If a little girl had kidnapped her infant sister in order to protect her, the parents would be out in full force to find their younger daughter. Except—

These kids were neglected. Abused. The father, if that's what he was, would be brought up on charges if he claimed the baby now. And where the hell had the newborn come from? Not from a hospital—she'd still had the umbilical cord attached. Home birth gone wrong?

Petrosky reached into the box behind him and felt for a blanket. *Poor baby.*

"Boss—"

"Gonna yell at me for messing up a crime scene, California?"

They locked eyes. Morrison shook his head.

Petrosky laid the blanket on the baby just below her neck and pressed his fingertip to the carotid artery. He knew what he was going to find, but ... He felt nothing. Pushed harder.

"Boss ..."

"Gotta make sure." He was sure. He just didn't want to accept that he'd lost another kid. Would she have been alive last night? But they'd had no reason to think someone had tossed a baby inside the house. No reason to think the basement was actually a crime scene. He'd let Courtney Krakow-whatever-the-hell-her-name-was convince him not to do his fucking job with her sad eyes.

He was a fucking pushover. Maybe he'd lost his touch.

Petrosky pulled the blanket over the baby's face and started for the stairs. "Call the techs. Ask for the black-haired one." Maybe he didn't care enough anymore. About anything. No matter what he did, he failed.

"Katrina? Why?"

"She's smarter than the others."

Morrison pocketed his phone and the light went with it, reducing the room to an orange-washed tomb. "How do you know?"

"I'm a fucking genius. That's why you should feel luck—" Petrosky turned back to the window. "Did you hear that?" Morrison stared, wide-eyed, at the back wall.

Petrosky bolted back to the window and hit his knees. The blanket was still, unmoving, the outline of the child barely visible in the dim. Same as when he'd left. But—

The noise came again, the sound of mice. Of kittens? But it wasn't kittens.

Oh god.

He yanked the blanket off the kid. Her mouth was moving, tiny gasps, barely there. Behind him he heard rustling, the beeps of three dialed numbers, and Morrison's voice: "Need a bus."

Petrosky tucked the blanket around the child and over her head like a hood. She was limp, way too gray and way too cold. Nothing else moved. Just her mouth.

He cradled her in his arms and stood. "It's all right, baby girl. It's all right."

The infant opened her mouth and mewled.

7

KATRINA SHOWED up just after the ambulance, shot silent daggers at Petrosky, and went to work on the basement, tweezing, bagging, dusting. Courtney still sat dumbstruck in the kitchen with bleary-eyed Spiros. But her expression oscillated between confusion and an irritation that made Petrosky's neck hairs prickle every time their eyes met.

Morrison took Spiros into the other room, though he clearly wasn't their guy. But Courtney ... there had to be a reason the missing girl had chosen Salomon. Opportunity, maybe, but he needed to be sure.

"Do you have any idea who the child is?"

Her mouth dropped open, closed again. "No, of course not. And I can't imagine that my mother did either."

"Why, doesn't she like children?" Petrosky fought to keep his voice even but he could feel the heat creeping into his face and neck. Was Salomon enough of a chickenshit to close the door in the face of a panicked child? But even if she'd shooed the girl away it sure hadn't kept the woman from getting hacked apart on her own front lawn.

Courtney looked behind Petrosky at the wall, refusing to meet his eyes. "She ... kids were always more a burden than a blessing." Her gaze turned glassy.

"Do you have children?"

"Two."

"And how was your mother with them?"

"What does that have to—"

"Getting a feel for who she was. Whether the child who showed up here might have known her and been comfortable with her—comfortable enough to come for help."

She nodded slowly. "My mother doesn't—didn't—see my children much. She came over for holidays, birthdays, but she kept her distance, if that makes sense."

"It doesn't."

Courtney sighed, finally glancing Petrosky's way, her mouth forming a tight line. "She's always been distant. It got worse after my father died, especially with the cleaning. Kids weren't even allowed in her house because they'd mess things up. Even when I was a kid I couldn't go into the living room because she worried I'd stain something. Worst beating I ever got was for spilling juice in the hallway. Not that she was violent, but a wooden spoon wasn't out of the question."

"Sounds violent to me."

"Yeah well, that was the era she came from." Her voice dripped with bitterness. Yesterday's sorrow and shock had morphed into agitation. Resentment? Anger, or even lack of love, didn't mean intent to kill, but the rage suggested by Elmira Salomon's murder screamed something beyond a mere slight. Who else had Salomon upset? Maybe it was more sinister—she'd been involved in the kidnaping itself. It was unlikely, but stranger things had happened.

"How old are your kids?"

"Twelve. Twin boys."

"And where were you last night? For our records," he amended when her eyes narrowed.

"At home. With the kids and my husband. We wanted to spend some time together before he left on his business trip."

"Where's he going?"

"Brazil. That okay with you?" She practically spat the words.

Petrosky let it go without so much as a scowl. Grief hit everyone differently, especially when they'd had a less than perfect history with the deceased. Going after a grieving

daughter on nothing but the notion that she wasn't sad enough
—the chief would have his ass. At least he didn't have to worry
about the exterminator reporting him for brutality, or going
anywhere near the precinct. That guy was high as fuck and paranoid enough to believe Petrosky wanted to lock him away. He
wasn't wrong.

After securing Courtney's promise to contact them about
her mother's bank deposit boxes, Petrosky and Morrison
headed for a diner on Third where the waitresses were mean
and the food was so greasy it could make your napkin transparent in seconds.

Morrison frowned at his plate of egg whites, took a tentative
sip of coffee, and grimaced. "Courtney seems to be taking this
whole thing rather ... well." His lips were tight as he set the
cup down.

"Sure is. Wants to wrap everything up quickly too. Not that I
blame her."

"Maybe Valentine can follow her."

Petrosky raised an eyebrow.

"I checked out her husband. He'd fit the profile—just under
six feet and stocky, probably right around two hundred pounds
and Brandon said one-ninety. It's close." Morrison set the coffee
aside. "I figured we'd throw Valentine a bone too. He finally
takes the test to get into the bureau next month."

Petrosky shoveled bacon into his maw. Salty as hell. Fantas-
tic. "You must be so proud of your little pet project."

"If friends are pet projects what does that make you?"

"Don't push your luck, Cali. I might be old, but I can still take
down a surfer boy."

"You can't even work your phone."

Petrosky speared a hefty slice of pancake. He watched the
butter and syrup drip to the plate then shoved it into his mouth.
"Maybe we do need to look harder at family. Salomon was
mostly a recluse."

"So are you."

"Yeah, but no one's shoving kids through my basement
windows. And I'm probably just as cantankerous." On his plate,
the sausages were swimming in syrup. Petrosky grabbed one

between his index finger and thumb and shoved it into his mouth.

"Frazier was pretty clear that Salomon wasn't personable," Morrison said. "Actually, only one person in the neighborhood said she seemed friendly. Elderly woman, probably got twenty years on Salomon. And she answered the door in bright green overalls and a purple shirt, hobbling on a walker, convinced she was going to go get the mail."

"Fancy."

"Indeed. But not fancy enough to really help—she vouched for Salomon's awesomeness, then admitted she didn't know her. All in the same breath. I think she was just excited to have company—sat me down in her kitchen, tried to feed me cookies. I actually think ..." His cheeks reddened.

"What?"

"Well, she was kind of hitting on me."

Petrosky stared. "Should have taken her up on it. Gotten a little AARP ass."

"Who says I didn't?" Morrison stifled a smile. "But seriously, Boss, I don't think Salomon was as fearsome as you think. Just kinda alone. Like old people are sometimes."

"You really are a bleeding heart." Petrosky wiped his sticky fingers on his napkin. "Maybe the kid went there because she knew Salomon was a bitch—figured she'd be scary enough to protect them all." He was stretching. A lot. How often would an abused kid get out of the house, let alone socialize with the neighbors?

He pushed his eggs around on the plate. "To find our killer we need to figure out where these children came from. Who they are." But the biological father—he'd know they could match his kids to him using DNA. Probably. If he'd known his baby was in someone else's basement, he'd have tried like hell to get rid of the evidence, especially after Salomon was dead. Then again, they'd had officers driving by the house all night—maybe the killer had wanted to get to the baby but hadn't been able to.

"I'm betting on abduction for the older child," Petrosky said. But the infant ... how had their killer found a baby that young? Maybe he'd kidnapped a pregnant mother. But then ...

Morrison pushed his untouched plate away. "How the hell did that child snatch the baby immediately after birth? The baby's mother …" His face clouded. "Unless the mother was dead already, and the girl thought whoever hurt mom was going to kill the baby next. Those puncture wounds on the infant's belly and groin say she had a good reason to believe that." Morrison rubbed a hand over his face and for a moment he looked almost as old as Petrosky felt. "So where did the girl come from?" he said. "No houses nearby that seem suspicious and we can't search every home within a five or ten-mile radius. No judge will give us a warrant."

"Warrant shmorrant."

Morrison ignored him. "But if our guy was trekking down the street with a struggling child, someone would have seen that."

"They didn't hear the asshole beating up the house with an axe."

"No, but that would have happened quick, right? Within a few minutes. They'd have woken up but thought it was a dream when there was no more noise. If he was trying to drag a child away after that, a child who was ballsy enough to run from him and shove a baby through a window … she wouldn't have gone quietly."

"Unless he incapacitated her."

"He still would have had to carry her limp body down a street where someone might have seen him. And he would have had that huge weapon."

"So he chased her down in a car. Drove off quietly to avoid drawing attention to himself. Maybe they were even driving when the kid leapt out. En route to the hospital with the infant."

"Maybe with the mother too," Morrison added hopefully.

Petrosky shook his head. "I don't like it."

"Why? Because it's optimistic?"

"That and it's implausible." If the mother was present, the girl probably wouldn't have taken the infant. And though the birth might have forced the killer to make a midnight run to the hospital or a drugstore for supplies, why would the girl leap from the car before they got there? It would be easier to get help in a fully lit emergency room or a drugstore parking lot. No, it was more probable that the girl had escaped from a nearby home with the kid, forcing the killer to give chase. "We'll call for the hospital records," he said. "Women brought in after childbirth without their infant. Look into hospitalizations of little girls too—if the one in the socks was injured in the struggle she might have been taken in. Though again, I highly doubt it." Petrosky stabbed another sausage. Oil squirted onto the plate like blood from someone's jugular.

"Too optimistic again?"

"The actions of this older child were not normal. Abuse, neglect, bad enough to risk her life. And the baby being born in isolation, away from the prying eyes of medical professionals— that was deliberate. The last thing our perp wants to do is take the older girl in to get her injuries looked at."

"You think the baby's mother is the killer's partner, victim of domestic violence maybe? Too afraid to cross him because he'd hurt her?"

"Maybe. Or he abducted a pregnant woman and forced her to have the kid. Or cut it out of her. There's also lots of money in child porn. Pedophilia shit or even those live torture videos."

Morrison put his fork down and pushed the plate away. "I was thinking the same."

"You're on your way to the dark side, my friend. Add Salomon's Russian son-in-law, a guy who's routinely out of the country to places like Brazil ..."

"Child trafficking? That's more statistically likely than baby snatching?"

"It's more common than people think, and Brazil has one of the highest rates of trafficking—top dozen, anyway. And last year we had that girl from ... Bangkok, maybe? She was found because she got away; ran just like our kid last night, nude and bleeding. Only difference is he didn't come after her because he didn't know she'd escaped. Maybe this girl didn't get so lucky." Petrosky shoved the meat into his mouth and chased it with tepid coffee. "The hospital is only a few blocks from Salomon's. If the kid knew the area, she might have run that direction. Tried to get help."

"She was probably just trying to get away, circling the house because she knew she couldn't escape."

The thought of the girl frantically streaking through moonlit yards, desperate for help ... had Julie tried to run from her attacker? Petrosky shoved the thought aside.

"She's young," Morrison continued, "maybe not thinking clearly or logically, though she still had the presence of mind to break the window." He shrugged. "She probably thought she'd be able to fit, too."

Petrosky grimaced, trying to ignore the sharp pain that had taken root in his gut. Could still be abuse, but they should check the trafficking angle, too. "We'll ask Freeman about it. See what he's gotten on the trafficking front lately, look for similarities." He nodded to Morrison's plate. "You all done there, Kid?"

Morrison winced. "You want it?"

"Fuck no." Petrosky frowned at his last piece of sausage and shrugged into his coat. "Let's make some calls, then we can go to the hospital and visit our latest break."

A break. Not someone's baby. He was just as heartless as whoever'd abused a child until she'd shoved an infant through a broken window.

8

THEY MADE call after call en route to the hospital. No luck with the hospitals themselves; records were sealed without patient consent. But the docs were legally bound to report abuse, and they definitely would have reported a recently pregnant woman without her child, or a sliced-up kid admitted without parents. The other precincts nearby had nothing of help either—they hadn't taken any reports from hospitals about postpartum women without babies, and they had no missing pregnant women, no stolen infants, no reports of little girls with injuries consistent with their case. They'd try a larger radius around Detroit, but he wasn't counting on that panning out. Their killer wouldn't bring in an injured child when he was the one who'd hurt her, and if the mother was still alive, he couldn't take her in for treatment sans infant.

The hospital smelled of alcohol. It wasn't vodka, but close enough to make Petrosky drool as they entered. He flared his nostrils as if he could pull the poison into his body, felt guilty for the thought, and then blew his nose using a tissue from the emergency room end table. He was in good company—twenty other people in the waiting room sat sniffling and hacking, or bleeding into towels. Morrison was the only one who looked healthy—though tired—tapping away on his laptop in the corner, jotting occasional notes onto his pad.

"Detective?"

Petrosky turned. A woman with short, spiked hair walked toward him. "Doctor Rosegold, pediatric intensive care." She extended her hand. Her blue-green scrubs had tiny splotches of what might have been blood, shit, or vomit. "Follow me."

Morrison was already standing, laptop and notepad under his arm.

They followed her down the antiseptic hallway past stretchers with long-faced men clutching one limb or another, then took the elevator to the seventh floor. The hall was filled with photos of happy families and posters proclaiming "Get your flu shot!" and "Pertussis is one kiss away." Herpes was one kiss away too, but that probably made for a shittier poster.

They stopped in front of a plate glass window. At the far end of the hall, a woman stood, wearing two hospital-issued gowns, one with the opening in the back, one wrapped around to the front to avoid that pesky ass-baring thing. Her eyes were vacant, staring through the glass, hands clutching a single brass bar that ran the length of the wall below the window. She was only wearing one sock.

He followed her gaze. Inside the room sat a dozen huge bassinets, six on each side, made of bulky plastic. Wires snaked from the tiny bundles inside to the surrounding machines, some of the equipment hissing intermittently, loud and halting, like a first—or last—breath. Half the bassinets were lit up like tanning beds, but the babies under their glare were tinted blue as death, crisscrossed with tubes, cannulas shoved into their noses. Monitors beeped. Scrub-clad nurses looked on warily.

Rosegold gestured to the right side of the room. "In the back."

Her bassinet was different, transparent—like a clear coffin—and separated from the others by a few feet, though whether done purposefully or accidentally as nurses shuffled the cribs around he couldn't tell. Her body was more bandage than skin, all of her bathed in blue. His heart spasmed, tightened, and he rubbed at his chest like he could massage the awful away.

"She's alive," Rosegold said, low enough that the woman at

the far end of the window couldn't hear. "But only time will tell. We're worried specifically about infection."

"How old is she?"

"Three days, tops. The passing of meconium usually happens soon after birth, but the cord was dried enough that it's probably been a couple days. We've contacted Child Protective Services. And I already sent over her blood sample with an ... Officer Valentine, I think it was."

Valentine? Petrosky raised an eyebrow at Morrison who shrugged. At least they'd have DNA sometime in the next few days, if not today. "Thanks for that. What else did you find?"

Rosegold stared through the window. "She has compound fractures in her arm. The admitting doc said she went through a window?"

"Shoved through a basement window. Small space."

"That explains it. The break wasn't clean and there was more than one, not usual for a simple fall." She turned back to them. "If someone broke her arm trying to get her in there, the injuries make more sense. Well, those injuries, anyway."

Rosegold swallowed hard, glanced down the row at the woman in the gowns and lowered her voice still further. "She had abrasions on her thighs and back, like rug burn. Like someone had dragged her over something. But I'm more concerned about the puncture wounds on her belly and groin. She has them on her buttocks, too, and her chest."

"Can you tell what made the marks?"

"Almost looks like a sewing needle." She dropped her eyes to Petrosky's chest and he realized he was still massaging his breastbone.

Petrosky dropped his hand and side-eyed Morrison who had gone still beside him. It had been two years since Morrison's wife and child had been abducted. Two years since the kidnapper had sewn Shannon's lips closed. Since then, any mention of needles made Morrison's nostrils flare like an angry bull's.

"Signs of sexual abuse?" Petrosky asked softly, as if whispering would make the conversation less awful.

She shook her head. "No penetration or tearing, but the puncture wounds ... there were a few around her labia."

Fucking sadist. Bile rose in his throat. Few looked at newborns as sexual objects—this was done to torture. For the pain.

Morrison turned away from the window and rested the back of his head on the glass, his Adam's apple moving like he was trying not to puke. Petrosky glared at him until he straightened up, though his own stomach was churning with now-sour coffee and disgust. Vomiting sausage and eggs all over a hospital hallway sure as shit wasn't going to help them find a missing kid. Or help this one.

"Some of the wounds are newer, but some have already scabbed. That's another reason I can tell it's been a few days since her birth." That pain—Jesus. Petrosky watched the monitors as Rosegold continued. "As it is, the physical injuries are minor, but significant in terms of psychological trauma and pain. And we are fighting some infections from the needle sticks. My biggest concern is that a few were deep enough to puncture internal organs. We've stopped all the bleeding but sepsis is a possibility though we're doing everything we can. This is just ..." She shuddered. "I've seen a lot, detectives, but to stab a newborn over and over again ... it says a lot about whoever did this to her."

Petrosky drew his eyes to the back bassinet, where blue lights made the tiny figure look ... well, dead. Like she almost had been when he'd found her. When he'd almost left her in that basement, cold and alone and ... alive. Petrosky waited for her monitors to go off, signaling her heart had stopped, but they kept blipping, silently. The hand on her uncasted arm moved sluggishly then stilled.

He dragged his eyes away, willing his gut to settle.

"Please call me directly if anything happens." Petrosky handed her a card. "Good or bad."

"I will."

Morrison's eyes bored into him as they walked down the hall.

"What?"

"Call good or bad, eh?"

"We need to know if we should upgrade from child abuse to homicide."

"And the good? You're coming to the brighter side of life, old timer."

Petrosky ignored him and stepped into the empty elevator. She'd been stabbed repeatedly immediately after birth and the older child had managed to get her away, at least long enough to throw her into a basement. The girl must have known what was in store for the baby. They could expand the search for Child Protective Services calls, but he doubted they'd find what they needed. Either this guy was hiding them—his own personal stash to abuse at will—or it was something bigger. Child smuggling. Kiddie porn, maybe, with the injuries to the labia. That's what was bothering him most—the needle sticks.

The elevator door closed. Petrosky leaned his head against the back wall and stared at the mirrored ceiling. He looked pale. Sick. "I think the stabbing thing is most telling, especially if it is a fetish."

Morrison shuddered. The asshole who'd taken Shannon and Evie had piquerism, a fetish where stabbing became a source of sexual satisfaction—like Jack the Ripper.

But the Ripper and Norton had both taken grown women. And though Norton was into iron collars and spiked boots as forms of torture ... were those things really medieval like that billhook weapon the ME was so certain about? But he had liked to stab ...

The lighted elevator numbers continued down, one floor at a time, mirroring the sinking sensation in Petrosky's belly. There was no way Adam Norton had stayed around here after they'd rescued Shannon. They'd had no other related kidnappings, nothing with needles or torture like that, no homicides that fit his MO. And Norton would have escalated, killed someone else; they'd surely have had more cases if he was here. The food churned in Petrosky's belly and he coughed, deep and wet, then swallowed phlegm that tasted suspiciously like iron.

Morrison put his hand on his stomach. "Aw, fuck." The kid's face had gone green.

"You all right there?"

"Yeah, I think it's just ... breakfast didn't ..." The elevator doors opened and Morrison bolted for the restrooms.

He'd probably been having the same thoughts about Shannon and Evie. *Victims.* Survivors, yes, but though Morrison's family had lived, the guilt never really went away. *I feel you, Kid. I do.* Petrosky hacked, once, twice, and pain seared through his lungs like they were tearing apart, bloody fissures widening with every cough. He tapped a cigarette out of the pack and stuck it between his teeth. He should probably quit smoking. But the butt was damp with his saliva by the time Morrison emerged wiping his mouth.

They remained silent until they'd left the hospital, their competing footsteps echoing through the lot like a crisp, uneven heartbeat.

"You need to go home?" Petrosky asked him, lighting up and inhaling the acrid smoke as if it were a balm against the burning sensation that lingered, hot and aching, in his chest.

"I'm fine."

The tightness in Morrison's eyes said he was anything but fine. Petrosky inhaled more smoke, coughed, recovered. "Good. We'll go back to the station and do a little research. You expand the hospital search for the mother, but don't spend too much time on it—the baby didn't even have her umbilical cord cut, so she wasn't born in a hospital. I'll pull the rest of the child protection cases, then we'll work on child abductions together." That part would be tricky. Most girls on the kidnapping rolls had no blood types on file and it would be difficult to narrow down the pool outside of shoe size—they didn't even know exactly how old the girl was or when she'd been taken.

"What about the child porn stuff? The trafficking?"

"I'll look into that too, see what I can get from Freeman over on that side. We'll pull pedophiles as well, but I don't know if I'm buying that." No sexual abuse on the baby, just the sadistic pain shit. Pedophiles often believed they were in a relationship with their victim, that they loved the child. Not that they never caused pain for fun, but the balls on this guy—holding a kid, holding a pregnant woman—not your standard pedophile. But psychopaths tortured kids for the fun of it.

Ash Park. *Goddammit.* He should move. Maybe they had fewer psychos in Canada.

Morrison pulled open the car door and Petrosky plopped into the driver's seat. Through the windshield the clouds burned white but the air remained frigid with the waning afternoon. It was the kind of cold that got into your soul and froze you from the inside.

"Don't let this shit get to you," Petrosky said as he merged onto the freeway, not entirely certain the words were meant for Morrison. But words were empty anyway. And from Morrison's frown, the kid knew it too. Never fucking ended. The pain, the struggle. The guilt. The grief.

Petrosky's chest tightened, and this time the pain behind his rib cage shot bolts of lightning up into his neck. He rubbed at it as he drove. Old man aches and pains were a small problem. Life was one big problem, and Jack Daniels was a cure—for a while. But not tonight; he'd live with his problems a little longer. One day at a time. One hundred and thirty-one days clean. *I'll make it one hundred and thirty-two, sweetheart.*

"You say something, Boss?"

Petrosky shook his head. "Let's get you a doughnut. You'll feel better with a little sugar in you."

Morrison leaned his head against the window and nodded.

Dark side, here we come.

BIG-SHIT FORENSIC ANALYST Brandon rang Petrosky's desk just after they arrived back at the precinct. Five fifty. Ten minutes before the cops with pictures of pudgy babies on their desks would head home for the night and thirty minutes before the guys without pudgy babies would arrive back from some greasy spoon or from a quick fuck at their girlfriend's place.

"Got some blood test results for you," Brandon was saying.

"Looks like both females—your infant and your missing child—are of Caucasian decent. Both unrelated to Salomon."

"I figured as much." Petrosky opened the drawer and grabbed his cigarettes, careful to avoid his daughter's gaze. "Are they related to one another?"

"That's the interesting part. We were thinking the prints you found were a child, that maybe they were sisters, but the baby is the *daughter* of the other girl at the scene. And I checked the paternity line, too, for both—different fathers." He paused. "Sick asshole." Then hung up.

The missing kid was the *mother* of the infant? Petrosky tapped his box of smokes. He'd thought she was seven or eight, but she might be older, just small. Eleven, maybe twelve? Julie'd worn her mother's shoes starting at nine or ten. But that didn't mean everyone did.

How old were most girls when they started ovulating? He punched it up on Google to be sure. Looked like some started puberty at age eight while others were as late as thirteen—but by then her feet would have been larger. Next, he called up shoe size information for the nine or ten age range—eight to ten inches, give or take, about the size of the fuzzy sock prints in the snow. *Damn.*

He pictured a girl, third grade, running through the frost in socks, still-swollen abdomen flapping, carrying an infant she had been forced to watch her own abuser touch—*stab.* His gut felt like someone was trying to rip his last meal out through his belly button. She hadn't stolen the baby; she'd given birth to her rapist's child and run away to protect it. The fact that she'd carried to term was an anomaly, but it was the one bit of luck in this whole hideous case. What the hell was he dealing with? Child bride? Or just horrendous fucking abuse?

Petrosky clicked off the shoe size chart and ran a hand over his face. He felt tired. And old. He could almost hear Julie crying. He rubbed the spot on his shoulder where the tattoo of her face was, gently, as if he could comfort her. But it was far too late for that. His entire body was aching, burning, hot with the knowledge that Julie had suffered because of him, and now, this other little girl was suffering too.

Fuck this shit. He looked at the clock. Six twenty. Plenty of time for a date with Jack Daniels. He stood so fast his chair toppled over behind him. Without bothering to right it, he strode from the precinct to his car. He was fucking incompetent. And if she wasn't dead already, somewhere a little girl without her baby was paying the price.

9

Petrosky parked, lit a cigarette, and watched men and women file into the white brick building. Sweats or suits or jeans, all walks of life, most with caps or hoods pulled low over their faces as they approached the front door. The wind whipped snow-drifts into tented piles at the side of the lot and beat snowflakes against the streetlamp, but the hats had nothing to do with the weather. Nothing like running into a neighbor on your way to AA.

He'd been here before, his ex-wife's winter scarf hiding his face, more times than he wanted to admit—not that it had done much good. AA was for those willing to give their shit to a higher power. Not him. What kind of God would allow such suffering? With all the fucked-up people in the world, the abused kids, the murdered mothers—if there were a God, that fucker was pouring the shots.

The door opened and closed, each time spilling light as yellow as cats' eyes on the walk. He could drive down the street to the hole-in-the-wall bar where no one would know him. Without his badge, he was just some guy, as noticeable as a pimple on a whore's back.

Tempting. He could almost taste the first sip, feel it burning down his gullet. Then he'd wake up tomorrow woozy and one step further from helping the missing girl. The girl who'd risked her life to save her baby when she was just a baby herself. Heroic. The least he could do was try to find her.

A man in a suit strolled up to the building, a Rolex sparkling gold in the yellow light. The guy touched the watch's face as if it was some kind of life preserver, like the jewelry could keep him from sinking. The door clanked shut behind him. Wind lashed snow against the walk and obscured his footprints as if he'd never existed. As if none of them had.

Petrosky tried to focus on what remained for him: The job, maybe. And Morrison, Shannon, Evie and Henry. He'd walked Shannon down the aisle. Been in the waiting room for both births. But even the love of a family—and that's what it was, a family—was marred by a dusky veil. He could see their support, knew it existed, but he drove their affection away before it could make a home in his chest.

He had failed before—with liquor, with cases, with relationships. Morrison and Shannon and their happy family would be all the happier without trips to the hospital and broken promises; there was no doubt they'd be better off without him. Maybe Julie would have too—if he'd divorced her mother earlier, they might have moved far from Ash Park. Far from the man who had slit Julie's throat.

He had failed his daughter. And Julie was far from the only one.

It had been four years since he'd failed Hannah Montgomery, a young woman who was so much like Julie it hurt to look at her. After months of searching for the serial killer who had been after Hannah, he had arrested a man who fit the description. Mountains of evidence, and he'd been wrong. And while that wrong man was in jail, Petrosky had lost Hannah for good. No, not lost—she'd been *taken*. He'd spent fruitless hours searching, desperate for any scrap of information that would lead him to her. When he came up empty, he'd drunk himself into oblivion, followed by a leave of absence from the force. He'd come back ready to take a few more criminals down, ready to do ... something. But it wasn't enough. It was never enough. Shannon and Evie, so close to him they might as well have been his blood— even they'd been taken on his watch. Tortured. There was always another criminal ready to take the place of every bad guy he collared. There was far more bad than good in this world—the good was doomed.

Petrosky gripped the steering wheel. He wouldn't let them win, not all of them. He'd save at least one heroic little girl, even though there'd still be more assholes out there who could hurt the people he loved.

He'd fucked up with his own family. Lost Julie. And now he was watching Shannon and the kids just drift away from him, blowing them off like he'd blown off his ex-wife after Julie died, not out of some naive belief that they'd always be there, but because he knew they wouldn't. He could see them now, picnicking in the park while his corpse rotted in the earth. It would be better that way.

They wouldn't even miss him.

10

PETROSKY ACCOMPANIED Salomon's daughter Courtney, whose last name only Morrison could pronounce, to the bank to look through her mother's safe deposit box. As she had told them, there was very little jewelry and nothing out of the ordinary paperwork-wise. They did find a life insurance policy for two hundred thousand dollars. Courtney cried and laughed at the same time. A little jarring, but normal—people reacted weirdly to both grief and cash.

All the way back to the station Petrosky thought about what he'd do with two hundred thousand dollars, but most of it involved building elaborate torture chambers for child rapists and maybe getting one of those massage chairs to help with his aching back—some mornings his ribs felt like they were trying to burst outward on either side of his spine. That might have been from the cigarettes, too, but no amount of money would make him give those up. Maybe with two hundred thousand he'd also get a new coffee pot. *Nah, fuck that.* He and Old Bessie had been through a lot together even if she was a little bitch.

When he got back to the station, the forensics report was on his desk. Morrison pulled up a chair while Petrosky flipped through the papers. "Shoe prints outside Salomon's look like boots." Hardly unusual in the middle of a soul-sucking Michigan winter. Petrosky squinted at the page, the words blurring, then sat back as Morrison grabbed the file. At least the kid didn't say something new agey about eating carrots to restore his vision. "Pink cotton-polyester fibers, socks available at any store. And some dust in the kid's footprints, looks like cement or clay."

"Maybe from the window?" Petrosky thought back to the basement, the crevices and corners of the encasement where dust and grime had gathered. Had she tried to climb in too? How close had she gotten to safety when she was snatched away again by her abuser?

Morrison flipped a few pages and scanned at the print. "Some dust matches the window, but not all. Looks like they haven't finished complete analysis of all the particles, but we'll have that soon."

"Hopefully they get something good." Petrosky stood. "I'm going to go see Freeman, get a little more on the trafficking angle." Hopefully that would pan out. Their expanded hospital search had yielded jack shit, not that Petrosky had expected different. No newborn kidnappings from hospitals recently, or even up to ten to twelve years ago in case their killer had abducted the first child as an infant as well. No baby girls unaccounted for, no mothers admitted under exigent circumstances aside from one case nine years ago, but they'd later found that woman's infant in a dumpster. They'd struck out with Child Protective Services too, but that wasn't surprising—you'd hardly let a pregnant ten-year-old out and about on the town. And if the killer had abducted the girl to begin with, he had all the more reason to keep her isolated.

Petrosky took a step toward the stairs, then glanced back. "Do me a favor and call Katrina—have her double-check the encasements around the windows and doors. The houses next door, too." The girl might have tried another house first, or been trying to get in the front door when Salomon came out. They didn't want to be on a wild-goose chase if the dust from the socks came from a neighbor's or another entrance.

"Got it." Morrison pushed his chair back. "By the way, you should probably get a vision test. There are places you can do that for free. And vitamin C—"

"My eyes are fine."

"But you were—"

"Don't sass me, California. You guys wear glasses just to fit in with the fucking hipsters who think their shit don't stink."

Morrison's grin caught the overhead lights. "Can't stink worse than you after a plate of chili dogs." He started away.

"Fuck you, *Dude*," Petrosky called after him. Irritable, but sincere.

DAN FREEMAN'S office was downstairs next to the offices of Harold Terse, head of the undercover group lovingly referred to as "The Hooker Patrol," and George Wallace, who ran most of the drug stings. The offices were identically small and nondescript with no windows, presumably because some cokehead might be strolling by the precinct on his way to a fabulous new job at the courthouse and catch them. Or maybe incognito operations meant you had to hide from the sun, too, like a goddamn troll.

Dan's pasty white skin, gray eyes, and limp albino-like hair gave him the look of a vampire. He stopped shuffling papers and peered at Petrosky from behind glasses with cheap plastic frames.

"Nice glasses. New look?" Petrosky said.

Freeman pushed the glasses up the bridge of his nose, which shone in the fluorescent overheads. "Trying to get used to 'em. Otherwise I'll have to wear one of those stupid mustaches next time I go out."

"Or get a tan. They'll never recognize you then."

Freeman grinned, showing crooked—but white—front teeth. "Or that. But who wants skin cancer?"

Petrosky took a chair across from Freeman's goofy ass. "I'm looking for some information on child trafficking. Got a case with a couple of kids. One newborn, puncture wounds immediately following birth, and the child's mother is probably nine or ten years old."

Freeman's nostrils flared. Agitated. "Child bride?"

"Don't know yet."

"You sure it isn't just domestic abuse? Incest, rape within the family?"

Petrosky frowned. "The girls have different, unrelated, fathers. But I can't rule out stepparents and the like. So, no, I'm not sure."

Freeman pulled the glasses off his dewy nose and tossed them on the desk. "I hope you find abuse—a lot easier than trying to locate a trafficker in it for the cash."

That much he knew—trafficking was an industry worth about thirty-two billion dollars every year, right behind illegal drugs. And the Motor City, Ash Park included, was number two for that shit. Petrosky cracked his knuckles. *Dirty fuckers.* "What do the current recovery rates look like?" He almost hoped Freeman wouldn't answer.

"Fucking terrible," Freeman said. "And much of it is right in plain sight." He grimaced. "They're homeless or under threat of severe abuse if they fight back. And they're brainwashed. Broken. And afraid we'll arrest them for prostitution if they tell the police, so we keep it going inadvertently." He rubbed the indentation left behind by the glasses. "As for the ones who are exported ..." His face darkened. "More of the same. And once they leave here we almost never get them back."

Petrosky rubbed at his chest, though it did little to ease the ache. "Tell me about the younger kids specifically. Maybe in the eight to twelve age range."

He nodded. "Trafficked kids tend to be kept at home. A few are put in school to keep up appearances, but not usually, because then we can identify them." He shook his head, frowning. "And you don't necessarily need a kidnapping either. Sometimes kids are picked up, drugged, threatened with violence if they tell, and brought back to their parents' home—over and over. I have no idea what you're dealing with on the girl, but your infant is more likely to be sold on the adoption black market than used for sexual exploitation. Big payout a hell of a lot faster."

"This infant was abused. Stabbed with needles hours after birth. I doubt there was any plan to sell her to prospective parents." The killer could have abused her, let her heal, and sold her later, but his gut said otherwise. This guy was conditioning another victim to play with.

"Sometimes you see photos—pornography. But the stabbing …" Freeman shook his head. "That isn't so common. I could see someone sadistic enough taking pictures or a video as it's happening—some live streams take requests on the type of pain they should inflict." He shook his head again as if ridding it of whatever ghastly images had been imprinted on his brain. "Still, I'd bet on in-home abuse. Maybe even someone using the infant to hurt the mother. Break her spirit."

They had done that to Shannon during her kidnapping, too, locked her up and made her listen to the wails of her starving child. Never failed—every new case felt just like an old case, every teenager was his daughter, every kidnapping from now on would always be Evie or Shannon. *Fuck.* This was going to get him in trouble. He couldn't take much more stress.

"But, Petrosky, this—this isn't really my area. You should get a profile from McCallum."

Dr. McCallum, department shrink. "I'll do that too. But if our stabber was going to put the photos or the video of the abuse out there—what sites would he use?"

"Well …" Freeman pulled out a sticky note, scribbled on it and handed it across the desk. "Most of the sites are so heavily encrypted that we have a hard time finding the original posters. Plus they get shut down every day. These ones are the newest, but I doubt they'll be up later this week. Check out the sex offender database—we get some overlap there. I'd also see if you have any world travelers nearby, though they probably have a false passport for themselves and the kids."

False documents didn't come cheap, but neither did kids. Maybe Courtney's well-traveled Russian husband knew a thing or two about fake passports. "Can you shoot me a list of names? Guys you might be investigating?"

"You can't interfere in those investigations, Petrosky."

"I promise I won't." Petrosky was lying, and from the way Freeman narrowed his eyes, he knew it too. "Listen, I just want to see if any of them knew Salomon or live near her home.

Maybe find someone who likes his victims especially young. I've got one live kid and one baby in the hospital that deserves—"

"Hell, they all deserve better, Petrosky." Freeman sighed. "I'll get it done, but half these guys are turning the kids over—selling them. Your guy sounds like he's keeping them for himself."

Petrosky nodded and stood. "I'll run down missing persons while I'm waiting for your list."

"I'll look through our database for stabbing injuries too. Most of those get kicked over to homicide, though." Freeman picked up the glasses and slid them back onto his nose.

Homicide. Because once children got feisty, they didn't last long.

11

———

THE WEBSITES FREEMAN had listed were difficult to access. Two required passwords and verification of identity before you could enter. The one that didn't was full of home videos and pictures. He found three photos of infants and toddlers that would have seemed almost normal if he had been looking through a photo album—one in a bathtub, two of the children lying in bed, nude or diapered. But with the type of man who'd taken the pictures, the little kids staring at the camera were doomed, marked, their innocence soon to be scarred by misery. Those later photos might sell even better—after the children had been broken. His fists balled at the thought.

"Shit. That's messed up," Morrison said behind him.

Petrosky clicked off the site. "Get ahold of Katrina?"

"She was over on another scene. I called around and got Bill."

"Who the fuck is Bill?"

Morrison plopped into the extra chair beside Petrosky's desk. "The one you call 'the Asian.'"

"The Asian's name is Bill?"

"He was born here, Petrosky."

"No one said he wasn't. What are you, some kind of fucking racist?" Petrosky waited while Morrison shook his head. Were all surfers that gullible? "So's the Asian there already?"

"He's on his way now. And you probably shouldn't call him that."

"It's not a slur. He *is* Asian. Just like I'm the fat, white asshole."

"You're white, but you're not *that* fat."

"No argument on the asshole part, eh?"

Morrison shrugged in response. "I swung by Freeman's office, but you had already left."

"It didn't take long. We'll probably go talk to him again, I just needed enough to get started."

"Got it. And where're we starting?"

"Kiddie porn. Sex offenders. Why don't you start with the kidnappings."

Morrison nodded as his phone buzzed—he pulled it from his pocket. "Morrison." Morrison's brows furrowed, cell pressed against his ear. Then he snatched a pen and wrote on the back of the file folder. "Be right down."

"What was that?" Petrosky asked as Morrison pocketed the cell.

"Katrina."

"Ka—"

"We've got another victim, over near Union Street. She's got cement dust all over her."

"Dust. I told you Katrina was fucking good," Petrosky said, but the jelly doughnuts in his stomach slithered around. *Cement dust.* They were too late.

12

BY THE TIME Beck Avenue gave way to Union Street, Petrosky's hands hurt from his white-knuckled grip on the wheel. He parked on the shoulder a block away from where officers were milling around and yelling at gawkers to move it along.

The old cobblestone street was patched with asphalt, and pockmarked with deep puddles of stagnant slush. Icy wind howled through the alleys, each one like a dark hallway leading nowhere good—tunnels lined with pawn shops and gun stores and greasy Chinese restaurants, the air reeking of urine. They walked past a few other cop cars and a station wagon with a green hood and a rusted red door that looked as if it had been put together in a junkyard. At least the rats were hiding.

Petrosky flashed his badge at an officer who didn't look old enough to have a driver's license let alone a gun, and squeezed between the barriers into an alley that smelled like the mildew around old fishing docks under that urine stink. Frozen piss was still piss.

Their view was blocked by a set of enormous dumpsters, taller than he was and wider than a car, pea green and lined with black mold or maybe the remnants of thousands of leaky trash bags. Petrosky wrinkled his nose at the scent of ripe trash. Had it not been for the floodlights, they wouldn't have known anything was back there at all—you could hide an entire fucking couch on the other side of the trash bins.

A swish of black hair from around the side of the dumpsters revealed the location of their body. Katrina straightened and waved them over into the spotlight. Their shoes clapped hollowly against the bricks. Closer. Closer.

Morrison gagged.

Red curls stuck to one intact cheek, a dusting of freckles visible amidst spattered blood. But too much blood and too little flesh to determine much else about her appearance. Her face was pulp where it was present at all; deep canyons split her eyebrows, fracturing the skin of her forehead. Her nose was a flattened mess, her lips cracked in two, a man-made cleft palate. Two teeth, or maybe other bone matter, shone dimly under the techs' lights from behind her ear, absolutely not where anything mouth related should be. A wound gaped between neck and shoulder, probably from a missed strike at her face.

Morrison knelt slowly, hesitantly, beside the body. "Looks like someone didn't want us to know who she was."

"Or he did it for fun." The mess their killer had made of Salomon had nothing to do with hiding identity, and nor had the injuries on that baby. And the gouges in the skin of this girl —*woman?*—told a tale Petrosky didn't want to have to read.

Her arms lay above her head. Deep bruises encircled her wrists, some scabbed-over yellowed skin and some fresh purple and still-wet lacerations. Her fingers were bloody nubs, half the fingernails missing as if she had clawed her way through something. Hash marks on her palms might have been splinters. Katrina squatted near her right hand.

"Able to get any prints?" Petrosky asked her quietly.

"They're pretty chewed up. But I think we might be able to lift a couple partials. The ME's on his way, but there's no way she was killed here. Nowhere near enough blood on the ground."

Petrosky drew his eyes downward, avoiding the victim's mangled face. Her breasts lay like bulbous implants, dark, swollen nipples pointing skyward. Stretch marks on her distended abdomen glowed purple under the techs' lights. Recently pregnant. Had to be their girl.

But this was no child. Could be a teenager, but definitely not the nine or ten-year-old he'd assumed. He'd gotten it all wrong—missed a clue that might have led them to her, failed to see some critical bit of information. Fucked up yet again, and he'd lost another girl.

Petrosky stared at her knees, at the scrapes and bruises—consistent with a number of falls as they'd noted at the Salomon place. Gaping wounds, more splinters—deep and fat—inside the one knee he could see. And ... her feet. *Tiny.*

He knelt beside Morrison, who was still crouched next to the body. No, her feet weren't small. They just weren't all *there. Fucking hell.* Petrosky's insides lurched but he snorted instead of gagging and shifted to get a look at the injuries from another angle. Each of her toes had been amputated. Open wounds covered the pads and heels of her feet, along with more thick, ropy slivers of what looked like wood—but where the toes had been removed, the skin was scarred, pink, not bloody or angry. Someone had done this a long time ago.

"Guess we know why she kept falling," Petrosky said. She wouldn't have been able to balance with mutilated feet.

"Like Chinese foot binding," Morrison said, and his voice was soft, pained.

"What the fuck is it with you and the Asians?"

Katrina huffed from her spot near the woman's smashed head, but Petrosky ignored her. Morrison remained still, staring at the body. *What the fuck's going on with him?* Having kids was turning him into a goddamn sissy. Not that Petrosky's own thoughts hadn't run soft lately—but he was sure as shit better at hiding it.

"In China, they used to bind their daughters' feet to ensure they couldn't grow," Morrison practically whispered. "Taping the toes down, forcing the bones to contort. It's a sign of submission, obedience. And the girls can't run to get away—have to take small steps or they fall."

Someone had kept this girl inside. Hidden her. Made sure she couldn't escape even if she managed to get away.

Behind them, a clank echoed off the buildings, jarring something in Petrosky's chest. He stood and watched the stretcher approach from the ambulance at the mouth of the alley. Even when they lowered the body bag, Morrison remained squatting on the cement.

"You going to sit there all day, Cali?"

Morrison raised his eyes and met Petrosky's gaze, and Petrosky's blood ran cold. Unbridled fear. And … rage. A rage he hadn't seen since the night they'd rescued Shannon and Evie from a madman.

He stepped around Morrison and knelt as Morrison pointed to the underside of the victim's hip, cast in shadow.

And then he saw it, pink and shiny, and bubbled as if the wound had been made by a needle, puncturing the skin over and over again. An old scar. A familiar one.

Petrosky's heart stopped as he stared at the *#1* scored into her flesh. He'd seen that mark before, carved into the skin of a murdered child and a murdered woman two years before by a man named Adam Norton. Then Norton had kidnapped Morrison's wife and baby. Tortured Shannon. Sewed her fucking lips shut.

Morrison lowered his hand. "He must have taken this girl right after we rescued …"

Petrosky nodded. Shannon had never mentioned another girl being held with her, and they'd found no one else in the home. But this girl had been trapped a long time, given the healed wounds and the fact it took nearly ten months to make a baby. That was a long time to keep a girl … unless she'd been pregnant when he snatched her. And Petrosky couldn't dismiss either possibility. With this killer there was little he could assume—he didn't even know if the bastard was working alone.

Last time Norton'd had partners; one was dead, the other locked up for good. But Norton himself had escaped. Petrosky had let him get away, thought him long gone, but the bastard hadn't stopped. He'd only gotten more ruthless. And now this girl was dead, and her baby was fighting for her life, all because of him. Because he'd been lost, addicted—too fucked up to do his job.

Petrosky put his hand on Morrison's bicep and Morrison met his eyes.

"Call your wife, Cali. Right now."

13

HE'S BACK.

The old case file was dry and cracked and dusty. But Norton was still there, whispering from the pages as if the words in the file had taken on a life of their own, more frenzied, more insane, with each passing day. *Their killer.*

In the file photographs, Dylan Acosta's body lay facedown in the mud, naked, back punctured with ugly gaping wounds from where he'd been stomped to death with Norton's boots—boots equipped with removable copper spikes. Acosta had died of a punctured lung, drowned in his own blood. Eleven. Eleven fucking years old.

Petrosky turned the page. The following week, a twenty-nine-year-old woman, Natalie Bell, had been stabbed to death with the same weapon used on Acosta. Punctures to the belly. The groin. Just like the infant.

He can't be back. Petrosky had convinced himself, somewhere in the far reaches of his brain, that this fuck-o was gone. That after Norton's partners were put away, the killer had taken off forever, and he'd surely never show up on their beat—Petrosky had *seen his face.* Spoken to him. The fake IDs Norton had used for work might not have looked like him, but they still had composite sketches.

And they'd been closing in. Wasn't that why Norton had

outed his partners to begin with? He'd told Petrosky exactly where to find Shannon. Though Dr. McCallum had told him afterwards that Norton had likely gotten bored.

Seems Norton had found something more exciting, more perverse, than torturing a cop's wife and sewing her lips closed. Unless ... was it possible they had a copycat instead? Though the department had tried to squash it, Shannon's lips being sewn shut had hit the papers—too juicy a story to pass up. But the department had managed to keep much of the rest off the news, including the #1 etched in the victims' flesh.

He flipped the page to Dr. McCallum's profile. *Piqueristic tendencies*—stabbing as a source of sexual pleasure. *Suspect insecure, threatened by any challenges to his manliness.* Probably why he went after vulnerable—read: young or slight—victims. *Attacks about control, possibly paying back those who rejected him in one form or another.* And a paragraph detailing McCallum's concern that Norton had been learning to kill, learning to groom a victim, by watching his partners. *Will kill again, escalation likely.*

Escalation. Norton had never raped his victims before, but they'd find out if he was a rapist soon enough—the DNA from the infant should be back today. They'd know whether he raped this girl and forced her to carry his baby before hacking her apart. But if the baby wasn't his, then what? A copycat could have found out about the #1 and taken the rest into his own hands. Adam Norton had never hacked a woman apart like the gruesome scene they'd just come from. And Norton would have to be a fucking idiot to stick around here where the cops already knew his face. Then again, Norton had made it a point to meet Petrosky in person during their investigation into Shannon's abduction ... He was going around in circles. Petrosky massaged his throbbing temples.

"Shannon's at home with the kids." Morrison dropped into the chair beside Petrosky's desk looking more haggard than even an hour before. "Valentine's parked in front of the house, and later they're going to stay at his place with the dogs. In case. Roger freaked a little when I told him, said he'd pick up the slack at the office."

Roger McFadden, Shannon's ex-husband and the lead prosecutor, was probably worried he'd be dragged into it—last time he'd been at the scene when they pulled Shannon and Evie from the house where they'd been kept prisoner. Not that Roger had minded being the hero—that narcissistic asshole would probably do it all over again just for the fame.

"Valentine's going to be the detail on Shannon and the kids, until we catch Norton. Chief's orders. But I think this killer has moved on from our family."

Petrosky nodded. *Our family.* Including him? And had Norton really moved on?

Probably. Norton hadn't had a grudge against Shannon or anyone in particular. He'd tortured and killed whoever was convenient, or whoever his partners told him to. And if he was back, without partners, it meant Norton had learned to take his own victims. Now he had a type. Shannon didn't fit it ... did she? If he'd been after her, he would have made another play for her sometime in the last two years. Again ... if it *was* Norton. Though better to assume Norton was back for round two and take appropriate precautions than risk fucking up and costing another innocent girl her life.

Petrosky could see the guilt in Morrison's eyes—Shannon had been taken and tortured, because of Morrison. Because Norton's partner, a woman from Morrison's past, blamed Morrison for the death of a man she considered her brother. She'd watched and waited for years until Morrison had something to lose—then tried to take it from him for good.

But she'd underestimated Shannon. So had Adam Norton.

"I ran the social security number Norton used at Xtreme Clean too," Morrison said. "Not being used. No taxes filed. Either he's moved on with a different social, or he's got work that doesn't require one."

Xtreme Clean. Norton's last known place of employment— where he'd been working while he had Shannon locked in an iron collar in his closet. The job that had given him access to many buildings he wouldn't have been able to enter otherwise— like the rehab center where he'd shown himself to Petrosky. Had Norton stumbled upon a good hiding spot during his cleaning gigs? They'd look, but that was too obvious and those buildings were occupied: offices, clinics and the like. Not like you could just stash a kidnapping victim in the janitor's closet.

Petrosky flipped another page and glowered at the composite sketch. Young, *god*, Norton'd been so young, only nineteen or twenty when he'd taken Shannon, which is why they'd checked every high school in the area, every college, to no avail. He was probably around twenty-two now, and slight—five-nine or so, gangly. A lanky computer nerd that no one would ever look at and think "murderer." But based on the footprints, he was heavier now. Fatter? Or had he put on muscle? He could have changed other aspects of his appearance, too—glasses or a beard could make a big difference, so could growing out his hair. He was bald in their picture, with dark eyebrows, dead eyes. A crawl of pimple scabs along his jaw. Petrosky could almost hear him speaking in that growly voice he had. If Petrosky had his way, the fucker'd never speak again.

"I want to go talk to Janice," Morrison said suddenly. The blind fury in Morrison's eyes burned so hot Petrosky could practically feel it. The kid hadn't forgotten how Janice had conspired to kidnap Shannon and Evie. "She's up in Ypsi now. I can be there in an hour.

Petrosky nodded and smacked the file closed. It'd be a little while before they got anything from the autopsy, and at this point Janice was their best lead—she was the only one who'd been close to Norton in the months before he'd kidnapped their latest homicide victim. "I'll go with you."

"You don't have to."

Morrison was trustworthy, but when it came to his family … *Yes I do need to go with you. And you know why.* Petrosky stared him down until Morrison averted his eyes.

Besides, instead of helping California, this bitch would probably try to slice the kid's balls off. At least Petrosky could choke her out first.

Maybe he'd strangle her anyway.

14

Janice looked the same as she had the night Petrosky had slapped the cuffs on her, right down to her enraged blue eyes.

The guard unlocked the barred cage—like a prison cell with a table instead of a bed—and led Petrosky and Morrison inside. The guy's eyes lingered a touch too long on Janice's chest—even shackled to a metal table in prison scrubs, she commanded attention with her brilliant red hair flaming under the harsh fluorescents. He'd almost forgotten about that: redheads. The killer had a thing for the gingers. Adam Norton had been shacked up with this one when they'd arrested her. And Natalie Bell, his second victim, had red highlights. Their current vic fit that profile too. Or had, until she'd been reduced to brutalized meat, her red curls plastered to what was left of her face with dried blood.

Morrison sat across from her, but Petrosky stood at the head of the table, examining her stiff posture, the way her knuckles stayed white even as she tried to feign calm by relaxing her mouth. But her eyes remained narrowed. *One move, it's over.* He'd be ready in case she lunged for Surfer Boy with a homemade shiv.

"I know you hate me," Morrison said.

"You killed Danny, and you got away with it. Of course I fucking hate you."

"Danny tripped. He hit his head."

"You could have saved him, and you didn't."

"I'm not here to make amends for the past." Morrison's face hardened and he hid his balled fists under the table. Maybe Petrosky should have stood behind Cali instead, ready to pull him off the woman who had almost killed his family. Morrison couldn't go down for assault—he still had a family to go home to.

Unlike Petrosky.

She crossed her arms. "Then why are you here?"

"It's about Adam Norton."

She licked her lips, nostrils flaring. Apparently she hated Norton too.

"We know he hasn't been to see you," Morrison said, and her mouth tightened along with her eyes. "We think he's responsible for abducting a girl. Raping her. Forcing her to have his child."

Her hands balled into fists, and Petrosky prepared for her to leap from the chair. Janice was fiercely jealous—she'd gone stalker more than once. She'd even tried to have ex-lovers arrested or killed for leaving her, including Shannon's ex-husband. Petrosky rather wished she'd succeeded in making Roger's stupid ass disappear.

Morrison's shoulders relaxed and he leaned forward, but the kid wasn't calm—he just knew how to get suspects talking. "You might hate me, Janice, but I suspect you hate him too. He sold you out. Repay the favor and tell me where he is."

"He'll kill you." Quiet, cool. The clouds cleared from her face and she half smiled. "And I don't know where he is."

"So you said during the trial."

"I was trying to stay out of jail—even had the chance for a plea if I told them where he was." She leaned back and crossed her arms. "Why would I refuse them then and tell you now?"

Because she had wanted to protect him. And she had. She'd fought them every step, wasted their time, and they'd walked away with no new information.

"Maybe something has changed," Morrison said. "He send you any letters? Care packages? He ever even consider coming to see you?"

"No." It was a whisper. Her lips were a bloodless line.

"What's the significance of the number one?"

She looked at the tabletop. "I don't know. I never knew. I told you that before."

"It was carved on our victim this morning. And it was carved on Dylan Acosta's body and on Natalie Bell's."

"I didn't do that to ... her. To either of them." She shook her head, violently, but it didn't hide the quiver in her chin.

"Shannon heard him call *you* his number one girl when you had her locked up." Though he'd spoken softly, Petrosky could hear the challenge in Morrison's tone.

"We were in a *relationship*. He wasn't in a relationship with ... them."

That was true enough—probably. If Adam Norton was indeed the man they were looking for, he had imprisoned their victim until she'd run from him in the middle of the night. Then he'd murdered her. He'd killed Natalie Bell without raping her, killed little Dylan Acosta without raping him either. Norton's pleasure came from the pain no matter who he was hurting.

"How do you know he wasn't in a relationship with them?" Morrison asked her, voice low and tight. "He's been fucking some little girl, Janice. Why did he carve a number one into her flesh?"

"I—"

"Just because he wasn't in a relationship with Acosta—"

"I had nothing to do with Acosta! That was Adam and his fucking pedophile friend." Even then, Janice had no control over Norton. Maybe Norton hadn't been in control of himself.

"Looks like Adam's a pedophile too, Janice. Makes me wonder what he saw in you." Morrison's words were almost whispered but the challenge was as loud as if he'd screamed it.

Her face darkened. "He isn't a—"

Enough. Petrosky stepped forward and slammed his fists against the table so hard that both Janice and Morrison jumped. "Stop protecting him," he growled.

Her eyes widened.

"He doesn't give a fuck about you," Petrosky hissed at her. "Never did. He was in it for the blood. He would have killed you too once you'd stopped being useful." He walked around the table, behind Morrison's chair. "But you gave him the house—a place to play."

"He wasn't there because of my money," she snapped.

"He couldn't have afforded anything on his own," Morrison said.

"He had funds. I don't know where they came from, but he had money. That's how he bought all that weird stuff."

Weird stuff. The collar fitted with razor blades that had almost ended Shannon's life. The mask, like the kind doctors of death wore during the black plague—bird-like and horrid, painted with the garish colors of a circus clown. And now that nightmarish billhook, the splintered doorframe, Salomon's rib bone spearing from her flesh like a monument to the world's depravity.

"What else did he buy?" Petrosky said. If they could track a few new purchases, they might have a shot. They'd looked into the weapons angle years ago, and had come up with nothing— just a few oddball collectors, a few museums. No one with ties to the murders or Norton.

"Old jester's masks. Stuff like that."

The masks had been a dead end too. But they'd meant something to Norton—they had a role in his game. "Why did he have the masks, Janice? What did he use them for?"

"He …" Her gaze flicked from one side of the barred cell to the other. "He wore them when he was hurting people." Morrison's back stiffened. "It almost made him seem … more confident, somehow. Stronger."

Sensitive and insecure, worried about slights to his manliness, McCallum had said. Disguises, then—to be someone else, someone who couldn't be touched by rejection.

The blush on her cheeks grew hotter.

"He wore them when you were fucking, too, didn't he?" Petrosky said.

She bit her lip.

Morrison cleared his throat. "He's still here, Janice. Nearby. Instead of running away, he stuck around, busying himself with other girls, and left you to rot in a cell."

Janice drew her gaze to Petrosky's, hurt radiating from her, like she was imploring them to stop aggravating her heartache. But Petrosky saw Shannon's mouth the day they'd found her—lips sewn together with upholstery thread, wet and bloody and dripping with pus—and any burgeoning hint of sympathy evaporated. Yet he and Janice had a common goal. He needed to exploit it.

"It isn't like he ever loved you," Petrosky said. "Let me find him. Maybe I'll kill him for you."

The hurt in her eyes brightened to rage. "If I knew where he was, I'd tell you." A single tear slid down her cheek. "But like you said, he never loved me." She sniffed and wiped her face, then leveled her gaze at Morrison, venom sneaking in beneath the pain. She took a deep breath. "So," she said, a smile touching her lips. "How's Evie?"

15

THEY STARTED with the last two years, since Shannon's abduction, searching for any missing girls who fit the profile of their victim—she was their only real lead. The ginger thing helped, though there were still far too many missing redheads in Ash Park and the surrounding area, if she was even from here. So many girls—photo after photo after photo. Twice, Petrosky picked up his phone to make sure it was working in case the morgue tried to call.

Janice didn't have shit that would help them. She hadn't seen Norton in years—they'd checked the logs. No one but her attorney had come to visit. They had to be sure, and Morrison wouldn't have been able to sleep if they hadn't gone up there in person, but the dead end still stung.

And they still had a corpse without a name. Identification would be tricky—they were looking for a young woman who'd been missing for an indeterminate amount of time, based on a body with no fucking face. She sure wasn't going to look like her school pictures.

Two hours later, the Taco Bell he'd inhaled on the drive home was gurgling like a volcano ready to erupt, but with more noxious gases. Petrosky was standing to rush to the bathroom when Morrison ran up with a picture: a teenager in a sundress, small, thin, freckled. Eyes smiling. Curly hair the color of dying autumn leaves.

"Lisa Walsh. Found her in a stack of missing persons from two years ago, a month after Shannon was taken." Morrison clenched his jaw, then released it as he pointed to the image. Still agitated. "See that pattern of freckles on the front of her shoulder? I think the body had the same pattern. Almost like a connect-the-dots rectangle."

Kid had good eyes. Petrosky started to nod approval but his stomach gave another lurch and he abandoned the head shaking and rushed past Morrison to do his business.

Afterwards, Morrison was waiting for him outside the men's room door. "I grabbed the Walsh folder so we can take it to the morgue."

"Haven't heard dick yet from the ME."

"I did. They're ready for us."

"Who the hell called you?" Although ... Katrina was pretty cozy with the ME. "That tech must be hot for you, Surfer—"

"I took the liberty of answering your desk phone."

"What in the ever-loving—"

"Let's go, old man." Morrison headed to the elevator, folder under his arm.

16

THE DRIVE to the hospital took thirty long minutes and the brightly lit lobby did nothing to assuage his nerves—every noise seemed amplified. Petrosky paused at the elevator, wondering if they should go upstairs to check in at the NICU. Hopefully the baby was okay—she didn't even have a name yet, and dying without one suddenly seemed a hundred times more terrible. Instead they headed to the basement, where, as of now, Baby Doe wasn't on a slab in the room with her toeless mother.

They signed in at a small counter and flashed their badges to be admitted to a cold, gray room with stainless steel tables and drawers full of people. Probably full of people, anyway. When Petrosky called to put a rush on an autopsy, the medical examiner's office always acted like the drawers were stuffed with bodies, but you never could tell if the morgue was really backed up or they were all just lazy assholes.

A short, spindly man with thick glasses and the face of a ferret stood at the head of the table above the girl, her body now completely hidden under a blue sheet. Dr. Woolverton had been working with the force for ten fucking years and he'd always been a dick. Petrosky had disliked him from the start.

"All right, Woolverton, what have we got?"

"Dr. Woolverton," he spat, lips so tight they were almost as white as the bloodless people he spent his days carving up. The guy had the defensive expression of a kid who'd been bullied all his life. Woolverton was probably just waiting for an excuse to take it out on someone now that he was big and bad and grown-up.

Kinda like their perp.

Petrosky maintained eye contact, like he always did, watching the bastard's mouth twitch like he was uncomfortable but trying not to show it. Maybe Woolverton would file another complaint against him. If he did, Petrosky would use it as an excuse to finally punch him in his fucking glass jaw.

Woolverton blinked first.

Morrison cleared his throat. "Dr. Woolverton, good to see you again. I'd shake your hand but ..." He gestured to the medical examiner's gloved digits, where specks of blood—or something more grotesque—clung to the latex. "Well, you know." He paused. "Did you find anything on the victim that might help us catch her killer?"

Woolverton looked behind Petrosky, face softening just a touch, as if the only reason to be pissed in this room was Petrosky's bitch ass and not the fact that this girl's life was over. "She's had a baby recently, but you already knew that." He glanced at the sheet and gestured almost nonchalantly to the middle, probably her belly. "And there are scars, injuries, that are older."

Petrosky gritted his teeth. *Here we fucking go.*

"Muscle atrophy, likely due to long-term imprisonment. What you'd see if you had someone in a cell or a cage where there wasn't much freedom of movement."

No surprise—the ligature marks on the girl's wrists and ankles had hinted at extended captivity.

"There's also a ton of tearing in the vaginal area," Woolverton continued, voice louder than it needed to be delivering this kind of news—his tone felt obscene. "New stuff, from the birth and whatnot, but old cuts and tears that are totally healed. And multiple healed stab wounds all over, many of them small and thin like he used a needle, and a few that look more like a round spike—a railroad tie maybe. Again, old and new." Woolverton shrugged like it was no big whoop and Petrosky resisted the urge to clock him.

"It's impossible to tell exactly how long ago most of the scars happened." Woolverton finally lowered his voice, perhaps because he was beyond the realm of verifiable fact. "Same with the toes. Amputations heal more slowly for obvious reasons, but I'd say he mangled her feet at least a year ago, probably longer."

"How old is she ... was she?" Morrison's voice was strained as if he were struggling to force out each syllable. Probably imagining what might have happened if they hadn't found Evie and Shannon.

"I'd put her around eighteen, give or take."

"Lisa Walsh would have been seventeen this year," Morrison said, eyes on the far wall as if he were speaking to himself. "I'll contact her parents, see if we can get dental records, hair ... something."

If Morrison was right about the freckle pattern, Walsh would have been just fifteen when Norton ripped her off the street. Two years with this asshole. Shannon had only been with Norton for a week, and she'd been changed forever. *Fifteen.*

Petrosky flashed to the scene in the alley—the girl's carved-up mouth, what remained of her face—and swallowed hard. He stared at the blue sheet. "We'll try to avoid making her parents see ... this." He hadn't been able to look at his own daughter's body—no way he could expect someone else to.

"Might want to avoid telling them the cause of death, too."

Petrosky's rib cage tightened and he rubbed at a sore spot in the middle of his chest. The stress would fucking kill him. "Yeah, no one wants to hear their kid was hacked apart."

"She wasn't."

Petrosky met Woolverton's gaze, trying not to recall the bloody gashes on her throat, on her face. "Come again?"

"I mean she was hacked up, but that wasn't the cause of death. Most of those wounds were done postmortem." Pink tinted Woolverton's cheekbones. "I've never seen anything like this."

He lifted the sheet. She was facedown, her back surprisingly clear of injury save for a series of punctures near her buttocks—

the marks could have been freckles if they weren't so ... deep. "Up here, this is your cause of death."

Near the top of one shoulder, between the blade and her neck, a gaping hole—gelatinous and still wet. Another stab wound? Looked like she'd been pierced by a fucking spear, and their guy did have a thing for old weapons. "What the hell is that?"

"Again, I had to do a little research because I've just—"

"Save the bullshit, Doc. We need concrete information. Something to help us."

Woolverton's eyes flashed. "I'm the one who's here on their day off trying to help out."

"She's the one chopped up on your fucking table, Woolverton. If it's so damn sad, help us find the guy who did it or so help me I will take you downtown for impeding an investigation."

Woolverton's face was nearly purple with rage. He looked directly at Morrison and spoke in a monotone. "We know that your guy has a penchant for medieval weapons, so I started there. She was killed using an old medieval method of torture. Everything is consistent—I even found splinters of wood in the wounds on her legs and arms."

"Wood splinters?" Petrosky said. "So it was a spear."

"Not exactly. The weapon didn't enter her body from the shoulder." Woolverton pulled the sheet back up, hiding the girl and her wounds, though his eyes remained bright, almost ... fascinated. Excited. *Horse-fucking piece of shit.* "The official murder weapon looks like a stake with a sharpened point. Probably had it upright and secured to the ground. He bound her hands and feet, inserted it into her vagina and just ... let her go."

Petrosky choked. Tension rolled from Morrison's frame, wrapping around them both and squeezing the air from the room.

Woolverton was still talking, apparently oblivious to their disgust. "Over the next day or so, the spike tore through her womb and organs, finally exiting the shoulder. She has splinters internally, but also in her calves and palms and the pads of her feet like she struggled against the—"

Petrosky put up his hand. "Okay, enough, we've got it. What the fuck, Doc?"

Woolverton closed his mouth but his eyes glittered. *What in the fresh hell is wrong with this guy?* Woolverton was almost … smiling? No, maybe a twitch at the corner of his mouth, but surely it was Petrosky's imagination. Woolverton might be a spindly dick but only a fucking psycho would be excited by the murder of some poor girl. He was probably just thrilled at the prospect of making Petrosky gag—it made him the big man in the room.

Petrosky stared at the table, avoiding Woolverton's bright eyes lest he punch the fucker's nose into his brain. A breeze from the heating duct ruffled the blue sheet, making it look like the girl was struggling to breathe.

Petrosky's stomach was a sponge squeezing further toward his throat. This girl had tried to get away from her abductor. She'd saved her baby from the hell she'd been living in. And the killer had used that to punish her. Barbarically.

He'd turned her love for her child into an excuse to impale her.

17

Morrison drove Petrosky's car back to the precinct. Petrosky smoked like a meth dealer's trailer and tried to ignore his rancid gut.

"Fifteen," Morrison muttered. "Can you imagine? A high school sophomore, and someone snatches you on your way home from band practice?"

Morrison had turned to chattering, surely to avoid thinking about how this girl could have been Shannon. And her infant could have been his daughter.

"Is that what happened?" Petrosky said. "Band practice?" Half of it came out like a belch.

If Morrison noticed the burp, he didn't show it. "If our victim is Lisa Walsh, yeah. She was walking home after practice, never seen again. But one of her classmates saw her with an older guy in the park a few weeks before she disappeared."

"Get a description?"

"She only saw him from behind and he was wearing a hat. About the right build, though—five-nine-ish and thin. That's all the witness saw."

Thin. Sounded like Norton. Though Norton might have gained some weight in the last two years, he would have been slight when he took Walsh—if he took Walsh. Though appalling,

Petrosky almost hoped they'd find Norton was the father of Walsh's baby. Then they'd know for certain they were looking for him and not some copycat or a random partner Norton'd had over the years; a partner who'd been privy to the details of Norton's past crimes.

Petrosky flipped open the folder and looked at Walsh's face. He pictured her alive, walking home, a clarinet or maybe a flute under her arm. *Fifteen.* The age Julie had been when she died. In another life, Walsh could have been Julie's friend—maybe, had time not separated them, they'd have been walking home together and the killer would have passed them over. Let them live and sought another girl walking alone.

Lisa. Julie. Despite the fact that Julie would have been in her twenties now if she'd lived, Petrosky was suddenly certain that Lisa would have been maid of honor in Julie's wedding. But Julie would have waited until after graduation to get married; she'd have been on her way to becoming a doctor, maybe a writer. But not a cop. Never a fucking cop.

"Boss, you all right?"

Hell, maybe if Petrosky hadn't become a cop, Morrison would have a partner who knew what the hell he was doing. Maybe without Petrosky, Morrison would have found his wife and daughter right away, before Norton had tortured them. Maybe they'd have caught Adam Norton before he'd had a chance to rape and torture Lisa Walsh. He could almost feel the spike tearing through his innards, and his breath caught. He coughed, hacked, gasped for breath.

"Boss?"

Years of abuse. Torture. Lisa had been murdered for the sake of a child she'd no doubt been forced to have. He slid the picture back into the folder and set it on the console, his teeth grinding together hard enough to make his temples throb. Julie had been lucky.

I'm glad they just used her and killed her. I'm glad it was fast.

Jesus Christ, what the hell am I thinking?

Morrison touched his arm.

So much evil and he was incapable of fixing it. Useless. His work would never be done—his life was a sham. Petrosky pictured Julie's face, peering up at him from his desk drawer next to the cigarettes he wasn't supposed to smoke but still did every fucking day. *Sorry, honey.*

Four months sober. He wouldn't make it to five.

PETROSKY WAS STILL TRYING to force Julie's face from his brain when Morrison pulled up at the precinct. The crimson sky of impending dusk felt ominous, like the entire world could sense his failure and was disturbed by it.

"You want to go get some coffee or something, Boss? Maybe some pastries at that fudge place over on Beeker? We can swing by the Walshes' and—"

"Get out, Morrison."

"It's just about dinnertime, Boss. We can go get some soup. I know that Taco Bell isn't sitting right with you."

Petrosky ran a hand down his sweaty face. "You go see them. I'll catch up with you in the morning."

Morrison hesitated with his hand on the driver's door.

"Get the fuck out, Cali. I won't say it again." Petrosky stared out the front windshield at the bloody sky until he heard the door open and slam. Then he walked slowly around to the driver's side and settled in, put his foot on the gas, gently, and puttered out of the parking lot, giving fate plenty of time to intervene. But the sky stayed red, bloody like the body in the alley, the mess at Salomon's, and Julie's throat, Julie ... He pushed his foot down harder.

The roads were clogged with the beginnings of rush hour. A sea of brake lights stretched out against the dusk as the sky dimmed and finally blackened. *Four months. Four.* It wasn't a lot, but it was a start.

But a start of what? A life where every day competed for the most fucking miserable? A life where he was just biding his time, draining the patience from the people he cared about until they finally gave up on him too? It wasn't like tomorrow'd be the start of some bright new future where his kid wasn't dead. Where his wife still made dinner sometimes and walking the goddamn dog was the worst of his problems. He'd never wake up to a world where people didn't kidnap kids and cut off their toes for fun.

He passed the building where AA meetings were held, passed a restaurant he'd visited with his ex-wife before everything had gone to shit, and stopped at a glass and mortar building with an obnoxious chalkboard sign that proclaimed "Beer! Wine!" in bubble letters. Petrosky resisted the urge to leap from the car and smash the shit out of it. The lights through the black bars on the windows cast a zigzag pattern on the walkway.

Then he was outside the car, breathing in the tang of rust and dirty snow. The wind froze his cheeks. And when Julie's face resurfaced in his mind, his despair solidified like ice between his shoulder blades. It wasn't just the existence of kidnappers, of killers, that spurred this helplessness—it was that the force was unable to catch them, *he* was impotent to catch them. *Adam Norton.* Petrosky hadn't stopped him from kidnapping Shannon and Evie, he hadn't kept someone from kidnapping and killing the Walsh girl, he'd not even been able to protect Julie from whoever the fuck had left her brutalized and cold in that lonely field. *Protect and serve.* He couldn't protect anyone. Why did he even bother trying?

The bell above the liquor store door jangled then stopped abruptly like a cat getting hit by a car—one jingle of a collar, then silence forever. The cases of beer were stocked as he knew they would be, but that wouldn't do tonight. He thought about getting back into his car. About the meeting down the street. His shoulder itched where Julie's face was probably trying to whisper to him from under his shirt sleeve.

"Jack, the big bottle." His words were strained, hollow, like they belonged to someone else.

Petrosky kept his eyes on the counter as the bottle disappeared into a brown paper bag. He slid cash onto the gray countertop. A gnarled old hand took it, its papery skin almost translucent under the garish fluorescent lighting. Half a ghost. One more human on their way out. The gun at the small of his back felt suddenly heavy, but comforting and warm, like an extension of his body.

Petrosky snatched the bag and his change and bolted for the car, death on his heels, then stopped to let the frigid air cool his blistered face.

Might as well let death catch up.

18

Petrosky wasn't immediately sure where he was, he just knew he was cold. *Damn cold.* He pushed himself to sitting, his head swimming as the world receded and then pulsed back in jagged gasps of color. The shower curtain. The showerhead. His arm on the side of the tub.

And someone was stabbing him in the temples. Fucking Jack. *You, sir, are a dickwad.*

Petrosky gripped the edge of the tub and peeled himself off the frigid fiberglass. His hand slipped. His shoulder smacked the side. He adjusted his grip and hoisted his body up again until his feet hit the tile floor, one at a time. *Success.* Then the world wavered.

Nausea slithered through his stomach and he lunged at the toilet, filing it with bitter clumps of some carbohydrate he didn't remember eating and slimy yellow bile, tinged with red. He retched once more and sank onto the floor next to the toilet, leaning his head against the wall. The room swam and solidified in the hazy way of a city trapped under the baking sun.

He was fully clothed in the button-down and jeans he'd been wearing the day before, though the shirt now bore discolorations that looked like food or maybe booze. His feet were bare. And his clothes weren't wet—there was no water in the tub.

Petrosky turned his head and his skull tried to explode. He touched his cheek to the wall and pressed one hand against his other temple as if he were trying to push his brain back into place and halt the relentless pounding.

Jesus fucking Christ, the light. His shoes were inside the tub. From their placement, he must have taken them off and put them under his head like a goddamn pillow. His gun was on the edge of the tub, the little red dot on the barrel showing the safety was off. He wondered how close he'd gotten this time. Pretty fucking close, probably.

But not close enough.

He stood on jelly legs and dragged himself along the wall back to the shower. The pattern of light on the floor suggested it was midmorning, nine at the earliest.

The dead girl was waiting for him.

He undressed, still leaning against the wall, turned the shower on cold, and staggered in, letting the icy water wake him. By the time he emerged, shivering, the world was less wobbly and his head was almost clear.

It took him three tries to button his shirt correctly, and by the time he finally got it he was ready to tear the thing off and grab a sweatshirt. But he wasn't quite ready to be the guy at AA in sweatpants and a backwards cap complaining about how the people at his work just didn't understand him. He headed for the door, made it to the couch, and sank onto the sofa. Put his head against the arm. *Five minutes.*

A dull thud sounded on the door, like someone kicking it with a shoe. His head pulsed in time with the knocking.

He didn't move. "You selling cookies or Jesus?" he yelled, and the strain in his temples stretched down through his voice box and into the tendons in his neck.

"I can go get some cookies, but Jesus might run from your cranky butt." Petrosky hauled himself to sitting and staggered to the kitchen as Morrison let himself in, carrying two stainless steel coffee cups and a box of granola bars pressed tight against his chest. The kid kicked the door shut behind him.

"You can head right back out if all you brought is chicken feed, California."

Morrison sighed. "Shannon said you'd say that. She's got the doughnuts."

"You brought your wife here? She should be staying in where it's warm." And where Norton couldn't find her.

"She was worried about you." Morrison set the granola bars on the counter next to Julie's night-light. The rosy hue was more red than pink this morning, glaring like an evil eye—like it was angry at him. Or maybe just angry at what he'd become.

That was fair.

Morrison held out one coffee and took a sip from his own, the peace sign brilliantly blue, almost grinning at Petrosky.

He resisted slapping the cup to the floor. "Where is Shannon?"

"In the car with Henry. Said she wanted to change his pants before she brought him up here."

"She can't be out there alone! This guy is—"

"Valentine's here too."

"It's a fucking party, huh?" Petrosky took the coffee and put it to his lips, but his hand shook and he lowered it before Morrison could notice. "So fill me in."

"Verified the girl as Lisa Walsh—three intact molars and a few other teeth on one side gave us enough to match dental records. Also ... parent identification. Her father came down." Morrison's eyes were haunted—he seemed to be staring past Petrosky altogether as if Petrosky had suddenly become so insignificant that he'd disappeared entirely.

Petrosky raised the cup again, quickly, and sipped the coffee. His stomach rolled, but the fog around his vision lifted some.

Morrison shook his head, unwrapped a bar. "We've also verified Walsh as the infant's mother," he said around a mouthful of granola. "Though we knew that already. And Adam Norton is the baby's father. Matched him from trace he left behind during his last crime spree."

Confirmation. Norton was definitely their guy. But they still had no idea where to start and suddenly his incompetence was a living thing, climbing up his throat along with the bile from his agitated guts.

"We also got something else from forensics," Morrison was

saying. "The dust we found on the baby and on Walsh isn't from the Salomon house or from any of the neighbors' places immediately surrounding."

Petrosky set his coffee on the counter, hoping Morrison didn't catch the way it clattered before he let it go.

"They identified the unknown compounds at Salomon's; the mortar around the basement windows contains asbestos." Morrison glanced at the counter and back at Petrosky. "Courtney will be none too happy about that when she tries to sell the place."

Petrosky belched. *Enough bullshitting.* "What about the dust found in the indentations on the lawn and on the victims? Tell us anything about where they came from?"

"Portland cement, they called it."

"Portland, huh?" Petrosky shifted his weight. His left leg was numb.

Morrison sighed. "It might not help us much because that cement is sold pretty much everywhere. It's the standard home improvement special—even used by the bigger construction companies now. It would have been more useful if it had been the other way around—asbestos on the kids instead of that house, but as it is ..." Morrison tossed his granola wrapper toward the trash can. It landed on the floor by Petrosky's feet. They both stared at it until Morrison stooped and snatched up the wrapper.

"Anyway, Decantor and I spent a lot of time harassing hardware store employees and going over surveillance videos."

"Decantor?" Irritation cleared the last of the fogginess. That chatty fuck was a homicide detective and one of Morrison's workout buddies, but since when did Morrison call him in on their cases? The chief must have put him up to it.

"Valentine helped me out, too, in the last eighteen hours—so many hardware stores that it's taken a while to pull credit cards on the cement purchases."

Eighteen hours? "What time is it?"

"Lunchtime, Boss."

"You've been up since yesterday? Didn't you sleep?"

"I wanted to get a jump on this. In case the guy decides to

grab someone else—or in case he already has some other girl, which he probably does."

A lump formed in Petrosky's throat. Norton had snatched Walsh soon after he'd lost his first captives. Of course he'd be after another girl. And Morrison knew that—from the grim look in his eyes, he'd probably spent his off hours watching his family sleep, thinking that it could have been them in the morgue. Or that it might still be.

"I'm going to check out the surveillance videos from the closest home improvement stores next, look at the times around cash purchases of that product and see if I can make out any license plates." He glanced at the granola box, at the night-light, back at Petrosky. "Right now, we don't have much else. Forensics doesn't have any prints at all, just the cement dust and the wood slivers in the girl's skin. Nothing unique about the wood either, by the way. Oak, available at any hardware store in the form of a curtain rod, and that looks to be the size he used; all Norton had to do was sharpen it into a point." He shuddered almost imperceptibly, then sipped his own coffee, blinking bloodshot eyes. "There were some other splinters that were different, though. Pine slivers along Walsh's sides, like she was dragged along a wood floor."

Petrosky pictured what was left of her feet and swallowed hard to avoid retching. "He was holding her captive. Might have squeezed out of a cage or through a wooden door."

"Or a cell. Maybe she dug a hole with a spoon like in one of those old prison escape movies. If the floor was concrete and the base or the frame was made of wood—"

"A spoon?"

"She had almost two years to do it."

"He would have noticed. If he built a jail cell in his house, it wouldn't be that big."

The door swung open and Petrosky jerked his head toward the sound, sending a lightning bolt of pain from his neck to his sternum.

"I'm not interrupting, am I?" Shannon strode into the house with Henry in a carrier on her chest, doughnuts in her hand. Evie followed, skipping, her blond curls bouncing over her cherub cheeks as she clapped her hands and squealed, "Papa Eddie!"

Shannon grabbed her arm before she could run to Petrosky. "Go use the bathroom, okay, honey? I know you have to go." Evie shot him another look.

"Go on! Do you need help?" Shannon asked her.

"No! I do it!" Evie yelled, and scampered off.

Shannon tossed the box of doughnuts on the counter and slapped Petrosky in the back of the head so hard he had to grab the counter to stay upright. In the carrier on her chest, Henry flailed his arms and kicked his feet.

Petrosky rubbed his skull. "Fucking hell, Taylor, you got some—"

"Stop scaring us like that. I can't run you down every time you decide to fuck up."

Morrison stepped beside Petrosky. "Shanny, just—"

"No, goddammit. And you know better too." Her blond hair was in a disheveled ponytail, her eyes glassy. She raised her arm again and Petrosky reared back, hand in front of his face for protection. But instead of hitting him again, she threw an arm around Petrosky's neck—a hug, fierce and strong—then released him and shoved him away.

"Fuck you, Petrosky. And I'm glad you're alive. But you keep it up, I will turn you in myself, so help me."

"You had to marry a prosecutor," he muttered to Morrison, then turned back to Shannon. "You could have changed the baby in the house, you know. He's got almost as much control of his bodily functions as your husband here."

Her face softened, but her eyes remained tight. "I wanted to give you guys a minute," she said as Henry blew spit bubbles at Petrosky. The baby's blue eyes danced—so full of promise, of hope, that Petrosky's gut clenched. Eventually the world would beat that joy out of Henry too, and there was nothing Petrosky could do about it.

Petrosky forced a smile. "What's up, little California?"

Morrison took Henry from Shannon and kissed his forehead. "Don't listen to him, Henry. He's just mad that his hair is nowhere near as golden—or evident—as yours."

Henry gurgled and Morrison kissed his nose which made Henry scrunch up his face.

Shannon brushed her hair from her cheek. "I got you lemon, Bavarian cream, and a few crullers."

"Thank you."

"No problem." She narrowed her eyes. "You look like shit."

Morrison put his hand over Henry's ear.

"You need to care of yourself," she said to Petrosky. "We need you to stick around."

Petrosky's stomach contracted. Bile and phlegm stuck, thick and metallic, in the back of his throat. "I'm fine. Besides, I can't walk you down the aisle twice. My work is done." He smiled.

She didn't. "When was the last time you ate?"

"Last night." Petrosky grabbed a doughnut, shoved half in his mouth, and raised his eyebrows at her.

Henry put his mouth on Morrison's neck and whined.

"I'm fine, Taylor."

Shannon took the baby and plopped into the only chair not covered with clothes or empty pizza boxes. When were those even from? The pizza was probably moldy as hell, but least he didn't have mice yet ... he didn't think. He eyed the boxes suspiciously.

She lifted her shirt to put Henry to her breast and the baby quieted. "Come have dinner with us tonight. It'll be a houseful at Valentine's, but I'm sure it'll be fine. The kids would love to spend some time with Papa Ed."

"Not tonight, Shannon. I have to get a few things done on this case."

"If you were that worried about the case, you would have stayed up and worked with Morrison all night."

Ouch. "I guess I better make it up to your husband tonight." Tonight would be a rough one. Already the doughnut was trying to make a comeback.

"Tomorrow, then."

"Maybe." He sighed when she stared at him. "Let me figure out my schedule and I'll let your husband know later toda—" He jumped as little hands circled his knees.

"Papa Ed!"

Petrosky knelt beside Evie, one hand on the ground to steady himself against the dizziness. She threw her arms around his neck, then drew back suddenly, her tiny nose wrinkled. "You smell weird."

Probably the reek of cigarettes that clung to everything around him—like King Midas, only everything Petrosky touched turned to ash. He smiled at her hoping she'd manage to stay unburned, unhurt—though if she did it'd be her father's vigilance that saved her, not Petrosky. *Julie, I'm so sorry.* "Still like me even if I smell funny?"

She pursed her lips, thinking. "Yeah. I like you. You have more toys?"

"Evie!" Morrison shook his head. "Leave Papa Ed alone. He just gave you—"

"Look in the hall closet." Petrosky winked at her and Evie's eyes lit up. She darted off and they all listened to the sound of the closet door banging open, the scuffle of things being pushed around.

"You really got her something else?" Morrison looked after her.

Petrosky shrugged. "You know I have a stash just in case."

Evie scampered back with a baby doll. "Look what Papa Ed got me!" Shannon smiled at her, pulled her shirt down and set a now sleeping Henry against her shoulder. That was fast—Henry was not a nap lover. Maybe the kids had been up all night too.

"What do you say, Evie?" Morrison whispered.

"Thank you!"

Another hug. Her hair smelled like baby shampoo, and something about that made his heart seize.

"Don't forget about dinner, Petrosky." Shannon stood and nodded to Morrison, who scooped Evie up and moved to follow her out. "Meet you at the precinct, Boss. Half an hour?"

Petrosky nodded. When the door closed behind them, he lurched to the sink and vomited.

19

THE CEMENT DUST was a major fucking headache. Or maybe it was just … him. Petrosky put his fingers to his temples, pressing hard enough to bruise the skin, but the throbbing did not relent. Eight aspirin hadn't done shit to make the pain stop.

He slammed the folder shut. It sprang open again. Possibly because it was stuffed beyond capacity with Morrison's million-and-one notes. Everything was trying to piss him the fuck off today.

Morrison had done his due diligence, though. None of the credit card holders who'd purchased a weapon or closet rods or anything remotely medieval lived close to the Salomon house, and Petrosky couldn't imagine Lisa Walsh had run more than five miles—or even one mile—to get to Salomon's in the middle of the night. Perhaps if she had been driven, but no one had seen a car, hadn't even heard one. Plus, there was no trace of automotive fabric on Walsh or the infant, which he'd expect if the girls been driven to the scene. They'd canvassed the neighborhood. Interviewed every person within ten blocks. No one knew where Walsh or the infant had come from.

But they hadn't appeared out of nowhere.

Petrosky picked up his coffee cup and brought it to his lips. His hand twitched, and coffee sloshed onto his shirt, then his crotch, where it burned hot as a cigarette in hell.

"Fuck!" He leaped up as the coffee spread over his workstation.

"Here you go, old man." Morrison yanked the keyboard and the folder to the other side of the desk and tossed a wad of takeout napkins over the spill.

"Where'd you get all the napkins? You been eating the fast-food you yell at me for buying?"

"I save them from your takeout bags." Morrison grinned. He handed a few more napkins to Petrosky for his roasting nuts.

"You going through my trash, California?"

"Reduce, reuse—"

"Shut the fuck up, Surfer Boy."

Morrison's smile faltered. He blotted the remainder of the coffee from the desk as Petrosky wiped at his scalded junk.

Morrison threw the napkins into the bin at his foot, then extracted the papers and peeled the soggy manila folder from the desktop. "I'll grab another folder in a minute."

Petrosky sat back down, trying to ignore the pressure threatening to clamp his rib cage shut. Withdrawal was a bitch, but it could have been stress. Loss. He'd had the same issue after Julie died, like a gaping black hole had opened in his heart, the pain throbbing throughout the night, stabbing at him when he woke and realized she was still dead, aching whenever he considered all the things she'd never do. Every time he saw someone else's child, murdered as horribly as Julie had been, he felt its sharpness—a reminder of the horror. Maybe it would never go away. "What are you on over there, Cali?"

"Running down abductions that have the flavor of Walsh's, specifically the ones with older boyfriends like in the Walsh case; Norton's young, but visibly older than these girls." Morrison kept his gaze on his desk as if trying to recall specifics —or maybe he was just avoiding Petrosky's eyes. "I had breakfast with Freeman this morning too, for cross-referencing. With the baby and the kidnapping and the severe abuse, sexual enslavement seems a strong possibility. We know this guy, we know he probably isn't a trafficker, but with his fear of rejection, he might not be above getting his ladies from someone else, buying them to ensure they won't say no. So far we have a couple dozen cases that look promising."

Petrosky opened his mouth to respond, then cocked his head. "You went out for breakfast with Freeman? I thought that albino fucker would turn to ash if you took him outside."

"He smoldered a little, but he survived. Besides, I had to eat, and you weren't here."

I had to eat? "I'm not jealous, asshole, just trying to figure out why Freeman thinks you know what the fuck you're doing." The pain in Petrosky's chest intensified, shot through his shoulder blade, and finally eased. He belched a wretched sourness into the back of his throat and pulled his keyboard closer. It rattled in his hands. Morrison stared at him and frowned, then turned on his heel and headed off, presumably to get the folder.

Get it together, old man. You've already lost half a day feeling sorry for yourself. He couldn't let the stress get to him. Norton could be torturing some other girl while Petrosky sat on his ass trying to keep his pulse steady. If Norton didn't have another victim now, he would soon, and Petrosky already had enough blood on his hands.

Morrison returned with a folder, ripped the old cover from the file, and slapped his notes into the new one.

"Sorry, Kid. Really. Bad coffee. Looks like I need to stick to that hippie shit you bring."

Morrison's eye twitched, but he nodded.

"So the abduction cases you're looking at—you find evidence that Norton kidnapped someone else? I'm worried he'll take another girl to replace Walsh." The way he'd replaced Shannon. Who had Shannon replaced?

"I had the same thought, but it was just a gut feeling. At first." Morrison stepped to his desk and returned with two folders under his arm. The classifieds. "Then I found *her.*"

The file was thin, but all Petrosky needed was the photo. Ava Fenderson. Red hair and freckles, just like Walsh.

"What's so special about this case?"

Morrison pulled up a chair. "The night Ava disappeared, she ran out of the house after arguing with her parents, wearing fuzzy pink socks with treads just like the ones at the Salomon crime scene."

"But she wasn't at Salomon's—we know it was Walsh. We found her blood."

"Right. But if Fenderson had the socks wherever these girls were being held, Walsh could have grabbed them if she knew she was going to run." He looked down. "It doesn't feel like a coincidence, Boss, and if we can use the information to find him…"

The kid needed more coffee—or sleep. But that wasn't happening for either of them. "Tell me what else you got."

Morrison closed Fenderson's folder and met Petrosky's eyes. "I started within a thirty-mile radius of the Salomon place, even though Walsh's house was only eight miles from where we ended up finding her."

"Lisa Walsh grew up eight miles from Salomon's?" Shannon and Evie had been kept a few blocks from there too. Acosta and Natalie Bell were both killed less than five miles from the Salomon house.

"Yep. And Ava Fenderson lived less than four miles from Salomon's place and five from the Walsh dump site."

So Norton was local—and keeping the girls here. Just like before. He'd been right under their noses for more than two years. *Son of a fucking—*

Morrison handed Petrosky the file, the kid's back straightening as he went on. "These cases are all girls in a similar age range to Walsh, similar physical appearance. And they all seemed to be … uh … growing up faster than their classmates."

"Growing up?"

"Development-wise. Some were thirteen or fourteen when they disappeared but they looked like college kids."

Petrosky tried to clear his throat, but it turned into a hack and he spit phlegm into a napkin. Shoved it into his pocket. "So he's after younger girls, but takes the ones that look older." Because even if they looked like adults, younger girls were more vulnerable. Their killer was still insecure, still terrified of rejection, and yet, Norton had attacked a grown woman in the past. He'd also stomped a little boy to death, though that appeared to have been a crime of convenience. They'd have to chat with Dr. McCallum again.

Petrosky held up the folder—looked like about two dozen possible vics. "How'd you narrow it down to these?"

"I focused on cases where an older boyfriend was mentioned in the files, like for Walsh, hoping Norton had kept a similar pattern. Then I pulled the ones where the parents didn't know the boyfriend or where the boyfriend matched the description from Walsh's file—under six feet and thin, though I kept an eye out for heavier guys in later abductions too, because of the weight we got from the boot impressions at Salomon's."

Petrosky flipped to their composite. Lanky. Thin. Bald, with thick black brows that looked more like a pair of ridiculous hipster mustaches. He tried to picture Norton heavier, then stockier. Hitting the cake or the gym? And those eyebrows ...

"We'll have to be cautious about the physical descriptions on our guy," Petrosky said. "Not just the weight. His hair from the Natalie Bell scene, blond at the root, black at the tip—he was changing his appearance then too." Dyeing his eyebrows. Shaving his head.

They needed a new composite. Probably a whole slew of them.

Petrosky massaged his temples.

"I thought about that too, Boss. The difference in appearance. Hopefully, a witness saw the boyfriend in one of these other abduction cases, but for now, I released our original description and the composite, along with a statement that he might be heavier."

"Released? To who?"

"To the press. At the chief's urging," he added when Petrosky balked.

"The fucking press?" Norton was still in the same location as he'd been last time—if the media hadn't helped before they weren't going to help now. "Are the phones ringing off the hook?"

"Yup, but nothing promising. The chief got us some volunteers to cover the calls while we chase down the rest of the leads. Got Decantor and Valentine to help us out too."

As much as Petrosky hated to admit it, Decantor was genuinely good at his job. And he had picked up the slack on the Natalie Bell case two years ago, so he was familiar with Adam Norton. If only Decantor didn't tend to chat like a schoolgirl with a crush—they couldn't all be Brandon in forensics.

Petrosky popped his knuckles and his pinky stuck. Arthritis too? "The press release, the new leads, this all happened between last night and this afternoon?"

Morrison shrugged. "Life happens quick."

If only the good came as fast as the bad. Petrosky sifted through the folder and wide-eyed girls stared at him from glossy school photos—lips painted in bubblegum pink, the hard planes of adulthood beginning to show through their baby fat. One had her eyes closed, as if she'd been photographed mid blink. Another had a tiny stain on her shirt, breakfast gone awry. Endearing imperfections, in what were likely their last school photos. Were any of them still alive?

"All these girls seemed popular from the outside," Morrison said. "School clubs, band, cheerleading—but they were also troubled, according to the files. Drug use, promiscuity, school suspensions, and the like."

On the fringe of popular, then—trying desperately to fit in, but only partially succeeding. "He probably chose them because they'd think it was cool to have an older boyfriend. And with their histories, everyone would know they had issues and write it off as a runaway thing." Runaways got little priority with police departments—the responding officers would have filed a report, looked for a few weeks, then moved on. No follow-up, unless there was reason to think something terrible had happened to them.

"Runaways. Exactly. He didn't just pick randomly. To go out with an old guy, the kids had to be at least a little bit messed up, right?"

"Maybe, but he's still pretty young—young enough they wouldn't consider him old. And I think most teenage girls are into older guys anyway." Had Julie been into that? Petrosky's head threatened to split, the stress causing pain, pain causing more stress. He needed to stop taking everything so goddamn personally.

"Boss? You okay?"

Petrosky rubbed his temple. Nausea tugged at his gut. "Yeah. Just a ... headache."

"I've got some aspirin. Hang on." Morrison disappeared toward his desk, and Petrosky rested his head in one hand and paged through the folder with the other until he returned with coffee, a doughnut, and a medicine bottle. "This should do it. And if it doesn't, I've got an extra yogurt in the fridge."

"Yogurt? Dammit, California, I was just starting to like you."

Finally, a half grin. "Likewise, Boss."

Petrosky popped a few aspirin and washed them down with the coffee. He stared hard at the doughnut. Too bad it wasn't a shot of Jack—a little hair of the dog never hurt anyone. He put his hand on the drawer that held Julie's photo. *Half a day sober.* And counting, because Ava Fenderson, another little girl like Julie, needed them. *Needed him.* Maybe.

"All right, so we've got a starting place." Petrosky tapped the folder.

"I figured I could get going with the interviews," Morrison said. "It might take a day or two to get through this batch, but hopefully—"

"What's this 'I' bullshit? Gonna leave me here?"

"I can take care of it, Boss." But the fire in Morrison's eyes burned hotter than the coffee had on Petrosky's junk.

"Like hell you can. This is the guy who took your wife. Your kid." Last time, Morrison had flayed the skin off a dead man and set fire to Shannon's ex-husband's house to appease the kidnappers. California was no innocent when you fucked with his family. And if Morrison's bloodshot eyes were any indication, he wouldn't rest until he had Adam Norton's heart in a jar.

"Two sets of eyes are better than one," Petrosky said. And tired men made mistakes, no matter how many notes they took. "We'll do a little more canvassing too. Maybe look at house plans, see if there are any likely suspects nearby, basements, sheds, places he could be hiding these girls. A bomb shelter?

Somewhere he doesn't have to worry about escape or noise, like a cell or a set of rooms that can be locked securely."

"It must not be too secure if he had to take her toes."

"He probably did that for fun." Petrosky tapped the folder to hide the tremble in his hand.

Two years ago their killer had taken Lisa Walsh right after they'd rescued Shannon. If Norton didn't have another of these girls already, he'd sure as hell be hunting now.

20

MR. WALSH HAD a head of dark hair, a face thin as a meth addict's, and a nose three times wider than it needed to be. His blue eyes were rimmed with red, making him look as stoned as a Bob Marley fan. Walsh's lip trembled when he found out why they were there.

"When they called I just ... I couldn't believe it." Walsh led them through a front room strewn with laundry and into the kitchen where he motioned to the bar stools, then attacked the crumb-covered Formica countertop with a filthy sponge. A gray stain spread across the top. He wiped again, and the stain widened.

Morrison sat on one of the stools and laid his notepad on his lap. Light from the afternoon sun filtered through the kitchen window and onto the countertop and cabinets. It also lit up an old Ruger rifle, the wooden barrel scuffed and dusty, mounted over the stove.

Petrosky leaned against the counter and motioned to it. "Interesting centerpiece."

"After Lisa disappeared ... I guess you can never be too careful." Walsh turned back to the sink, shoulders slumped as if he were carrying something heavy on his back.

Petrosky's gaze swept the cabinets, the floor, the wall. The sticky floors would have made Ms. Salomon hurl, but it wasn't the dirtiest kitchen he'd seen. Nothing unusual. "So you always suspected foul play?"

Walsh's shoulders hunched, but he didn't turn from the sink. "Of course I suspected foul play. She was headstrong, but a good girl. She was in the band, got good grades."

Her grades had been As and Bs—they'd checked. But they'd fallen to Bs and Cs the semester before she disappeared. That drop in grades had been deemed evidence enough of a troubled teen; a runaway, not a victim of abduction. "What happened to her grades that last year?"

Walsh stiffened. "There was just something ... off, I guess. She never wanted to come home at night. Got frustrated with me for trying to keep her home to study. She started getting angrier ... jumpy, almost."

Sounded like normal teenage bullshit, though here it was probably a response to Norton's attempts to groom her. But still, what had taken Walsh away from homework and band practice and led her into the arms of a psycho?

Petrosky stared at Walsh's back as Walsh turned the water on and sank his hands into the soapy sink.

"What do you think happened, Mr. Walsh? With her grades?"

"I thought it was the change of scenery." He sniffed. "Once middle school started she was a different person: happy one minute, screaming the next. I figured it was all the hormones, you know? Girl stuff."

Morrison's pen scratching at the paper mingled with the clattering dishes and the wet slap of soapy water. Drip, scratch, clang—a musical almost as awful as *Cats*, the one Julie had dragged him to the year before she—

Stop. "What'd her mother have to say?" Petrosky asked. Sometimes moms had more insight into their daughter's dating situations—boyfriends. Had his ex-wife known anything he hadn't about Julie?

"Her mother was ... angry. At the acting out." Walsh picked up a bowl and attacked it with a brush, though it looked clean already. "She blamed me, I think, for being too hard on Lisa." His voice caught. Regret? Agitation? Probably both.

"Where's your wife now?"

"Ex-wife." He sighed. "She left the year after Lisa disappeared. Said she needed to get away. As if you can ever get away from losing a child." His voice cracked.

Petrosky shoved the ache in his chest into the deepest recesses of his belly. Walsh still hadn't answered the question. "We'll need to speak with her, Mr. Walsh. Where does she live now?"

"Sterling Heights. But I called her when I heard from your … morgue." He choked, swallowed, and finally turned toward Petrosky, his eyes as wet as the dishes. "She'll be here soon so we can figure out the funeral arrangements."

Petrosky gave Walsh a moment to compose himself. Then: "You mentioned Lisa's moods were unpredictable?"

"Yeah. But she was still a good girl. Just got a little boy crazy."

Boy crazy. So he did know *something* even if he wasn't aware of Norton in particular. "Could you be more specific?"

"I overheard her telling one of her little friends that she had a boyfriend. I didn't think much about it, figured it was a school-yard crush—I mean, she was only *fourteen*. I didn't think it was serious." He glanced at the countertop in front of Morrison and grabbed the sponge again. Dirty water pooled, spilling onto the linoleum at Walsh's feet with a tinny sound like someone peeing on a plastic bag. "But I really started to worry after I heard from Becky's mom."

"She's the one who told you Lisa might be involved with an older man?"

"Yes. Becky was one of Lisa's friends. She saw her at the park with some older guy and it scared her because she didn't know him. She said he had his arm around Lisa." Anguish touched his features. He stared at the dripping water but made no move to sop it up.

"Did Becky tell you what he looked like?"

"She didn't get a good look. Just said that he was older. I think she mentioned a goatee?"

That part hadn't been in the file. A goatee was a great way to disguise one's appearance on short notice, and knowing that Norton had used it in the past might help them when creating the updated composite sketch.

"What color was his facial hair?"

Walsh furrowed his brows, shook his head. "No idea. Not sure she ever said."

"Did you talk to Lisa about it?"

"Of course I did!" He threw up his hands, his still-wet fingers flinging droplets of water onto the upper cabinets. "It didn't help. First she said that Becky's mom was lying, then that she was wrong, and finally she told me that she was practically fifteen and it was none of my business, and then slammed her bedroom door." A wan smile touched his lips. "I would have thought that feistiness might have helped her, but maybe it just made things worse." His eyes filled. "I was thinking that was why he ... messed up her feet. She would have given him hell." Petrosky's gut twisted. Fucking Woolverton must have told Walsh about the toes, and he'd probably loved every second of it, that sick, dweeby bastard. Hopefully their hack ME hadn't shown Daddy the gaping hole in Lisa's shoulder—or told him what had caused it. Petrosky knew better than anyone how those details ate away at your heart.

"How long after Becky's mother called did Lisa disappear?"

"A couple days. The police thought she ran away, but I knew better. She wouldn't have left her friends or school, not for anyone." His voice rose on the last words as if his rage, his grief, were building into a storm that might at any moment explode from his body. "But if I had known then what I know now, I would have locked her up until she turned thirty."

"Do you know where Becky is now?"

"She died last year." His voice had softened. "Leukemia."

There goes our new composite sketch. "Do you recall anything unusual around the time of Lisa's disappearance?"

Walsh shook his head. "I wish I could. I wish I could remember everything. I'm constantly going over every detail, replaying our conversations, looking for something I could have done differently. But ... I obviously wasn't watching closely enough."

The slam of the front door made Walsh jump so violently that the clean bowl on the counter behind him caught his elbow, fell into the sink, and shattered against another dish.

Petrosky jerked around to see a tall woman, five-nine without heels, come careening into the kitchen, her face hot pink and glowing with sweat or tears or both. She skidded to a halt when she saw Morrison and Petrosky. Petrosky flashed his badge and her eyes widened more.

"I didn't know there'd be cops here. Why are—"

"Now, Stacey—" Mr. Walsh began.

The woman aimed a finger at Petrosky as if it were a gun. "Aren't you supposed to be out there trying to find whoever did this?"

"We're here trying to find whoever did this," Petrosky said with a calm more pronounced than he felt. "Perhaps you can help us."

She crossed her arms, trembling so hard Petrosky feared she'd fall over. "Why don't you have a seat, ma'am."

"I don't need a seat." But she moved to the dinette behind her and slumped into a chair. "This is just awful. And to think that he ... that she ... I mean, I think I knew somehow that she might be dead, but it feels like I'm missing a part of me, that something is horribly wrong and ..."

The words came fast, almost manic, like she'd been hitting the pipe. Hard. Her feet vibrated with enough energy to kick a sumo wrestler's ass, and her mouth was constantly moving: biting her lips, chewing her cheek. Anxiety, trauma from the news about her daughter, or just grief? But from the twitch at the corner of her eye, Petrosky could almost believe she felt guilty. Had she known more about her daughter's boyfriend, maybe been sympathetic to Lisa dating? Maybe she'd even suspected the boyfriend was older and hidden it from her husband.

Petrosky stepped toward her. "Do you know why your daughter started acting strangely in those last few months?"

"Him." She jabbed her finger toward Mr. Walsh.

Him. Behind Petrosky, Mr. Walsh gave a startled cry, but Petrosky didn't turn. Had Walsh ... hurt his own daughter? Was that why she thought it was normal for a kid her age to be involved with an older man? Maybe Lisa was looking for someone to protect her, to love her. "What did he do to Lisa?"

Petrosky snapped, far harsher than he'd intended. He held his fist at his side to avoid punching the bastard.

"Yelled at her all the time. Tried to make her stay home after school."

"She had homework," Mr. Walsh piped up. "She was failing—"

"She was a *kid*." The woman leapt up so fast Petrosky had to jump back to avoid getting hit by her flailing hands. "She needed to be a kid. You pushed her away."

"What about abuse?" Petrosky asked, practically whispering so Mr. Walsh didn't overhear. The question wouldn't be a secret for long, but at least he could observe their reactions separately.

"Abuse?" Her brows furrowed. "Like hitting?"

"Or sexual."

Her jaw dropped. Pure shock.

Mr. Walsh huffed from the kitchen. "Now you wait just a—"

"Don't move, sir," Morrison said, and the guy's shuffling stopped.

Petrosky backed up and turned so he could see both of them. And the gun on the wall. Petrosky studied Mr. Walsh, the man's mouth open in horror, eyes less defensive and more surprised. "This isn't an attack. But we need to cover all the bases if we're going to find your daughter's killer."

At the word *killer*, the former Mrs. Walsh practically fell back into the chair and buried her head in her hands. Mr. Walsh crossed the kitchen, and put a hand on her back, awkwardly, his face a mask of pain.

"I appreciate that you're just doing your job," he said finally. "But I don't think I have anything else that can help you." He gestured to the hall. "You asked about her things; her room's the last on the right. Everything's the same as the day she left. Please try to keep it that way."

Petrosky and Morrison left the couple in the kitchen and headed for Lisa's room. Paisley walls, frilly duvet. Too girly for Julie's taste. The room itself had that rancid pre-teen vibe, but there was an undercurrent that was disturbingly ... vacant. In used rooms, the potential seemed to emanate from things themselves, every item reflective of life and new discovery. Here, like in Julie's room, the emptiness howled at him from the deepest corners: stolen potential, discoveries never made. Maybe one day Lisa's dad would turn it into an office, or maybe he'd sleep in here under her posters and try to remember what it was like when she was still alive. Maybe eventually dear old dad would bring the rifle to bed too.

Petrosky and Morrison searched quickly, under the bed, around the vent, through drawers. In the pockets of Lisa's coat, they found two lollipops and a telephone number, though it proved to be disconnected. Morrison said he'd check on it later. In the back of the closet, a few sheets of notebook paper, folded into hexagons or paper Pac-Mans—girl talk in a scrawl messy enough to have been done years before she'd disappeared. Homework that could have been from elementary school. Nothing of use to them.

Petrosky handed Mr. Walsh a business card on the way out. "If you think of anything else, please call."

"Do you think you'll catch him?"

"That's the plan," Petrosky said.

But plans failed.

"If you do, give me five minutes alone with him." Walsh's voice was strange. Probably helplessness; he surely knew he'd never get that chance.

"I would leave you with him if I could, sir," Petrosky said. *Maybe I'll kill him myself.*

THEIR NEXT STOP was the home of Harriet Smith, one of the girls on Morrison's list of possible kidnap victims. Her father answered the door—black hair and deep-set eyes that darkened when he saw Petrosky.

"Mr. Smith?"

He glared.

"I'm Detective Petrosky, and this is Detective Morrison. We need to ask you some questions about your daughter." Petrosky's chest vibrated with too much hippie coffee. He shoved his hands in his pockets to steady himself.

"Harriet? Or Monique?"

"Harriet."

"What's that girl done now?"

Petrosky and Morrison exchanged a glance. "This is about her disappearance. We need to ask you about the man she was dating."

Smith crossed his arms and smirked. "I scared that punk right off. Wasn't no man when he was pissing himself all the way home to his momma."

"He was a boy?"

"You're goddamn right. Some punk from the next school. I told her she wasn't dating him no more."

"You had this conversation before she left?"

"Yep. And again once she came back."

Petrosky's back clenched. "You never called the police to report her return?"

"They said don't call us, we'll call you." He smiled. "I figured I'd return the favor."

"Sounds to me like you're trying to waste the city's time. Perhaps you'd like to come downtown for filing a false police report."

"I didn't file—"

Heat seared into Petrosky's chest like hot pokers. "You reported your girl missing. She's not missing, motherfucker."

Morrison grabbed Petrosky's arm.

Mr. Smith's face contorted with rage and trepidation—they were cops after all.

"Say hello to your girl for us." Petrosky spit off the porch. Smith wasn't fucking worth it.

MORRISON MADE phone calls while Petrosky drove them to a burger joint for a late lunch—or early dinner. He was still on the phone when Petrosky parked.

"I'll get us a table." Petrosky left him in the car and strode into the restaurant where he was greeted by a far-too-smiley woman with brilliantly white teeth, ebony skin and lipstick the color of fresh blood. "One?"

"Two."

"Right this way."

The clamor of couples and children and silverware followed them through the restaurant. They stopped at a corner booth upholstered in squeaky orange vinyl—sticky looking, but at least the adjacent booths were empty. Petrosky left the menus on the table and went to the restroom to splash water on his face, his heart shuddering around in his chest. His skin looked a little green too, but it might have been the fluorescents above the sink. The withdrawal. It'd be over soon. He thumped his breastbone with a fist, like a gorilla, and glowered at his reflection.

The waitress was at the table when he returned. "Coffee?"

Why is she smiling so goddamn much? "Sure." Petrosky picked up an individual serving of cream, thought better of it, and tossed it back in the bowl.

Thankfully Morrison didn't keep him waiting. "Telephone number's a dead end. Just another little girl from Lisa's school back then, since moved out of state. With a few other calls, I crossed four more stops off the list: two runaways deceased— one overdose, one drive by—not our guy. Both deaths occurred in other states which is why they didn't show up in our files. Got two other successful returns that went unreported. A few other parents with nothing else to tell us, though we'll still go search whatever's left of the girls' things. We can meet a couple more families today, including Ava Fenderson's parents—the girl with the pink socks." He picked up his menu.

"What can I get you guys?" The waitress's lipstick had smeared onto one canine as if she'd just torn someone's throat out.

Petrosky's stomach rolled.

"Wheat toast, dry," Morrison said.

Petrosky frowned. "Toast? What are you, a vegetarian now?" But toast did sound pretty good.

"I just need a few grains to get me through the afternoon. Not sure I can stomach a fatty burger." Morrison looked up at their waitress. "No offense."

Her smile didn't reach her eyes—like it was plastered on. Her facial muscles probably hurt like a bitch by the end of the day.

"I'll have the same," Petrosky said.

When she left, Petrosky turned to Morrison. "You done good, Kid."

"Was that a compliment?" Morrison fluttered his hand to his chest. "Be still my heart!"

"Don't get used to it, Nancy."

"Really, you're going to keep on with all the Nancy—"

"Not like you need your manhood." Petrosky sipped the coffee and it blistered his gut like burning oil. "Let's face it, son: your wife's got enough balls for the both of you."

21

THE FENDERSON HOME was in a neighborhood struggling toward well-to-do. Ava's parents stood beside scuffed, but clean, tan leather sofas in front of a flat-screen television. The room smelled of lemon furniture polish over the boiled hot dogs someone had probably made for lunch. From the spotless white mantle, Ava's flaming orange hair practically screamed "Look at me!" above the brown-haired child, probably a sibling, on her lap. The younger kid was four years old, tops. Too young to know anything useful. Petrosky averted his gaze from the photo when Ava's bright blue irises morphed into the milky eyes of a corpse. The socks. Norton had her, right? Her, and how many more? How many girls would die before they finally caught him?

Mrs. Fenderson had the same red hair as her daughter. She sat across from Petrosky on the love seat, hands clasped between her knees like her fingers might run off if she didn't squeeze them tight enough. Her husband perched on the arm of the sofa, one burly arm over his wife's shoulder. Stoic. Protective.

"Thanks for seeing us on such short notice," Morrison said.

The Fendersons nodded like a pair of goddamn synchronized swimmers. But where Mr. Fenderson wore a mask of sorrow, Mrs. Fenderson's face was pinched like she'd just tasted something sour. "So," she began, "you have something about Ava? Maybe?"

Petrosky glanced at Morrison's impassive face and back at the Fendersons. "We're not sure, ma'am. I'm sure my partner didn't mean to give you the impression that we—"

"No, no, he didn't. I just hoped." She sniffed. Her eyes stayed dry.

The toast gurgled in Petrosky's stomach. "We need some information on the man your daughter was dating when she—"

"Dating!" Mr. Fenderson boomed, his sorrow morphing into rage, his face darkening until it was nearly purple. "That wasn't dating. That was ... that was ..."

Explosive. Not that he'd expect anything less from a grieving father. "Mr. Fenderson, I agree that whoever your daughter was seeing was a piece of shit. What I don't know is if he was enough of a piece of shit to kidnap her."

Mrs. Fenderson paled. Mr. Fenderson's face returned to a more normal hue though the pink remained high on his cheekbones.

"What can you tell me about the man?" Petrosky asked.

Mr. Fenderson looked at his wife.

"I only saw him once, a month or so before Ava disappeared," she said, softly, hesitantly, as if trying to keep from vocalizing her worst fears. "I went to pick her up from the library and she was walking out front with him. Holding hands." She grimaced. "They saw me and he took off."

"We'll need you to come down to the station. Give us a composite sketch."

Mrs. Fenderson sniffed again. "I'll go today. I wish someone had done all this earlier." She looked at her hands. "I mean, I guess they did take his description and talked about it on the news. I think they really looked for her, she was just gone. Still ... I can't help feeling like if we'd done more, if the police had done more back then, we'd have her home."

Petrosky ignored the slight. He wished the same. "Did she give you a name?"

She pursed her lips. "Not at first. But I found a note in her pocket once, when I was doing laundry. From an Andy. I wish I'd kept it."

Andy. Not Adam. *Dammit*. But though it wasn't the same, Andy was close to Adam, the name Norton used when he was shacked up with Janice and kidnapping a cop's wife.

"Last name?"

Another synchronized head shake. "Ava said she didn't know it," Mrs. Fenderson said.

"Did he ever call here?" Most teens used their own cells for that shit, but the police had surely looked at that already.

"Never, that sneaky bastard." Mr. Fenderson this time. "Nothing on her phone either."

Norton had to have another way of contacting her. Maybe he'd given her a burner phone. "What did he look like?"

Mrs. Fenderson squinted. "Twenty, maybe. He had his hat pulled down, so it was hard to see his face. I remember he had a goatee though."

Just like Lisa Walsh's friend had said. "Color?"

"Blond."

So he'd gone back to his natural hair color. "Height and weight?"

"Average. Maybe five-ten? He had on a coat too, but he seemed ... big. Not fat, but stocky, like he worked out."

Ava Fenderson's abduction had come more than eight months after Lisa Walsh disappeared. Plenty of time to bulk up. And from the weight profile from forensics, it looked like Norton had kept the weight on. Good information, but Petrosky would have preferred a perp who'd been hitting the drive-through instead of one who'd embraced weightlifting. That determination didn't bode well for the victims. If Norton still had other girls hidden, he could use that same driving force to make more sinister plans and carry them out. And bulking up took time; he was not only determined, he was patient. Deliberate. *Bummer*. Impulsive men were easier to catch—they made more mistakes.

"Any distinguishing marks? Tattoos, scars? Acne?"

"Um ... he was wearing long sleeves, so I'm not sure on the tattoos," Mrs. Fenderson said. "But I think he had acne along his lower jaw below that hood—his facial hair was thinner there, anyway. Not that a few pimples would help you now."

Pimples might not help, sure. But Petrosky had met Adam Norton and the guy'd had the same marks back then too. And they hadn't been pimples—they were scars.

He waited until she averted her eyes before he spoke again. "Did Ava meet him often?"

Mrs. Fenderson lowered her head as Mr. Fenderson raised his. "Not that I know of," he said. "But she was having some ... issues. Her grades went down a little. She was smoking pot and drinking. Even cut class a few times and started running off without telling us where she was going. We'd called the police twice before that last time, but she always came home before we even finished the paperwork. I'm sure it was because of him. If he hadn't ... if we'd known ..."

Norton might not have been solely responsible for Ava's problems, but he surely hadn't helped. Grooming a victim took time, and patience. If he could get her to cut school, maybe he could get her to come to his house. And once he did that ...

"That's why they thought she ran away, right?" Morrison's voice was soft.

"Yes," Mr. Fenderson said, just as quietly. "And she did leave that night, ran out of here in socks and sandals even though it was snowing. I tried to follow her, but by the time I grabbed my boots, she was gone. Must have headed around one of the neighbor's houses, and I went the wrong way. I really thought she'd get cold and come back." He grimaced. "We never believed she meant to leave for good. Did we, Nora? We never believed it. She wouldn't do that." He stared hard at his wife. She looked at her knees.

"We'd like to take a look through her things," Petrosky said.

Mr. Fenderson stood. "I wondered why they never did before. They just looked to see if her bag was gone, even though I told them it was by the front door—that she grabbed it on the way out." He frowned. "The officers did take her computer. Gave it back when they didn't find anything incriminating, no evidence that she'd been conversing with a boyfriend online.

And she ran off in the middle of a fight—didn't look like she'd planned it ahead of time."

So Norton hadn't seduced Ava via online chat or email. And with nothing on her phone, texts and calls were out, and there probably wasn't even a payphone for five miles. *Sneaky fuck.* Had to be a burner cell. And those were next to impossible to trace. "Her room, sir?"

"Down the hall, last door on the right."

Another little girl's room left exactly as it had been, though the vacuum tracks told a different story from the Walshes'—someone was in here regularly, tidying for an unlikely homecoming. It made the room that much more gut-wrenching.

Morrison grabbed the knob on the closet door while Petrosky pulled open the top drawer of the dresser. He pushed aside socks and underwear. Nothing besides clothes. *Please let her just be a runaway.* He could only hope Ava Fenderson wasn't with the man who'd impaled Lisa Walsh. The man who'd watched Lisa die, listened to her screaming as a stake slowly ripped through her insides. *Jesus Christ.* Petrosky coughed to cover a retch.

Morrison shook out one coat and replaced it. Pulled out another.

Petrosky knelt and peered under the bed. *Too easy. Think like a teenager.* He pulled aside the duvet and lifted the mattress. Nothing. He dropped the bed and climbed on top, running his hand between the mattress and the headboard.

"Jackpot," Morrison mumbled, and Petrosky rose so quickly the room spun and he had to grab the end table to avoid falling over.

"Boss?"

Petrosky shook off the dizziness. "Stood up too fast is all." *I need a drink.* "What do you have?"

"Box of CDs." Morrison lifted the container with one hand. "What kid listens to CDs?"

Petrosky stared. What the hell did kids do instead of listening to music?

Morrison was already on his knees in front of the box, checking one CD at a time. Three cases were empty. Five more had the disks intact. One held a dime bag of weed. Morrison stacked them on the floor.

Petrosky looked around the room. No disk player in sight. And she'd have been too young for a car that might have made CDs necessary.

Morrison flipped open another case. "Money."

Shit. If she'd left her cash, she'd planned to come home. Petrosky peered at the Squirrel Nut Zippers CD and the stack of twenty dollar bills inside it. "Gotta be two hundred bucks." *And what kid listens to this shit?*

"That's a lot of cash for a fourteen-year-old to be hiding."

Petrosky nodded. "No job, and I doubt Mommy and Daddy know about it." He reached into the box and pulled out his own stack of CDs, opening one, then another. Just the music.

Then—

His heart stiffened, seized, and fluttered back to life. White notebook paper. And here he'd thought these kids all texted.

But it wasn't a child's handwriting. Block letters: *AVA.* He would have thought they were typed had it not been for the indentations, the slight thickening of the ink at each start and stop point. Pen. A leaky one maybe, but definitely not a laser printer.

Petrosky squinted at the words, then flipped the page over. "Fuck," he whispered. His chest was on fire.

On the back, the guy had signed *Andy* in a loopy scrawl. And he'd written another line in block letters:

Enjoy the music. Never forget you're my #1 girl.

139

22

MONDAY DAWN BROKE COLD, gray, and miserable. Petrosky sat on the edge of his bed and stared at the half-full bottle of Jack. His head swam, not as badly as yesterday morning, but enough to make him wish for another hour or thirty of sleep.

Get it together, Petrosky. But he couldn't. He would be the same piece of shit he'd been yesterday, fumbling around and asking questions while Morrison wrote because they both knew he wasn't steady enough to write legibly.

Fuck.

They'd hit four more houses the night before, but found nothing—no notes, no one else who'd seen the boyfriend. Hopefully the note from Ava Fenderson's bedroom had already been processed by forensics.

They needed something to go on.

Petrosky's brain tried to pound through his skull. He stood, but dizziness forced him down again.

Why hadn't he registered the CDs as an important clue? Ava hadn't even had a CD player in her room; Norton had probably snagged the whole box at Goodwill for five bucks. At least their killer was as tech-challenged as Petrosky was.

But still—he should have caught that. He needed to do better. Morrison and Shannon and Evie and Henry ... If not for them, maybe he'd have given up completely by now.

The bottle winked at him, practically screaming "Drink me." He didn't believe in signs; they were for new age hippies and guys like Morrison.

But that tiny glint on his Jack—that was definitely a sign.

Petrosky grabbed the bottle by the neck, throttling it the way he wanted to throttle the asshole who abducted little girls and turned them into his own personal harem, or maybe the way he wanted to throttle himself. The guilt, the grief—they never ended. Never would.

Petrosky cracked the cap and put the bottle to his lips. The fire burned its way into his stomach and his gut clenched, tried to refuse the liquor, then relented. *Good*. The booze would surely settle better than granola. And today he had a job to do—he had to try, no matter how inept he might be.

MORRISON APPRAISED him when he jumped into Petrosky's car at the station, but the kid said nothing. Petrosky pulled another breath mint from the pack in the dashboard and popped it into his mouth. Morrison stared at that too, then opened his manila folder. "Got the composite from Fenderson," he said.

"Not tired of your classifieds yet, eh, Cali?"

Morrison pulled out the picture and smiled. "Nope. Keeps me organized. Unlike you, who probably doesn't even know who we're going to see right now."

"That's why I have you, Surfer Boy." Petrosky glanced at the new composite of Norton. A hat covered his head, but blond hair stuck out at the base. Thin, blond goatee, scraggly, like the stippling of scars along his jaw had damaged his hair follicles. The scars were probably what Norton was trying to hide with the facial hair in the first place. And below the neck, broad shoulders, far larger than what Petrosky remembered. This time, Norton would be harder to take down.

"So who are we going to see?" Petrosky asked as Morrison replaced the sketch.

"Kim Nace, the mother of Margot Nace, who disappeared just over a year ago—most recent potential abductee I found.

She was thirteen. Last seen by her mother during an argument over an older boyfriend. Margot snuck out that night, never came home."

"Mom know we're coming?"

"Yeah, I called her last night. Followed up on a few others, too—crossed a couple more potential kidnapping vics off the list. I also visited the family of Casey Hearn on the way home, but there was nothing there. They'd moved to a smaller house, and all her things had been purged except for a few boxes of toys and clothes. And her parents didn't meet her boyfriend, though they suspected he was an older boy from another school."

"You went alone in the middle of the—"

"Mr. Hearn works during the day. He said that was the best time. And the other families we can see today."

"Don't get cocky on me, California."

"Not a chance, Boss. Just trying to be efficient."

Petrosky grabbed the coffee from the cupholder and took a deep swallow. His hand was steady for once. "I thought you were going home to Shannon when I dropped you off last night."

"I did, just later." Morrison eyed the cup as Petrosky put the coffee back. "She understood; she wants this guy behind bars as much as we do."

The whiskey and coffee rolled in Petrosky's stomach, a thick, burbling liquid, but his head was clear. "I know she does, but she needs to be important too. So does Evie. And Henry." Then Julie was begging him to come see her in the talent show—*Please, Daddy, please?*—and he felt like he was drowning in a deep, dark void. Against the small of his back, his gun was heavy and cold, and held more promise in that moment than he wanted to admit. He pushed at the thought. It pushed back.

Focus. He'd find Ava. He'd put Adam Norton away. Then maybe he could drift off into the big sleep more peacefully knowing Shannon and the kids would be safe from this maniac.

NACE LIVED IN A TRAILER PARK, ten miles from the Salomon place. Pockets of snow and rivulets of hardened ice cleaved through the dirt in the walk. A curtain snapped and billowed in an open window, like Nace was trying to get rid of the smell of weed—or something harder—before the cops arrived.

A woman opened the door, sporting orange curls so bright they looked like a frizzy clown wig even with the white streaks at her temples. But her face was sallow, the gray of dirty dishwater, and her eyes were bleary, dull, and stupid. Drugs? Booze?

Do I look like that?

"Ms. Nace?" Morrison said.

She nodded, mouth slack.

"I'm Detective Morrison, and this is Detective Petrosky. We spoke last night."

She stared.

"About Margot?"

She backed up. Petrosky thought she might slam the door in their faces, but then the screen door squealed open and she gestured for them to come in.

Inside the trailer, the surfaces sparkled. Hand towels in the kitchen hung neatly over the oven door handle. No lingering marijuana smoke like he'd expected, nor the burning-plastic stench of crack cocaine—just the breeze from outside, whipping against the blue walls. You never really knew about a person.

A school photo of Margot had been tacked above the love seat. She had an unfortunate face, the kind that will always be dowdy even through pancake makeup. Maybe she was compensating for that with her low-cut tank top and a bra that pushed her cleavage together in a porn-star way. Had Morrison said ... *thirteen?* He wanted to give the girl a jacket, tell her to cover up, tell her his own face was a shitshow but that didn't mean he had to show everyone his balls. But then the wind whipped through the room again and the photo sighed in the breeze as if it were alive.

Petrosky winced.

"Sit?" Nace asked.

Petrosky looked at the love seat, at the table. No other chairs. "We'll stand, ma'am." Petrosky said.

"Drink?"

"No thanks," they said in unison. He hoped they didn't start moving their heads in unison like the Fendersons, though he supposed that happened in families sometimes. Or ... with partners.

Morrison whipped out his notebook, but Petrosky motioned to him. *Give it to me.* For once his hand was steady, and he didn't trust his voice—his lungs and throat felt suddenly tighter, like he was coming down with a cold. Or the plague.

Morrison raised an eyebrow but handed the notepad over and turned to Nace. "As I mentioned yesterday, we're looking for the man who was seen with your daughter last year."

Ms. Nace said nothing, just sank back farther into the couch. *Come on, lady.*

"We know you're aware that your daughter was seeing an older boy."

Slow nod.

"You argued with her the night she ran away?"

Another nod.

Morrison glanced at Petrosky.

Petrosky slapped the folder against his palm. "Wake up, ma'am. We don't care what you're on, but you need to cooperate with us so we can find this asshole. If you can't do it here, we'll take you to the station until you sober up and we can get what we need."

Her vacant eyes cleared incrementally, as if finally realizing where she was. She swallowed hard. "I'm not ... on anything. I'm just ... I can never sleep. Can't go outside." She shuddered. "I keep thinking I'll walk past a street and she'll be lying there and... sorry." She inhaled sharply, blew it out. "I never met him —never even saw the man, but I knew he was older than she was by the way she talked about him. Said he didn't go to school, so I thought he'd graduated already. I told her it was a bad idea, but..."

Of course it was a bad fucking idea. But predators knew which girls to target. Wasn't even the clothes, the push-up bras and the short skirts. It was in the eyes—an unspoken vulnerability.

"Any phone calls to the house?" Morrison asked.

"We never had a phone. She was always mad about that, but it was a luxury I couldn't afford."

Morrison pulled out the photo and showed it to her. "Does this man look familiar?"

She squinted, shook her head. Then her eyes widened, brightened, finally alive—and furious. "Is that him? The guy you think took her?" she said, each word louder than the last.

Nothing like rage to wake a motherfucker up.

Morrison put the photo away. "We're not sure yet. What did Margot tell you about the man she was seeing?"

"Not much; I found out most of it the night she left. She'd wanted to go to the movies, and I asked who she was going with. She was only thirteen, not like she was ready to date no matter what she thought with all her short shorts and ..." She blew orange frizz from her cheek. It lifted and settled back onto her face. "Anyway, she said he was nice but that he didn't go to her school, didn't go to any school, which made me wonder. And she had this necklace, like a heart kinda thing? At first I thought it was from her school, maybe for winning a contest. It seemed too nice for that, but she had been cutting classes, messing up on tests, and I guess I was ... hoping it was from school, hoping that things were changing for her."

Were necklaces a normal prize at schools these days? Morrison's brows were furrowed over narrowed eyes. "Why would you think her necklace was for a school contest?"

"Well, she always did well in school." Her chest puffed up, then deflated just as quickly. "I mean, before. It was more the engraving: First Place."

Petrosky's heart jolted, sending a bolt of painful electricity into his jaw. Great. His whole goddamn body was falling apart.

"Did it say first place or was it just a number one?" Morrison said, quietly, slowly.

"The number, but with the number sign."

So Margot Nace *had* gotten the necklace from Norton. Petrosky thought back to Dr. McCallum's psychological profile —the doctor had been concerned that their perp was escalating, that he had learned from the predators he'd been hanging out with.

And Norton had. Now he was grooming his victims, finessing them until they came to him willingly. No abduction necessary if they called you after a fight with their mother. No fuss in the street. And what a rush for his self-worth, to finally have women—*no, girls*—who wouldn't reject his sorry ass. Norton had been getting cocky, too, showing his face in public—like the fucking library.

Then going home to a torture chamber Petrosky hadn't found.

Yet.

"Do you have the necklace here?" Morrison was saying.

Petrosky gritted his teeth against the pressure in his chest.

"No, she took it when she ..." She shuddered, though the wind had stopped blowing. Margot's photo was still.

"Can you describe it? Color, size?"

She put her fingers in an "okay" sign, the hole about the size of a quarter. "About this big, silver. On a silver chain. Hung to here." She touched the center of her clavicle.

"Would you recognize it if you saw it again?" Petrosky asked. They'd check out local jewelers. How many people were engraving the number one on a charm? And though the charms probably weren't expensive, to purchase jewelry for each girl took a little bit of cash—looked like Janice was telling the truth about him having his own money unless he'd found some other woman to mooch off of.

"Yeah, I think so." She locked her gaze on Morrison. "You think you'll ... find her? I mean ... alive?"

Morrison looked away, probably envisioning the alley and Lisa Walsh's body. Maybe seeing Shannon's sutured mouth. "I'm not sure, ma'am, but we hope so."

She sighed. "Now I wish I would have kept her things. Not that she'd still fit in the clothes, but ..." Her eyes filled. "Maybe she'll come home. Maybe then I'll finally be able to sleep."

It was a pipe dream, but if their guy had Margot and was keeping her for a purpose ... maybe she was alive. *For now.* Norton had kept Lisa Walsh alive for years, before she'd done something to piss him off. Same with Ava Fenderson—probably.

But if Norton's blatant display with Salomon and Walsh was any indication, they'd know when he killed again.

Petrosky rubbed his aching jaw and flipped the notebook closed as Morrison handed Nace a card. "If you think of anything else, ma'am, please call."

"You all right, old man?" Morrison asked on their way to the car. "You're looking a little pale."

"I'm fine." He wasn't fine. He needed more Jack. "You drive, California."

THE REST of the afternoon was a bust, with no other leads. One father eyed them suspiciously over the head of his infant daughter as if they'd come to bring up a past he'd tried to forget. The man had nothing to offer besides insisting his daughter had been using drugs and that he had warned her about trouble. He didn't seem particularly surprised or upset that she was still missing.

The father in Petrosky wanted to punch the fucker. The cop in him figured the man was probably right to assume his daughter was dead of a drug overdose somewhere and that shutting off the pain was the best choice. He'd certainly wished for numbness after Julie's death, and when it hadn't come, he'd found it at the bottom of a bottle.

Not much had changed.

Morrison pulled into a Thai place at two o'clock. Their table was in the middle of the restaurant next to a long, algae-infested tank where an enormous goldfish stared at them with the boggle eyes of a tweaker.

Petrosky wondered if the goldfish were like the lobsters in a grocery store tank, if someone would be by shortly to turn the googly-eyed bastard into sushi.

He frowned at the fish. "You sure about this place?"

"You talking to me or to the fish?"

Petrosky turned back in time to see Morrison raise an eyebrow at his shaking hand. He put it under the table where it could tremble on his knee with a little privacy. Stupid dumbass fish—he was just hungry, that was all.

They ordered from an Asian kid who looked twelve but probably wasn't, with straight black hair cut in a bowl over cheekbones and a chin sharp enough to slice glass. Three minutes of confusion between Petrosky and the kid over which soup would be the most like chicken noodle, then Morrison ordered for both of them. The kid scampered away.

Petrosky trapped his still trembling hands between his knees, keeping his eyes away from Morrison's face and the bastards in the tank. He needed to think. Not a goddamn thing had come from the press' involvement—goddamn waste of time. And time they did not have. Finally, he said, "After lunch, let's check out the jewelry stores. He had to get that necklace engraved somewhere."

Morrison nodded as the Asian kid returned with a teapot. When the kid left again, Morrison whipped out his phone. "I'll make a list now." He took a sip of something that was supposed to be green tea but looked an awful lot like piss.

Petrosky grimaced at it. "We can print a list at the station."

"This is way faster." He was already tapping on his phone. "And we don't have to waste the trip."

Petrosky sipped his water. Some asshole had put lemon in it. He set it back down.

"Holy cow, there are tons of jewelers." Morrison tapped frantically on the face of the phone with his index finger—how the hell was one-fingered typing more efficient than a fucking keyboard? "Hang on, let me see if I can look up the engraving bit. The nicer ones will do it, but some stores might not. Plus, it looks like a few of these are pawn shops which might not have the same equipment."

Petrosky stared at the goldfish until his middle school waiter put a bowl in front of him. Green pieces floated in a clear-ish broth. He took a spoonful. It tasted like lime ... and something sort of like chicken. Pretty tasty, actually, but his stomach clenched. He choked down another bite.

"How many miles you want to go out to start? If we do ten we can always expand."

"Fine."

Morrison tapped a few more buttons, set his phone aside, and grabbed his fork. He gestured to Petrosky's dish. "Good, eh?"

"Just fucking delightful." Petrosky's phone chimed. He pulled it out of his jacket. "You texted me?"

"In case you wanted the list of where we were going."

"I'm going with you in ten minutes, California—"

"Just being thorough."

Petrosky shook his head, picked up the bowl and slurped the remaining soup before he could change his mind.

23

THEIR FIRST STOP was a strip mall three miles from the Salomon house. Petrosky parked in front of another Asian food restaurant, this one advertising the best egg rolls in town. Maybe they should have eaten there instead—at the very least there'd surely have been less fish watching them eat. The banner flapped over their heads as they walked into the Tiger's Eye jewelry shop next door.

An elderly man with three chins and hawk eyes watched them enter. He grinned.

"Afternoon," Petrosky said. He flashed his badge and the man's smile fell. "Are you the owner?"

"I am. Horowitz is the name." He drew his shoulders up.

"Mr. Horowitz, we're looking for a man who may have purchased a necklace here." Morrison showed him the new composite of Adam Norton, but Horowitz shook his head.

"Maybe you'll remember the necklace," Morrison said. "Silver, a heart on a thin chain. Engraved with a number one."

Horowitz pursed his lips, nodding. "A few like that I suppose, but I don't recall any number engravings."

Petrosky and Morrison followed on the outside of the glass display cases as Horowitz made his way to the center case, slid the door open, and removed a velvet pad bearing a heart-shaped locket smaller than Petrosky's pinky nail. A tiny diamond sparkled in the overhead lights.

"White and rose gold, quarter carat. Opens on the hinge there. One of my own creations." He beamed.

"Pretty small to engrave, right?"

Horowitz shrugged. "It can be done. I engrave the insides of wedding bands all the time."

"Anything a little bigger?"

Horowitz lovingly settled the charm back on the velvet pad.

"What about this one?" Morrison said from near Petrosky's waist. The kid's nose was nearly touching the glass.

Horowitz replaced the board and pulled another heart pendant from the case—larger, silver, no diamonds.

"This?"

"Yes." Morrison straightened and snapped a photo with his phone.

Horowitz raised an eyebrow but said nothing.

"This another of your own creations, sir?" Petrosky gestured to the piece.

He shook his head. "Those I get from a distributor. Shriner's the name, an outfit out of Texas. I just call and tell them what I want from the catalogue. I don't have one handy, but I'm sure you could get one mailed—maybe they have it online too."

"How common are pieces like these?"

Horowitz slid the case closed. "They're popular everywhere, all over the country—available in gold, silver, white gold, you name it. You can even get the charm on a bracelet if you want to. The quality is subpar, but it's cheap."

"Ever engraved a number one on any of these?"

Horowitz furrowed his brows. He shook his head. "Not that I recall, and I don't keep records of that. Usually sell these to high school sweethearts, sometimes from parents to daughters for sweet sixteens. If I engrave anything, it's initials or a first name, maybe. But not numbers."

No engraving records and even if the guy had purchase orders from his distributer, knowing when he bought the pieces wouldn't help them. Petrosky glanced at Morrison, whose pen was flying over the notepad.

"Why are the police looking for that necklace anyway?" Horowitz said. "It get stolen by that guy in the picture?"

"No, sir. But if you see him, don't approach him. And call us right away. Same if anyone comes in about a number one engraving."

Horowitz nodded knowingly. "I got an old dog at home, used to leave her up here at night. She ain't much to look at but she'll get the job done even if someone disables the alarm."

"That shouldn't be necessary, sir. We have no reason to think it's a burglary situation."

Horowitz nodded again, but his eyes were wary.

He'd have his old dog up there before nightfall.

THREE MORE JEWELERS yielded similar results. Every one of the stores had at least one necklace or bracelet that could fit the description given by Margot's mother. No one remembered engraving a number on anything, though one owner kept records of engravings and agreed to look through them that evening. No one recognized Adam Norton.

The fifth store was decidedly fancier than the rest, with crystal sconces hanging along the back wall. Behind the cases hung abstract art that looked like it'd been done by a three-year-old and probably cost more than Petrosky's house.

Petrosky frowned at the twenty-something underwear model who smirked at them as they entered. His tailored gray suit combined with the less cultured stubble shadowing his jaw surely made his female customers swoon—the ladies liked that "I'm good but bad" bullshit. He identified himself as Reginald Beckwith III, but his self-important smile fell as soon as he saw the badge, and he looked downright confused when he heard what they wanted.

"You're looking for a heart without any stones?"

"Yes." Petrosky tapped a finger on the glass.

Beckwith frowned at Petrosky's finger tapping, or perhaps at the greasy smudges he was leaving on the case. "If you're looking for something like that, you can find it anywhere. I'd try the mall." He said the word *mall* with the same level of disgust he'd use to tell them where they could purchase a box of fresh shit.

Pompous asshole. "What store?"

"Try Forever Memories. On Hoover."

The mall on Hoover, four miles from Salomon's. Petrosky handed him a card. Beckwith's hand was as smooth as a baby's ass. Even his breath—slow and sure—was privileged. Cocky.

Cocky. Audacious. Like the man who'd taken girls off the street as if they belonged to him. Hidden them away like they were his personal toys.

But Walsh had clawed her way out of Norton's hiding place. Was another girl trying to escape as they spoke? Ava Fenderson? Margot Nace? Even Casey Hearn, the girl whose family Morrison had met with on his own.

Or maybe they were too late. Petrosky started for the door and drowned out Beckwith's egotistical breath with the howling wind.

24

IT WAS WELL past dinner by the time they arrived at the mall. Morrison had wanted to come over immediately but Petrosky had resisted—he didn't want that prick Beckwith to be right. He'd relented after three more jewelry stores had yielded jack shit.

They entered through the glass doors, the solid white linoleum echoing under their feet as they approached the building map. Across the way, music blared from some teeny-bopper store with mannequins wearing torn, but new, jeans.

Petrosky jerked his head at the dummies. "That's fashion now, California?"

"It is."

"I should sell my old work jeans. I'll make a fucking fortune."

Morrison found the dot for Forever Memories on the store directory, and they took the escalators to the second floor, skirting gaggles of teenagers punching buttons on their phones. "Look, California, it's your people!"

Morrison glanced at them, then back at Petrosky. "Nah, I like to look at you when you talk."

"Watch it, California. I'm not your type," Petrosky grumbled.

Forever Memories boasted T-shirts and novelty key rings out front. In back, it was set up like a jewelry store, with cases of necklaces, silver tongue rings, and belly rings running the length of the back wall. In the middle of the floor in front of the cases were multi-tiered stands adorned with silver picture frames, silver flasks, and cheap pocket watches just waiting for someone to come along and grind initials into them. Half of them already bore sappy romantic bullshit like "Always" or "I Love You" or lame example initials like anyone would forget which tool had brought a pocket watch to a party.

A sales clerk approached—bottle-blond hair and a nose ring —wearing those new, but torn, jeans and a new, but faded, tank top. Looked like Petrosky could sell his worn-out undershirts too.

"Can I help you?" A metal tongue stud glinted in her mouth like she was chewing on a bullet.

Petrosky flashed his badge. "We need to see the manager."

Her eyes grew wide. "Um ... kay. Hang on." She headed for the back of the store, where a door proclaimed Employees Only in red block letters.

Morrison elbowed Petrosky in the ribs. "I think you scared her."

"She'll live." Unlike Walsh or Julie or—

The door opened again, and a lanky man emerged; not much older than the girl, but with far less metal attached to his face. He pushed huge green-rimmed glasses up a beak-like nose, brown eyes darting from Morrison to Petrosky as if unsure who to address.

Petrosky cleared his throat and the guy turned his way.

"How can I help you, sir?"

"Your name?" Petrosky said.

"Um, it's Gerald."

"Last name?"

"Last name?"

His head throbbed. "Yeah, genius, pretend your parents weren't the only ones on the planet to use the name 'Gerald.'"

"Oh, um, Kent. Gerald Kent."

Gerald Kent. Pretentious but not near as pompous as Reginald Beckwith III. "All right there, Mr. Kent, we're looking for a man who purchased some jewelry items to be engraved a couple years back. This guy."

Morrison showed him the sketch.

Kent examined the image, wrinkling his nose, then finally shook his head. "Doesn't look familiar, but we get tons of people in here and two years ago ... I mean ... that's a long time."

"Do you guys sell silver heart pendants?"

Kent nodded far too vigorously—like a nervous Chihuahua. "Lots. This way."

They followed him to the right back corner of the store, where he opened a glass case and produced two boards that looked like they were made of black plastic or shiny card stock. Four hearts of various sizes, all on chains, lay along the middle of one board. On the other, smaller hearts were attached to bracelets. All were silver. Any could have been the one Ms. Nace described.

"These are our best sellers, but we have a catalogue in the back where people can order specific things from the warehouse for engraving."

Petrosky squinted at the pendants. "How often do you change the types of hearts you carry?"

"Not often." He pointed to the ones on the left. "We've had these since I started here three years ago."

"You keep records of purchases?"

"Of course."

"I'll need to see those. We're looking for a specific engraving —the number one, either alone or with the pound sign in front of it."

Kent cocked his head and his glasses slid again. "The pound sign?"

"Hashtag," Morrison said.

Kent's eyes lit up. "Oh, *that*. Yeah, we can look at the computer." He scampered ahead of them to the other corner of the store where a register was set up next to a flat screen.

"Hashtag?" Petrosky whispered.

Morrison shrugged with one shoulder.

"We need to have a serious talk, Surfer Boy."

Kent typed frantically on the keyboard, shoulders hunched like it was his dream to be the next Quasimodo. "All right, it looks like I have seven necklaces with that particular inscription. All purchased within the last"—he scrolled, clicked a few keys—"two years or so."

Jackpot. But ... *seven*. Dear god. He glanced over at Morrison. The kid's jaw was tight, his pen frozen over the notepad.

Petrosky's heart raced. "Were they paid for with a credit card?"

"Sorry, I can't tell."

His arm tingled, throbbed. "We'll need to meet with the employees who sold the merchandise."

Kent shook his head so fast Petrosky thought it might fall off. "Can't tell who did it. Here's what I got." He turned the screen toward them, pointing to the left column. "Here's the date on the far left. Then this column here is the code for the actual piece itself, the next is the cost, and the last is the engraving."

Petrosky squinted at the tiny type. "So you keep track of the item and the engraving itself but nothing on the people who purchased it?"

"It's a marketing thing, looking for patterns." Kent swiveled the monitor back to its original position. "We stock a bunch of pieces already engraved. Some people are really impatient, just want to grab something that says "I love you" or "With all my heart" or whatever, instead of waiting to get it personalized. If we know what people are engraving, we can tell what others might want and put it out there."

Fucking romantic. What woman wouldn't want a piece of shit jewelry with some stranger's words scrawled on the front? "We'll need to speak to all the employees who were here during the time of those purchases."

Kent winced. "Well, there's a pretty high turnover. It'll be almost impossible to—"

"We'll need the sales records too. All the necklaces and charms. A place like this has to have a way to track purchases of their jewelry, even if it isn't in your nifty little chart."

"But—"

Petrosky whipped out a card and planted it on the glass case next to Kent. The keyboard chattered as Kent jumped.

"Lives may depend on your cooperation, Gerald. This needs to happen today."

"I—I'll call corporate in the morning. As soon as they open."

"You work tomorrow afternoon, Gerald?"

"Yes … yes, sir."

"You call me in the morning or I'll be back tomorrow afternoon to bring you down to the station, got it?"

Petrosky turned on his heel and stalked out the front door. Across the linoleum, a shoe store was pulling down barred gates over the plate glass.

Morrison fell into step beside him. "If only they kept records as thorough as mine, Boss. We'd be in much better shape."

Better shape, but not good enough to save Lisa Walsh. And there was no note-taking that could have saved Julie. Pain radiated through Petrosky's arm in time to his footsteps and he rubbed at his chest. His hand was shaking again. "If only."

25

THE NEXT MORNING, he hadn't even made it to his desk when the chief's alto voice rang through the bullpen.

"Petrosky! My office."

Ambushed before he'd even had a jelly doughnut. Tuesday was shaping up to be worse than Monday—all he needed was a dead dog and he'd have a damn fine country song ... if you liked that kind of shit. Which he didn't.

Petrosky followed Chief Carroll's black braid down the hall to her office, glad that he'd done a shot before work so he wasn't a shaky mess. Even gladder that he'd followed up the shot with four slugs of mouthwash. He blew a breath up toward his nose, just in case. *Minty.*

At least Stephanie Carroll was a step up from Chief Castleman; that asshole had been taking kickbacks from the mayor's office. Castleman ended up indicted, the dominoes fell, and the department had been left without a chief until Carroll's appointment. Though a few in the boy's club had been annoyed when she'd taken over, their chagrin hadn't lasted long—Carroll had as much balls as any of the men, and as she was always quick to remind them: vaginas were tougher. Petrosky didn't give a shit one way or the other as long as she wasn't a fuck-up. He was already fucked up enough for everyone.

He settled into the chair in front of her desk, but she stood behind her own chair, five-six on her best day, and stared him down with eyes the color of malt liquor. "Been trying to get ahold of you."

"Been busy."

She met his gaze, eyes narrowing slightly like she thought he was full of shit. "Sure you were. Tell me about the Walsh case."

"Still working on it."

Her full lips formed a tight line. "It's high profile, Petrosky. We've got a dead grandmother, a murdered teenager and a newborn in critical care. People want answers—justice."

"We're going as fast as we can." His voice was smooth, but Petrosky's skin was jittering like it wanted to slither off. He glanced at his arm. It looked perfectly normal.

She sighed and finally sat in her chair, crossing her arms over her chest. "What have you got?"

"Found a few other cases, possibly related. One girl who disappeared wearing socks that might match the fibers found at the Salomon crime scene. A few other troubled teenage girls who might fit the profile—abducted. Found a note in one of their rooms about her being his number one girl." Walsh's carved flesh blinked into his mind, then her smashed skull— blood and bone and gore. He inhaled sharply through his nose. "Another got a gift from an older boyfriend prior to her disappearance—a necklace with an engraved number one."

"The number carved into Lisa Walsh," she said quietly.

He nodded. "And the one carved into Natalie Bell last year. It's been his calling card since Dylan Acosta."

He waited for her face to show disgust, but it remained blank.

"We've also got a potential lead on the jewelry," he said. "The corporate office is going to send us some information this morning—we'll try to track down the kids who sold the charms to our guy, and hopefully we can get a credit card from the purchases." He rubbed his forehead and his fingers came away damp. "That's the best case scenario. I'm betting on him paying cash. And it's unlikely that any security tapes will have been saved that long, but we'll check."

"I see." She adjusted the collar of her suit jacket like it was trying to choke her. "What else?"

"That's what we're chasing. I'm going to go visit Dr. McCallum for a little profile review this morning, too."

She nodded. "Get on it. I want updates. Have Morrison send them over—he's better at the paperwork than you are. Though you really shouldn't get him to pick up the slack on that. He'll be begging for a transfer before you know it."

Petrosky stood and made for the door, calling, "He loves it," over his shoulder.

On his way back across the bullpen he drew a few questioning looks from those who'd overheard the chief's summons. Probably wondering if he'd been suspended—he'd been close to it far too many times.

Petrosky flashed his gun. *Still got it, motherfuckers. No one took my badge today.*

But Surfer Boy sure seemed to think he was gone—the kid was sitting in Petrosky's chair, phone to his ear, pen scratching away. Petrosky put his hand on the back of the chair as Morrison replaced the phone and slid the chair backwards into Petrosky's knee. *Fucking shit.*

"Oh ... sorry. Bad news, Boss—"

"You're answering my desk phone again? Don't they teach you any manners in California?"

Morrison ignored him. "It's a no-go on Forever Memories. We have the dates, but the purchases were all in cash, so no card trace. They don't have security camera footage from that far back either—oldest is from a year ago. The guy said they'll pull up the employee punch cards to find out who was working those dates, but for each shift, we're looking at six or seven employees." He grabbed the folder from the desktop. "Even with duplicates, we'll end up with at least thirty kids to ask what they remember about an engraving they did at a part-time job as much as two years back. Unless he was really outlandish—which we already know he isn't, from his composite—I'm not thinking we'll get much."

"Probably not. We'll try anyway." They couldn't ignore that

lead, even if they believed it was a waste of time; they didn't have the luxury of being wrong.

"How was Carroll?" Morrison asked.

"Bitchy."

"So are you."

"True. Maybe more than she is." Petrosky tapped his fingers on the back of the chair. "When did Forever Memories say the employee names would be ready?"

"They're going to email them over to me as soon as they have them. I'll get them on my phone."

Petrosky squinted at the cell. Nodded. "Good trick."

Morrison stayed silent until Petrosky said, "Okay, Mr. High Tech, let's go take five minutes downstairs with McCallum."

"You call him to make an appointment? Last time you forgot."

He hadn't forgotten—he'd been drunk. Same as this time. "I texted him," Petrosky said.

"Really?"

No.

THE PSYCHIATRIST'S office was located next door to the precinct on the ground floor of the prosecutor's office where Shannon and her intolerable ex-husband worked. The place itself was uglier than sin—boxlike and squat, painted an uneven brown, like a rectangular block of shit. Even McCallum's single window glowered like it was pissed as hell to be part of the hideous building.

But having McCallum this close was convenient for the cops who were assigned to therapy after burying a partner, or for the softies who felt guilty about shooting some asshole during a robbery. Easier, too, for the brass to check up on those cops forced into therapy—he'd been Petrosky's mandated shrink after Julie's murder.

Petrosky yanked the handle hard against the blustery wind. Inside, three old dining room chairs sat along a paneled wall painted a blue-green color that reminded Petrosky of mold growing on an orange. Rot and decay—so fucking relaxing.

The wind howled against the exterior glass as Petrosky listened at the office door for the mumble of voices, the rustle of a tissue box, someone blowing their nose. He heard only the wind—nothing on the other side of the door to indicate the doctor was with a patient. He rapped his knuckles against the frame.

McCallum was close to three hundred pounds, what a hug would look like if you brought it to life and gave it a green tweed jacket. He opened the door and his fleshy face stretched into a grin. "Ed. And Curt too. To what do I owe the pleasure?"

Petrosky could feel Morrison's eyes on him. "How are you, Doc?"

"I'm just fine, just fine." McCallum stepped back around his desk and eased into his chair, presumably to avoid breaking it. Morrison followed Petrosky into the room and they took seats across from the doctor, the legs of Petrosky's wingback creaking as he lowered himself into it.

McCallum looked at Morrison. "I hear that little baby of yours is growing up fast."

Probably from Shannon. She still came to see McCallum every week, Petrosky knew—postpartum depression was a bitch, and her kidnapping ordeal sure hadn't helped her nerves. But at least this time she wasn't dealing with those things while locked in Norton's closet.

Because Lisa Walsh had been the one locked up. And Ava Fenderson. And Margot Nace.

It could have been Shannon.

It could have been Julie.

Petrosky cleared his throat. It sounded syrupy and tasted like rust.

McCallum's face turned solemn. "I heard Adam Norton is back. Double homicide this time, yes?" He examined Morrison, eyes narrowed. Shannon must have been down here already, no doubt re-experiencing her own trauma with Norton's reemergence. McCallum was surely helping her feel better about the situation, even if he couldn't promise her things would be fine. They'd done all they could—she was surrounded by cops and would be until they found Norton, but there were never guarantees in life and death. He'd learned that the hard way.

"Catch me up," McCallum said.

Petrosky did his best, starting with the Salomon crime scene and working through the medical examiner's disgusting report on Lisa Walsh's death, and their leads on the jewelry. All the dead ends that weren't helping shit.

McCallum sat back and tapped his sausage fingers on the desk. "So he took the Walsh girl immediately after Shannon's escape. And Fenderson and Nace the following year." He leaned forward with effort. "I think it's clear his MO has changed since we last spoke. And his victims—there are more of them. And they're getting younger, though he's never been picky about who he harms." For a few seconds there was only the sound of McCallum's labored breathing over Petrosky's erratic heartbeat. Petrosky rubbed at his chest as memories seared through his brain—Evie locked in Norton's dog cage, Shannon, her lips sutured together, an iron collar around her throat. Morrison didn't seem to be breathing at all.

"You want to know what kind of person does this," the doctor said.

The silence stretched. McCallum actually looked like he expected an answer. Why else would they be there? This guy wasn't simple—not some Romeo pimp, buttering up girls with jewelry so he could groom them to fuck a john. "Yeah. We need to know who Norton is." They needed to know how to catch him.

McCallum cleared his throat, apparently satisfied. "During the last case, Norton was exposed to things he might not have had the guts to do by himself. Rape. Murder. Kidnapping. Watching Janice in action, he figured out what turned him on." He'd been watching. Learning. Now, Norton knew what he liked —and exactly how to get it.

"Your guy might be numb to empathy, but he feels the rage and pain of rejection more deeply than you can imagine. It's consumed him. He's made it his life's mission to avenge himself against a sex he sees as threatening—their rejection is the ultimate cause of everything wrong with his life."

"He doesn't even know these girls before he starts grooming them." Morrison's voice trembled, almost imperceptibly, but enough that Petrosky's own heart squeezed like it was in a vise.

"Ah, but don't you see? He doesn't have to. They represent something to him. And because his victims are all girls, young teenagers … that may be the time in his life he was hurt. Perhaps he feels entitled to their affection—common in a culture like ours."

Petrosky coughed, his throat irritated by the stale heat now huffing from the vent. McCallum had a point. With the way western women were sexualized nowadays, young men were groomed to see them a certain way—and to expect a certain response. When women didn't return their affections, it wasn't merely a blow to their self-esteem. It felt like they were being mistreated. Petrosky saw it every week, some dickhead claiming he was entitled to rape a woman behind a dumpster because she'd been dressed provocatively, or a college girl beaten for refusing her boyfriend's advances. Norton wasn't different or new, even if he thought he was; that asshole was a product of their fucked-up society.

"Fine, so how does this help us?" Petrosky said. "We're looking for a misogynist. A guy who thinks women should be subservient."

"Hence his crawl back to the torture devices of the middle ages, where women would have been expected to meet his demands."

"But these aren't women we're talking about. These are little girls. I know we assumed he wasn't a pedophile in the past, but the infant we found is definitely his child—he raped Lisa Walsh."

"Lisa Walsh wasn't that little."

Heat flooded Petrosky's face. "She wasn't even fifteen when he took her."

"Teenagers would have been perfectly acceptable as brides during the medieval period. Remember that. And not to say that he isn't a pedophile, but he's choosing girls who look like women—it's more about vulnerability and fear. Let us not forget that his first solo victim, Natalie Bell, was twenty-nine, but small in stature—frail. Childlike. An older woman might reject him or be more able to fight him off. These girls can't. Might even be why he told you how to find Janice. He wanted to punish her because he felt slighted by her, even threatened by her, because she was stronger than he preferred."

Weak men hated strong women. Made sense. "He's refined his tastes since then," Petrosky said slowly.

McCallum nodded. "Norton might have found a position where he has unfettered access to the type of girls he's after: a camp counselor, a bus driver, even a Sunday school teacher. He picks one girl and grooms her. Gives her gifts. Then he waits for her to come to him—less risk of rejection."

And once he had them, he took whatever he wanted. Because he thought they owed him that.

"He's staying local—or at least hunts locally," Petrosky said.

"He may also be hunting locally and taking them to a secure location elsewhere; he's proven himself to be rather intelligent, and he knows you've seen his face." McCallum studied the ceiling, and when he drew his eyes back down, his face was solemn. "If these girls trust him, it'd be easy for him to get them into his car and take them for a ride."

Maybe that was how Lisa Walsh had escaped with her child. Had he taken her with him as bait for someone he wasn't sure would go without a fight? A girl could lure another closer simply by being female—that was why baby-snatching rings always included women. None of that was really Norton's MO, but then again, neither was having children, or giving gifts, or grooming his victims—Norton had snatched Shannon and Evie off the side of the road. Petrosky didn't know shit for certain outside of the fact that Norton was a sadistic asshole who'd take as many little girls as he could. *Girls. Daughters.* Petrosky rubbed his shoulder where a dull ache pulsed with every beat of his heart—weak but persistent.

McCallum cleared his throat, one harsh, staccato bark. "Though he thrives on the energy of others, it's hard to say whether he's living alone. He may desire emotional reinforcement as he did when he was working with Janice, but I suspect he would rather avoid the complication of a partner after last time." McCallum's brows furrowed. "He's keeping these girls at his home or another place where he can access them—he might be leading a rather normal life that allows him to garner emotional support in other ways."

A normal life, aside from snatching kids every once in a while and running them through with an axe. Paper crinkled to his right. Petrosky glanced at Morrison who was scratching notes as fast as McCallum was talking.

"We'll start with the schools," Petrosky said. "He had to have a way to meet these girls." With the Dylan Acosta case, Norton had known exactly how to position himself to avoid being seen. Likely he knew his way around these other schools too.

Morrison nodded but didn't look up from his writing.

Petrosky stood, unsteadily enough that he had to rest his hand on the desk to stay upright. He needed some fucking sleep… and another shot. "I'll come back and hash things out once we get a little more information."

"Come back either way, Ed." McCallum said, examining Petrosky's hand. "You and I should have a good sit-down one of these days."

Petrosky ripped a cigarette from the pack in his shirt pocket. "I'll be back."

"See that you are," McCallum called after him.

Petrosky tongued the roof of his mouth. It tasted like peppermint.

26

LISA WALSH'S former middle school was sandwiched between a dilapidated library and a brand-spanking-new liquor store. A dichotomy, as Morrison would say. Also a testament to where the people of the city put their cash.

Petrosky and Morrison entered through a creaky double door and stopped before the metal detector, where a pudgy rent-a-cop with a smashed pancake face and a Tom Selleck mustache looked up from his spot behind a folding table laminated to look like wood.

"The principal's office?" Morrison asked.

Petrosky showed his badge. The guy waved them through with barely a glance and went back to his crossword.

"Third hall on the left, all the way down."

Petrosky and Morrison exchanged a look. "Don't you have to watch carefully to make sure no one shifty gets in here?" Petrosky said.

"You're the cops," the guard muttered at his page. "Can't get more careful than that."

The yellow halls echoed with their footsteps and the occasional metallic clang of a locker somewhere in the vicinity. From behind closed doors, voices rose and fell in waves, students and teachers doing the school thing. When they passed the bathroom, Petrosky caught the slightest tang of nicotine on the air, and he inhaled deeply—then rested his finger on the pack of cigs in his pocket and pulled out a piece of gum. Not the fucking same. It was like drinking lemonade instead of vodka; gave you something to do with your mouth, but you might as well have been sucking ass for all the pleasure you got out of it.

The scent of cigarettes gave way to a faint dust-bunny smell as they entered the main office. The place was clean, though, with flattened green carpet and a plywood counter as high as Petrosky's rib cage. To their left was a lone door with a gold plaque that read "Principal E.G. Cummings." Well beyond the counter in the back corner of the room, a woman wearing a bright orange turban raised her head. The tag on her desk said "Mrs. Nwosu." She stood.

"I'm Detective Petrosky, and this is Detective Morrison. We're investigating the kidnapping of a former student—"

Her hands fluttered to her face. "Oh, you're here about that poor girl on the television." Her voice was husky and deep like a lounge singer's, with a melodic accent that might have been South African though he could barely identify regional accents in America let alone in other countries. But he always knew Boston—an entire city pronouncing every goddamn vowel wrong pissed him off. Though that was still better than calling everyone "dude" like they did in surfer country.

"I remember when that happened, sir. Terrible, terrible thing." She stepped around her desk and approached the counter.

Petrosky waited for Morrison to get his notebook ready. "Were you here when Lisa Walsh disappeared, ma'am?"

"I was."

"What do you recall about the days before she went missing?" The tiniest bit of information could turn into a lead. Was there something she hadn't told the police before, anything she hadn't thought pertinent?

"Not much. The police came then, too, asked us questions, but they said she ran away. We get lots of kids who run away." She leaned in. "It wasn't right, though. That girl was trying to get better. Working harder on her homework. Even came in here occasionally, after the rest of the faculty left for lunch. I let her eat with me. Helped her." Her eyes glassed over.

That wasn't in the file. "Did you mention this to the police?"

She closed her mouth, jaw tight enough that he could make out the tense muscles in her lower face. Petrosky's back stiffened. Was she lying now? Or had she purposefully held back this information before?

"No," she answered finally. "I did not tell them."

"Why not?"

"It didn't seem important and the girl deserved a little privacy. The police asked me about her boyfriends a dozen times." She squared her shoulders. "She never spoke about her life, just did her schoolwork. I think she needed someone to believe in her." Her mouth trembled, but without the telltale guilt-twitch of the lip. Only sadness.

Morrison produced Adam Norton's picture. "Ever see her with anyone? An older man?"

She shook her head. "Never." It came out *Nevah*.

"Adisa?" A woman with salt-and-pepper hair in a tight bun stood in the doorway to the principal's office. Black suit, no makeup, but the same tight jaw as the woman in front of him, and a stiffer back than Petrosky's own. She narrowed her eyes, clearly not pleased with the interruption.

"Ms. Cummings?" Petrosky showed her his badge. "I'm Detective Petrosky. We're here investigating the death of a former student."

Her eyes softened. "You're here about Lisa." She stepped back through her office door and waved them in.

Cummings's office had the same green carpet as the lobby, with a carved wooden desk in the center. A scent like lemon and rainwater wafted from a candle in the corner. Petrosky cleared his throat to avoid gagging and sat beside Morrison in the leather chairs facing the desk.

"How can I help?" She folded her hands on the desktop, much like McCallum did when he was about to analyze the hell out of you.

"Were you the principal when Walsh disappeared?" Petrosky asked.

"I was. Been here nearly ten years now."

"What can you tell me about her?"

Her knuckles went white. "To be honest, I didn't know much about her until she disappeared. She wasn't sent down to the office too often; when she did get into trouble it was small enough to be handled by her teachers. She was bright, a good student for the most part. Quiet."

"What about the people she associated with?"

"The crowd she hung with wasn't the best—some drugs, cutting class and such, but she was well-liked. Pretty." She shrugged. "The police asked those questions, talked to her friends. After she disappeared, I spoke to the faculty, too, but no one had anything useful to say and I can't remember anything that'd be helpful."

"What about strangers hanging around the school? An older boy, maybe twenty?"

Cummings waved her hand as if shooing off the question. "Now, Detective, you know they asked that already. And, no, we didn't have anyone hanging around our school. The only thing that was strange was a janitor who up and left around the same time." She raised one shoulder as if a staff member vanishing along with a student couldn't possibly matter. "He didn't come to work the day after she disappeared. Normally, it wouldn't have raised any questions—those people leave all the time, no notice at all. But with him disappearing right when she ran off, well …"

A janitor. That's what Norton had been doing for work when he'd kidnapped Shannon. Was he brazen enough to maintain the same occupation? If he was a janitor in the school system, he'd have unfettered access to victims, though … he'd have been fingerprinted. And then they'd have caught him already.

"Did you contact the police about this?"

"I did. They said they'd look into it."

Petrosky had read the file—no mention of a janitor that he could remember. He glanced over at Morrison, wondering if he'd missed something, and Morrison shook his head. If the kid didn't know about it, it wasn't in the file at all.

Petrosky leaned forward in his chair, hands on his knees. "Tell me everything you can about the janitor."

She sat back and crossed her arms—putting distance between them. Hiding something? Or just … regretful? "His name was Carlos Reyes. He was quiet. Stuck to himself, but they aren't usually the most talkative types."

"They?" *Those people,* she'd said. *Those people leave all the time.* He'd assumed she meant the janitorial staff, but—

"Mexicans." She eyed the ceiling. "I do remember thinking that he might not speak much English, but he always understood instructions just fine."

Petrosky's heart sank. Norton couldn't pass as Mexican— even with dark hair, the guy was as pasty white as Petrosky's sun-deprived ass. Then again, Norton'd gone from naturally blond hair, to bald with black eyebrows when Petrosky had met him, and then back again by the time he was running around the library with Ava Fenderson. Maybe wearing makeup wasn't out of the question, even if it was highly fucking unlikely.

"Did Reyes ever seem particularly interested in the kids? The girls?"

"If he was, no one noticed. He just came in, did his job, and went home."

Reserved. Fearful of rejection. Smiling shyly until someone seemed receptive? The quiet, non-threatening girl might have smiled at him. Then *bam,* there went Lisa. But that didn't feel right. Someone would have called in after Morrison passed around the composite even if his coloring was off—Norton wouldn't have been able to hide the scars on his face. Unless … he'd disguised that too.

"Did Reyes have facial hair?"

Cummings examined the ceiling again, then shook her head. "Clean-shaven."

There went that. "Height? Weight?" he asked.

"Maybe … five-seven, five-eight? I'd say two hundred and twenty pounds."

Height and weight weren't right either unless Norton was wearing a body suit—not their guy's style. But Reyes might have accidentally seen something, or maybe he'd been watching the girls for Norton, picking out potential targets. McCallum thought Norton had a partner. Was that why Reyes hadn't shown up for work the day after Lisa disappeared? He felt guilty? But Norton had a habit of choosing partners that didn't stick out; surely he'd have vetted Reyes and discovered the janitor worked with assholes who would have suspected him just for being one of "those people."

"The police said they stopped by his house," Cummings was saying, "but he wasn't there. Mrs. Walsh threw a fit about it, both here and with the police, I heard, though I suppose she had complained before."

"Complained about what?" Had the guy come on to her daughter or …

"About him being an immigrant, even though he was legal— we always check. But she came in here muttering about people who live here speaking English or going back where they came from."

If that argument held, they'd all be speaking Native American. Mrs. Walsh sounded like a real gem. Her nervous babbling at the house settled uneasily in Petrosky's belly like bad fish. "I understand you have a high turnover rate, but was Mr. Reyes specifically prone to absences before that?"

She bit her lip. "You know, I don't think he was ever late a day. Not until Lisa disappeared."

So the things Cummings had just said about Reyes were bull-shit stereotypes that didn't fit him at all. Awesome. "We'll need that file, ma'am." Hopefully there'd be less bullshit on paper … but he doubted it.

She stood. "I'll be right back."

As soon as she closed the door behind her, Morrison pulled out his cell and peered at the screen.

"Got the list from Forever Memories. Thirty-six employees. I'll pull their phone numbers after we follow up on Reyes. Unless we happen to find the janitor with a basement full of little girls, which is doubtful." Morrison pocketed the phone. "Sounds like Mrs. Walsh is a little xenophobic."

"Enough with the big words, Cali."

"Bigoted."

"Gotcha." It was their job to be suspicious of everyone, but race and nationality were shitty fucking reasons. Petrosky heaved himself to standing and walked to the corner. He blew out the candle and sat back down.

"What'd you do that for?" Morrison asked.

"What, are you sad you can't smell pretty?"

"I smell pretty all the time."

"How does Shannon feel about that, Nancy?"

"Better than she'd feel if I smelled like you."

The door clicked open. Cummings glared at her candle and the tendril of black smoke now wafting toward the ceiling. "Adisa is making copies for you now."

Copies that would probably lead them nowhere unless this bastard had become a master of disguise—or Reyes was actually involved. Hopefully Forever Memories would give them something better. Every hour that passed was another hour of torture for these girls.

If they weren't already dead.

27

CARLOS REYES DID NOT HAVE a Michigan driver's license, just a social security number. His last known address—or the one Cummings had on file–was a section eight apartment building two blocks behind the school.

"Want to hike it, Boss?"

Petrosky glowered at him until Morrison started for the car.

"Just asking."

Petrosky pulled out of the lot and headed east while Morrison's knee bounced a steady rhythm against the side door.

"What the fuck's wrong with your leg, Cali?"

"You know, I can take this, and you can start on Forever Memories. Or vice versa."

"I need your eyes."

"You need my notes."

"That too. Carroll wants you to do the reports. And if we actually manage to find Norton …" He didn't have to say they'd need backup. That if either of them went in alone, this guy would be ready with a fucking spear to take their heart out. And Norton wasn't the only concern. Petrosky glanced over. The last time Morrison had gone after Norton alone, the kid had set Roger's house on fire and filleted a pedophile with a fishing knife. Not that Petrosky was complaining, but still.

THE FIVE-STORY APARTMENT building loomed the same ash gray as the crestfallen sky. Along the street side, pink-and-blue graffiti encouraged Grace to fuck off while dingy snow left by a plow turned the curbs into mountains of filthy slush.

They parked in the lot next to a Pinto with half a bumper and a tarp covering the back window, and picked their way across the icy lot and through a swinging screen door. A piece of yellow caution tape hung from the upper corner of the elevator, fluttering in the frigid breeze.

Morrison glanced at it, pulled open the door to the stairwell, and headed in.

Petrosky's throat felt thick. Heavy. Even his tongue was tired, and he sure as shit wasn't going to feel any better after this trek upstairs. "Hey, Surfer Boy."

Morrison turned, mouth working like he was chewing on the inside of his cheek.

"Can you talk to Reyes and write at the same time?"

Morrison's eyes lit up, though his lips remained tight. "I can, Boss."

"Good."

Morrison's phone rang. He whipped it out, then relaxed. "Valentine." He shoved it back in his pocket.

Petrosky raised an eyebrow at him.

"I asked for updates every few hours. He said he'd text if it was critical." The tightness had crept into the corners around his eyes—even if Valentine had just been calling to make a playdate for their rug-rats, Morrison was haunted by whatever was going on in his head. Probably remembering Shannon's lips the day they'd found her—the stitches, the black thread, crusted with pus. His infant daughter locked in a dog crate.

Petrosky grabbed the railing and panted up another step.

"You sound like you're in tip-top shape, Boss," Morrison said, fast enough that he might have been trying to distract himself too. "You really should hit the gym with Decantor and me."

"Fuck that." What he really needed was the airplane bottle of Jack he had hidden under his passenger seat.

At the top of the stairs, Morrison pulled open the door to the hall. The air smelled like Spam. Petrosky sucked in a few painful breaths, cursing the stairs and his out-of-shape ass all the way down the hall to a deeply scarred door. At some point in the past, someone had broken it in. Maybe even the police, back when they were searching for Lisa Walsh.

Apartment 303 was opened by an older man with skin the color of pissed-on snow. A cannula hung from one blue-veined nostril, the tube leading to a wheeled oxygen tank on his left. If he was spry, he could heave it at them … but he wasn't. The man leaned heavily on the doorframe and looked at Petrosky, probably waiting for him to speak, but Petrosky's lungs were still on fire from the stairs.

Morrison cleared his throat and brandished the pen like a weapon. "Good afternoon, sir. I'm Detective Morrison and this is Detective Petrosky. We're looking for a Carlos Reyes."

"Don't know him." His voice held the whispery rasp of emphysema. Petrosky pulled out a piece of gum.

"Your name, sir?" Morrison asked.

"Martin. Martin Ellsworth."

"How long have you lived here, Mr. Ellsworth?"

Ellsworth took a Darth Vader breath. "'Bout a year, I'd say."

"Did you know the previous tenant?"

He shook his head.

"Any mention around the building of Carlos Reyes?"

Ellsworth shook his head again, the bags under his eyes darkening.

"There an apartment manager here?"

"Used to be. I think we got bought by the bank or something. Had to change the address where I send the rent."

"Can you give us that address?"

"Sure." Ellsworth reached behind the door, probably toward an entry table piled high with overdue hospital bills, but Petrosky stiffened and Morrison shot him a glance. He relaxed when Ellsworth's hand reappeared palming an envelope. *Get it together, old man.*

"Already paid this one," Ellsworth said. "You're welcome to it."

Morrison traded the envelope for his business card. "Thank you, Mr. Ellsworth. Sorry to have bothered you."

"No problem."

The door clicked shut.

"What do you think?" Morrison asked as they descended the stairs.

"We'll call the bank, and try to find the manager from a few years back." But it probably wouldn't help much. Manager of a place like this didn't give a flying fuck who lived here as long as he got a check.

"If Reyes disappeared," Morrison was saying, "you think the police at the time just didn't follow up?"

"I think they probably did and didn't write a fucking novel about it. A janitor left, sure, but they might've already figured Lisa as a runaway and didn't do much investigating."

"Only one way to find out."

Petrosky sighed.

THE RIDE back to the precinct was thick with Petrosky's agitation and Morrison's unspoken worry. Petrosky drove, inhaling his cigarette like a starving man, until he felt the kid's eyes boring into him.

"Problem?"

Morrison pointed to the window.

Petrosky glared but rolled it down, then hit the cigarette and blew the smoke out on a hard exhale, loud and violent. Violent, like Norton.

The unease he'd been battling all day expanded into a more intense foreboding as he watched the freeway slide by, every bush, every building a reminder that some things went on, and some did not. Bricks and mortar and cement remained but blood and flesh and bone decayed like the memories of the person who'd once owned that outer shell. It'd happened to Dylan Acosta and Lisa Walsh. It'd happened to Julie.

And Norton was relishing that decay, and not only during death—oh no, that would be too easy, too kind. He was relishing the annihilation of the individual, abusing love and joy and hope until these girls probably wondered if those things had ever existed. If only they'd caught Norton sooner. If only they hadn't stopped looking. It was their fault—*his* fault. Petrosky's stomach constricted. All those little girls probably thought it was their fault too. They'd run off, disobeyed their parents. They'd smiled and encouraged Norton and met him somewhere secret because they believed they were safe. How many times had Norton told them it was their fault they were locked in a cell? Brainwashed them, made them believe that if it hadn't been for their own stupidity, he wouldn't be hurting them? And somewhere in the back of his head, Petrosky heard *her* voice: *Sorry, Daddy. I didn't mean for them to get me.* Had Julie known her attackers too? Had she felt that same irrational guilt he'd seen over and over throughout his career—attack victims saying, "It was my fault" as they sat there, tearful and unfocused, blood trickling down their legs?

"You coming?"

Petrosky jerked forward and looked out the window at the precinct. He hadn't even noticed they'd arrived. "Head in and get started. I'll be up." He tossed his cigarette butt out the window and lit another smoke.

Morrison hesitated, then got out. Petrosky's stomach twisted like there was a knife in his gut as he watched him stride across the lot. *Sorry, Surfer Boy. I never was one to rely on.* The car shrank around him. *Just ask Julie.*

When the precinct door closed behind Morrison, Petrosky put the car in reverse, moved to the back of the lot, and stuck his cigarette-free hand in the console. An extra lighter and a few ketchup packs. His chest ramped up like a suspect's right before a confession.

He jerked open the glove box. Registration. Six parking tickets, months old. *Fuck.* Petrosky threw himself over the seat and bent his hand underneath the passenger side. Nothing. But ... wait.

Cold, small.

He fumbled for the bottle, tried to slide it out, but his hand stuck on the seat adjustment bar. He pulled harder, wincing as the underside of the seat tore at his knuckles. But that didn't matter, not now that he had the bottle clenched in his fist.

Petrosky heaved himself back against the headrest. The sky watched him through the windshield like an angry parent, able to convey disappointment without uttering a word. He unscrewed the little bottle and tilted it up, ignoring his bleeding hand.

The liquor burned into his gut. Maybe this would be his last case. Maybe he wouldn't see tomorrow. There was a comfort in that, but he was still too much of a chickenshit to do anything about it—while he was sober, anyway. And as long as there was a chance he could help Ava, help Margot … he'd try. But he couldn't do this shit sober; the pain was too much to bear.

Petrosky smashed the butt of the cigarette into the ashtray, tossed the empty bottle to the floor, and thumped his fist against his breastbone—his heart was trying to squeeze itself through his ribs. The wind blew at his face as he headed for the precinct, but by the time he got to the bullpen, the Jack had eased the erratic thumping in his chest.

Morrison wasn't at his desk, but the case file was.

Fuck it, I'll run down the janitor myself. Petrosky snatched the file, then headed to his own workstation and plopped into the seat. The steady beat of his heel on the floor and the beeps and buzzes of the computer booting up were lively, chaotic. But the black screen was a reminder that no matter how much noise you made, how hard you tried, you were still at the mercy of the dark.

The screen lit up. *Finally.*

Petrosky punched up the social security number for Carlos Reyes that Cummings had given him. Thirty seconds later, he had an Arizona driver's license and a current Arizona address. But the photo didn't look anything like what Cummings had described—or like Norton, either. The Reyes on the screen was tall and thin and decidedly white. His height was listed at six-foot-three. What had Cummings said? Five-eight? No way she'd be that far off. And the license put Reyes' birthday at eighteen years ago. Two years ago when Walsh was taken, Reyes would have been … fifteen? Sixteen?

Petrosky leaned back in his chair. False social. Not uncommon with illegal immigrants, if that's what Reyes was. He opened his drawer, pushed aside old gum and a napkin and ran his finger down the laminated directory sheet Morrison had glued to the bottom of the drawer. Maybe someone in immigration might—

"Whatcha got, Boss?" Morrison peered over his shoulder.

Petrosky slammed the drawer. "Check this out."

Morrison's face was pained. Petrosky pointed at the screen where Reyes stared back at them, sullen. "Got Reyes here, address in—"

"Arizona, yeah I know. I called him five minutes after I came in. Not that I needed to, I guess. Obvious fake. But here's the kicker." Morrison set half a dozen sheets of paper on the desk in front of Petrosky. "I called Hernandez—"

"Who?"

"The original investigating officer on the Lisa Walsh kidnapping, the one who deemed her a runaway. He's retired but still consulting over in Warren. Turns out they didn't follow up on the janitor because they found Reyes's body a few days later, probably killed the day he disappeared." Morrison flipped the folder open and turned a few pages. "Shotgun wound to the chest, listed as a robbery because his wallet was missing. Without a real social, he would have stayed a John Doe if they hadn't already been checking the area for him."

Had Norton killed Reyes for suspecting him, for seeing something at that school he shouldn't have? Maybe Norton killed him because he feared Reyes would turn him in, whether they were originally working together or not. But … a gunshot wound? That wasn't even close to Norton's MO, especially not two years ago.

"They nail anyone for the murder?"

Morrison shook his head. "Not sure they tried too hard on that either. But get this—he was shot with a Ruger 10-22 rifle."

A rifle. The gleam in Morrison's eyes said it all. "Like the one over Mr. Walsh's stove," Petrosky said.

While he'd been in the car drinking his pain away like an

asshole, Morrison had solved a cold case. The kid didn't need him at all. "You did this in ten minutes?"

Morrison closed the folder. "You were out almost an hour, Boss," he said quietly, voice laced with a subtle disappointment that made Petrosky's heart hurt.

Petrosky fumbled in the desk drawer for a pen. They'd go grab Walsh in five—he wasn't going anywhere. But first ... He flipped through the file, pausing to mark one of the maps Morrison always printed when they started a case. "I don't like how close all this is." He ignored the tremor in his fingers and pointed at the page. "The school, the abductions, the girls. Acosta and Bell were farther outside this zone, but—"

"Norton was working with someone else back then."

"Right." Petrosky tapped the map. "Here's the Salomon house. Here's where Margot Nace lived." He marked each spot with a determined jab, trying to disguise the shaking. "This one is the Walsh place. We've also got the dump site for Walsh. And here's the last place Casey Hearn was seen, since you took the liberty of talking to her folks without me." He scowled at Morrison to show his displeasure, though he didn't really give a shit that he had missed that interview.

"Boss, Hearn's parents didn't know anything. I know we can't rule her out conclusively, but—"

"We've got the library, too, where Mrs. Fenderson saw our guy, and here's each of the girls' schools and the mall where he purchased the necklaces."

Morrison squinted at the page. "Makes a pretty cozy circle around the Salomon place."

A headache was creeping in behind Petrosky's eyes. He didn't give a shit what McCallum said about Norton being smart, about their perp knowing they'd recognize him—he was staying local. Hunting local.

"We canvassed the neighborhood," Morrison said, "even went inside most of those houses with the owners' permission. And nothing. Decantor went over there again with the new composite, showed Norton's picture around. Got jack shit."

"I know, I know. But this guy doesn't like change." Norton was still reliving high school wrongs, wasn't he? Punishing girls

who reminded him of the girls who had hurt him in his forma-
tive years. Or those he imagined had hurt him—*entitled prick.*
"My money is on his place being within a ten-mile radius of the
Salomon house, but it's densely populated. If we base it on how
far a girl with mangled feet could run before someone caught
her, I'd say ... two miles? Three? Providing she had a head start;
she sure as shit didn't outrun him."

"True. But we've been looking." Morrison's voice still had
that edge of concern. "And ... I mean, McCallum thinks he might
just be hunting there. Maybe Norton is taking his victims elsewhere to—"

"Fuck McCallum."

Morrison refused to meet Petrosky's eyes. Petrosky tried to
pretend it was because the kid had a headache too—the piercing
pain behind his own eyes was getting worse by the minute.

"We need to go back to square one—back to Salomon's,"
Petrosky said. He was in the neighborhood, Petrosky could
almost taste the truth of it, feel it coursing through his blood
along with the Jack. "Maybe we should just fucking sit on the
street corner until we see him."

Morrison glanced toward Decantor's area then back at
Petrosky, his mouth half open.

"Got something else to say, Surfer Boy?"

Morrison shook his head and closed his mouth. "Let's go get
Walsh's gun."

28

"WHERE IS IT, MR. WALSH?"

Walsh hadn't seemed particularly happy to see Petrosky or Morrison once he found out they weren't there to give him his "five minutes" with the man who'd killed his daughter. Though knowing now that the guy had already doled out vigilante justice to his daughter's kidnapper—or the man he thought was the kidnapper—perhaps Petrosky should have taken that "five minute" thing more seriously.

"Where is what?" Walsh said.

Petrosky gestured to the blank spot above the stove, the outline of the weapon almost visible if you squinted. "Your rifle."

Walsh looked at the stove and back at them. "Stacey has it. She said she felt unsafe so I let her take it. Why?"

His ex. Petrosky and Morrison exchanged a look. "Where is she now, Mr. Walsh?"

"At home, I assume. What's this all about?"

"Were you aware that a janitor at Lisa's school, one Carlos Reyes, went missing the day after Lisa's disappearance?"

"What?" Walsh's brows furrowed. "I don't think I've ever heard that name. Do you think he ... hurt Lisa? Is he ..." His voice cracked and he wiped his eyes. "Sorry, it ... comes in waves, you know?"

Petrosky did know. What he didn't know was why this guy's

posture remained slumped—defeated. Not a hint of anxiety, even when they'd asked about the gun. Then again …

Cummings had said *Mrs*. Walsh was upset about the janitor. She'd said nothing about Mr. Walsh at all.

Jesus. Petrosky leaned against the counter, his arms suddenly leaden. "Did your ex-wife ever mention Reyes?"

Walsh paused. His jaw dropped. He closed his mouth again.

"Mr. Walsh?"

"Stacey … right after Lisa went missing, she said something about someone at the school taking her, but she … I mean, she didn't say anything to me about a specific person. She said there were people there, taking girls, turning them into drug mules. Bringing them to Mexico." Walsh shook his head. "I told her it was crazy, but—"

"You didn't buy into her story? Maybe you considered going after a man you thought could have hurt Lisa?"

Walsh reared back like someone had slapped him. "Go after… who? For what? I mean, if I knew who had Lisa, I would have tried to get her back, but what Stacey was saying didn't make any sense. Then a few weeks later, she was hospitalized— they said the stress from Lisa's disappearance had caused some kind of a psychotic break, and … well, she hasn't been right since. I guess I figured those accusations were … part of the same brand of crazy." He sighed heavily. "I'm not sure what you're asking me."

Petrosky heaved himself away from the counter and leaned close enough that he could smell Walsh's soap. "Let me be more clear, then: Did you kill Carlos Reyes?"

Walsh stepped to the dinette and lowered himself slowly, incrementally, into the chair at the table. "Oh my God. What did she do?" He put his head in his hands. Either he was a psychopath or he truly was clueless. Petrosky's money was on the latter.

No wonder his ex had been so nervous last time they were here. Her racist ass had gone after Reyes the moment she found out Lisa was missing. Probably decided to threaten him into giving back her daughter. Hell, maybe she'd shot him accidentally.

And now she was on the run. Because she knew she'd killed the wrong man.

"We'll need her address, Mr. Walsh. Now."

STACEY WASN'T HOME. Of course she wasn't. She was probably out shooting some other innocent brown-skinned laborer for being in the vicinity of her kid at one time or another.

God-fucking-dammit. Like they didn't have enough to deal with. Now he had some crazy racist running around, armed to the teeth.

"Can't we give this shit back to Hernandez?"

"Maybe if he hadn't retired, Boss." Morrison was eying him strangely. Petrosky didn't give a fuck. The exhaustion in his limbs had intensified since they'd left the Walsh house; every step was unwieldy, like he was trying to wade through glue. Tomorrow he'd get back on the wagon and try to get a little more fucking sleep before he actually passed out on the job.

"I thought I'd start with her work, her friends," Morrison said. "If I don't get her by the morning, I'll pass it over to Decantor for follow up." He was still staring at Petrosky, brows furrowed. "I'll text you in the morning, let you know how it goes?"

"You trying to get rid of me, Cali?" Petrosky was aiming for sarcastic, but the words came out strained. Weak. Defeated.

Morrison shook his head. "Not necessarily. But you don't look well, old man."

He didn't feel well. Might have been the booze, might have been the stress. "I'll get some rest later." But the earth was trying to suck him down, like the ground was made of quicksand.

"I can handle this, Boss. This is easy shit—just tracking cell phone location, APBs and the like. And if I find her, I'll take Decantor for backup. I won't go in alone."

"Shannon's going to have your ass, staying out all night again."

"I can't sleep. I just lie there, staring at the ceiling, worrying about Shannon, the kids. Maybe if I was staying with them ...

but I'm afraid I'll lead Norton to her. And after further consideration, we decided to move her again. Valentine's wife, too, just in case."

Further consideration. Morrison didn't feel that his family was safe—wouldn't until Norton was locked up for good. No wonder the kid looked like he'd slept with his eyelids pried open.

"She's at Decantor's mother-in-law's place; the house is in her new husband's name," Morrison said. "Valentine's still on them all day long, plus she has our three German Shepherds and Valentine's Rottweiler. The sooner I close this, the sooner they can come home."

Morrison put a hand on Petrosky's shoulder, suddenly looking as tired as Petrosky felt. "Go home. We can't both be wrecked. Text me when you wake up. Hopefully by then we'll have collared Reyes's killer and be back to tracking Lisa Walsh's."

Petrosky frowned and the muscles in his face twitched. But the kid was right. "You know I hate that texting shit."

"It's more efficient." Morrison smiled—only his red-rimmed eyes showed his concern. "And I can tell you where I am, even send you a map with a little GPS dot for you to follow."

"You think I don't know my way around, Surfer Boy?"

Morrison shrugged. "Just saying."

Petrosky sighed. "Fine. But if that jerkwad GPS voice in the phone lands me in the river, I'm coming after your ass."

Morrison was staring at Petrosky's hand and Petrosky followed his gaze to the gouge across the back of his knuckles where he'd caught them under the car seat. The bottle had been worth it.

He put his hand behind his back. "Caught it on the car door," he said, though Morrison hadn't asked. He stood. "You're going home when you're done with Stacey and her rifle?"

"After a little. I've got one more thing to check on."

"On the case?"

"I'm not sure."

Petrosky's body vibrated. His mouth was a desert. He sucked his teeth to hide a yawn, tasted salt and sand and something sour. "Fill me in tomorrow. And in the morning we'll head over to Salomon's neighborhood, scout the place out."

"Sounds good. Get some sleep, Boss."

Sleep wouldn't cure what was ailing him, but he was no longer functioning without it. Even the room was starting to fade in and out—fuzzy. A drink and then bed. Maybe a bullet, if his balls miraculously grew into cantaloupes before dawn. Either way, the kid would be fine.

29

WHEN PETROSKY AWOKE, his balls were exactly the same size. Maybe even smaller—whiskey wasn't known for its restorative properties when it came to your junk.

He texted Morrison three times, but the kid wasn't responding. Probably worked too late and finally passed out. Petrosky took a swallow from the bottle by the bed—just one, hair of the dog—and dragged himself through the house getting ready for work. Texted Morrison again, just in case the phone had lost the first few messages. In the kitchen, he appraised the coffee pot, jabbed the buttons, and watched it sputter. He left before it finished brewing.

He parked at the precinct, scanning the lot for the kid's car. Not there. He glared at the phone, considered dialing again, and then shoved it in his pocket. Some things were better done in person. Old school, like good shoes or wooden toys before they started mass-producing shit. Not that it stopped him from buying cheap Chinese toys for Evie and Henry. He was principled, but not stupid.

The dash clock read 7:44. Morrison never got in after seven —he'd probably ridden in with Valentine or that fuckface Decantor, whose stupid Jeep Wrangler was already in the parking lot. No doubt he and Morrison were up there jawing about the Kardashians, wasting everybody's goddamn time.

Petrosky stalked up the steps and into the building. Morrison's desk was empty. Eyes followed him as he marched through the bullpen, looking for Decantor's chummy ass, irritated as shit that he had to search for his partner like a lost cat. *I'll give them something to gossip about.*

Decantor glanced up as he approached. "Hey! You talk to Morrison yet?"

"Haven't heard from him."

Decantor smiled but his eyes stayed guarded. "I heard congratulations were in order. He came in last night with that Walsh woman."

He got her? Again, without him—apparently without anyone since Decantor hadn't given him the congrats last night. *Won't go without backup, my ass.* "He recover Walsh's weapon?"

"Nah, I hear she tossed it in the river."

"You hear? He interrogated her?"

"Yep. Full confession's the word on the street. She's in lock-up now." Decantor smiled. "Your boy's good."

Carroll was right about the kid moving on without him. And Morrison did deserve a better partner—or at least one not quite so fucked up. Maybe it really was time for Petrosky to leave the force.

Petrosky nodded. "He is good." But he still wasn't fucking *there*.

Petrosky ambled back to his desk, eyes on his chair. After he'd arrested Mrs. Walsh, Morrison had probably gone home to sleep. Maybe he needed a wake-up call. Nothing said good morning better than being jolted out of bed by someone ramming their fist into your door.

Petrosky would even bring him coffee.

MORRISON'S HOUSE WAS EMPTY. Valentine hadn't seen him since the day before. And when a bleary-eyed Shannon answered the door at Decantor's mother-in-law's place, unease began writhing in Petrosky's stomach like a nest of rats, scrambling into his chest and up and down his arms.

"When was the last time you saw him?"

"Yesterday before work," Shannon snapped. "I assumed he was pulling an all-nighter. With you."

"Relax, Shannon, he still might be."

"Relax? The maniac who took me and caged Evie is still out on the street. I'm off work—I'm in a goddamn *safe house*. And now you're telling me that my husband is out there somewhere and you have no fucking idea where he is?" Her voice was shrill. From the other room, one of the kids started to cry and she looked back, then out the front door again as if trying to decide whether to comfort the kid or throw on her shoes and come with Petrosky instead.

"I'll find him, Shannon." He squeezed her arm. "If he'd been hurt, we'd know by now."

But he didn't believe it. And from the look on her face, the tremble in her lip, she didn't believe it either.

She knew what it was like to be hidden; you could be dead and no one would have any idea.

THE COFFEE WAS long cold by the time Petrosky drove through Salomon's neighborhood, on the lookout for Morrison's Fusion or for the man himself. Last night, Morrison had succeeded in finding Lisa Walsh's mother, which left this morning's plans to check out Salomon's hood. Maybe the kid had decided to get a head start. But where? They hadn't located any bomb shelters or sheds that might have made good dungeons, and every house over here had a basement. *Dammit.* Petrosky's chest tightened as he circled Salomon's block. All quiet. Some homes seemed abandoned and some had lights on inside, though nowhere did he see Morrison's ride in the driveway.

But the kid sure as hell hadn't walked there.

The next block was more of the same, and the next, and the one after that. Petrosky lit cigarette after cigarette and tried to focus on what he knew—which was jack shit, though his confusion might have been from the anxiety, raging through his chest so hard he could barely breathe, let alone think. Had Morrison come here without him in the first place? Had he seen something? Had he followed someone out of the neighborhood? But Norton wasn't showing his face—couldn't be, not around here. The area had been canvassed twice, once with a composite sketch. These people knew who the cops were looking for.

It was nearly nine now, and every breath drove icicles of frigid air into Petrosky's lungs. The window was still open, as if he thought he'd hear Morrison's laugh on the breeze if he listened hard enough. But there were only the sounds of the block awakening—front doors slamming, cars starting as people headed off to work.

Morrison had seen something. Gone somewhere.

But he'd have called. Sent a goddamn text. And even if he was in one of these houses, locked up like Shannon had been—like Lisa Walsh had been before she'd been...

Dumped. In the alley. And Norton, if nothing else, was a creature of habit. If he'd hurt Morrison—

No. Petrosky didn't want to go there, literally or figuratively. He didn't want to see the alley. Didn't want to smell Walsh's frozen blood on the earth.

Didn't want to be right.

He headed in that direction, every pothole a jolt through his skeleton, screaming at him to turn around. Decantor called when he was halfway there, and Petrosky's heart leapt—or maybe just ... shuddered. *Please let me be wrong.* Because if he was right ...

"Petrosky."

"Hey, you got anything?" Decantor's tight voice echoed the cold fear that Petrosky had been trying to tamp down all morning. "I put out an APB on Morrison's car already. Nothing in yet."

"Nothing here either," Petrosky said. "Headed to the alley where we found Walsh."

Silence on the other end. Then: "You think he—"

Petrosky hung up before Decantor could finish the thought. He couldn't put it into words. And he sure as fuck couldn't hear it from someone else.

NONE of the businesses around the alley were inhabited yet. They'd be rolling up their bars around ten o'clock probably, if they still bothered to open at all.

No police barricades or tape obstructed his path this time, and Petrosky squealed onto the cobbled street, the chassis clanking over potholes, icy piss-water from the road spraying droplets up into his open window. He spit out the cigarette along with the foul-smelling slush and slammed the car into park at the mouth of the alley. The wind blew around him, tearing at his cheeks as he exited the car. He barely felt it.

The alley was deathly silent, except for the wind—the wind and the water that dripped from a drainpipe onto the icy ground with a steady *tick, tick, tick. Get back in the car.* He stood, listening to the water, gripping the door handle like it could tether him to a different life, a life where he wasn't doing this. *Just get back in the car.* Where he was at work, bullshitting with his partner and not in some alley looking for his partner's—

He released the car door and dropped his arm. He was being ridiculous. He'd walk down there to satisfy his curiosity, then head back to the station to find Morrison at his desk. He'd give the kid hell for worrying everyone. Morrison was too good to get blindsided by a goat-fucker like Norton, too watchful. The kid had probably pulled an all-nighter doing the paperwork on Lisa Walsh's homicidal mother and finally headed somewhere to get some sleep—maybe even a motel since there wasn't a lot of bed space at Decantor's mother-in-law's, and at his own house... *I just lie awake all night staring at the ceiling.*

With a final glance at his car, Petrosky steeled himself and headed up the alley, the subtle moan of the wind behind him. Here and there, a varmint skittered away from his footsteps. But no human noises—no bustle of crime techs, no irritable sigh from an overworked ME. Just the blustery breeze and the hollow thunk of his shoes on the cement.

The dumpsters loomed even larger than they had the first time he'd come here. *With Morrison.* Petrosky's breath panted from him in short gasps. He quickened his steps, the sound amplified tenfold by the high walls that echoed the noise back to him. Then he was running, feet flying, every frigid breath he sucked into his lungs tinged with electric panic.

He lurched around the dumpster, and the world stopped. Tucked close behind it, the same place they'd found Walsh, was Morrison's car, the blue-gray paint reflecting off the ice-crusted buildings. The tick of water was suddenly unbearably loud. Petrosky stumbled and kicked aside a garbage bag full of god knew what, and the plastic crackled through the air like buckshot.

He didn't want to touch the car but there was no choice, and somewhere behind him another car door slammed even as he was putting his hand against the door handle. Was Morrison here, then? Just walking around, investigating?

His throbbing heart muted every other sound as he ripped the door open. Images came at him in slow motion: The plastic wrap—Visqueen, rolled up like a rug. One of Morrison's hippie shoes sticking out the bottom. And Morrison's face, beneath the plastic, mouth gaping.

Jesus fucking Christ. No, no, no.
He can't breathe, fuck, he can't breathe!

He leapt inside the car, ripped at the plastic, failed to clear it, and whipped out his knife, every zip of the blade against the thick sheeting reverberating back down at him from the walls above. His heart was burning, slamming against his breastbone, trying to explode from his chest.

The plastic tore away from Morrison's face, then from the rest of him, and Petrosky yanked at it blindly, tossing some outside the car and some to the floorboards. Petrosky scrabbled for Morrison's hand, the kid's palm curled toward the sky.

Still. He was so still.

Petrosky put his head on Morrison's chest. Nothing. No movement, no pulse, no warmth. He touched Morrison's face. Pressed his fingers against Morrison's neck and touched not skin but something wetter, more gelatinous—the kid's neck was sliced open, the tissue around the wound so cold. But the kid's lips were still red.

Blood.

No, please no.

"Hey, Kid, wake up." Petrosky said it loudly enough that Morrison should have been able to hear him. But he didn't respond.

The throb of Petrosky's heart was deafening, but his breath was louder still. His vision flickered and returned in shuddering waves: Morrison's blue eyes, open, unseeing. The gaping wound bisecting the kid's neck. Deep lacerations across his chest, just like the wounds on Salomon, bits of bone visible through the severed skin. Slash marks clear to the bone on his forearms like Cali had tried to protect himself from a machete blade.

Morrison. The kid was cold. He was so cold. Like the baby in the basement, but the baby was going to make it. Maybe Morrison could make it too—there was always a good side, right? The kid was forever telling him there was always a good side.

Not again, please not again. Petrosky should have been there last night. He should have been with him. *I'm so sorry, Cali. I'm so sorry, son. I'm so ...* Petrosky readied his fists, one on top of the other, for CPR, every thrust of his hands manic and more hopeful than he felt.

Someone grabbed at his leg from outside the car. Norton was there to finish what he'd started. Right now, Morrison might still have a chance to make it, but if Norton had come back ... Petrosky whipped around, Swiss army blade drawn, ready to slash the fucker to death.

Decantor released him, eyes wide as he leapt away from the arc of the knife. "Petrosky!" Decantor tried again, grabbing Petrosky's arm. "Wait—"

Petrosky threw an elbow, connected with bone. Decantor's hip clipped the car door as he fell to the frozen ground.

Petrosky put a hand on Morrison's throat. He could stop the bleeding, at least. But there was so much blood, scarlet stains on the kid's shirt, on the plastic tarp, the gore slimy on Petrosky's hands—

"Petrosky!" Someone was yelling at him blathering some shit about evidence and fingerprints.

"Get a bus!" Petrosky yelled. He needed a towel. A shirt.

Anything. He released the pressure on Morrison's neck, and his hands came away … sticky. Not wet. He stilled, squinted at the wounds. Morrison wasn't bleeding.

Not anymore.

Petrosky reached for him, his hand moving too slowly through space as if the air had turned to molasses. His arm muscles burned as he stretched closer, closer … he touched Morrison's forehead. Cold. Clammy. *I'm so sorry, Kid. I'm so, so sorry, son.*

Then his vision went red, bloody—Morrison's blood, then Julie's blood, the pain mingling and smearing across the surface of his brain, images of their bodies twisting like a gory reflection in a funhouse mirror. His chest was alive with an agony so sharp he was certain it could cut anyone who came near. He took his hand from Morrison's face, reached for his holster and jerked out the weapon. The safety clicked off easily, almost as if of its own accord. *See you soon, Kid.* He shoved the weapon between his teeth.

Someone grabbed him from behind again, yanked his leg, and this time he was pulled off balance, the weapon careening to the floorboards with the dull, heavy thwack of metal on rubber. He kicked, tried to retrieve the gun, but was jerked back again. He went for his knife.

Then Decantor had his arms, and his knees hit the pavement. "Stop fucking with me!" Petrosky reared back into Decantor and the fucker released him as they toppled backwards.

"Fuck you, Decantor! Fuck you!" Petrosky screamed it over and over again, spittle flying from his lips. And then there were others at his elbows, just standing, not pulling, just holding his arms against the car. Flatfoots maybe, not detectives. Where the fuck had they come from?

"I'm sorry!" Decantor was yelling. "I shouldn't have—"

"Get off me!" Petrosky's voice was like the howl of a wounded animal against the alley brick. He threw his arms, his legs, heaving with all his strength but the men on either side held tight.

The pain in Petrosky's chest radiated down his arms, grounding him. Black faded in and out around the edges of his vision. He stopped tugging. They loosened their grip, and he jerked his arms free.

Decantor's eyes were on the car, a single tear on his stupid fucking cheek. "Let me take you back, Petrosky."

Petrosky turned and panted back the way he'd come, past the greasy, stained dumpsters, past the tick of water, past the scrambling rats.

It took four tries to get his key into the car door. Then he was sitting in the front seat with the engine alive and rumbling though he didn't remember getting into the car or starting it. He didn't remember vomiting on the front seat either, yet there it was, the sick everywhere.

He threw the car in drive and squealed away from the alley, from his partner, from his boy.

Home. Home. Home. He needed to be alone with his fucking gun.

30

DECANTOR WAS FOLLOWING HIM—AROUND every turn, over every hill, that jackass was back there, headlights off but reflecting the dull gray sky like a pair of dingy moons. Petrosky swerved between cars and in and out of lanes, but there was no way he was going to beat Decantor's newer car in his old-as-dirt Caprice. Not that it would really matter in the end.

His entire body felt numb. Tingly. His senses came back to him occasionally but just long enough to register that the car smelled like someone had yacked in it. That his rib cage was in a vise. That he couldn't fucking breathe.

He wanted to stop breathing. He just needed a quiet moment. A quiet place. He glanced in the rearview mirror. If he had to, he'd take Decantor's nosy ass with him, that motherfucking piece of shit.

But he wouldn't. He couldn't. Not yet.

I have to tell Shannon.

She needed him. Except ... she didn't. She had Lillian there with her, Valentine, the kids. And surely someone had told her already—what could he offer her that they couldn't, fucked up as he was?

The answer revealed itself like a rolling fog pulling back from a mountain as day broke, exposing the rock, lighting up its gouged, devastated surface. He missed the turn to Decantor's mother-in-law's place. Passed restaurants where he and Morrison had eaten. The breeze sighed over his car and he felt the chill even with the window closed. He knew what he had to give.

Petrosky headed for the precinct, Decantor still on his tail.

Fucking leech. But numbness was creeping over him, dampening the fire in his chest, expanding his lungs though he wished his broken body would just give up and stop working once and for all.

None of it mattered. Nothing mattered—nothing besides Shannon and the kids. And he could take care of them better if he was dead.

———

PETROSKY MARCHED to the human resources office amid twitters of old mother hens gossiping about him being there, or maybe trying to figure out who he was going to punch. They kept that shit up, it would be all of them.

He shoved a piece of gum into his mouth, hoping it covered the shot he had taken in the car but not really caring if it didn't. At the back desk in the HR office, a beady-eyed little prick sat typing on his keyboard. Greg Teeple. The guy looked like a fucking rat.

Teeple stood when he saw Petrosky coming. "What can I do for you, Petrosky?"

"I need to change the beneficiaries for my insurance policy and my pension."

"Ah, okay." Teeple gestured to the chair, sat, typed.

Petrosky drummed his fingers on the desk, again and again and again, until Teeple paused his typing and looked over. *Come on, fuckhead.*

"I see you have no eligible beneficiaries for your pension." Teeple delivered the news like he was ordering a sandwich, like that wasn't the saddest fucking thing he'd ever heard. "Is this still accurate?"

Petrosky nodded, his fingers tapping faster now, foot bouncing beneath the desk.

"So you're looking to have one lump-sum payment of your benefits to another person besides"—he squinted at the screen—"Curtis Morrison?" He raised an eyebrow. "Or did you just want to add another person?"

"Morrison's dead." It rolled off his tongue too naturally, as if it had happened years ago instead of moments before.

Teeple's jaw dropped. "Morrison? Dear god, when—"

"This morning."

Teeple went white as a sheet. White as fog. White as a dead guy wrapped in plastic.

"I—I'm so sorry for your loss. He was such a good man, a good, good man."

Teeple babbled on as the numbness was punctured with a sharp and poignant sorrow, as real and hard as if someone were actually stabbing at Petrosky's chest from the inside. He lost his breath. *Hold on a little longer, Petrosky. Almost over.* For there was no point in trying, not now. He'd failed, catastrophically. No matter what he did, no matter how much he tried, he was incapable of protecting those he loved. He was incapable of helping … anyone, at least not while he was still alive. He recovered his voice, though it sounded flat and hollow. "I want to transfer all my benefits to Shannon Morrison."

Teeple appraised him, fingers over the keys.

"Problem?"

"I just …" Teeple swallowed hard and shook his head. "Should we wait to do this? Perhaps later this week or after the funeral?"

"We can take care of it now."

"But—"

"What do I need to sign, Teeple?"

"Uh … I'll print some things. While you're here … will you be taking leave? We can take care of that now, too."

"I'm not taking leave." *I'm just leaving.*

Teeple stared at him, lips pursed.

"Can we hurry this up?" Petrosky barked.

Teeple took a deep breath and averted his eyes. Typed. "Do you have Shannon's social security number?

"I don't."

Teeple paused, biting and releasing his bottom lip. "Really, perhaps we should wait until you have all the—"

"You have everything you need in that damn computer of yours. Shannon's information will be on Curtis Morrison's policy, and you'll have to pull that up today anyway."

Teeple chewed his lip harder.

"When will this change take effect?"

"I ... have to get everything in, obviously. It'll be a bit. Then we have to do the notary stuff, and—"

"How long?"

Teeple hesitated. "Tomorrow?"

Petrosky stood. "I'll be back tomorrow."

One day more.

31

THE PHONE on Petrosky's desk was ringing when he approached. He ignored the clanging and rifled through the drawer for antacids. The rest of the bullpen was so quiet you could have heard a rat fart.

Petrosky jerked his head around, daring one of those fuckers to say something, anything to set him off, but no one made eye contact. When he peered around the corner, Decantor wasn't at his desk—probably sitting in the parking lot waiting to follow him home. Maybe Petrosky could lose him. Worst case, he'd go too fast and wrap his car around a goddamn tree.

His cell rang, playing "Hail to the Chief," and Petrosky's heart tried to claw its way from his rib cage. He could almost see Morrison's face the day the kid had set that ringtone. He clicked the phone to vibrate and let Chief Carroll go to voicemail as he headed for the stairs.

"No coat?" Dr. McCallum blocked his path, three hundred pounds of calming stares and platitudes that didn't do dick. The psychiatrist was red-faced with the effort of walking from his office next door and up the stairs to the bullpen.

Who the hell had called him? Decantor? But if Decantor had called once he realized where they were headed, the doctor would have been waiting for him in the parking lot when he arrived.

Petrosky glanced behind him at the bullpen where a dozen sets of eyes snapped back to imaginary tasks as a dozen idiots tried to pretend they weren't watching. "No coat," Petrosky said. But he didn't recall taking it off—or feeling cold. Maybe he couldn't feel anything.

"Didn't it feel chilly outside to you this morning?"

"What are you, my fucking grandmother?"

"Not taking leave?"

"No." *Get the fuck out of my way, goddammit.* The hush wrapped around them like a damp cloth.

"I hear you shoved your service revolver in your mouth."

Petrosky glanced behind him, at the bullpen—was it more quiet than it had been moments ago? The silence was probably part of a tactic McCallum was using, trying to jar him into responding—responding to something the doc shouldn't even know about. *Fucking Decantor.*

"Want to talk about it?" McCallum said.

"No, I don't want to talk about it. Now move."

McCallum turned and headed down the stairs and Petrosky had no choice but to follow at the doctor's pace. When they emerged into the lot, the cold stung his cheeks but not the rest of his body, and even on his face it didn't feel good or bad, it just was. Everything else—his hands, his arms, his chest—was a void. A gaping, bleeding hole.

"Come to my office and sit with me a minute, Petrosky."

"Fuck off."

McCallum squared his shoulders. "We can do this here, or I can have you hospitalized involuntarily as a danger to yourself."

They wouldn't keep him—and McCallum knew it. "All I have to do is say the thoughts passed. I can't be the first one to freak out after finding ... finding ..." Petrosky's breath left him again, his lungs imploding into white-hot pain. And his chest ... *fuck.* Maybe his heart had actually stopped and the rest of him was trying to catch up. Something was happening, he could feel it instinctually—somewhere inside him, a dam was cracking, getting ready to burst. And when it did, he needed a gun. He'd dropped one in Morrison's car. He had another at home—two actually. And thanks to Decantor, he now required those backups to splatter his own brains against the wall.

Home, home, home. But he had to wait until tomorrow anyway, after the life insurance policy was finalized. So now what?

Petrosky stared into the gray lot. People walked by on their way to court, but he couldn't register discerning features—they were aliens on a foreign landscape.

McCallum cleared his throat and tried again. "Why were you over at HR?"

"Making some changes."

"To what?"

A paper cup turned end over end across the lot on the icy breeze. Petrosky watched. Dumb. Mute.

"Would it happen to be your pension? Perhaps the benefactors to your insurance policy?"

Teeple. That rat bastard had called, and McCallum had probably run into Decantor in the lot—or the doc had called around to get the details. Petrosky finally met his eyes and shrugged. "It needed to be done."

"Not today it didn't. Not an hour after you found the man who was as close to family as you've got."

"It's none of your—"

"That's where you're wrong." McCallum shifted his weight and narrowed his eyes. "You have a history of substance abuse and depression, and you've just lost one of the only people you loved. That's a red flag. When I see you wrapping up loose ends, it's even more concerning. And after this morning ..."

Petrosky stared at him and ground his teeth together.

McCallum shook his head. "Let's stop bullshitting, shall we? I was here after Julie. I know you better than you think I do. And you're not fooling anyone right now, walking around smelling like wintergreen over a bar."

Petrosky shoved his trembling hands in his pockets. "I just took a little sip this morning. Not that I have to justify it to you."

"Did you take that sip before or after you found your partner's body?" The words punched a hole in his lung. McCallum's face softened as Petrosky gasped for air.

"You took a little nip to avoid alcohol withdrawal, is what you did. You can't be on duty like that, and you definitely can't be on duty after finding your partner murdered."

"So, what, you're going to tell me to stay the fuck home? You think that'll help, Doc? Sitting around with my gun? Watching the glint of the straight razor in the bathroom?" Wouldn't help, but it couldn't hurt to immerse himself in the act of dying—he'd been close for years just hadn't had the guts to fucking do it. But he did now. He'd pull out the extra gifts he had hidden for Evie and Henry first, set them on the dining table. Maybe he'd even wrap them.

McCallum shook his head and his jowls trembled like gelatin. "You never did respond to reason, Petrosky."

"Oh yeah? And what do I—"

"Justice. Vengeance. When Julie died—"

"That was a long time ago."

McCallum put up his hand. "When Julie died, the only thing that kept you going, through the funeral, through the grief, through your divorce, was finding the guy who hurt her."

"Which I never fucking did," he spat. "I stopped looking because you said I was on a downward spir—"

"You didn't find her killer, but you put a lot of other bad guys away." McCallum shifted his weight and his shoes squealed like a stuck pig.

"Like it matters how many. I didn't find *Julie's* killer. And I sure as shit didn't catch Adam Norton before he killed my son."

"You mean your partner."

"That's what I said."

McCallum lowered his voice. "Putting away the guys you *did* catch, though, that matters. It matters to the people you helped. It matters to those victims, those parents. And keeping those criminals from hurting anyone else, seeking justice … it kept you alive."

"That's not much consolation."

"Do you want to die, Ed?"

The silence stretched between them, an ocean of unsaid things.

"You think you'll do it?"

"I don't know."

McCallum's face hardened. "You're a fucking coward, Petrosky."

Petrosky balled his fists, but McCallum continued.

"You're a coward, but not because you want to die. You're a coward because you can't see beyond your own misery to do your damn job and catch the asshole who did this. You're letting your personal bullshit get in the way—so worried about the dead that the living don't matter at all."

Petrosky straightened, the tendons in his neck singing. "Now you wait just a goddamn—"

"Morrison loved you like a father." McCallum's soft voice was barely audible over the wind that howled through the lot like an agitated spirit. "Shannon loves you like a father. You're Papa Ed to their kids. She needs you more than ever and you're abandoning her by wallowing in booze and self-pity."

"I'm not—"

"You treat other people like morons when they don't work fast enough—crime techs, hospital personnel. But when bad shit happens to you, it's perfectly acceptable for you to bow out, hit the bottle, and forget."

His heart. Jesus, his heart. Someone was pulling on it, stretching it like a rubber band until it seemed it might snap in two. "I need to forget."

"You need to remember. You need to deal with what happened to Morrison. You need to feel the guilt and the blame and eventually you will need to move on." McCallum leaned toward him and pointed at Petrosky's chest.

McCallum shook his head. "Enough's enough. You never came to see me so someone would pussyfoot around things with you. You came because you needed someone to tell it like it is. Morrison worshipped you—he didn't challenge you. And the shit you're thinking right now ... you're going to let him down, let his family down when they need you most, all because you feel like being a selfish—"

Petrosky squared his shoulders, chest expanding with newfound fury. "I don't have to take this shit."

"No, you don't. But if you die tomorrow under suspicious circumstances, they'll know you did it yourself. And I'll make damn sure the insurance company knows it too. They'll void your policy."

"You fat, fucking piece of—"

"Call me all the names you want, Ed, but don't test me. I'm not going to stroke your wounds and tell you that it doesn't matter. It does. Help someone else. Save another kid instead of feeling bad about the ones you couldn't help. Make Morrison's death mean something. Make the world safer for Shannon. For Evie and Henry."

"Fuck you, Doc." He stepped off the curb, adrenaline coursing through his body, every nerve trembling.

"And, Ed?"

Petrosky stopped but didn't turn, just peered into the spot where Decantor had parked his car. Decantor wasn't inside. Looked like someone finally realized they couldn't follow him around the whole damn day.

"Stay alive, and clean yourself up," McCallum said. "Shannon won't get your pension if they fire you for alcohol abuse, either."

Motherfucker. Petrosky ripped a cigarette from the pack and smoked himself across the parking lot. His chest throbbed in time with his head. He pulled smoke into his lungs and the caustic burn centered him, though not enough to stop him from shaking.

He needed to make some more calls. He'd leave Shannon his house, so even if he got fired, she'd at least come away with something. But that fat fuck was right about one thing: if he blasted his brains all over the wall, his personal insurance policy wouldn't pay. And while Shannon and the kids would be better off without his drunk, fucked-up ass, that was the biggest chunk of money he could give them. It was the least he could do. For Morrison.

But if he managed to stick it out and died in the line of duty…

The pressure in his chest lightened and there was no more fear.

He smiled, crushed the cigarette under his heel, and got into his car.

Soon enough. And if he got to plug the guy who got Morrison first, all the better.

32

SHANNON WAS SITTING on his front porch, her lovely face contorted with grief, her eyes red and swollen as if someone had hit her.

Petrosky parked behind her still-running car and got out. She stood, walked over to him, and collapsed in his arms.

He held her while she sobbed against his chest, but he had no words, no gestures of kindness, nothing. He was as frozen as the snow that swirled around their legs.

"Where are the kids?" His voice was strained. On the surface, it was a reasonable question, one that seemed important, yet it didn't feel reasonable right then. Nothing was reasonable. Maybe nothing would ever be reasonable again.

"Evie's at the house with Lillian. Decantor's there too. And the dogs. And I just ... I couldn't—" She gasped for air, and he put a hand on the small of her back, but he couldn't feel his fingers. Or the cloth of her coat.

"I'm staying here. With you," she said.

"You have the kids—"

"Henry is still tiny, so I brought him. And Valentine's on his way here to play lookout. But Evie is safe where she is, there's a whole army of cops there, and she doesn't need to see me like this. She's fine with Lillian, and Lillian's son, Mason, is Evie's best buddy. Evie didn't even mind when I left." She swiped at her eyes. "I haven't told her yet," she said, her voice thick with tears. "She needs one more day of ... happiness. Of playing. Of not knowing Daddy is gone." He could hear the message implicit in that: It wasn't just the kids. Her world would never be the same. A funeral fucked everything up.

A funeral. Petrosky could still see Morrison's face, his milky eyes, the blood around his mouth. He didn't want to live to see the funeral. Didn't want to see the makeup covering his partner's wounds, trying to hide the horrors but not succeeding.

No, they'd close the casket. Or they'd burn the body.

The body.

He waited for the jolt of pain in his abdomen but felt nothing. He glanced at his hand, at the snowflakes melting against his skin. His bare fingers registered no cold or wet—he didn't remember that from when he'd lost Julie. Had he not been so numb? Or had he forgotten? "Is your brother-in-law coming in?"

"Tomorrow."

Morrison couldn't be dead. But Shannon's grief-stricken face was proof enough that he was.

He followed her to the trunk and grabbed her bag, brought it inside to Julie's room. His phone rang, and his breath caught as he pulled it from his pocket, wishing it would play "Surfin' USA" one more time. It was the precinct—the chief. He shut the phone off.

Shannon was behind him when he turned around, Henry asleep on her shoulder.

"I'm going to have to wash the sheets," Petrosky said.

"Later." She laid Henry on the bed, near the wall. He seemed so small. Petrosky had a flash of Morrison cradling his son against his stocky frame—the gentle giant Petrosky had never been, even with his own daughter. Pain shot through his heart again, and he winced.

"You going to offer me a drink, or what?"

Petrosky's mouth dropped open.

"One shot to take the edge off," she said. "Then you're going to tell me why my husband is dead."

THEY SAT at the kitchen table. Petrosky poured the liquor, one paper bathroom cup apiece.

She sipped hers and grimaced. He slugged his back all at once.

"He was in the alley where we found the last victim," Petrosky said finally. "In the backseat of his car. Wrapped in plastic." He didn't recognize his own voice.

A tear trickled down her cheek. She met his eyes. "Why was he out there last night?"

He should have had that answer. He should have been there. *It should have been me.* "I don't know."

"But you know what you were working on. So what was he doing? I mean, was he …"

So much pressure. So much pain. He forced air into his lungs. "Last night, he arrested a woman on a related cold case— she killed a janitor when her daughter went missing." Every word was labored, like he was puking them onto the table one by one. "I texted him this morning so we could meet, but he never responded."

"He must have done something else after he arrested that woman. You have to know what he was working on."

What had Morrison told him? That he was going to get Lisa Walsh's mother and then … "He said he was going to check something out," he said slowly. "But he didn't say what it was."

"You didn't ask him?"

I was exhausted. Sick. I needed a drink. "No."

She stared at the paper cup and tapped her finger on the brim. "Morrison found Norton." Not a question. Her mouth twisted with a fury he had never seen, even after her own kidnapping. She panted through flared nostrils.

"Yeah." Morrison had found Norton, or at least gotten close enough to scare the guy into killing him. Morrison had been right to send Shannon away—to send his kids away. Maybe Norton had it in for all of them. But why?

Come and get me too, you sorry motherfucker.

Shannon ran a finger around and around the brim of her cup. Tears fell freely down her face. "Did he suffer?"

Petrosky couldn't breathe. The blood smeared across his

memory—the gaping holes in Morrison's neck, the wounds on his chest. His forearms and the exposed bone. His lips painted crimson.

"Did he?" Sharper now—desperate.

Petrosky reached across the table, grabbed her cup and downed the rest. When Julie died, McCallum had told him to forget what had been done to her. To ignore the rape. To pretend her genitals had not been burned. But Brian Thompson, the medical examiner, had been truthful—and no matter how much it hurt there was a comfort in that, in knowing that he had the information, that there was someone he could trust to give it to him. And after he'd known ... he'd taken McCallum's advice and pushed the horrific details aside, ignored them every day until his little girl was reduced to a photograph in his desk drawer and a night-light on the wall. The forgetting had kept him sane, though he'd never trusted McCallum the same way.

And Shannon—glassy-eyed, destroyed, but determined. There was no protecting her from this. She'd get the truth from someone. Or maybe he just didn't want their last conversations tainted with his lies. "Yes," Petrosky whispered. "Yes, he suffered."

She stood and walked around the table to his chair.

A brick in his chest was growing, heavy and sick with unsaid things, with mistakes, with sorrow. "Shannon, I wish I knew ... I wish I'd been there, I wish ..."

She put her arm around his shoulders.

The heaviness reached his throat.

"He loved you so much," she whispered. "He didn't have a dad. You were it. And he made me love you too." Her voice cracked. She gasped, choked.

Petrosky wrapped his arms around her waist, turned his head into her belly, and wept.

SHE LET him have the rest of the Jack, something about pump and dump, but he didn't really care why. He chugged it all and tried to let the fuzziness calm the ache in his heart—but even with the booze, there was this awful hole with jagged edges in his chest, making every heartbeat sharp and bright with fresh agony. This wound would never heal. Not that he'd have to worry about it for too much longer.

Petrosky stared at his spare gun on the bedside table. He needed his insurance to pay. But did he? Yes, he did. Plus, Shannon couldn't be the one to find him—he'd not wish that on anyone and he'd always thought it was a dick move when he interviewed a widow after her husband plastered his brains all over their bedroom. Still ... he traced a finger over the barrel like he was caressing a lover's cheek, and the action brought with it a fresh wave of memory.

Morrison's face. He could almost feel the boy's pasty skin, cold and dewy with the early morning damp. He coughed, spat phlegm into a sock. Touched the gun again.

He dropped his arm when she knocked at the door. "Yeah?"

Shannon pushed the door open, hair frizzy and wild in the orange light from the streetlamp outside. She crept in as he pushed himself onto his elbow.

"Shannon, you okay?" Stupid question. She'd never be okay again.

"Move over," she said, pillow in hand. She stood unmoving by the bed, then sat on the edge. "Please."

He heaved himself back against the wall and she got into bed next to him, shoving her pillow beside his.

"I don't want to be alone. I mean, I know Henry is in there but ... I just need to not be the strong one."

But even now he wasn't sure she was the weak one. She probably didn't want him to be alone with his gun.

He slid down on his back until his head hit the pillow, and she put her cheek against his shoulder. "I miss him so much already."

He put his free hand on her shoulder, awkwardly, but that didn't matter, not now. "I miss him too."

They lay there, Petrosky listening to their breath mingling and disappearing into the night. After a time, Shannon closed her eyes, her head still on his shoulder, crying softly once she thought he was asleep. All night long he watched the clock and the weapon on the side table and tried to decide to stay longer.

"Why did this happen?" she whispered as the dawn crept into the room. "Of all the ... It's always the good ones."

Sharp, hot pain radiated out from his heart. Shannon would rather have had Petrosky die. Not that he could blame her.

He'd rather have died in Morrison's place too.

———

SHANNON WAS in the kitchen when he got up. He opened cabinet after cabinet, searching for more alcohol, but there was none. From the wall, Julie's night-light teased him. He wondered what Shannon had of Morrison's that would tear her heart out every fucking time she saw it.

Petrosky would never eat granola again.

"I want to run over to the church next to the precinct," she said, and Petrosky nodded—he'd been to more than his share of cop funerals at that place.

"You don't want to wait a day? I can go with you or—"

"No, I can do it. After the way my brother died, with everything being dragged out because of the cancer and then the arrangements... I just need it to be super fast and simple. And over."

He glanced around at the soiled counters, the bottles in the sink. *Arrangements.* A life reduced to paperwork and a wooden box.

"What are you planning for the day?" Her voice was soft, strained, as if she was learning how to speak again after a bout of laryngitis. "I can grab us lunch after I'm done with the plans, and—"

"I'm going to the precinct."

"Today?" Her eyes filled with tears.

"You just lost your husband. You don't need to be sitting here with me."

"You loved him too. As much as I did, whether you'll say it or not."

"Of course I loved him, Shannon." But had Morrison known that? *I should have told him. Just once I should have said it.*

"You need to take leave, Petrosky. You can't work like this."

"Who said I was working?"

She sighed. "Fine. But I'm coming over for dinner. Will you be back by then?"

"I don't know."

"Then Henry and I will wait outside the precinct until you—"

"Okay, okay. I'll be back by then."

"Good. I'll bring some of the stuff from the house. Lillian said people are dropping by with food."

"You sure you don't just want to stay there?" Petrosky said.

"I'm not leaving you alone."

Because he might put a bullet in his head. "Don't worry about me. That's the—"

"If Morrison were here, he'd be looking out for your testy ass too. Since he isn't—"

"I don't need looking after." He was a fuck-up, but he knew what he was doing.

She stared at the wall behind him like the spider webs in the corner were goddamn artwork, then dropped her gaze to the floor. "It's not you, okay? It's ... over at Decantor's mother-in-law's, Lillian and Isaac keep giving me these *looks*. All this fucking warmth and pity just oozing over me until I can't breathe."

Decantor. The man's name made the back of his neck tingle— the way he'd tackled Petrosky from the car. *I'll never forgive that asshole.* Decantor had stolen his perfect moment of courage. His perfect moment to go out, to die in the arms of his boy.

Shannon sniffed. "How the hell am I supposed to figure out this new ... *life* ... with them staring at me like I'm going to break?" Her lips puckered, and the scars around her mouth seemed to brighten. If Norton couldn't break her, no one could.

But maybe Norton had finally hit her where it hurt most. Maybe he'd hit them both in the one spot that would finally end them.

Shannon's eyes filled. "Everything feels so ... empty. Hollow, you know?"

Petrosky did. Over the years he had spent countless hours sitting in Julie's empty bedroom, feeling as if everything that was her had been sucked out of it, despite that poster on the wall. He felt that same ache now, but it was more barbed, poignant, if only for its immediacy. He nodded. "I'll be here for dinner."

She appraised him with bloodshot eyes. Henry squawked from the other room and she turned toward the sound, but paused in the doorway. "Are you going to be trashed when I get back here with dinner?"

He opened his mouth to lie to her, then closed it again.

"Try not to be, okay?"

Petrosky crossed his arms and stared at the night-light until she left the kitchen. Something was bothering him, something besides the grief and the bright agony in his gut. Something about—

Decantor. The name was still in his head, rolling around even as Shannon muttered something else about dinner, or maybe about alcohol, or maybe the fucking Tooth Fairy, he couldn't really tell, not with his heart suddenly picking up speed like a runaway train. Decantor had yelled that he was sorry when he was dragging Petrosky from Morrison's car. That he shouldn't have done … something. But what did Decantor have to be sorry about? It wasn't the whispered words at a funeral, the *sorry for your loss* that did nothing to ease the poignant ache of grief. This was something specific. And Decantor had talked to Morrison the night he'd taken off—the night the kid had wound up in that alley.

Decantor knew why Morrison was down there.

Decantor knew why Morrison was dead.

33

THE BULLPEN QUIETED when he entered. An officer stood by the water cooler, conspicuously trying to be inconspicuous. Petrosky scowled at him, marched to his desk, and picked up the case file.

Morrison had been looking into something last night. Human trafficking? Other abductions? Petrosky shuffled papers. From the third sheet, Morrison's tiny, exacting print leapt off the page and wrapped itself around his throat. Days old. He closed the folder. Whatever Morrison was on to wasn't in there. He must have had it with him. The classifieds.

He tossed the file on his desktop and headed back through the bullpen, avoiding even a glance at Morrison's workstation. He feared just seeing that empty chair would make his chest explode.

Decantor shot out of his seat when he saw Petrosky, the chair clattering to the ground behind him. He didn't right it, just squared his shoulders as if preparing for a fight.

"I'm not here to hit you, Decantor."

"I know." His shoulders didn't relax.

"I need to know what you told Morrison last night. He said he was going to investigate it."

Decantor eyed him warily. "I told him about … hell, let me

show you." He pulled a folder from the top drawer and passed it over.

Petrosky flipped the file open. A girl with ebony skin in a white tank top stared back at him: narrowed eyes, high cheek-bones, and a pert nose, a model if you could ignore the scar that ran across her forehead. A jagged reminder of all that was fucking wrong everywhere.

"Her name's Alicia Hart. I arrested her over on Baldwin, hooking with another girl."

The name wasn't familiar. She hadn't been on their short list of possible abductees, and appearance-wise she didn't seem to be Adam Norton's type—the fierceness in her eyes alone would have sent that little fucker running crying to his mother. "What does she have to do with our case?"

"When I talked to her in booking, she said that she was scared because she knew Lisa Walsh, that they were friends before Walsh disappeared. Friend of a boyfriend or some such. Seemed like a hell of a coincidence; I figured she was trying to get out of her own charges, but she was insistent. So I let Morrison know."

"And?"

"That's it."

"She have a pimp?"

"Yeah, Lance, she said, but all she would give us was the first name, and it's probably a fake." He held up a hand before Petrosky could ask how the fuck this would help. "I have to tell you, I ... They got forensics back on Morrison's car." Decantor's eyes were glassy. "No usable prints outside of yours."

Petrosky had probably obliterated anything usable trying to rouse a dead man. He squinted at Decantor, attempting to focus, but his brain suddenly felt hazy. Not that focus would make a difference anyway. He'd already fucked up the thing that mattered most. Petrosky waited for that old, familiar pain to rise in his chest, but felt only a throbbing void where his heart should be. "What else did they find?"

"Oil, in a fresh scratch on one side of the trunk. Identified it as a compound made specifically for bike chains, so the guy must have stashed his bike in the trunk as best he could, then ridden off after dumping the ... car."

Bike chains. Norton probably still had the same bike he'd ridden from the Acosta crime scene. But he wouldn't be using it regularly, not now; you'd draw a lot of attention to yourself trying to pedal through three feet of snow. "What else?"

"I talked to the ME. And he said ... well ..."

"Spit it out, Decantor." But he wanted to staple the man's goddamn mouth shut.

Decantor took a deep breath. "Morrison's service revolver is missing, but it wasn't used against him. For the arm and chest wounds, it was the same weapon used on Salomon and Walsh. But ... Morrison lingered for a little bit. Fought it." Decantor looked pale, almost green like he was going to hurl. "He got hit first in the arms—defensive wounds—and once he lowered his arms, Norton got him in the chest. But it was the jugular wound that killed him. And that looks like a different weapon altogether, some kind of knife."

Norton had stopped hacking at Morrison, then ... gone to get another weapon. While Morrison bled out on the floor, maybe begging for his life. Screaming. Gaping lips, coated with blood. *California.* No more coffee, no more jokes. Petrosky's lungs spasmed. He wheezed in a breath and tapped Alicia Hart's photo with a shaking finger. "You said you picked her up." His voice ... like he was trying to talk after running a marathon. "Did she already post bail?"

Decantor's brows knitted with concern. "Yeah, she posted yesterday. I've got her last known address, but it might be wrong —you know how it is."

Petrosky flicked the folder in his hand. "I'm keeping this." Without waiting for a response, he turned to leave, but glanced back as another thought occurred to him. "They find Morrison's case files in the car?" Any criminal would love to peek at what the cops had on them.

Decantor shook his head, then looked down. "Hey, if you find out that Morrison was killed because I ... because of what I told him ... you'll tell me, right?"

"If it's your fault, you'll be the first to know."

Petrosky left Decantor staring after him and carried the folder to his desk, wondering if he should go get a nip out of his car to cure the pain in his temples or try a few aspirin first. But the mere thought of tackling the stairs made his leg muscles ache along with his head.

He dropped into his chair and fumbled in the top drawer. Cigarettes. Thumbtacks. Half a pencil. A roll of breath mints, sticky and wet somehow. A cardboard container of rock-hard hash browns from a fast-food restaurant.

You okay, Boss? Need some aspirin? Petrosky was never the one who had the pills. He slammed the drawer, took a shaky breath, and approached Morrison's desk. The chair was empty, of course it was, but the shock of that hit him in some tender, hidden place deep in his belly. On top of the desk sat a photo of Evie on Shannon's shoulders, Henry in a carrier on Morrison's chest. In the drawer, ibuprofen, aspirin, and Pepto Bismol lay in an orderly row behind a basket of pens and a box of granola bars. Petrosky grabbed the aspirin and swallowed four dry. He fingered the granola bars, noticed the room had gone quiet again, and snatched the box. He took the picture of Shannon and the kids too, for good measure.

One more stop. He slid the photo from the frame and shoved it into his pocket.

TEEPLE STOOD when Petrosky entered and waited until Petrosky sat to ease into his own chair. He handed him a pen. "I have everything ready. I'll need your signature here"—he tapped the paperwork on his desk—"and here."

Petrosky snatched up the pen, each illegible scrawl of his name messier than the last. When the signatures were done, Teeple applied his notary seal. "Well, that's really it. I'll send you a copy and file the rest."

"Great." Petrosky stood and put his hands on the desk. "By the way, if you ever call McCallum on me again, I'll have your fucking head, got it?"

"I just thought—"

"No one asked what you thought. Do your job and let me do mine, you horse-fucking piece of shit."

PETROSKY DROVE past the address on Alicia Hart's file, checking out the surrounding neighborhood. Along her block, houses with boarded-over windows were interspersed with burned-out shells. Hart's address was of the former category, with an old jalopy, half-gray, half-rust, parked in the drive. He wondered if she was squatting. Petrosky circled the block then parked across the street in front of the fire hydrant, swallowed four more aspirin and got out, the file folder under his arm. A mangy dog appeared from behind a trash container and approached Petrosky tentatively, whining.

Petrosky stomped his foot and the dog skittered off over last season's leaves. He gazed at the path the animal had taken, at the scarlet foliage frozen to the earth beneath a layer of ice that was all too reminiscent of bloody Visqueen. No escape for those leaves until the seasons changed unless some compassionate soul put them out of their misery with a blowtorch. Trapped in the cold. Like all of them.

He scanned the rest of the street for movement. No sign of the pimp. Maybe he was inside already, or off grabbing another john. Or maybe no one was there, and the car was a permanent fixture; useless, but not important enough to tow.

Petrosky checked the gun in the back of his jeans and took the steps two at a time. The doorbell hung from a wire, and he pressed it, then pushed it again for good measure, letting his fingers brush the frayed ends. Absently he wondered if it would electrocute him as a faint buzzing sounded inside the house. He dropped his hand to his side. *Not yet.*

A patter of footsteps approached, and his back stiffened as a young woman opened the door and stared at him with heavily mascaraed eyes that bulged like those on a bullfrog. Not Alicia Hart—this girl was thinner, bony, swimming in a sweatshirt that sagged off her shoulders. No scar on her forehead.

"Lance sent me," he said, using the name of Alicia's pimp

from the file, and the girl nodded. So Alicia had told Decantor the truth about her address. Maybe she'd also been truthful about her connection to Lisa Walsh.

Petrosky followed her down a dimly lit hall to an open door on the right. Some bedroom—one exterior wall had no drywall, just the outside plywood boards showing behind skeletal wooden beams. A plastic space heater sat in the corner, the plug spliced into a cord that ran up one of the walls. The place was going to burn to the fucking ground just like the neighboring houses had.

The girl stood in the center of the room, staring at the wall as if deliberately trying to avoid looking at him. "Put the money on the bed. I'm going to use the bathroom." Her voice was dull. Half dead already.

Petrosky sat on the dingy comforter with the folder beside him, avoiding a dark stain on the mattress near the foot of the bed, and pulled out his pack of cigarettes. He lit a smoke with a jittery flame, wishing the vibration was from the lighter and not from his hand, though he didn't have anyone to hide his tremors from, not here. Not anymore.

"You ready?" She was back, wearing a cheap blue sports bra and white panties. A tattoo of a snake wound around her rib cage above ripples of stretch marks like the ones on Walsh's belly. Tracks like overgrown acne craters stippled her forearms.

He held the pack of cigarettes out to her.

The girl shook her head and knelt between his knees. She reached her hand down the front of his pants and sighed when she realized he wasn't hard. "Don't worry, baby, we'll get this up for you in no time."

He held the cigarette between his teeth and pulled her hands free of his jeans. "Not that kind of visit."

She stared at his hands, eyes glazed.

"Get up. Sit."

She eased onto the bed, frowning, but her gaze had sharpened from dull to suspicious. "You a cop?"

"I need to ask you a few questions." He exhaled smoke toward the single bare lightbulb above them.

She jumped up again, eyes wide, anxious. "Hey!" she protested when he grabbed her arm with one sweaty hand.

"I'm not going to arrest you," he said around the cigarette. "I need information on another case. A murder case. A girl who could have been you. Might still be you if I don't find her killer."

She slapped at his forearm, but it was the feeble protest of a baby bird pecking at a feral cat. Helpless. Hopeless. Halfhearted at best. "I'm not going to hurt you either," he said. But she clearly didn't believe him; she'd probably endured enough pain to cause suspicion for ten lifetimes.

Petrosky grabbed the gun from his belt, held it on his knee, and finally, she stilled. "You going to stay put if I let you go?" If she ran, he'd never get what he needed—he'd fail Morrison yet again. What a note to go out on.

She nodded, eyes on the gun.

He released her arm and she sank onto the bed. "Lance coming back here?" he asked.

She looked at the door.

"Is he?"

She shook her head.

"What's your name?"

Her gaze darted to the ceiling. "Laura."

Liar. He pulled the cigarette from his mouth and ashed it on the floor, half hoping it'd ignite. "I'm looking for Alicia Hart. Do you know where I can find her?"

Her lip trembled.

"You know we picked her up, right?" He put his gun back into his pants.

She nodded, watching his movements as if trying to discern whether his replacing his weapon was a trick. "Lance said we needed to work extra hard to make up for what she lost us." She grimaced and rubbed her throat. Small dark areas that he hadn't noticed earlier stood out along the sides of her neck beneath her hair. *That fucking shithead.*

"I need to find her. She knows the girl who died." If Alicia had seen Lisa Walsh, she might be able to lead Petrosky to Norton. And then ... An electric sensation jittered from his stomach to his neck, tensing his tendons and muscles. Petrosky rotated his head to release the cramp, but the pain became more acute, drilling into his spine like a hot poker.

"People die all the time," she said.

He met her eyes. "Not like this, Laura. This girl was kept for years as a sex slave. He carved her skin, cut off her toes, made her have his baby. And when she tried to save her child, he impaled her on a wooden stake and let her die."

She squeezed her eyes shut.

"Where can I find Alicia?"

"I'm ... not sure." She chewed her cheek, opened her eyes, stared at the ceiling. "She's here sometimes, but we're never together unless someone ... pays extra. Lance has her working double now 'cause of the bail money she lost him."

"Where's Lance?"

No reply.

Petrosky pulled out his wallet, slid three hundred dollars from the billfold. "Where's Lance?" He put the money on the bed.

"He ..." She gawked at the money. "That's not really his name, but I don't know what it i—"

"I need to know where to find him."

"Fifth and Dexter. Behind the thrift store. There's an alley, where the homeless guys ..." She wrinkled her nose. "He makes us work there if we screw up. For punishment. Even those guys can come up with a fiver." She shuddered and stared at his cigarette. He ashed it again and handed it to her.

"Did you know Lisa Walsh?"

She sucked on the cigarette through pursed lips, then exhaled a plume of smoke into his face. "No."

"Seen anyone unusual hanging around, here or on the street? Young, blond guy, stocky?"

"I ... don't think so." She hit the cigarette again, shrugged. "But there are lots of guys."

He pulled out the composite of Adam Norton. She shook her head and looked back down at the money as if to reassure herself it was still there.

"Take it," he said, putting the picture back in the folder. "And don't tell anyone."

"But Lance—"

"If I find out you gave it to Lance, I'm coming back for it."

She rubbed the crook of her arm.

"You gonna spend it on smack?"

She shrugged.

"Try not to fucking kill yourself, all right?"

He was a goddamn hypocrite.

34

THE ALLEY WAS empty save for two young men, strolling with a funny penguin walk because their pants were around their knees. The more modest one only had his ass hanging out, a belt tightened just below his poop chute, a bulge in his saggy back pocket that could have been a weapon but was probably a sandwich. Either way, getting shot wouldn't be nearly as horrible a death as getting hacked up by a fucking machete. Petrosky nodded to the taller one as he parallel parked in front of the thrift store. The guy nodded back and disappeared around the corner. By the time Petrosky got to the walk, the men would be too far away for him to chase down to ask about the girl—but he'd drive around the block and cut them off if the asshole inside didn't have something for him.

The storefront just off the alley was yellowed with age and the rust-colored water dribbling from somewhere up above— melting snow taking last year's grime off the roof. On a white pasteboard sign inside the barred window, someone had printed "Roscoe's Pawn Shop" in red Sharpie. He pulled Alicia's picture from the folder and stepped from his car into the gray afternoon, narrowing his eyes against the icy wind.

Inside, the place was no more than a thousand square feet, its walls lined with glass cases full of old guns, pictures, the occasional medal, and baseball bats signed by players that no one remembered or gave a shit about. A spindly man stood behind the nearest case peering at him from under Einstein hair and eyebrows. Distrustful. Cautious. Presumably Roscoe.

"Can I help you?" Roscoe asked, his leathery forehead wrinkling as he appraised Petrosky with eagle-sharp eyes. A lock of white hair slid in front of his ear but he made no attempt to tuck it back.

"I'm looking for a couple of people. This guy ..." He slid Norton's composite across the counter.

"Nope."

"How about her?"

The man glanced at Hart's photo and back at Petrosky. "You a cop?"

Petrosky pulled his wallet from his pocket and flipped out his badge. "I heard she was in this area today. Probably in the alley behind here."

The man shoved the photo back across the counter. One long fingernail rattled against the glass.

"Well?"

Roscoe looked toward the bars on the front window, maybe wondering how he'd ended up owning a place that might as well have been a jail cell. "Haven't seen her."

"You saw her."

The man met Petrosky's gaze. The corners of his eyes twitched.

"She blow you out back? Or did you let her come into the store to fuck you in the back room?"

His face flushed a sickly pink. "I didn't—"

"I'm sure you did if you're trying to protect them."

Roscoe was scared, and not of the girl. The pimp. Maybe Lance was the key here. Did Alicia know Lisa Walsh because they were both first taken by Lance? Had Lance sold Lisa Walsh to Norton? But no ... they knew Norton groomed his victims himself, and Mr. Fenderson had seen his daughter with Norton. Then again, Petrosky didn't know what Lance looked like. Even the name Alicia had given them was probably wrong. "Look, I know this is Lance's turf. Maybe he pays you off, gives you free rides on his girls every once in a while, am I right?" Petrosky leaned across the glass until he could smell the guy's rank breath. "I can arrest you for soliciting a prostitute or you can tell me where the fuck she is."

The man put his hands behind his back and shook his head.

"Put your hands where I can see them, sir, or I'll blow your head off and tell them you shot first."

Roscoe put his hands back on the counter.

"When was the last time you saw Lance and the girl?"

He shrugged.

Petrosky grabbed him by his stained shirt collar and yanked him into the counter so hard the glass case groaned like it might break.

Roscoe paled, mouth gaping. "Earlier today! She was working out back. I didn't do nothing, man. I was in here and she was out there."

"How long was she out there?"

"Most of the morning and early afternoon, I guess. I went to take out the trash an hour ago and she was gone."

Petrosky released him. "Lance here too?"

The man nodded. "I mean, not now. Was then—out in the front. Watching, I guess. For ... customers."

Pain danced through Petrosky's temples on spiked heels. "You know where they usually go after they leave? You've seen the direction they head. A car, something."

"I'm not—"

Petrosky banged his hands on the glass hard enough to rattle the whole counter. The little man leaped back into the wall behind him and his head smacked a flimsy shelf of terrible watercolors. It teetered and crashed to the floor, the pictures scattering at his feet. Roscoe cursed under his breath, rubbing his head.

"Goddammit," Petrosky yelled, "tell me where the fuck—"

"Down the street, okay?" Roscoe's eyes were wide and terrified.

"That tells me a whole hell of a lot. Down what street?"

"I ... I think I saw him going toward that apartment building once. Only apartment on the road."

Petrosky straightened his shoulders and leaned in again. "If you're fucking with me …"

The man cowered against the broken shelf like Petrosky had hit him. "I swear, that's all I know! I swear!"

"I'll be back later." Petrosky snatched up the photo of Alicia Hart and glanced at the back wall. "You might want to fix that shelf."

He was halfway to his car when he realized he never should have gotten away with grabbing that guy.

Morrison should have been there to stop him.

35

He left his car beside Roscoe's and headed up the road toward the apartment building on foot. The sky was orange, the air wet and cold, as Petrosky took the sidewalk past a café that had chairs attached to the wrought iron tables with bike chains. He peered around for an actual bicycle, maybe Norton's bike—as if he'd get that lucky—saw a place with a green-and-white sign boasting "Free money until payday!"

He glanced inside. A rat skittered across the floor. No bike.

The apartment building was small—an old house, probably converted into separate apartments to turn a profit. What gave it away were the exterior stairways snaking up either side of the place. Three, four apartments tops. He cringed at the fetid odor of urine on the front stoop and ducked into the foyer. Inside, the stench was stronger and accompanied by a musk and something else that could have been cigar smoke but probably wasn't. He stepped to the mailboxes on the back wall. No names, just numbers in consecutive order: *100, 200, 300, 400.*

Next to the mailboxes was a lone door with *100* painted above the peephole. Petrosky knocked. A male voice yelled something. Petrosky reached for the gun in his back waistband, but a spasm in his right shoulder shot pain into his fingers—he lowered his hand before a tremor in his index finger made him shoot himself a second asshole. *Twitchy.* He wanted to get the fuck out of Dodge, but not by slowly bleeding out from his back end.

"Who is it?" a trembling female voice asked.

"Police, ma'am."

A latch clicked. The woman was at least eighty, wobbling against a cane, her palsied legs barely sturdy enough to keep her upright. But her irises were bright behind the folds of dark skin around her eyes.

"Ma, who is it?" A tall, burly man in what looked like a fast-food uniform stalked from the back hall, eyed Petrosky suspiciously, and retreated to the kitchen when Petrosky flashed his badge. Either he had nothing to hide and was daring Petrosky to come in after him, or he was climbing out the back window. Petrosky didn't really give a shit which.

"Have you seen this girl, ma'am?"

She looked at the photo and said nothing, her head shaking in such a way that Petrosky wondered if she had nodded and he'd been unable to tell because of her incessant tremor.

Petrosky was opening his mouth to ask again when she said, "I think I've seen her. Maybe in the hall by the mailboxes."

"Was she with anyone?"

"A man." She nodded like a bobblehead as a toilet somewhere in the apartment flushed.

The pain in Petrosky's temple intensified in time with her nodding. "Do you remember what box they were using?"

"I think it was the one on the end, but my memory isn't so great."

"Would your son know?"

"Zeek!" The vibrato in her voice was more pronounced when she shouted.

Zeek emerged from the kitchen, his mouth so tight he'd about pushed the blood from his lips. Drugs, maybe. Probably pissed he'd had to flush them.

Petrosky handed him the photo. "You know this girl?"

He shook his head.

"You certain?"

Zeek looked him in the eye. "I mean, she looks familiar, but I never met her. Just passed by her's all."

"Where?"

"Here. I was bringing groceries for my moms."

"Know where she lives?"

Zeek shook his head.

"Thank you for your time." He stepped back as Zeek slammed the door in his face. So much for being the good cop.

Apartment 200 was on the other side of the foyer—not a sound from inside. He knocked, waited, banged again. Had they heard him across the hall? But unless Zeek and his mother were lying ... the girl didn't live down here. Though, like Roscoe, they might have been paid off to keep their mouths shut.

Upstairs, then. His shoes stuck to the treads on the exterior staircase, each step hammering into his brain. He avoided touching the railing.

The man who answered number 400 had the round face and nose of a pug and the puffy lips of a Jersey Shore socialite. Under his collared shirt, his spare tire was as big as Petrosky's, but he looked heavier. Slower. Though surely he wasn't— Petrosky could barely catch his breath after climbing one flight of stairs.

"What?"

"Are you Lance?" Petrosky's lungs felt like they might burst at any moment.

The man's eyes narrowed. "Who wants to know?"

The hair on Petrosky's neck prickled as though Morrison was right there beside him, breathing into his ear: *This fucker is going down.* "I'm Detective Petrosky and I'm looking for—"

Lance heaved the door at him. Petrosky took it in the shoulder and shoved his way into the room, bulldozing Lance over a coffee table. They landed on the floor, Petrosky on top. White powder flew. Cocaine. Bags. Weights.

"Aw, fuck." Lance tried to hit Petrosky with an elbow, and Petrosky brought his fist down against Lance's nose, splattering blood across his knuckles. *I'm going to get arrested.* Maybe he should be arrested. But this guy was standing between him and his partner's killer and even now he half expected Morrison to walk up and strong arm him away from the guy, cuff the fucker, and convince Lance to talk—calm, diplomatic. But Morrison was not there to balance him out. Morrison would never be there again. And every nerve ending in Petrosky's chest burned hot with the pain of that—and the guilt. *I should have been there.* He would not lose another lead, another girl. He would not.

"Get the fuck off me, man! I don't have to answer shi—"

Petrosky clocked him in the jaw hard enough to jam the fucker's teeth together and the guy sputtered and opened his mouth so wide Petrosky could see the glint of a gold crown on his molar.

"Help! Someone! Police brutali—"

"I don't have time for this shit, Lance!" Lisa Walsh's body flashed through Petrosky's brain—the smashed skull, the split skin, the smell of iron. And Morrison. Morrison's face. So cold. His crimson lips that looked warm and alive but were only coated in blood.

"I. Don't. Have. Time." Petrosky shook the man hard, too hard, whaling the back of Lance's head against the floor with a hideous *thunk.*

Lance stopped struggling. *That's right, motherfucker.* But hopefully he hadn't killed the bastard—he needed answers. Petrosky pulled one eyelid up. The man's irises had rolled back, but Lance's pulse was strong and steady. The pimp was out, but he'd live.

Asshole.

Petrosky stepped to the door and peered down into the street below. No one. He closed the door, locked it, and returned to the bastard on the floor, feeling the rush in his veins, his blood as searing hot as boiling acid. Morrison would have called an ambulance. He would have said they needed to keep this guy alive so they could ask questions. That much was true. They—*he* —did need to keep Lance alive. But Petrosky's trigger finger was twitching in a different kind of way than it had outside the apartment downstairs. Norton needed to pay, but this bastard, exploiting women, hurting them, humiliating them ... Lance didn't deserve to live either.

Lance groaned, and Petrosky kicked him in the gut. Lance threw his arms in front of his head.

"Knock it off, fuckface," Petrosky barked. "I'm only going to hit you if you don't give me what I need." He might have been lying, but he didn't give a shit.

Lance peered over his elbows, cringing. "What the fuck do you want?" His words were muffled by his arms.

"Lisa Walsh."

Lance dropped his arms. "Who?" He shook his head, wincing at the movement. "I don't know no Lisa Walsh." He was probably telling the truth. If Norton had taken Walsh himself, he wouldn't have had a reason to introduce her to this guy.

"How about Alicia Hart?"

He furrowed his brows. "Aw, fuck that bitch, man! She's already fucked me ov—"

Petrosky kicked him again, this time in the shoulder. "Where the fuck is she?"

"I don't know, man! She's off today, okay?" There was no tell-tale guilty twitch of the eye, just the raised brows, the widened lids of a thousand lying sociopaths. "You really a cop?"

Petrosky took his gun from his belt. Lance tried to scramble back but Petrosky pinned him to the ground with his knee on the prick's chest.

"Jesus, man, I swear, I—"

Petrosky pointed the gun at Lance's forehead. "All out of time, motherfucker. Where is she?"

"Fuck man, you don't gotta get so upset! She's over on Finn, at the motel with another bitch." His voice was a high-pitched whine.

Petrosky pressed the barrel into Lance's head hard enough to leave a bruise. "Room number."

"Jesus, hang on … twenty-three. I think."

"Be more sure." Petrosky cocked the gun.

"I'm sure! I'm sure! Goddamn!"

Petrosky released the fucker, uncocked the weapon, and jammed it back in his belt. "You lay a hand on her, Lance, and I'm coming back for you."

"You ain't no cop. I know a cop when I see one." Lance clambered back to the wall and rubbed his head, the vehemence creeping back into his face. "Why the fuck do you care so much about some street skank anyway? Bitches are a dime a dozen."

The pain in Petrosky's head intensified and sank into his chest, a deep, throbbing abscess. "They're replaceable, are they?"

Lance's lips were a straight, tight line.

"What about the ones who get beaten?" So many cases, so many hurt girls. "The kids who get left in some fucking alley like trash?" Walsh. Morrison. "What about the girls left dead in a field, left after someone used them and threw them away? You think they didn't matter to anyone?" *Tell me you could have killed Julie, motherfucker. Tell me it doesn't matter.*

"It's just business."

Petrosky whipped the gun from his belt. Before Lance could raise his hands, he brought the butt of the gun hard against the bastard's skull. Lance's eyes rolled back in his head as he slumped to the floor and lay still.

If he couldn't catch Julie's killer, this piece of shit would have to do. Petrosky kicked Lance in the ribs one more time for good measure, then kicked him again. Then again. Ribs. Belly. Groin. Lance wheezed a stream of something pink onto the floor. *Sorry ass motherfucker.* He kicked him again and again, feet flying, the dull thud of impact echoing through the air until the sweat poured off his face and soaked the collar of his shirt and he could hear nothing but his heart hammering in his ears, feel nothing but the searing pain in his chest, like his ribs were on fire. And then Morrison's voice: *Enough, Boss. Enough.*

Panting, he knelt and felt for a pulse. Thready, but there. He was moderately disappointed. Maybe a lot disappointed.

"Dad?"

Petrosky turned.

A boy of six or seven stood just outside the hallway, an over-sized T-shirt hanging off his thin frame. One bare foot was pale with white powder.

Fuck. Petrosky straightened and the kid jerked back into the wall. "I won't hurt you."

The boy kept his eyes on Lance.

"Where's your mom?"

"She's working."

"What's her name?"

He drew his eyes away from Lance, slowly, then took a step toward Petrosky.

"Hey, don't move, okay? There's some glass, and you'll hurt your feet." The coffee table was shattered—blood spatter coated the floor, stained his knuckles.

The boy froze as if unsure whether to listen or to run like hell.

"Here." Petrosky stepped over the shattered glass, the powder, and a stray razor blade. The baggies shuddered around his shoes as he scooped the boy up and set him on the couch to brush his feet off.

"What's your name?"

"Peter."

"Like from *Peter Pan?*"

"He's a guy in the Bible."

Looked like all that biblical reading was helping his mom a whole hell of a lot. "When will your mother be home?"

Peter's shallow breathing was his only reply. The boy seemed to be done talking.

"I'm going to call someone to take you out of here, okay, Peter? I'll bring you downstairs to wait."

Peter nodded. He stood and leaned toward Petrosky's ear. "I'm glad you hurt him," he whispered.

36

PETROSKY TOOK the side streets four blocks over to Finn, his hands aching—at least his heart had slowed. Zeek from downstairs had taken one look at little Peter and cradled him to his barrel chest, promising to look after him until Child Protective Services and an ambulance could get there. Hopefully Lance would stay unconscious until backup arrived.

Petrosky parked in front of the motel, a two-story L-shaped building, and reached into the backseat for a fast-food bag. Lance's blood glowered from his knuckles. Pulling the napkin free, he spit on his hands and wiped them, frowning at his cracked skin. The man was probably a cesspool of disease. At least Petrosky'd be gone before that would matter.

Room twenty-three was on the second floor, third to the left from the top of a rickety set of stairs that whined under Petrosky's weight. His worn-out legs whined back. He was getting far too old for this—and far too tired. But the thought of bringing Norton down spurred him on.

Room twenty-three had a scarred metal door and a stain that might have been piss on the cement beside the entrance. Petrosky put his ear to the door. Silence. *They better still be here.*

He knocked.

A scuffling, and then a voice, high and light, on the other side of the door. "Yes?"

"Police. Open up."

The scuffle turned to scrambling, like rats in a cage. A man's voice shouted something unintelligible. A female voice answered, tentative, halting. Nervous.

The man flung the door wide. His pants were hanging open under an untucked button-down. A wedding ring glinted in the dim light from the room. "I met them at the bar! They told me—"

Petrosky grabbed him by the throat and slammed him against the wall—just like he had the high-on exterminator at Salomon's house—and for a moment he thought he felt Morrison's hand on his arm. He inhaled sharply, blew it out. "You pay them already?"

"Pay? He rasped under Petrosky's knuckles. "But—"

Petrosky peered into the room. Alicia Hart stood just inside the door wearing a halter top with a picture of a cartoon skunk and a pair of leggings that looked too thin for the weather. Another girl sat on the bed behind her, hastily wrapping herself in a bedsheet.

Petrosky addressed Hart. "He pay you?"

She looked at the ground and nodded.

"Aw, fuck, I didn't—"

Petrosky released him, and the man staggered back. "Go home to your wife, asshole." The man was still tripping down the stairs when Petrosky pushed inside and closed the door. "Alicia Hart?"

She nodded again at her feet.

"I need some information."

"Are you gonna arrest us?" the other girl asked from the bed. Even with the sheet around her shoulders, he could see rolls of belly protruding over a pair of Daisy Dukes three sizes too small. Two perfect circles of blush glowed against her pasty cheeks. Her red lipstick had smeared across her lower jaw.

"No. I just need to ask you some questions." He looked back at Hart. "About Lisa Walsh."

"Lisa?"

Petrosky rested his hand on the wall. His knees were soft—

jelly-like. Maybe there was a bar nearby to perk him up. But the bed looked even better.

He shuffled to a threadbare wingback chair and eased into it. The chair protested by jabbing him in the ass with a renegade spring. *Figures.* "Tell me about Lisa."

"I know her from way back. She went to Harris. I went to Our Lady right up the street."

"How'd you know her if you went to different high schools?"

"Oh, well, there was this dance? And I got asked by this guy who knew my cousin. So I went, and she was there. Said she liked my dress." Hart smiled wistfully. "It was a pretty dress. I got it from my grandma for Christmas."

"Right. What happened after she complimented your dress?"

"Oh, sorry. Well, we just kinda talked, you know? Girl stuff. She was a little younger. Impressed that I had come as someone's date. But I didn't know anyone else there and the jerk I went with was out back smoking with his friends, so I just talked to her. And I asked her why she wasn't there with anyone, and she got all quiet with this sneaky look on her face, you know? Like when you know someone's got some kind of juicy secret? And she whispered that she had met this ... guy. And that he was *older.*"

"Why would she tell you that if you'd just met?"

Hart shrugged. "I mean, I always thought she was trying to impress me"—the smirk of a girl remembering her heyday—"but maybe she was just dying to tell *someone.*" Hart's face fell. "I guess she was kinda weird about it. After she finally told me, she clammed up, begged me not to tell anyone else."

Lisa Walsh had wanted to be special. But Norton had probably told her that secrecy was part of what made her that way. Of course she'd clammed up. Typical grooming bullshit. *Manipulative prick.*

"Did you have contact with her after that?"

"I saw her around. She was at laser tag one night with another girl, but I was with my friends, so we didn't really talk."

All fucking day on this. Petrosky ground his teeth. "So you knew her from one night?" His stomach was rancid. "You told an officer that you knew her because of one isolated interaction?"

"I just thought—"

"You thought you'd get off easier if you threw around the name of a dead girl like you were pals? You have other friends like that? Girls who disappeared that you've got ready for next time?"

Her lip trembled. The other girl tried to sink deeper into the sheet.

Fuck it. He'd arrest them both.

"I do," the chubby one said.

He snapped to her. "You do what?"

"Know other girls who have disappeared."

He massaged his temples. "I imagine you do." The police only saw a fraction of the crimes against these girls. Some just vanished, anonymous, without anyone to even report them missing.

"People don't know, you know? How dangerous it is. Better than anything else going, but still ... I don't know what we'd do without Lance."

"Yeah, he's a fucking hero." Petrosky's heel tapped against the worn carpet. He took a deep breath.

Morrison had died chasing this lead. How had it led him to a killer?

"Either of you talk to another cop yesterday? A Detective Morrison?"

Blank stares. Head shakes.

Fuck. "What's your name?" he asked Hart's friend.

"Francine."

"Francine, who else do you know that disappeared?"

She sat up straighter. "Well, there was that one girl a few years back. One day she was just gone ... remember her, Alicia? She used to work Emery Street."

"Tequila," Hart said.

Like the drink? Tequila wasn't on their list of possible abductees, but that didn't mean they hadn't missed one. And a name like that—probably an alias anyway. "How about younger girls, Francine? The guy I'm looking for likes them younger."

"There was Antoine's girl. She couldn't have been over fifteen. That was like a year ago, though. Or maybe more."

"Name?"

"Casey."

Electricity winged through Petrosky's chest and down his arm. "Casey Hearn?" The girl whose parents Morrison visited without him.

Hart shrugged and the other girl looked down. "I knew her too," Hart said quietly, "but I never knew her last name."

Petrosky thought back to the files that were keeping the frost off his front seat, wishing he had Morrison's classifieds, wishing he still had the kid to take notes. "Long red hair? Green eyes? Thin?"

They both nodded.

He leaned forward in the seat and the spring tugged at the seat of his pants. He'd hammer that fucker down before he left. "Anyone strange hanging around before she went missing?"

Hart glanced at Francine. "No, I don't think so. Not any weirder than usual."

"What about someone who gave out lockets? Little hearts?"

More blank stares. Head shakes all around.

What would Morrison do? "Maybe a guy who tried to be a sweet talker, someone who called you his number one girl?"

Francine's eyes brightened. The sheet dropped from her shoulders revealing a pink push-up bra, her breasts swelling from the top. One brown nipple was already visible. He averted his eyes. "I heard about that guy from Whitney," she said.

"Whitney what?"

"I ... I don't know, but she used to talk about this guy who would say shit just like that; that she was his number one girl. Guys are always saying you're their favorite or whatever, but the way he said it was ... goofy."

His heart was throbbing, frantic, against his breastbone. "Where's Whitney now?"

He waited for Francine to say *dead of leukemia* like Walsh's friend Becky, or some equally inconvenient thing. Inconvenient to him. More so for her.

"She's over on Clayborne now at the ..." She squinted at Petrosky. "You sure you ain't gonna take her in?"

"All I care about is finding the person who hurt Lisa." *And who killed Morrison.* "Whitney's in danger if she knows this guy."

Francine gathered the sheet around her again, covering her exposed nipple. "The massage parlor. Right over on Clayborne and Seventh. I think it's called Purple Lotus."

Hart nodded.

Petrosky stood. "I'm going to grab a picture from the car so you can tell me if it's Casey." He glanced around the room. "Then you guys lock up and get some sleep."

Francine shook her head. "Can't. We have to—"

Hart elbowed her.

"You have a quota?" Petrosky said.

Hart studied her hands.

Petrosky pulled out his wallet and handed her four hundreds. "Enough?"

She nodded. Her eyes were wide.

"Order a pizza or something too, okay?" He paused. "And ask for a woman delivery driver."

His stomach rolled at the thought of food. He retrieved the folder from the car, and both girls confirmed Hearn was the girl they had met on the street, the one who'd disappeared eighteen months ago without a trace. He also showed them the photo of Adam Norton—nothing. It had been a long shot.

As he turned to leave, Hart used the sheet to wipe off her garish lipstick. Without it, she looked younger. Innocent.

But looks were deceiving.

Petrosky pulled the door shut behind him.

HE HAD JUST COLLAPSED into the driver's seat when Shannon texted him.

"Where are you? I got us Mexican."

Petrosky turned the phone over in his hand, glanced in the back where some numb-nuts had tossed his jacket on the seat. Shannon needed him. But did she need him there, or here?

He texted back:

"Got a lead."

Her response came immediately.

"Nail the fucker."

37

THE PURPLE LOTUS was sandwiched between a greasy spoon that probably served more maggots than coffee and one of those Korean convenience stores with the chicken feet and bull cocks or whatever they had there. He could almost hear Morrison saying "Try the feet, Boss, you'll like them," and for a moment he swore he heard the kid's laugh rumbling on the breeze. He shoved the thought and the pain deeper into his gut.

A picture of a grinning Buddha was taped to the Purple Lotus's front window. The place was dark inside, but he could make out the paint peeling from the eaves like thin, blistered strips of skin—like a bad sunburn that someone had taken a garden rake to. Like the flesh of an innocent girl torn apart by a machete. Then he saw that alley, Walsh, then Morrison, then Walsh again. His breath caught. *Get it together, asshole.*

The door shrieked as he strode in, his file tucked under his arm. Four stick candles on a low table illuminated a slim white woman with the severe face of a school principal. The shadows stretched behind her, dissolving to pitch dark in the lower corners of the room. Above her, candlelight flickered against the ceiling and walls, like the fire was attempting to burn the place to the ground and put them all out of their misery. Petrosky wondered if the power was out or if they were hiding the spider veins and aging bodies of their workers.

"I help you?" The woman's words were halting, but more like a terrible impression of an Asian accent than the real deal. Faking it? He wasn't entirely sure he'd be able to place the real deal.

"I'm looking for Whitney."

"Ah, she with customer. You wait."

Petrosky nodded and looked around. No chairs in the room or down the lone hallway that faded to black on his right.

"You pay first."

"How much?"

"Depend."

"Just the normal in-and-out package."

She smiled. "In and out, eh? You funny."

"How much, ma'am?"

She squinted at him, looked down at his shoes. "Sixty."

"I'm not giving you the scam price. I'll give you forty."

Her mouth tightened—not so funny anymore. "Forty. You be out twenty minute."

Petrosky handed her the cash. She pocketed it, her eyes resting on his wallet until he put it away. The room was hushed, like the place was full of little girls keeping secrets, and that thought made his skin crawl. The woman watched him. He glared back.

They both turned to the far wall as a scarecrow of a man slipped out the middle door. He tucked his chin to his chest and tried to push past them, but tripped on Petrosky's extended leg and went sprawling. *What a fucking shame.* The guy scrambled to standing, and this time escaped into the night.

When Petrosky turned back, the woman was frowning at him. "You go now. Twenty minute or you pay more."

Petrosky walked through the open door and closed it behind him. No lock.

It smelled of sex: the musk of sweat under the muted chlorine tinge of semen. Whitney was smoothing a sheet over a massage table in the middle of the room. She wore a negligee in some dark color. Light corkscrew curls hung around her face— she was beautiful, but it might have been a trick of the candles in the corner.

She smiled. "First time?"

"Yes."

"Come on and have a seat."

"I'd rather not, ma'am." He flashed his badge in the dim light and put a finger to his lips when she opened her mouth. "I'm not here to arrest you," he said, low and gentle. "I'm looking for a guy. I heard you might know him." He wiped sweat off his neck. "He's a very bad guy. A killer. Someone who called you his number one girl."

She wrapped her arms around herself. "Oh Jesus, *him?* I haven't thought about him in forever."

So Morrison hadn't made it here either. Petrosky whipped the sheet off the bed and handed it to her.

She draped it around her shoulders, still shuddering. "You can't forget guys like that. He was ... something was wrong, you know? He didn't even act that weird, but I just ... knew he was off. Gave me the creeps."

"Do you know his name?" Maybe Norton was using an alias they could trace.

"I don't think he ever gave it."

"Where'd you meet him?"

She sat on the table, hunched over like the weight of the world was hunkering down on her back. "He used to troll the street. He approached me a few times, asked me to get in his car, but I said no, that I was meeting someone." She looked up. "Even though I never was."

"Did he come back?"

"Yeah. I mean ... you have to be nice, so maybe I led him on a little. The third time I was with another girl, and he gave me this box. With a necklace."

Electricity zipped up his spine. "It have a heart on it?"

She gaped at him. "Yeah. With a number one engraved in the middle."

"You still have it?"

She shook her head. "I sold it right after. It was all so creepy. When I said thanks, he told me there was more where that came from."

"What'd he look like?" *Give me something I can use. Help me catch this fucker.* He inhaled sharply when he realized he was holding his breath.

"Shorter for a guy, just a couple inches taller than me."

Petrosky appraised her—five-five, maybe five-six. Norton's profile was five-nine.

"Was he thin?"

"No. He was kinda stocky. Strong-looking. Not like"—she looked at Petrosky's belly—"huge, or anything. Just bigger."

Petrosky swallowed back bile—the fresh spunk smell was making him ill. "How old was he?"

"Twenties? Not much older than me."

Norton. Had to be. "Any tattoos? Scars?"

"I don't think so. But he had marks on his face. Like the welts you get when you're allergic to something. My brother used to get them from eggs." Something almost wistful stole across her face and disappeared.

Everyone was missing someone. "Hives," Petrosky said.

"Yeah, but it was weird because they were always there, every time. And they moved around too, on different parts of his face."

So were they hives? Or merely acne spots? Petrosky thought back. Had Norton been itchy when they'd met? *Yes.* How had he forgotten? He'd had scars along his jaw, but when they'd started talking, the welts had popped up on Norton's neck and face— subtle, but there. And the guy hadn't eaten anything that Petrosky knew of. He pulled out the file and flipped to the composite sketches.

Whitney brought the picture to her nose and winced. "Yeah... I think that's him." She bit her lip and looked at the door as if she expected him to show up at any moment.

Norton had been more than a little creepy if she was still looking out for him years after the fact.

"When was the last time you saw him, Whitney?"

"Maybe a year or so. After the necklace he only came once more and I hid when I saw him walking up. He looked ... angry." She swallowed hard. "I started working another street after that. But I saw him there too. He was one of the reasons I ended up here. Inside—where not just anyone can see you. And where I never have to be alone." She thrust the photo at him, as if she wanted nothing more than to get it away from her.

"So he followed you? Stalked you?" Of course he'd followed her. If he had sensed that she was rejecting him, he'd have wanted to slice her open.

"Yeah." She nodded. "Yeah, he did. I guess he was upset that I didn't go to see him after he gave me the jewelry."

Petrosky froze, the composite sketch still held in the air between them. "He told you to come see him? Did he tell you where to go?"

"Wasn't an address—just a street corner. But he said I couldn't miss it."

"Whitney, this is really important." She knew where Norton was. Would he still be there, in the same house? The guy had been a creature of habit so far. "What corner did he live on?"

"I can't remember exactly. But one of the streets was Beech because I remember thinking it sounded nice—like an ocean vacation."

Beech. A block behind Salomon's place.

"What else did he tell you about the house? Color? Brick? Two stories? Anything?"

"He didn't say. Only that it was on the corner." She frowned. "The corner of Beech and ... something."

The small room was crackling and spitting with energy. None of those corners had just one house. How the hell was she supposed to find it with no other information? Petrosky needed to leave. He turned to the door, and she grabbed his arm.

"Wait ... do you think he'll ... I mean, is he around here now?"

"Not sure, ma'am. In the meantime"—he handed her his card—"let me know if you hear anything else. And if you see him ... run. Don't take any chances."

She handed the card back. "I can't take this. They check my pockets."

He crumpled it in his palm. "My name's Detective Petrosky. Call the 56th precinct and ask for me if you see him or if you hear anything."

She nodded. "I know where it is. I've been there enough times."

THE WOMAN at the counter looked at her watch and nodded approvingly as Petrosky emerged.

He whipped out two hundreds and tossed them on the counter. "For her time. She better see every penny."

The woman's eyes widened. "Whoa. Thanks a lot."

"What happened to your accent?"

She shrugged.

Faker. He should have tripped her lying ass too.

Back at his car, Petrosky vomited a thin stream of bile and half-digested aspirin onto the crumbling asphalt and locked himself inside. Dizziness washed over him. The car was getting smaller. Withdrawal was a fucking bitch. He took a slow, shaky breath and rummaged around on the passenger seat, pulled out the box of granola bars, and ripped one open. His stomach protested before he even swallowed.

He needed to find a bar.

No, he needed to find this fucker, shoot one fatal round into Norton's gut, then let the guy smoke him. *Even a dumb shit like you can handle that, Petrosky.*

But he couldn't. Every one of these girls unscrewed something hidden in a deep, dark corner of his brain. He couldn't help them, not really. He had never been able to help anyone— especially not the ones who mattered.

I can't do this.

But he had to try. For Morrison. For Shannon and line-of-duty insurance. For Julie, so some other little girl didn't die the way she had—at least not at the hands of this fucker.

McCallum was right: he was a coward. Wallowing like a fucking prick.

But just one drink should get him back on track. Just one.

38

THE SALOMON HOUSE WAS STILL, not the way a house is still when no one's home, but in that way of silent abandonment. The walk and the driveway had the same untouched snow as the lawn, which no longer bore any trace of hacked-up bodies or frantic, toeless feet. Visqueen plastic covered the empty basement window casings, and the glass had been removed, the casings stripped between what looked like new bricks. Presumably to take care of the asbestos the forensics team had found; Courtney'd have to fix that so some hippie buyer didn't sue her in ten years when he got cancer.

He parked in Salomon's snowy drive and locked the car. The wind whipped stinging slivers of ice onto his cheeks—not even eight o'clock and no hint of warmth, just biting winds like someone was taking a pressure washer to his goddamn face. He checked the safety of the gun in his jacket, oddly pleased at the spatter of Lance's blood grinning at him from his shirt cuff. Nothing about this week would ever wash out.

Petrosky flipped the collar of his coat up against the wind and strode down the sidewalk trying to picture the night of Walsh's escape. Dark, like this, streetlamps reflecting off the snow and tingeing everything yellow. It would have been cold, but not quite this cold. Which way had she come? Lisa Walsh was found nude in the alley, but that didn't mean she'd been nude when she'd run from Norton, carrying her tortured newborn. She'd at least worn socks—and fallen because she couldn't balance on her mangled feet or maybe because her muscles had been wasting away for years in a torture chamber.

He walked, scanned, trying to ignore how sick and painful his heart felt in his chest, though the ache might have been the granola, ready to make a comeback. He squinted at the bars scoring the windows on the opposite side of Pearlman. At a few shoveled walkways. At another home covered with aluminum siding. Could Walsh have gotten out through a loose piece of siding? He pictured Lance's place of business—the shitty mattress, the space heater, the raw framing with only plywood as protection from the elements. Walsh might have been able to squeeze out of that, depending on the interior.

Salomon's road dead-ended at Pike Street. Petrosky approached the corner and glanced back at the Salomon house. Walsh would have spent a lot of time in the open, under the streetlights, if she'd come from Pike. It had been late, but surely someone would have seen her if she'd come this way.

Were the other roads more private? Not so much. She'd probably stayed off the main walk, hiding from Norton. Most of the yards didn't even have privacy fences to slow her down, and in the shadows behind the houses, lots of shit would go unnoticed, even a girl running for her life during a sleet storm.

He turned left down Pike at a house with boarded windows. Next to the corner house, another home was in the early stages of abandonment—a foreclosure sign hung from the door but the windows remained intact. His boots crunched over the icy sidewalk, then through the salt of a shoveled drive, then sidewalk again. From the west, the wind roared ever louder. He swung his gaze side to side, noting the occupied houses with clean ground level stoops and spots for potted plants come spring. Like Salomon's place. She sure wouldn't be putting out plants this year. And here it seemed the ice would never melt—it was perpetual winter, forever burdened with snow and sorrow, a wasteland under the two broken streetlamps along this stretch. He squinted through the gloom which seemed suddenly harsher than the blustery wind.

Was Norton watching? Petrosky looked behind him, scanned the houses on either side. Nothing. He put his hand on his gun anyway, the black around him too laden with invisible menace for him to let go of the weapon completely. Norton had killed Morrison. How had Morrison gotten here? And why? Unless ... had he driven over to scope out the place and stumbled upon something by chance? Had Norton just happened to see Morrison and taken him out?

Corner of Beech and something. He was almost to Beech. Petrosky crossed a drive crusted with ice when something leaped at him from behind a barred window, face planting on the glass. Barking.

Oh god, his heart. *Stupid fucking twat dog.* He left the yappy jerk and continued on, finally removing his hand from his gun as he approached the next corner. Beech and Pike. If Norton's place was on the corner of Beech ... Petrosky narrowed his eyes against the wind, looking for the twitch of a curtain, for signs of a man watching his neighbors, for the glint of an outdoor camera. Norton would want to know if anyone suspected what horrors he was hiding. But there were no pock-marked douchebags running the streets tonight. Just the film of frost and snow reflecting yellow in the glare of the streetlamps.

He gritted his teeth and turned left up Beech toward the Salomon place, trying not to be obvious. The corner house across the road appeared abandoned—no way to keep a girl prisoner when half your windows were gone. The house next to Petrosky was well-maintained: no bars or shutters, just a table with a lace tablecloth visible through the window. But wide-open lace curtains, a definite no-no for someone with something to hide. No basement, either, just red bricks, the ones near the earth damp with melting snow from the salted drive.

"Hello?"

It had come from that house. From the dark of the porch.

He heard the door latch click and grabbed for his gun.

"Hello?" The voice was hushed, barely loud enough to be heard above the wind. Trying to draw him closer? Petrosky kept his hand on his weapon. A light went on inside the house and as the door opened wider, Petrosky raised his gun.

A woman, shrunken but sinewy, appeared, leaning on a walker. No shakes like the woman at the apartment building; despite her cane she looked steady, strong. Her shock of white hair was almost fluorescent under the porch lights. Bright orange housedress, neon yellow slippers.

Her eyes lit up as he replaced the weapon and approached the house. She stuck a finger in her ear and started tapping. "Hang on now, let me turn my ears up."

Hearing aid. If anything had happened on her lawn, this woman would have been none the wiser.

"I'm Detective Petrosky with the Ash Park PD. Sorry to bother you, ma'am—"

"Now, now, don't you start that ma'am bologna with me. That's my mother. I'm just Gertrude to you … *sir.*" She winked.

Petrosky paused. "I'm … investigating a crime down the street. The attack on Ms. Salomon."

She looked at him blankly. "Who?"

"Ms. Salomon. She was killed early Thursday morning, just around the block from here." How could she not know that?

She shook her wrinkled head. "Oh yes, poor, poor woman. But I'm sure you can protect us all." She winked again, and Petrosky fought the urge to pull his jacket tighter around himself as her eyes ran him up and down.

"Your full name?" he asked her.

"Gertrude Hanover. If you want to buy me dinner, I'll tell you my middle name too." So this was the woman Morrison had met his first day canvassing the neighborhood—the one who had hit on him. Who had made him eat cookies in her kitchen. At least Petrosky knew the house had already been searched.

Instead of responding, he pulled Norton's composite sketch out of his jacket and held it out to her. "Do you know this man?"

She scrunched up her face. "Of course, yes."

"Yes?" Petrosky's heart was hammering. "When did you last see him?"

"Oh, it's been quite some time now. Looks just like my nephew, Richard. Used to come help me around the house—building things so I wouldn't fall down the stairs and whatnot."

But Gertrude Hanover had a fire in her eyes—the type of

woman who'd plow over any barricade just because she could. And Morrison had said she'd been getting the mail when he saw her. She wasn't afraid of falling down stairs or anything else.

"When was Richard here doing work? This week? This month?" Was Adam Norton the alias for a guy named Richard? Or the other way around? And if Richard was here recently, he might be staying nearby—maybe he'd stayed in this house.

"No, no, it's been a long time since he helped me out." She frowned. "Months."

The excitement in Petrosky's chest fizzled into the dull ache of defeat. *Months.*

"You know how it is," she was saying. "People get busy with their lives, and the military—well let's just say he's very private. I've got the whole place to myself, if you know what I mean." She cocked one eyebrow.

Petrosky might have known what she meant but he wanted no part of it. He sighed. What the hell was he thinking anyway? To hide these girls away, Norton'd need a place long-term, somewhere he could keep them hidden, not under the nose of his aunt. And Norton was twenty-two—young. This woman's nephew would be far older. But he still had to follow up, if there was even a chance …

"Can you tell me how to get in touch with Richard?"

"Who?"

"Richard? Your nephew? Or is it great-nephew?" What the fuck was this lady's problem?

"Oh, no, just nephew. I'm not that old, *Detective.*"

He waited for her to answer his question and when she didn't, he said, "Where can I find him?"

She shook her head. "He calls sometimes. But I don't call him. Too many numbers to keep track of, you know."

Petrosky could get Richard's number from the phone bill and locate him that way.

"You remind me of my Richard a bit, though you've got more muscle," Hanover said. She laughed.

He didn't. Apparently everyone looked like her nephew. But his heart had slowed, and thank fucking god for that. "Have you seen anyone, anything, out of the ordinary? Someone out walking that you didn't recognize or—"

"Just you." She smirked. "I'm usually in bed early, though. Tonight I heard Justin Bieber was on the television, so I stayed up for that. Can't mess with the hot on that man, no sir." She patted Petrosky's arm, her grip lingering on his bicep, and then she squeezed hard enough to make him jump. "Anyway, you want to see unusual, wait until spring. That's when they all come out again, don't you worry."

What the fuck is she talking about? "What happens in the spring?"

"Oh, you know. Just people coming out of hibernation. Stop wearing these thick jackets." She eyed his coat and leaned heavily on her walker.

Petrosky backed up before she could maul him. "Thank you for your time, ma'am."

"And if you happen to see my Richard, tell him I'm making pie. I always tell him he deserves all the goodness in the world, and pie is right on top of that list." She winked again. "And you're welcome to come on back for some too. It's cherry."

Petrosky nodded. "I sure will." *Crazy old coot.* "And if you see someone else who looks like Richard, call me." He handed her his card. "The guy I'm looking for is a bad man. You'll need to watch out for him."

Gertrude Hanover took his card and grinned, one eyebrow raised. "Son, any bad men out there had better watch out for me."

PETROSKY CONTINUED ALONG BEECH, the wind attacking his coat, but less aggressively than Gertrude fucking Hanover. Here, fewer houses were abandoned than on Pike; some drives had even been shoveled purposefully, while others had snow crushed down by car tires. Streetlights stood at the ready. No people. Though if you believed Gertrude Hanover, more folks would be out come spring. Maybe Norton would be among them this year.

But where was he now? Over here, there were lots more bars on the windows, and lots more aluminum siding. Many of the houses had their basement windows treated, some with glass block, some with holes around the window in a deep rectangle, surrounded by walls of brick and backfilled with rock to facilitate draining before any standing water could penetrate the basement. A few homes even had the window blocked some other way—brick and mortar, plastic sheeting, one sporting an actual drainpipe with a catch basin near the house.

From the slope of the drives, it looked as if the water here might pool at the house and flood the basements if they left the window casings as built. That was probably why Salomon had kept her boxes pulled so far from the wall beneath the windows. But ... if someone was attempting to block off a basement, they could just have used the brick from the rest of the house—it would blend perfectly and no one would be able to tell the lower level existed at all. He could pull the building plans, compare each home, maybe. See if one was supposed to have a basement but didn't appear to. But even if he just looked at the houses with altered basement windows, there were too many to get search warrants for; his only hope was to go door-to-door, begging to check out basement after basement. And his legs were already failing him. Every muscle hurt. His thighs. His calves. They'd probably give out before he made it back to the car. Thinking longingly of Gertrude Hanover's cane, he passed a red brick place, a drainage pipe visible by the east-facing basement window. Backlit by an indoor lamp, a little boy peered out at him from behind barred glass—his ears were hidden by the hood of a fluffy coat. A coat, inside. Petrosky looked away.

Think, asshole. Why had Lisa Walsh chosen the Salomon house? There were plenty of places to hide a child all along Beech if Walsh had run from this direction—plenty of windows to shove a kid through. He passed another boarded home with a foreclosure sign taped to the front door and a realtor's lock prominent on the doorknob. Really, did the house have to be on the corner? Norton certainly wouldn't just pass out his address. And each of these intersections had at least three houses on the corner, so even if Whitney had come knocking, she'd have no idea which place to approach. If Norton hadn't given her an exact address, he'd been ... watching. Waiting.

Petrosky peered across the street at another red brick house on the corner of Beech and Whitmore. The place had metal bars and full wooden shutters closing off every window but the one that now had his attention. The curtain flapped again in the front window. Someone was watching him.

Petrosky put his hand on his weapon and crossed the street, peeking around the side of the house as he approached. Glass blocks on the windows. Steel padlock on the unattached garage. The place was like a fortress, designed to keep someone out.

Or someone in.

He slid on an icy stair, righted himself against the banister, and treaded carefully to the door. No welcome mat, just the ugly gray cement beneath a layer of ice stained with winter grime. He raised and dropped the brass door knocker.

"Who is it?"

Petrosky flashed his badge at the keyhole. "Police."

The door flew open. "You guys aren't done harassing me yet?" The guy had stained buck teeth and squinty hazel eyes that darted from Petrosky to the street and back again. "I already told him everything I knew. Which was a whole lot of nothing."

Petrosky stood stock-still, hand on his gun. He swallowed hard. "Who did you talk to before, sir?"

"That big detective. Morrison, like the singer?" He crossed his arms and Petrosky resisted the urge to shake him. *The kid was here.* "But it doesn't matter—I don't know anything. And the people in this neighborhood don't know anything about what happened before, okay? I don't need that shit. I've already moved twice. I don't even let people come over—shit, I had friends show up for my birthday one year, brought their families. I threw them all out, yelling at them. Never saw a one of them again." His gaze shifted back to the road. "I'm doing what I'm supposed to do. And I called my lawyer, just so you know."

Petrosky took in the guy's clothes: T-shirt, pants hanging off a too-thin frame, bare feet. A tattoo of a hula girl quivering on one forearm, her face ugly and not even close to symmetrical.

This guy didn't have the funds to call a lawyer just because someone asked him a question.

"Your name, sir?"

"Ernest Lockhart." He cocked his head. "But don't you already know th—"

"Did your lawyer tell you not to answer questions in a murder investigation?"

Lockhart's mouth worked overtime behind a stubbly jaw. Acne scars stood out angry between the hairs. *Acne.* But this fuckhead wasn't their guy. Their killer was shorter, with a stocky build and the deep, dead eyes of a madman—Petrosky'd been face-to-face with the bastard himself. So who the hell was this guy and why had Morrison come here?

"Why don't you invite me in before your neighbors start to ask questions and you have to move again?"

Lockhart looked over Petrosky's shoulder into the street, grunted, and stepped back.

Petrosky pushed past him into the house. Small. A kitchen to his left held a food-spotted gray fridge stippled with magnets from takeout restaurants. A love seat covered in what looked like burlap sat in the center of the living room straight ahead. Around them, the walls were bare.

Lockhart waved Petrosky to the love seat, and sat on a folding chair, kicking a takeout box from between them. Petrosky tried not to think about the pizza boxes he had laying around his own house as he eyed Lockhart's hands, which were wringing one another with enough force to turn his knuckles white.

Guy was nervous as fuck. Petrosky forced his voice low, even. "When was Detective Morrison here?"

"Tuesday night."

Morrison had been here the night he died. *Why?* Petrosky rubbed his shoulder as the pain radiated through it on the way to his neck. Morrison's neck wound flashed through his mind and disappeared. "What time did he show up?"

"It was nearly ten." He'd stopped wringing his hands, but Lockhart's bare heel was *tap, tap, tapping* against the floor and

Petrosky wanted to kick him in the shin. "I was upset because I had to go to work the next day."

"What did he want to know?"

"Was he not a real cop?" Lockhart's eyes narrowed and his feet finally stilled.

"No, he was a real cop. But now he's dead." *Did you kill him, motherfucker?* "You were the last person to see him alive. So how about you stop wasting my fucking time and answer my questions."

Lockhart paled and put his hands half up like he was about to raise the roof but was too damn lazy to follow through. "Wait, wait, dead? He just asked me ... *fuck*."

"What did he ask you?" Petrosky's voice boomed against the empty walls. Morrison hadn't just wandered over here on a whim. So what had made him suspect this guy? The shutters? The fortress out back? The fact that Lockhart had probably denied entry to his place the first time the cops came by?

"He just ... he wanted to know if I ever went down to the west side over there. To see any of the ... the ... girls." Lockhart was panting. He looked like he might faint.

"Girls? Hookers?"

Lockhart nodded, panted harder.

"Did you know Lisa Walsh?"

"No! I told him that. He said he had met a girl who described me. Said she had seen me around down there with the ..."

"Hookers." The girls he'd spoken to hadn't mentioned this jerkoff. Had he not asked the right questions? Had the girls not told him everything? Or ... had Morrison been snowing the guy to get him to talk? *Way to go, Cali.* He wanted to high five the kid. His breath caught. He'd give anything for just one high five. Just one.

"Listen." Lockhart was babbling now. "He said he was looking for people who knew some girl, but I don't know her, man, I swear. Just because I'm on the list—"

"What list?"

"The registry," he said, more slowly. "Isn't that why you're here?"

The sex offender registry. An avenue Petrosky had abandoned once he realized they were dealing with Adam Norton. Petrosky appraised the man in front of him: pasty, meek, scraggly ... and a pedophile, right? Very much like Adam Norton's last partner, Stephen Hayes. Was Norton that much of a chickenshit, that fearful of rejection, that he simply couldn't do these things on his own?

"What'd you tell him, Lockhart?"

"Nothing! And I let him look around and everything, I swear." His heels were moving again, hands clasped between his jittering knees. "He said he didn't care about ... uh ... porn or anything else, just wanted to see the layout ... in case."

In case you were hiding a few girls in your basement.

"And I just said okay because ... he was nice about it. Not like some of the ..." He glared at Petrosky and looked at the arm of the couch.

"How about giving me the grand tour?"

"What? You guys can't just keep coming here, harassing me. I paid my debt to society."

"I'm sure you did. Maybe you also killed a little girl—a girl who bore your child." Petrosky knew it wasn't him. But if Morrison could bluff to get a little information, he could too.

"I didn't kill—"

"Come in and give us a DNA sample."

"Fine."

"Fine?"

"I mean, I'll call my lawyer. But I didn't do anything, and my DNA is already in the system, so if you were looking for me, you'd know already. If it makes you leave me alone—"

"I'll need to search this place too."

The guy shook his head. "What are you looking for?"

"Victims."

"Let me call my lawyer."

NOTHING. Absolutely nothing.

The attorney had arrived in a sweat suit, none too pleased about being dragged out in the cold. But once Petrosky ran through the evidence—much of it entirely fabricated—the lawyer must have thought they had enough to bring him back a few hours later with a warrant. Lockhart consented to the search so long as anything outside the scope would be ignored. Petrosky ground his teeth, trying not to consider how much kiddie porn Lockhart was hiding.

It took three hours, though he found out quickly that Lockhart wasn't hiding a human anywhere. No additional leads on Norton, either. Just a beat-up classic car in the garage—hence the padlock—and a basement full of old pinball machines. No signs of foul play, no place to keep a girl prisoner for two years or even two days, and no weapons outside of a set of kitchen knives that couldn't slice a tomato without smashing it. Petrosky did find a year's subscription to some teen magazine under the mattress—creepy as fuck, but not illegal.

He had nothing on Lockhart. There was nothing here. But this man was the last one to see Morrison alive, and that wasn't a coincidence.

Petrosky almost slipped again heading down the stairs, legs so wobbly he swore he'd never make it back to his car. It was only a block and a half from Lockhart's to Salomon's and he could barely breathe by the time he reached his Caprice.

He looked at his watch. Midnight. Hopefully he'd be able to figure out what this meant in the morning. Not like he was getting anywhere now.

He headed home to Shannon and cold Mexican takeout.

39

THE BULLPEN SEEMED quieter than usual the next morning, though that might have been because everyone and their mother was avoiding him. Or maybe the entire world seemed slower— the night before had kicked his ass. It had taken him three tries to haul himself out of bed, and he'd had to pull over on the way to work because of the residual exhaustion. Even now, the world kept going fuzzy on him.

Petrosky chugged shitty coffee like it was his job and pulled up Gertrude Hanover in the system to search for her relatives, specifically the elusive Richard. Who lived in Maine, apparently. According to Facebook, Richard had spent yesterday with his family, ice fishing. And his Facebook profile picture showed a guy who was much too tall, much too old, much too square-jawed. Much too not-their-fucking-guy.

Next he called up a list of sex offenders, cross-referencing them on the map he and Morrison had used when they'd charted abductions. That's what Morrison would have done, right? Lockhart was first, arrested for indecent exposure. The idiot had fondled his dick in front of some old woman at a bus stop. No rape, no assault, though looking at that pasty fucker's junk was surely an assault on the eyeballs. Petrosky went to work with a blue pen, marking the addresses of all sex offenders within a five-mile radius of their already marked dump sites and kidnapping locations and the girls' houses. If Norton had chosen a partner like Stephen Hayes, it was probably one of those guys. He wouldn't have agreed to work with a woman, not after Janice had proven too strong for him. And Norton didn't see women as accomplices. They were things to be used. Possessions to be disposed of at will.

He held the map back from his face and squinted. The red marks for each girl's abduction still looked like a bullseye ... but it could have been Lockhart's place in the middle, circled in blue. No other pedophiles' homes were close enough for Lisa Walsh to have run from.

But he'd found nothing at Lockhart's. And Norton wouldn't have needed a partner anyway, not once he'd taken the girls and imprisoned them for his own twisted games.

The phone on his desk rang.

"Petrosky."

"Where the fuck have you been?"

"I—"

"Get your ass in here," Chief Carroll barked. "Now."

"It was self-defense."

Carroll raised an eyebrow.

"That's right," Petrosky said. "I approached the suspect to get information on one Alicia Hart, a woman who claimed to know Lisa Walsh, the vic from last week and the mother of the infant we found at the Salomon house. He slammed the door on me, tried to run. I attempted to detain him, and he fought back. Perhaps it was the cocaine—it was all over the table in his apartment, as I reported when I called for assistance."

"Ah, yes, you called for assistance and then left the scene."

Petrosky shrugged. "If I didn't get to the hotel, Hart could have been gone. I needed to find her while I knew where she was."

"At what point were you threatened enough to pull out your weapon?"

"He lunged for one of the razor blades off the table."

"So you told him to drop it?"

"I was trying to restrain him. He fought back."

"Sounds like bullshit." Carroll stood. "I'll need your badge."

"But—"

"You're on leave. Effective immediately. I don't care whether you want to be or not. You can work out a return date with Internal Affairs."

Petrosky bolted to standing. If he was on leave, would his insurance still pay out? His pension?

Carroll silenced him with a hand. "I took the liberty of arranging a session with Dr. McCallum tomorrow afternoon. I know you and Morrison were close. And you're *too* close to this case, Petrosky. It was a bad enough idea to let you guys work this one knowing the perp was the same guy who kidnapped Shannon."

"We didn't know that in the begin—"

"And once we found out, I still thought the two of you could be impartial enough to work it. But I can't send you to investigate your partner's death."

"I'm investigating Lisa Walsh's death."

"The killer is the same person, Petrosky."

"I know this case. We need search warrants on every house in a five block radius of—"

"You know that's not happening. You need probable cause for any home you want to look through."

"Okay, just the ones on the corners, then." Whitney's statement might be able to justify that search. But sitting here, knowing Norton was still out there, knowing they had a lead and not being able to follow it … this shit was going to give him a motherfucking aneurysm. "And I've got probable cause: the place where Norton bought the jewelry said Norton picked up seven necklaces. There are more victims being tortured right—"

"You can't prove that those necklaces went to the girls or that he has any of them with him."

"Goddammit, you know he does, as well as I do."

"If we can't convince a judge to give us a warrant—"

"I have a witness who said that Norton told her to meet him at a house on the corner of Beech."

Her eyebrows hit her hairline. "Beech and what?"

"I ... she didn't remember."

Carroll's face soured.

"But it can't be too far from the Salomon place," Petrosky said. "Remember that the girl ran there. I just need ... even without a warrant, we can ask around again, canvass the street, just try to get the ones who refused a home search initially. Maybe—"

"It's not enough. And without probable cause or permission, anything we find will be inadmissible. You know that. You could find the entire garage full of girls and he'd walk away to do it again somewhere else. Is that what you want?"

"No, but—"

"You're going to give another detective the rundown and go home."

"But—"

"This is non-negotiable. I'll need any files you've got. Now get the fuck out of my office and get some rest. And keep your appointment with McCallum tomorrow if you ever want to come back here."

Petrosky swallowed hard. Handed over his badge. "You already have my service revolver." He started for the door.

"Petrosky?"

He turned.

"I'm sorry about Morrison. We all cared about him."

Petrosky gasped for breath, but someone had sucked all the air out of the room. Something—his heart?— jerked against his rib cage, twisted, and shuddered. His ribs squeezed back. The bones in his shoulders were on the verge of snapping, and—

"Detective?"

He grabbed at his chest and a sizzling pain shot from his shoulder down his left arm. His lungs had hardened into useless stone, forcing every molecule of oxygen from his body. The world wavered, then clouded, like he was trying to see through a pane of dirty glass.

"Detective!" Carroll yelled it into his ear. Her arm was on his elbow.

His chest lurched again, and he stumbled. He pictured

Shannon in one of those T-shirts that says "My friends went to Key West and all I got was this lousy T-shirt," but instead of palm trees, it had a photo of a casket. "My whole fucking family died and all I got was this." And then he saw Morrison, blue eyes smiling, his beefy arm around Julie as her dark hair whipped around their faces on some wind he could not feel.

See you soon, kids. The world went black.

40

EVERYTHING SMELLED OF ANTISEPTIC. Hushed whispers swirled around him like the rustlings of cockroaches in the walls, the words themselves a hissing gibberish. And his eyelids were heavy ... so heavy.

Petrosky squinted against the harsh fluorescents. A shadowy figure stood above him, a murky silhouette, but no features that he could see.

"Mr. Petrosky?"

"Ayuh." Had that come out of his mouth?

Pain shot through his lower back when he tried to shift his weight. His legs. He couldn't move his legs. Was he dead? Which ME would be in charge of the autopsy? Maybe Woolverton— that psycho prick would slice his sternum open for shits and giggles to see if his heart was really as black as he suspected it might be. If only his heart were black and cold—he'd surely feel better than he did right now.

The room came into focus in pieces. At first he couldn't see through the jagged lines that vibrated across his vision like an old, poorly tuned television, but then they softened into lines like thread or ... hair? Was there someone standing over his bed? A flash of green eyes behind the distortion, and then she smiled. An angel? Was he dreaming? If this was death, it was fucked up. He was cold—hungry. He tried to wrap his arms around himself but a sharp tug in the crook of his right forearm changed his mind. An IV?

A hazy voice mumbled something. Somewhere a monitor beeped, steady and incredibly annoying.

"Mr. Petrosky?"

The room was suddenly bright—violently bright. Someone's huge fucking head blocked the light like an alien in one of those old UFO movies. He squinted, trying to force his eyes to adjust, to see the girl again. But she was gone.

"Mr. Petrosky, do you know where you are?" The man had a thin face but a chin so wide it made his head look like a goddamn eggplant.

"Where's the woman who was here?"

"Woman? There was no woman."

But he'd seen her. Hadn't he?

"Sir, do you know where you are?"

"Of course I know where the fuck I am." He blinked hard, trying to clear the bleariness from his eyes. The hospital. Like he wouldn't notice the hospital bed and the doc with a clipboard and his arms, laced with IVs. *I'm a goddamn detective, motherfucker.* "I'm not an idiot, just ... tired."

"Well, after surgery you really needed to rest, so I gave you a sedative, too, which might explain part of the exhaustion." His voice was nasally, irritating like the buzz of an enormous mosquito. "Kept you calm while we ran tests, and probably helped you rest overnight."

Overnight? Petrosky jolted to seated, and the room and the eggplant-head doctor swam out of focus and came back, sharper than before. His heart writhed, vibrated, like it wanted to split apart. He put a palm against the center of his chest, and—

What the fuck? Bandaged. And a hard, swollen ... something under the skin in his chest. He collapsed back against the pillow.

"When you came in, your heart was beating irregularly. Judging by the level of damage, it's probably been that way for some time. I had to install a pacemaker to control the arrhythmia."

Petrosky dropped his hand. "I gotta get out of here."

"Mr. Petrosky, you need to rest."

He needed to find Norton. He needed to find him and take him apart before he killed someone else. "I don't need to be in the hospital."

"You just had heart surgery."

"Lots of people have pacemakers, doc. My ex-wife's brother got one too—home the next day."

"Listen, Mr. Petrosky, you have a condition called dilated cardiomyopathy. Your heart's left ventricle, the main pumping chamber, is enlarged and is having trouble pumping blood out of the heart."

"Doesn't sound that bad."

"It can be fatal, especially if you have certain risk factors. Do you have family with this condition?"

Petrosky tried to swallow, but his mouth was stuffed with cotton. "I'm not sure," he said. "My dad had a heart attack early."

"Any history of drug use? Alcoholism?"

History? Petrosky shrugged. *Shit, if I was home, I'd be drunk right now.* "We all have few watching the game, right?"

The doctor raised a spindly eyebrow and made a note on his pad. "We'll need to watch it closely to make sure it doesn't get worse." He looked pointedly at Petrosky's gut. "I'll give you some beta-blockers and diuretics to help with the pressure and fluid retention around your heart, but you'll need to make lifestyle changes. No smoking, for one. No drinking. Better food choices."

"What happens if I don't?"

The doctor furrowed his brows, not comprehending. "Sorry?"

"What happens if I don't change my diet. How long do I have?"

"It's ... hard to say." The doc frowned, eyes still narrowed. "If you just take the beta-blockers you might be okay for a while, but you need to make changes if you want to live a normal life. Keep going like this, and the condition can deteriorate to the point where you're too tired to get out of bed."

He was too tired to get up now, but he still managed to haul his ass to work. "And without the drugs?"

"Mr. Petrosky, you need the medications to survive."

Survive. *Right*. Petrosky stared at him until the doctor looked down at his clipboard again.

"I'll leave some pamphlets on the condition so you can read them over," he said. "Do you have any questions?"

"I don't want to read. I need to get back to work."

"You passed out at work, Mr. Petrosky. You're not going back there. I'd like to keep you another day for observation, but at the very least you'll be here a few more hours. We'll see how it goes."

I'll show you how it goes, jackass. Petrosky heaved his body to seated, disgusted at the grunt that passed his lips.

The doctor patted his shoulder. Petrosky would have punched him if his arms weren't so heavy.

"By tomorrow we'll have a day of monitoring and we can take it from there."

Petrosky leaned back in the bed and closed his eyes.

Mandatory leave. Internal Affairs. Fuck.

The beeping on the heart monitor accelerated. He took a deep breath and listened to the frantic rhythm slow—but not by much.

He wondered who had the case now. Maybe Decantor. But that asshole was close to the case too, and Carroll was no slouch. Maybe Freeman took it. He wasn't all that close to Morrison.

Freeman would figure it out.

Freeman would be the one who got to look Norton in the eye before he yanked him in. Freeman would get to see what Morrison saw. Maybe he'd get the privilege of putting a bullet through Norton's fucking forehead.

Petrosky's chest burned, and the monitor accelerated again. *Fuck this.* Insurance or no insurance, he'd kill Norton himself. Maybe he wouldn't even use his gun. Maybe he'd tie him up and cut off his toes and slash at Norton's chest until the room was sticky with gore. The monitor beeped, faster, more frantic, a metronome playing the soundtrack of his rage.

He pulled air into his lungs and it seemed ... easier than it had recently, though the hollow, scooped-out feeling in his gut remained. Lockhart wasn't their killer, yet Morrison had died after visiting his house. Norton had been watching—seen

Morrison. Gone after him. Norton knew Morrison was closing in.

Or else Norton knew Lockhart after all, and the asshole had tipped him off. Lockhart said he didn't recognize him, but he might have lied. Or had Norton changed his appearance yet again? Just because Lockhart hadn't taken the girls didn't mean he wasn't involved; maybe he was all too happy for a friend with a few teenagers in the basement.

Petrosky had to go back, badge or no badge.

He pulled the IVs from his veins, wincing at the sting, then peeled the suction cups from his chest. The monitor beeped shrilly, probably notifying someone at the nurse's station. Petrosky heaved himself to standing, snatched his pants from the chair and jerked them on. A wave of dizziness pulled at him and he steadied himself on the bed.

"What the fuck are you doing, Petrosky?" *Shannon.*

She stood in the doorway, arms crossed. No kids with her. She glared at him, but her lip trembled.

"I'm leaving," he said, but it came out more like a croak. He grabbed a tissue for his forearm, where a thin line of blood was trickling toward his wrist from the IV hole.

"Like hell. At least if you're stuck here, you have an excuse for missing the funeral."

"Oh fuck." He'd missed the funeral. Morrison's funeral. They'd put his boy in the ground and he hadn't even been there. "Taylor, I'm so—"

"Morrison won't mind either way."

"Won't—"

"You didn't miss it yet, Petrosky. When's the doctor say you can leave?"

"Now." He straightened and tried not to collapse. "Right fucking now." How the hell had she gotten the arrangements done so quickly? Families of fallen cops got special privileges, but she must have called in a favor or two ... or paid extra.

"Bullshit." She hefted a bag off her back and tossed it on the bed. "You've got less than two hours before the service, and I have to go get Evie and Henry ready. But you need an okay from the doctor, or I'm not coming back to get you, understand? I am not losing you today, too." Her eyes filled, and something in his already broken heart snapped hard against his ribs. She stepped to him and hugged him like she was trying to crush his sternum.

"Okay, it's okay, Taylor." Her back was shuddering. Crying? A lonely place deep in his chest tore open. "Listen, I'll get a cab. Go on without me." He needed a drink anyway.

As suddenly as she'd grabbed him, Shannon let go and disappeared through the door. Maybe she knew why he wanted to go alone. Maybe she wanted to be alone, too—not like he was much help anyway.

But he had no time to consider it. Another woman entered: brown hair with strands of gray, face wide and flat as a pug's ass, thin lips that didn't show her teeth when she smiled. *Can't these people leave me the fuck alone?*

She appraised the monitor, the abandoned IV tubes, then Petrosky's chest, free of wires. A name tag on her chest said *B.L. Curry, RN.* "Mr. Petrosky, you need to get back into bed."

"No, just …" God, the monitor was annoying, like the steady whine of cicadas. "Can you turn that shit off?"

She frowned but adjusted the monitor, holding the vacant suction pads out to him.

He shook his head. "I need to take a walk."

She looked down at his bare chest. He crossed his arms like Shannon had just moments ago, though it might have been as much to cover his nipples as anything else.

"You're very ill," Curry said. "You could pass out at any time."

He lowered his arms, zipped his fly. "Listen, my partner … he died. The funeral is today and I have to be there."

Her tight mouth softened. "I lost mine two years ago next month."

Petrosky narrowed his eyes. "Your …" *Partner.* He fingered the empty spot on his ring finger. Morrison would have gotten a kick out of that. "I need to go."

"You need to be ambulatory."

"I am."

"You're exhausted."

"I can be tired at home." *Or in a church, staring at my partner's photo over a casket that may or may not have him in it.* Had Shannon gone with cremation? Was she burying him?

The nurse sighed.

"I'm going to get dressed," Petrosky said. "Then let's see if Doctor What's-his-face is going to let me go or if I'm signing myself out."

She scowled. Nodded. Left.

Don't let the door hit you in the ass.

He dressed, watching the door for intruders, AKA nosy nurses ready to stick him with something or tell the boss on him. It took four tries to get his arm into the sleeve of his shirt. If he didn't get a drink in him soon, the tremors were going to give him away. Though … He glanced at the heart monitor, silent now, the line steady and flat.

Maybe he had a bigger problem than the liquor after all.

41

THE NASALLY, eggplant-looking doctor was not available, but he would be before it was time to take off. Petrosky headed for the seventh floor.

The pediatric intensive care unit vibrated with activity. In the waiting room, an anxious older woman wrung a knitted baby blanket. Next to her an old man was doing a crossword. He shot Petrosky a disapproving glance over his reading spectacles.

Without seeing his badge, no one wanted to let him back, so Petrosky asked for Doctor Rosegold and collapsed into a chair in the back of the room to wait for her. He'd just rest a few minutes. For though the room around him bustled with nervous visitors and chattering nurses, the air itself seemed to be as exhausted as he was, weighting his limbs, crushing his chest.

"Mr. Petrosky?"

Daggers shot through Petrosky's neck as he righted himself. He looked down. Looked at the clock. Twenty minutes since he'd gotten there. Had he fallen asleep?

"Sorry to keep you waiting. You must have had quite the night."

Yeah, an eggplant drugged me and told me to lay off doughnuts. Petrosky wiped the sleep from his eyes and followed her toward the glass-enclosed room where their youngest Jane Doe lay sleeping: lonely, still healing—but alive. Unlike Morrison. He peered through the glass, trying to ascertain which was her. They all looked the same. He tried to read the printed names, but either the words were too small or he was too old to see them properly.

"Back corner. Under the blue lights."

The infant's tank was a nest of purple and yellow wires. Under the UV lights, her skin was the blue of dead lips.

Rosegold put her hand on the railing. "You guys really take your victims seriously."

"Sorry?"

"Your partner was here the other day too."

"Morrison was here?"

"Mm-hmm. Just asked how the baby was doing. He called her Stella, said Jane Doe was no name for a baby." She cocked her head. "Why do you seem so shocked?"

"Nothing I just ... he's dead." *Dead.* How many more times would he have to say it before he believed it? He could almost hear Morrison's voice now: *Come on, old man. You've got this.*

Rosegold was frozen, her hand still on the railing. "I'm so sorry for your loss," she said finally, and touched his arm.

Petrosky stared at her hand a beat. "How's Stella doing?"

"She's stable. She still has a long way to go, but she doesn't appear to have been premature and didn't have any other complications."

Petrosky nodded.

"Any word on the bastard who did this?" she whispered.

"We're ... I'm working on it." *Just me.* His heart squeezed behind the bandage and shot a bolt of pain through his rib cage.

They watched Stella in silence. One tiny foot wiggled then stilled.

"I wish I could do more," she said.

"Maybe you can."

She raised her eyebrows.

"This has to stay between you and me, but the guy I'm looking for may have a ... condition. Is there anything that causes skin welts on a regular basis? Particularly on the face?" If he knew what it was, maybe he could figure out where Norton had contracted it—or if he'd been getting treatment.

"Skin welts? Like hives? Or like boils?"

"I think more like hives, but I'm not entirely certain."

Rosegold shifted her weight and drew her eyes back to Stella's bassinet. "Could be chronic urticaria," she said to the glass. "We see it sometimes in babies but I'd imagine it'd be more common in adults. It can look like acne, small bumps, though usually it's more welts, patterns of red and white weals or large sections of skin that become inflamed. It's common on the hands, arms and face, though I've seen it elsewhere too."

Sounded like their guy. "What causes it?"

"Allergies, often. Sometimes the rash doesn't really have a cause. It can get worse during activities that irritate the skin, like heat and sweating, and the welts might spread with high stress or excitement."

"Stress hives?" No wonder he'd broken out when he met Petrosky, and again as he'd tried to chat up Whitney. *Guy's a neurotic mess.* He tapped the railing, his head throbbing. "Can sexual excitement cause them?"

"In some, sure. But obviously that doesn't happen to everyone." She shrugged. "I wish I had a better answer, but it isn't fully understood as a condition. And it varies from person to person."

"Would someone need treatment for urt—for something like that?" *Please say yes. Give me something.*

"Not necessarily, though a few do seek help because it's incredibly uncomfortable. I'd encourage people to get checked out regardless—if their problem is caused by allergy or another underlying condition, they run the risk of a more severe reaction."

If Norton could avoid a doctor, he surely would. But that did explain the scars—constant picking. Stabbing himself, even. Petrosky's stomach made a horrid gurgling noise. Rosegold stared at Stella and pretended not to notice. Petrosky liked her more for it.

"Stella really liked your friend," she said. "She calmed right down last time he was here—he must have talked to her for an hour."

Instead of being with his own family out of fear he'd put

them in danger, Morrison had been here, comforting their smallest victim.

"Your partner would have made a good dad."

He was a good dad. A better dad than Petrosky had ever been. He looked at the blue-lipped girl in the plastic cradle—tried to stay in the present, tried not to think about his own blue-lipped girl in her own wooden box. And Morrison, everything blue and still and cold. Petrosky's air was gone. "Life fucking sucks sometimes," he croaked. "You get used to it fast in this business." But that wasn't true. You never got used to it.

She met his eyes and turned back to the glass. "In this business too, Detective."

They were both liars.

42

As PROMISED, Shannon held the funeral in the church two blocks from the precinct. Stained glass reached to the ceiling. Everywhere Petrosky looked, statues of a long-haired Jesus hanging from punctured hands stared upwards with anguish written on his face.

Everything felt foggy yet sharp, like pain from a phantom limb. The front pew where he sat was too hard, his heart was too loud, and someone's sniffling was grating on his eardrums. He could barely concentrate enough to focus on any one thing. His eyes kept going blurry. He let the world fade out until a flash of blond hair caught his attention—Roger, sauntering up the aisle in a black suit. Shannon's asshole of an ex-husband. But Petrosky didn't even have enough drive to want to punch that jackass—it didn't matter, Roger didn't matter, not anymore. His boy was gone.

Morrison. Closed casket, so he couldn't be sure the kid was inside. But that didn't stop Petrosky from thinking about his partner, cold and dead, his blood replaced with noxious chemicals until he was more Frankenstein than the man Petrosky had loved like his own child. He glanced at his not-trembling hands, thankful for the cabbie who'd agreed to swing by the liquor store first.

Shannon touched his knee. Henry gurgled and kicked Petrosky in the thigh with one tiny foot.

Morrison should have been the one getting kicked. *It should be me in that box. Why isn't it me?*

And what had Morrison found? The answer was near Lockhart's place, he could feel it. Norton had watched Morrison following up on the sex offender lead—had watched him walk to his car. And had … what? Stalked him? It had to have been Norton. If Lockhart had killed him, he'd have done it in his house. He wouldn't have let Morrison leave, then gotten into his own car, and followed Morrison without the kid noticing. Morrison had been a lot of things, but he hadn't been a fool.

Petrosky needed to go. The priest had been talking about the punctured hand guy's victory over death for what seemed like a goddamned hour. Victory? What the hell was that all about? Death was brutal and horrid and nasty. There was nothing victorious about it—outside of the fact that you didn't have to deal with the bullshit of *living*.

Petrosky stood when everyone else did. Some other prayer. Then someone was singing. No speeches, thank god—Shannon had kept shit simple. He swallowed the bile creeping into his throat, which still burned from the alcohol he'd slugged in the car.

Henry kicked his legs again, from his place on Petrosky's lap. Petrosky didn't remember offering to hold him and when he looked up, he saw Shannon talking to Roger, the man's face a mask of concern. Petrosky drew his eyes away and stroked Henry's hair, as golden as Morrison's. *Little California. Little Surfer Boy.* You can take the surfer away from the ocean …

Shannon squeezed his arm, and took Henry.

There was no way to be careful. No way to plan. *It should have been me.*

It would be him. He and Norton were going out together, and Shannon was going to put him in the ground and take his money and the world would be better off. And he could finally rest.

Shannon leaned her head against Petrosky's shoulder and turned her face into his neck. She smelled like Morrison, that herbal-scented shampoo of his, though before she'd always smelled of lemons.

He wasn't equipped for this. He wasn't. He squeezed her arm as her tears seeped through his shirt. His chest pulsed with a heavy, painful thud. Was he finally having the heart attack that would kill him? One could hope, though he'd prefer to stab Norton through the head first.

A slash of Morrison's face, his torn-apart chest, his bloodied lips, darted across his brain, and every weeping wound in his mind's eye felt like it was bleeding the life out of Petrosky too. *I'm just going to check on something, Boss.*

Morrison might have lived if he'd been paired with someone, anyone, who wasn't a total fucking failure. Someone who would have cared enough to stick around instead of going home to get hammered. He would have been better off if they'd never met.

PETROSKY CALLED another cab after the service, leaving Shannon in the care of her brother-in-law and the other law enforcement personnel. On the drive over to the precinct, he leaned his head back against the seat and closed his eyes. It wasn't that he was sick—he was tired. Just so damn tired. The entirety of his abdomen felt swollen and hot, the oxygen around him thick like he was trying to breathe through a wet cloth. He rubbed at the device in his chest, wincing at the pull of the stitches in his skin.

Okay, maybe he was a little sick.

"We'll need to swing by my house first," he told the driver. "Two miles up, make a right at the light."

They'd taken some of his things at the hospital. He needed to get another gun.

43

AT THE STATION, Petrosky pulled out his wallet and gave the driver a handsome tip for keeping his mouth shut during the drive over. Then he hauled himself from the cab to his own ride.

His breath misted through the air behind the windshield. The driver's seat froze his ass cheeks on contact like liquid nitrogen. But though the cold woke him up some, his movements remained stiff, like he was a bear coming out of hibernation. He shoved the key in the ignition and headed off toward Salomon's place. Again.

But he still didn't feel fully awake, and Morrison wasn't there to help with his hippie coffee. Petrosky hit the drive-through at one of those fluffy-ass specialty coffee places and ignored what he assumed was shock at his order of a large regular coffee instead of a half-caff Norwegian brew with bat's milk or whatever other people drank for eight goddamn dollars a cup. His stomach burned with the acid, but it steadied his hand as he drove. *Pearlman. Pearlman.* The pewter sky was ridged with the kind of electric stillness you get right before a storm. He peered out the windshield. Hazy, but no thunderclouds.

Maybe it was him that was electric—the anticipation of finding this guy, of ramming a bullet through that miserable little bastard, was fucking killing him. Maybe literally. Ironic to worry about that now, but passing out while trying to rid the world of a stabby, woman-hating fuck seemed more than a little pointless. He was ready to die, but first he wanted to see his hands coated in Norton's blood.

It wasn't too much to ask.

He passed Salomon's, pulled around the corner onto Pike and parked halfway down the block. Much closer to Beech, where he could see Lockhart's house on the right, its shutters now drawn. He still might not make it wandering around out here. He rubbed at his chest, at the device, at the stitches. Norton, or his heart? He almost laughed. Quitting was for assholes. And it wasn't like he was afraid of death. Not anymore.

Petrosky stared through the windshield at the waning afternoon sun—light, but no warmth. Had Norton followed Morrison to Lockhart's, hiding in the shadows until he could blitz him? On a dark night in a big coat, maybe a wind-protective face mask ... But Morrison would have been on his guard. Plus, this attack had been personal, intimate. Norton had stopped and gotten another blade to slit Morrison's throat. That took time.

So Morrison had to have died inside a house—a garage, maybe. Somewhere hidden. But how had Norton gotten him in there? And *where*?

Petrosky scanned the street and reached into his jacket, comforted by the cool weight of his Glock—the last weapon in his arsenal, the one he'd had with him the day Julie was killed. The one he'd almost put to his head back then. Even now it held that energy, as if despair had imprinted itself on the barrel. Everything was different now. Yet nothing had changed.

The barking dog that had scared the shit out of Petrosky the day before—*obnoxious little fuck*—was still at it, half-hidden behind the bars in a house on his left. Still angry. An abandoned home loomed on the other side of the street. But—

Over the howl of the wind, a garage door squealed, and Petrosky tightened his grip on the weapon. He leaned over the steering wheel, squinting at the house up the road.

Two doors down and across the way from where Petrosky sat, a man emerged from the garage with a snow shovel and a Labrador retriever. The animal pricked its ears at Petrosky's car

—or maybe at the godawful yappy racket from the house he was parked in front of. The guy walked around the red station wagon in his driveway and heaved a shovelful of snow onto the curb. He didn't look over. Petrosky put his phone above the dash, zoomed in as much as he could and waited. The wind picked up, wheezing icy breath on the windows. The guy turned toward him. Petrosky snapped the photo and pocketed the phone.

Nice catch, Boss!

Puffy coat, thinning white hair poking from beneath thick red earmuffs. Looked harmless, but you never knew. Petrosky climbed out of the car, disgusted by the way his legs threatened to buckle, by the soreness in his ribs. He shifted his weight to get the blood flowing. The old guy, far more spry than Petrosky, kept on shoveling. The dog stepped toward Petrosky and wagged its tail as the man looked up.

"Good afternoon," Petrosky said.

"Afternoon." The man had a chunk of snow embedded in his white beard. He glanced at the dog. "Sit, Mac." The dog put its butt on the icy ground. Petrosky winced and clenched his own butt cheeks, just a little.

"I'm Detective Petrosky, Ash Park P.D." He patted his pocket. No badge. He stuck his hands into his coat instead. "Checking out a case around the block. Had a few questions."

The man pulled an earmuff to the side, his gray eyes crinkling at the corners like your friendly neighborhood grandfather. That was who Henry and Evie needed: someone kindly. Stable. Petrosky balled his fists to overcome the sudden urge to punch the guy. He was too drained anyway, even with the coffee running through his veins—so profoundly tired.

"I sometimes work during the day, Detective, but I'd be happy to help any way I can." His smile lit up his whole face. One of those naturally happy geezers just delighted for the chance to plow the fucking snow. "What are you looking for?"

"Your name, sir?"

"Zurbach. Wendell Zurbach." He stuck the shovel in the snow and extended his hand.

Petrosky shook—hearty. Energetic. He replaced his hand in

his coat, already three times more tired than when he'd gotten out of the car. "Zurbach, huh?"

"With an "H". It's German. Not that I've ever been out there." Zurbach chuckled.

This giggly fuck was going to give him a headache. "What do you do for work?"

"I'm in accounting. Now I do more consulting than taxes."

Enough small talk. But where to start? Petrosky's thoughts were foggy as the horizon, but they solidified as he peered down the road to the shuttered house at the corner. Morrison's last known stop. "What do you know about Ernest Lockhart?"

Zurbach's eyes followed Petrosky's gaze. "I can't say I know much at all. Stays to himself. He doesn't like Mac here, either, does he boy?" Mac wagged his tail. "Glares at us when I walk him around the block."

"He ever have company?" *Like a machete-wielding psychopath?*

Zurbach shrugged. "Sometimes. Not that I've ever paid too much attention to it. He did have a party once, a year or so back. Almost called the police that night."

"Why?"

"People yelling. And when I looked out, there were some girls on the front lawn, looked younger than my granddaughters. I didn't like that." He shook his head. "I didn't like that one bit."

Girls. Was Norton loaning his girls out? Lockhart had said a few friends once dropped by with their families and he'd yelled at them to leave—but that could have been a ruse. Norton had to be making money somehow; maybe the Romeo pimp idea hadn't been so far off. Two years ago he'd let others have their way with his victims, waiting until his partners were done and then finishing them off. The stabbing was his thing. The torture. Would he care what happened to the girls before that?

"Any men there on a regular basis?" Petrosky asked.

"Every once in a while, I guess, though I can't say I ever paid attention to what they looked like." He raised one shoulder and his puffy coat hissed as the fabric rubbed against itself. "I think one drives a black car, though. Maybe a Honda? I see it sometimes during the week."

"No idea on the occupants of the vehicle?"

"I don't want to finger anyone wrong. If I had to guess, I'd say middle-aged. Sometimes he wears a suit."

A suit. The lawyer? Norton was definitely not middle aged. "You seen anything out of the ordinary lately, Mr. Zurbach?"

"Not really." He shook his head. "Mac here paces by the door or yelps a lot—couple times a week. We got the guys driving by with their bass up, and sometimes we get folks walking down the way toward the main strip, teenagers mostly, 'specially in the summer. Mac ... you know, he did that, the barking, the night it happened at Salomon's there. I keep thinking if I had actually gone outside I could have ..." He studied his boots.

"What time was that?"

"Can't recall. I woke up in the middle of the night to get a drink. Didn't check the time, just saw him pacing. I looked out the front window, but I didn't see anything, so I yelled at him to shut up and went back to bed." He scratched behind the dog's ears. The animal panted happily. "I probably should have ... But I've never had a problem. Mac's good for keeping trouble away, maybe." He nodded to his own place and Petrosky scanned the facade. Barred windows, but not on the upper story.

"By the way, you hear anything about the report I filed on Gigi?" Zurbach asked.

"Gigi?"

"The terrier there." Zurbach gestured to the house next to Petrosky's car, the one with the yappy dog. "Owners moved out a week ago, left her behind. It's cruel. I go by there, give her food when she'll let me get close enough, but she needs a home." He nodded like Petrosky should be the one to take that tiny jerk home with him. "Animal control keeps saying the shelter is full. I'd take her myself, but she's full of piss and vinegar—wouldn't want her to bite my grandkids."

A week ago. That'd make it ... "When exactly did her owners move out?"

"Friday I think? Right after ... well, you know."

The day after Salomon was killed. Had it been Norton, moving out, running with his victims? Why the hell hadn't this guy said anything before?

Petrosky looked back at the house. The overgrown grass, frozen stiff in the flowerbeds, had surely choked out any plants long ago. Most of the paint had chipped away from the window casings. "It looks like it's been abandoned for some time."

"I don't think they worked outside much."

Them. Had Zurbach seen Norton with one of the girls? Or a partner? How did these wackos find each other? SickFucks.com? "Have you been inside?"

Zurbach's smile fell. "Well ... I wanted to make sure they were gone. I knocked, but no one was there, and then I ..." He sighed. "Okay, I went inside. Through the back door. I was worried about ... Well, a few years back someone moved out just around the block and left their gas on. Place went up like a fireball." He crossed his arms. "Am I in trouble, sir? I just didn't want anyone to get hurt."

"You're not in trouble."

The smile returned. Mac licked his glove and whined.

"Do you know your neighbors' names, Mr. Zurbach? The ones who moved out?"

He cocked his head, squinting into the frosty sky. "No, can't say I do. Met them once but we never really talked much. Kept to themselves, like that fellow on the corner, there." He jerked a thumb at Lockhart's place.

"Can you describe them?"

"Young couple. She was pretty."

Young. And the woman was pretty, like Janice. Maybe he'd been wrong about Norton's choice of partner. "What about him?"

"Younger guy, dark hair. Real thin, like a beanpole—used a wheelchair too. I think he was in the Army. Damn shame, you ask me, the state of Veteran's affairs."

A wheelchair? Petrosky studied the porch. "There's no ramp up to the door, Mr. Zurbach."

"They used planks."

Of course they had. And if Norton had really wanted to play it low-key, what better way than as a quiet, brooding Army vet injured in the line of duty? But ... beanpole? That didn't sound like their guy.

He turned back to Zurbach. The dog had wandered away and was pissing in the bushes next to the porch.

"And no idea where they went?"

"Nope. Left in the middle of the night. Probably felt unsafe."

Zurbach gestured to the dog. "I got up to check that time—watched them go."

"And that was the last time Mac woke you up? The day after Salomon was murdered?"

Zurbach winced at the word *murder* and shook his head. "No, he was upset the other night too. But it was just someone walking home. Not doing anything strange."

Petrosky's back tightened. "Someone walking home in the middle of the night didn't seem strange?"

"Not really. People walk out here all the time, like I said. Not as much as in summer, but I wouldn't call it strange."

"Did you recognize them?"

Zurbach shook his head. "No, it was too dark. But he was walking normal, not running like he'd stolen anything."

Petrosky scanned the street. The main road was up a few blocks, but there was … what? A few fast-food places. They might be open late. Gas station too. Did the walker live on this street? Had he seen something? But Zurbach was an observant fellow; he'd probably have recognized the guy if he was out there regularly. "Could he have been coming from Gigi's house?"

Zurbach shrugged, pursed his lips. "No idea, sir. Just saw him heading down the walk."

Toward Beech. "Can you tell me what he looked like?"

"Probably about our height. Maybe a little thinner, though." He chuckled placing a hand on the belly of his jacket. "But I didn't see him that close; he was across the road and it was dark. That light over there doesn't work."

Petrosky drew his eyes to the streetlamp—broken. The one he'd seen the other night. Was that why Norton had chosen this part of the road? But he'd surely have heard Mac barking if the dog did indeed alert his owner as much as Zurbach claimed.

Zurbach's eyes widened. "You think he …" He glanced at the abandoned house behind Petrosky. "You think he came over here on purpose to do something? You got some burglaries? Someone else get ... hurt?"

"I don't know at this point, sir. Just trying to cover the bases." An unfamiliar man had been walking toward Beech the night Morrison died. That was a little too coincidental.

Petrosky pulled out his card. "If you think of anything else, anything at all, please call me." He started to hand the card to Zurbach, then pulled it back, searched his pockets for a pen, and crossed off the precinct number, leaving just his cell.

Zurbach shoved it into his coat pocket. "I will, sir." He picked up his shovel again. "And you'll call in about Gigi there, too?"

Petrosky nodded. "I'll go check on her now." Might as well see if there was anything worth sneaking away from under the cover of night.

44

PETROSKY CLOMPED BACK up the snowy sidewalk to the abandoned house where Gigi was still yawling from inside. A tiny idiot dog trying to be a badass. He was going to get fucking rabies.

The unattached garage sat twenty feet to the side of the main house. He crept up beside it and peered into the grimy window. Empty—to be expected if the place was abandoned. No sign of foul play. He squinted against the icy breeze at the backyard, where the snow had been blown into hills by the tempestuous wind. Any tracks—Morrison's or otherwise—were long gone. Might get some trace, but he'd need to call in the crime techs for that. And then they'd know he was here and haul him in before he could find Norton. *If* he could find Norton.

So had Norton been living here all along? He looked across the yard toward Pearlman, catty-corner from there through empty lots and missing fences, but he couldn't see the Salomon house. If Walsh had come running from this place she surely would have chosen somewhere closer—there were at least four other homes he could see that would have made more sense to run to, though maybe she'd been trying to put distance between herself and Norton. But they'd looked in the other yards and found no prints, and the sleet had obliterated anything on the sidewalks. She could have run around the entire block for all he knew.

Petrosky snapped a picture of the garage and picked his way around the side of the house to the back screen door. He pulled the screen and tried the handle of the inner door. Unlocked, like Zurbach had said. It squalled inward.

Something skittered out of the room on tiny paws and shot past him into the street, and Petrosky almost fell into the defunct flower bed. *Fucking rat dog.* "Come … Gigi!" he called half-heartedly. "You little bitch," he muttered, then shut the door to the outside and the seal around the frame silenced the wailing wind and the yapping dog.

He was in the kitchen; the refrigerator door hung open, but the interior looked clean. Dog shit in the corner of the room—*of course*—and a couple puddles of water or maybe piss. Petrosky walked through an archway into what might have been a living room, noting the blue carpet peeking between a few shredded takeout bags and torn newspapers. *Confetti a la rat dog.* But nothing strange.

Down the back hallway, he stepped over a broken crock pot that seemed oddly homey in the otherwise dreary house. There was a door on either side and one at the far end of the hall. To the left was a bathroom—no shower curtain, no … nothing. He frowned. Not even a dog turd. Nothing that looked like blood, but nothing that looked like mildew or toothpaste either. Petrosky stepped inside, and over the scent of dust in his nostrils he was assaulted by the chemical stench of bleach.

Why would a couple of squatters running away in the middle of the night take the time to scrub a bathroom down? No reason to—unless they were hiding something.

Like a crime scene.

In the bedroom opposite lay a mattress stained with god knew what. Blood or feces? Dog or human? But even if it was blood, the stains were small–not enough to cause death, though that might have happened in the bleached out bathroom. Petrosky's chest shuddered, and he rubbed at the device as he stepped farther inside the bedroom. In the corner, one used condom. Against one wall, a rope was screwed into a beam, low enough to attach to a dog collar—or a person collar. He peered at it. Not a bit of mold or rot. No rust on the nail. He took a picture and dropped the phone back into his pocket.

That left the door at the end of the hall, looming like a beacon, though of what he wasn't sure. He pulled it open: rickety wooden stairs, descending into the dark.

A basement.

Heart throbbing, he pulled the door farther and peered into the dim, the dull light behind him creeping over the upper steps. On the top stair, right next to the basement door, was a half-empty bag of cement mix. He shifted it so he could see the back —*Portland cement.* The same type found on Lisa Walsh.

Splintered stairs descended into the blackness below. The steps creaked under his weight and his heart responded with a weak kind of stickiness, as if with every beat it glued itself to his rib cage, then broke free. He'd probably pass out down there and be found half-thawed in the spring. Maybe that fucking dog would find him and eat him first.

Across from the stairs, light shone feebly through a narrow row of glass block, dirt and snow from the lawn outside piled to the middle of each. But above the snow line, the windows were clean enough to show him the center of the floor, though the light faded to nothingness around the perimeter of the basement. Cement. Dirt and sawdust. A few shirts and a kid's shoe, all too small for any of the potential kidnap victims. Garbage in a plastic grocery bag sat against one wall, emanating the rank scent of rot.

He walked to the farthest corner of the room and pulled his phone out, ignoring his chest, ignoring the way his belly was trying to crawl out of his body. Ignoring the voice that was so clear it could actually have been in the room with him: *Want me to show you how to do that, Boss? You'll never have to carry a flash-light again.*

Rat droppings along the base of one wall. He swung the light to the other side of the room where a tattered poster like the one Julie'd had lay crumpled in the corner. No ... not a poster—just shiny like one. *What the hell?*

He stepped over an empty paper cup and what could only be

a doll's leg, and peered at the back wall. There was a cylinder of cardboard on the floor, like a giant toilet paper roll as tall as Petrosky himself. And ... plastic. *Visqueen.*

Like the stuff used to wrap Morrison's corpse.

Petrosky's heart was no longer sticky—it was greased, blood like oil, every beat vibrating through his arms and into his fingertips. Behind the plastic, a glint of silver winked at him. Round, like ... the bottom of a coffee cup. The air was thin, every rapid inhale he wheezed into his lungs acrid, tinged with refuse and iron. No, not refuse. Not iron.

Blood.

He grabbed the edge of the cup and pulled it out. A coffee mug. Stainless steel, with a cheery blue peace sign stamped on the front. But it was cold—cold like his partner's face the morning he'd found him, frozen, slashed, dead. Fingerprints were smeared down the side of the cup, almost black. The flashlight beam shivered as he moved the light away, following the plastic to the roll and continuing over the floor to his feet and—

Aw, hell.

He stepped back. The dirt here was not the same color as that covering the rest of the basement. Some patches were creeping toward sienna, but the frigid temperatures had slowed the congealing process. A puddle in the middle still glowed a deep maroon. No one had bothered to clean it up—cocky bastard.

Maybe there was no way to clean it satisfactorily. To hide it.

Or maybe once someone came down here, they weren't coming back out. His neck prickled like he had someone else's eyes on his back and he jerked around. Nothing. He scanned the floors, the corner again. *Get it together, old man.* Morrison would have had his files with him. He might have found something Petrosky could use. But Petrosky saw only more trash, nothing that even resembled a folder—and no papers either.

And there was no way Norton would have let the folder lie there. A case file was a lot easier to get rid of than a basement lake of gore.

Petrosky scanned the room again, looking for shackles, rope, anything that might explain the marks on Lisa Walsh. Though ...

he'd seen a rope in the upstairs bedroom. Had the other victims been here at some point? Was this where he'd brutalized Lisa Walsh? This place, in a sea of abandoned houses, looked less abandoned than the others—no one would think there was a torture chamber in the basement. But the police had searched every house they could and that included the abandoned ones.

And this blood was fresh.

Norton had been here, but why? And when? Maybe he'd lured Morrison in with the promise of a lead on the case—then blitzed him, slashed him apart, dumped him in the alley like a piece of trash.

But Morrison wouldn't have gone with Norton. So who had he talked to? Who had led him down here?

Maybe the same person who'd told Petrosky about this place. *I'm a fucking idiot.* Like anyone would give a shit about that asshole dog. Was Zurbach Norton's new partner? Shit, that dog of his saw everyone—Zurbach would have known Petrosky's fat ass was here the other night too. There was no mistaking him, regardless of the gloom. Zurbach had known who he was the moment Petrosky walked onto his driveway.

Petrosky tapped the flashlight off, casting the room into hazy gray, but at least he couldn't see the blood any longer. He was turning to the stairs when above him, a door squealed. Footsteps thudded over his head.

He was no longer alone.

45

"DETECTIVE?" Zurbach's voice. *Of course.* Motherfucker couldn't just let him walk out of here if he knew what was in this basement.

"Detective? Are you here?" Zurbach called again, far too friendly. The guy knew where he was—had to. Zurbach had probably been watching from his place to see if Petrosky left. Hell, he'd probably watched Petrosky pull up, decided to shovel the drive just to make sure they met. *Accidentally.*

Petrosky pocketed his phone and pulled his gun, the metal clanking when he drew his hands together. *The fuck?* He looked down at the coffee mug, still clutched in his left hand, sucked in a breath, and crept to the corner farthest from Morrison's blood.

"Detective? Hey ... darn it!" There was a thunk above him, a yelp, and the patter of tiny feet, accompanied by high-pitched yipping that made Petrosky's teeth jam together. Fuck, Gigi was probably this guy's dog too, trained to search intruders out. Or maybe he'd lured Morrison here with that same fucking lost-dog sob story.

Goddammit.

The footsteps approached the stairs. Unhurried. Plodding.

The guy was old, heavy, but he was strong—Petrosky couldn't take him. He'd have to lure Zurbach down and disarm him. At least that dipshit dog wasn't trying to run down the open basement stairs to sniff him out. Perhaps the treads were too wide. Or maybe it smelled the death down here, like a shelter dog struggling as it was dragged to the back room for euthanasia. Petrosky lowered his gun but stayed next to the wall where the light from the block windows and the hallway above didn't reach. "Down here, Mr. Zurbach."

A sound like a snort came from above. Zurbach's feet appeared first, then his legs. Hips. Petrosky squinted, looking for signs of the billhook, a glint of blade, but when Zurbach's hands appeared they were clasped together, bare, no weapon at all. But… what was he holding?

"What's in your hand, Mr. Zurbach?"

Zurbach stepped off the stairs and cocked his head, peering around until he caught sight of Petrosky's silhouette in the shadows. "Sorry?" He looked down. "Oh, that little mutt bit me." He opened his hands and Petrosky's finger tightened on the trigger, but Zurbach's hands were empty, one leathery palm trailing blood from a set of puncture wounds. "Never done that before, though I guess I've never picked her up. But she was in the road." Zurbach's eyes narrowed in the gloom, like he was accusing Petrosky of trying to kill the little bitch.

"Why didn't you mention you saw me walking down the street last night?" His jaw was so tight he almost couldn't get the words out.

"Well, I didn't think that's what you meant. You said you were the police. I figured you had a reason to be here."

I sure as fuck do have a reason to be here. Petrosky kept his gun cocked at his hip, itching to blast Zurbach into oblivion. They were standing in the room where his boy had bled out and Zurbach didn't even have the decency to look sorry? His finger tightened on the trigger. No, not yet—he had to find those girls. He had to find Norton. Adrenaline sang through his veins, tunneling his vision. The dog was still barking, but Petrosky only registered it remotely, the way he was aware of the wind outside, the weight of the coffee cup in his hand. He couldn't really hear much of anything over the thumping whoosh of blood in his head, and his chest, *fuck*, a sharp pain there was burning, spreading—

Zurbach twisted his face away, taking in the room. *Like you don't know what's down here, motherfucker.* But without the flashlight, the space remained dusky, murky, like they were underwater. *Enough.* Zurbach turned back to face him, and Petrosky stepped into the light, weapon raised and trained on Zurbach's forehead.

"Hey, hey! What's—"

"Hands behind your back."

"Hands? But—"

"Now!"

Petrosky reached for his cuffs and came up short. *Fuck.* They'd taken those along with his badge. Zurbach stood motionless, waiting, eyes wide with shock or maybe fear. Faking it? Petrosky could tie him up with the rope from the spare room … maybe.

I need to get out of this basement.

"Listen, if you're going to cooperate, I won't cuff you. Walk upstairs slowly."

Zurbach glanced at the gun but turned. The dog barked once, like an exclamation point.

"I don't understand." The man's voice shook. Why—"

"I need you to answer a few questions." *Like why you sent me into the house where my partner was killed. And where you have the weapons hidden.*

And where the hell is Norton?

"Walk upstairs." Petrosky put his hands together on the weapon, and again hit the barrel of the gun on Morrison's coffee cup. The hard steel, the sticky surface against his fingers—it was all that was left of his boy. "And Zurbach?"

"Yeah?" the man said without turning.

"Don't run."

THEY STOOD IN THE KITCHEN, the cold seeping into Petrosky's bones, but at least they were protected from the wind and from the prying eyes of the other neighbors. It was possible Zurbach had a weapon hidden here, but more likely he would keep a gun or a machete at his place. And at Zurbach's there was also a much bigger, much more well-trained, dog.

Petrosky tried to calm his itchy trigger finger, his hand inside his coat pocket, still on the gun. Though now, in the light of the kitchen, Petrosky's suspicions seemed unfounded; Zurbach had turned back into a kindly grandfather. Not that psychos weren't good at faking shit.

He set the mug on the countertop and watched Zurbach's eyes—the man barely glanced at it. "You seen this before?"

Zurbach shook his head. "I don't think so. But ..." He swallowed hard. "Is that blood?"

It's gonna be your blood in a minute. "Why did you want me to come over here?"

"I told you, I wanted to report the dog." Zurbach's voice was low, wary. "And I never said for you to come over, just to get animal control out here."

That ... was actually true. He hadn't sent Petrosky into the house, only alerted him to the dog. But still ... He scanned the kitchen. The terrier had tired of barking at them and had run into the other room. *Good.*

"Where were you Tuesday night?"

"Home." He said the word slowly, like it had two syllables, and each one quivered just a little.

"Anyone who can verify that?"

"Just Mac." Half smile, but his eyes remained nervous. "Since Blanche died—"

"Who?"

"My wife." His eyes went glassy. He looked at his hands.

Good trick, the watery eye bit. But ... Petrosky wasn't getting the fake vibe, and his freak-o radar was pretty good. Or maybe Zurbach wasn't setting it off in the afternoon light the way he had when they were standing in the darkened basement mere feet from Morrison's blood.

"Did you allow the police inside your home when they canvassed the neighborhood?" Zurbach was nodding, but Petrosky already knew the answer. He didn't recall Zurbach's name being on the list of those who refused the search, and it was unique enough it would have stood out. So the guy wasn't stockpiling weapons in his garage for Norton. He didn't have the girls at his house either. And if the girls weren't there, Norton wouldn't be there—he'd want to keep his victims close, maintain control. If Norton was living with a partner, if was someone who refused the search. Someone as fucked up as Norton.

"Tell me again about the man you saw walking," Petrosky said.

"I don't know what else to say!" Zurbach raised his hands in exasperation and Petrosky gripped the gun tighter until Zurbach lowered his palms to the table.

"He was coming from the direction of Pearlman?"

Slow nod.

"Past this house?"

"He was almost directly across the street from me when I saw him."

"Did he see you?"

Zurbach squinted at the ceiling and shook his head. "Nah, I don't think so."

If he'd been spotted peering out his window, Zurbach would be dead. If it even was Norton he'd seen. "And you didn't see where he went?"

"No, he was just walking. Though I can't imagine he'd have gone too many places. It was late, after all. Most of us around here get to bed early."

But not everyone—Zurbach had mentioned a party at Lockhart's, a party with young girls. Too young.

And Morrison had gone to Lockhart's the night he died.

What if Lockhart was the one who'd hinted at this place? Helped lure Morrison to the basement of an abandoned home? Norton could have ambushed Morrison and murdered him, then walked back to Lockhart's to get help loading Morrison into the car. But then ... where were the girls? Had Norton gotten rid of them already? When the crime techs got here would they find a myriad of blood types in that basement? Or did Norton have his own place around here with some kind of secret dungeon? Even a storage unit would work.

But maybe he was wrong altogether. Petrosky had zero evidence that Norton and Lockhart even knew one another.

And it was a stretch for Lockhart to go from misdemeanor indecent exposure to murder, especially since Lockhart was a nervous little bitch, getting his rocks off by shocking old ladies with his package. He wasn't psychotic. He hadn't even been convicted of touching anyone.

But if not Zurbach or Lockhart, then ... who? From the current sketches, Norton was more physically capable than he'd been years before. Stockier. But still, Morrison was a big guy—Norton would have needed help moving the body.

The body. Of his partner. His friend. Of his ... son. *Breathe, Petrosky. Think, you useless sack of shit.*

Petrosky's heart seized, and he tapped on the plastic embedded beneath his chest wound, as if that would help if he was really having a heart attack. *Not now. Another day or two.* He'd finish with Zurbach, chase down a few more leads, and find out where the hell Adam Norton was hiding. Then, with Norton's blood on his hands, he could finally eat that bullet.

46

THE SUN WAS low and orange in the bruised sky by the time Petrosky pulled in front of the precinct. The building itself stared down at him from rectangular window-eyes on the second floor, the entrance below snarling like the maw of a rabid dog. The stairs made him feel like he'd been punched in the lungs. And someone had taken his desk chair. He grabbed another seat from the desk behind him, plopped into it, and flicked the computer on.

Fatigue pulled at his eyelids—the adrenaline from his visit to Zurbach's had barely lasted the ride over. More coffee. He'd get more coffee, then—

The screen changed and he typed in his password.

Access Denied.

Fuck. He tried again.

Access Denied.

He typed each letter of his password independently, but he knew the outcome before he hit *Enter.* Carroll, or Internal Affairs, had surely told tech support to block him until he was approved to come back. He tried Morrison's username and password.

Access Denied.

Petrosky sat back in the chair and tapped the barrel of the gun in his pocket. The gun he probably shouldn't be carrying.

He got up and left the useless computer. Decantor was sitting at his desk taking notes off a computer screen that obviously fucking worked.

"Who's on Salomon?"

Decantor jerked his head around. "I heard you were on leave. Didn't you have a heart attack or some shit?"

"I am on leave, and no." Petrosky's legs were like weights. He grabbed a chair and sat. "Well, kinda."

Decantor scanned the room around them. "Me. I'm on Salomon."

Petrosky balled his fists. *Of course, of fucking course.* "Why'd Carroll put you on it? You were friends with Morrison too."

"I asked for it, okay?" He lowered his voice. "I already knew some of the background, and Carroll thought I could be impartial. She also said you were going to drop off the files to her." He squinted. "Is that why you're here? To drop those—"

"I've got you a lead." *Because this is my fucking case.* "Crime scene—Morrison's murder. Pike Street, left side, two off the corner. Got a Jack Russell in the house, unless it ran away again."

"A Jack—"

"There's a bag of cement by the basement stairs and a witness who says someone might have walked from that house down toward Lockhart's place the night Morrison died."

Decantor's jaw dropped. "Lockhart? Who the hell is Lockhart?"

"Do me a favor, rook, and figure out who was in that house."

"I'm not a rookie."

"Maybe get forensics over there to dust the rope screwed to the wall in the bedroom."

"Wait, a rope in the—"

"Write it down, Decantor."

Decantor flipped his notepad to a new page and scribbled away, and the act was so like Morrison's note-taking that Petrosky's gut roiled. "Who lives there now?" Decantor asked.

"No one. They moved out the day after Salomon's murder."

Decantor stopped writing and stared. "Address?"

"No number on the house, no mailbox. Look it up."

Decantor clicked open a new tab on the computer and searched for the street, then wrote the address down and pulled up another screen: mortgage records, water bills, electrical bills.

Petrosky leaned in. "Mary Grant. Foreclosure." The last known legal occupant was four years ago. No water or electricity in the past year. But ...

Decantor was clicking again, typed something. Someone named Henry Wilt had turned on the water last year, shut it off six months later. And Wilt hadn't needed a house deed to turn on the water; just an ID and some mail in his name.

They both sat back.

"I'll go talk to the neighbors ... again," Decantor said. "See who knows what. I'll look at Grant and Wilt too, but I doubt that'll lead us anywhere."

Petrosky nodded.

Decantor met his eyes. "I need the other files, Petrosky. Let me try to catch him."

Petrosky stared hard at Decantor's face, and the determination in the man's eyes was so genuine that he lost the urge to punch him. He sighed, but it came out more like a yawn. "I've got the main file in the car. I'll get it." Not like the folders were doing him a hell of a lot of good.

Petrosky hauled himself from the chair and lumbered through the bullpen toward the exit. Someone else's coffee cup was on top of Morrison's desk. His hands shook with rage all the way to the car.

The cold from the driver's seat leached into his aching bones as he leaned back against the headrest and closed his eyes. Maybe if he fell asleep out there, he'd just freeze to death. Slow and easy.

"Not now, old man."

Petrosky jolted upright, convinced Morrison was sitting

beside him, but he saw only the files, the mug, the emptiness. He shoved the key into the ignition. The engine sputtered and caught, and he shook a cigarette loose from the pack in the console, lit it, and inhaled deeply. He coughed just as deeply— from the bottom of his lungs—and rolled down the window to spit something frothy onto the cement.

Petrosky sucked on the cigarette again and squinted through the smoke at the file on the front seat. Before he handed them off … he might as well. He flipped through to the first day's interview notes. If whoever lived in that Jack Russell's house had been there the day of Salomon's murder, one of the officers would have spoken to them.

Not that he should care anymore, right? It wasn't his case. They'd replaced him, sure as shit. Just like they had replaced Morrison.

Petrosky stifled another cough and ran his thumb down the page.

An officer who wrote in tiny cursive like a princess had taken that side of Pike, starting at the corner. Each house was listed along the left side of the page, notes on the right. No one home on the day in question at either Gigi's place or the foreclosure next door.

Of course.

Zurbach's, though:

Resident reports no activity.

Petrosky sat back. That fucker had been awfully talkative this afternoon. Told him all about his dog's jitters the night Salomon died. Why wouldn't he have told Officer Prissy that morning? Or had they just not thought it important enough to note?

Petrosky fingered the rest of the page, stopping at the longer notes. Just a lot of the same: *Resident reports seeing no suspicious activity.* No one else had a dog that'd barked. That was unusual, right?

Petrosky looked back at Zurbach's address. A misunderstanding? Maybe. And even if Zurbach had said something about the party at Lockhart's, the beat cop's notes might not

303

reflect it—they were looking for information on a recent crime, a specific crime, not some long-ago party. And a dog barking without anything concrete from a witness might not have merited a mention either. But ...

Morrison would have noted it.

Petrosky touched the stainless steel mug in his cupholder. Morrison's mug. He needed to get it to forensics, he needed to leave it alone—he was contaminating evidence but he couldn't seem to make himself care. Morrison'd had this when he died. He'd held it. His blood was all over it. Only—

Why would Morrison's blood be all over it?

Petrosky turned on the overhead light and examined the side of the mug. Morrison would have dropped it with the first slash of the weapon—he'd had defensive wounds all over his forearms, and it wasn't like he would've kept holding the cup once Norton started hacking him to pieces. He would have dropped it before it could get bloody.

Petrosky touched his finger to one long stripe of gore, the dried blood smudged all along the side. And the lid ... covered in crimson turned brown. Had the killer touched it? But why run a hand over the side of the cup and then grip the top like you were...

Opening it.

Petrosky unscrewed the lid and peered inside.

Paper.

He reached in with two fingers and carefully pulled out a crumpled sheet of notebook paper. The size of a small apple, blood on the outside, white paper peeking through—like a blotchy red baseball.

He put the mug back in the console and pressed a hand against his throbbing shoulder. *Fuck. Breathe.*

He still had his cigarette in his mouth, the tainted air climbing into his nostrils. Petrosky ripped it from between his lips and shoved it into the ashtray. He tried to peel apart the ball of paper but the corners stuck together. Blood. Maybe coffee. He turned it, looking for another corner, then used a fingernail to peel that part back from the rest. Slowly, slowly, with a sound like the whisper of an uneasy spirit, the sheet came apart. He flattened it against the steering wheel, his heart shuddering in the rapid way of a twitchy coke addict, every pulse sharp and hot and excruciating.

Three stacked sheets crumpled together, covered in Morrison's tiny, even, print. He squinted at the writing on the most recent page—the one Morrison had left on top.

11/12 6:45pm: Block casing complete. Three teenagers, African American, approx. 17-19 y/o, approached, all noted no suspicious activity in area.

11/13 2:20pm: Block casing: Hanover, getting mail—assisted back into home. Notes no suspicious activity, notes nephew will be home tonight. To follow up.

Block casing. Looked like Morrison had been circling the block every day, well before Petrosky had mentioned they should. The kid had always been one step ahead. He felt a fatherly pride in that, but it was extinguished by a new certainty: Petrosky had been a weight tied to the boy's ankle, pulling him down, hindering his career. And of course, another partner would have helped more, would have at least asked the kid about the lead that had ultimately killed him.

11/13 4:20pm: Decantor indicates Alicia Hart may know Walsh. Address in file. To follow up.

11/13 5:50pm: Jewelry stores: dead end. Untraceable. (Specifics in file.)

11/13 6:30pm: Alicia Hart not at residence. To follow up tomorrow.

11/13 7:45pm: Block casing: Caucasian male, approx. 65, walking Labrador, identified as Wendell Zurbach. Indicates suspicious activity at home on corner, party one year prior. Poss. trafficking/prostitution of underage females.

11/13 8:22pm Sex offender database identified owner of home at 584 Pike Street as Mitch Lockhart.

11/13 8:50pm: Mitch Lockhart interviewed, allowed search of premises, nothing suspicious. To look into underage party: Lockhart denies wrongdoing, to follow up with others present in the a.m.

11/13 10:30pm:

No more words, just a spattering of blood covering the bottom of the pages ...

Not spattered.

Letters. Notations.

In blood.

While Norton went to grab the knife to slit Morrison's throat, the kid had left a final message for Petrosky. *G*, something that looked like an *O* and ... part of a pound sign? Or what had Morrison called it? *Hashtag.* But it was missing the top horizontal line, so it almost looked like a square without its top. Even ... the number four maybe? The right vertical line of the symbol continued downward, ending in an arrow that pointed to the bottom of the page.

There were other bloody marks on the sheet, but they might have been haphazard blotches. Or maybe not. Two marks that looked like bloody thumbprints marred Zurbach and Lockhart's names, but not enough that they were illegible. Highlighting them or crossing them out? Another thick, brown streak smudged Morrison's note about the resident getting the mail and had dripped into the crease of the page. That one was probably an accident.

He flipped the paper over, hoping the arrow might point him somewhere, but the back of that sheet was blank. The other pages had no marks either, no streaks in blood or otherwise—just the occasional stippling of gore. Bile rose in his throat and he swallowed it back down.

Had Morrison tried to highlight those names? And what was with the *G*? Not Gigi—that damn dog sure as hell hadn't come at

Morrison wielding a machete. Mary Grant, the last known resident at Gigi's place? That wasn't right either. She'd been gone four years, and he wasn't looking for a woman, not this time. Maybe a working girl or another abductee ... but none of the girls he'd spoken to had seen Morrison. And if Morrison had found out about another girl, he'd have noted that for follow up along with his source.

In fact ... Morrison hadn't found any of the girls he'd gone looking for from Decantor's lead—that wasn't what brought him to Norton. Petrosky stared at the page. Morrison had been casing the neighborhood, and he'd run smack into their killer.

Petrosky jumped at a sharp knock on the driver's door, and his knee hit the ashtray, spilling cigarette butts over the console. He made no move to brush the soot away as Decantor poked his head inside the open window—worst goddamn timing. He opened his mouth to tell Decantor to fuck off, but his breath was gone.

"Carroll called to see if you gave me the files yet. I swear that woman has eyes everywhere."

Then he registered what Petrosky was holding. His jaw dropped. "Is that ... what is that?"

Petrosky watched him without seeing, his mind still on the page. He dropped his gaze back to the sheet. *G ... G ... What the fuck is G?* The arrow down ... the basement? Morrison had died in the basement, but that couldn't be what he was referring to. Whoever found his coffee mug would surely know where they'd picked it up.

The hashtag was a reference to their killer—had to be. And that arrow ... the girls would be in a basement too. Lots of privacy. And no one to hear them scream. But whose basement?

Decantor was talking to him, a thin drone outside the window. Petrosky reached out to roll the window up, but his arm was heavy, weighted by some unseen force. Everything was so damn heavy.

The hashtag. The arrow. The ... G.

The G.

Who else had he talked to in the neighborhood? Surely there were many with G as an initial, but only one mentioned in this section of Morrison's notes: The woman who'd tried to pick him up. *Gertrude.* That old lady? Petrosky reread the page: *Block casing: Hanover, getting mail—assisted back into home. Notes no suspicious activity, notes nephew will be home tonight. To follow up.*

Gertrude Hanover. *Is the hashtag an H?* Her nephew Richard lived in Maine—he wouldn't have been home that night for Morrison to follow up with. Was she demented, then? And if so... Norton could be living there with her. Couldn't he? If he were, would she even fucking know?

"Petrosky!"

Petrosky pictured the base of Hanover's house, the bricks against the earth, damp from snow—or so he'd assumed. But was it wet all the way around, or just in one spot? Maybe the damp bricks he'd seen had been wet because they'd been repaired after someone dug through the mortar with a spoon and their fingernails and pulled themselves through it prison-break style. Maybe instead of just damp from the snow, the mortar there was frozen and uncured. Because someone had reduced the previous mortar work to Portland cement dust.

Fucking idiot. The brickwork was not unlike the other houses in the neighborhood, but ... he should have seen it. Should have picked up on it. He should have knocked on every fucking door, forced his way inside, Chief Carroll be damned.

"Goddammit, Petrosky, for fuck's sake!"

Maybe Lockhart had nothing to do with this after all; Norton could have been walking to Gertrude's just as easily. Except ... Morrison had been inside that house ... she'd tried to serve him fucking cookies. Had the kid missed something?

"Petrosky!" Decantor reached through the window for the pages on the steering wheel. Petrosky put a fist on Decantor's chest and shoved, but it wasn't hard enough to knock Decantor from the car; the man's fingers still gripped the base of the window.

"Back the fuck off, Decantor."

"Petrosky we need to—"

He was after the cup. The pages. Petrosky shoved him again.

Decantor reeled back, one hand clinging to the bottom of the window to hold himself upright. "You crazy son of a bitch!"

Petrosky threw the car in gear, hoping he wouldn't run over Decantor's fucking leg but no longer caring if he did. That cunt would make him get a warrant. They'd have to follow procedure. And if he went in with a posse ... he'd never manage to kill Norton. *Not happening.* He was going to bleed out on that asshole's floor while he watched Norton die. Worst-case scenario, he'd have to put the gun to his own head, but at least he'd go out with a fucking smile.

Petrosky peeled out of the lot, chest screaming at him to calm down, to give himself time to process the adrenaline coursing through his veins, but there was nothing left now—nothing but the stinging of his throbbing heart and the empty ache where his family had been. Julie. Morrison. His wife. Even Shannon and the kids—better off without him.

Crazy son of a bitch. He'd show Decantor fucking crazy.

47

PETROSKY TOOK his last shot of Jack and texted Shannon from Salomon's driveway:

"Gertrude Hanover."

Shannon wouldn't know what it meant until later. If he died without killing this bastard, she'd ask Decantor about the text. And then Decantor could go in, guns blazing, warrant in hand.

But tonight, it was just Petrosky against a killer who'd destroyed everyone he loved. Who'd changed Shannon. Who'd murdered Morrison, taken him away from his children. Who'd caused the death of so many little girls. Far too many girls like Julie. And the atrocities he'd committed, Lisa Walsh, Ms. Salomon, Stella …

Norton deserved to die.

Maybe they both did. And god help him, both of them would die tonight.

Petrosky got out of the car and walked up Salomon's drive and past the garage where he could see the backs of the homes on Beech. The cement pavers covering Salomon's backyard seemed to shrink from him, as if chagrined; if the yard had been grass, there would have been no way to hide the evidence that Lisa Walsh had tramped through it on her battered half-feet. But

Norton had cleaned up here, obscuring the girl's path toward the house the night Salomon died—if he'd even had to with the sleet. Nature had worked in his favor that night. Sometimes the world was on the side of the beasts.

Petrosky paused, listening for the crunch of feet on ice. No lights from the back of Gertrude Hanover's place, just the murky gray of night over crusted snow. Frigid air scratched at his cheeks. He strode through the backyards and approached Hanover's from behind, stopping every few feet to listen to the night. The moon glowed above, full and ringed with a halo that seemed to stretch and reach for him as if whispering goodbye through tendrils of mist. And suddenly the whispering wind felt sweeter than it had in a long time, filling him with the quiet heaviness of a peaceful and well-deserved rest. It was a good night to die.

Gertrude Hanover's home glimmered like an apparition, the back door black and hollow against the white aluminum siding. Dizziness washed over him as he skirted the side of the house— the side he'd noticed from the front the other day, with the damp bricks. The deck box. His guy might be smart enough to use bricks that looked like the house, but he'd still hide his hand- iwork, especially while the repair job was wet.

The crackle of salt on cement growled at him as he shoved the box a few inches from the wall. He stooped beside the bricks and put a finger against the mortar: half frozen, but still moist— the hard damp of cement not yet fully cured. Muggy air would have delayed the process. The wet snow piling on the outside of the seal had probably slowed it further.

He wanted to sit. To rest. Instead he hauled himself up and crept to the front of the house, peering through the window beside the front door.

There was only darkness.

He knocked, his body pressed against the doorjamb in case Norton decided to use Morrison's revolver to cap him—that fucking coward wouldn't want to meet Petrosky face-to-face. But there wasn't a sound aside from the wind's icy breath and the violent vibrations of his chest that rattled his eardrums like thunder. He put his ear closer to the doorframe—still nothing.

Gertrude wasn't gallivanting about in the dark. Was she asleep?

Or already dead?

Petrosky pulled his Swiss army knife from his pocket, slid the blade beside the jamb and jimmied it open. He paused with his hand on the knob. Would Norton have set up an alarm? He examined the top of the frame, but saw nothing—not that you'd see alarm wires from this side. Then again, if you had a girl who might accidentally escape …

He pictured Shannon's sewn lips. Flashed back to the ligature marks on Walsh's wrists. And the coroner's report—impaled on a stake, suffering for hours, days …

No, this guy had better ways of subduing people. And there was no way in hell Norton would have an alarm that would alert outsiders to the house … though there might be something to alert Norton himself to Petrosky's presence.

He cracked the door and waited. Nothing. He slipped inside and closed it behind him, listening hard for the padded footsteps of a dog, the shuffle of Gertrude's stockinged feet, the steady breath of a killer.

Silence.

Linoleum slid under Petrosky's boots, leaving a trail of watered-down mud as he slunk through the front room. The lamplight outside illuminated a single couch in the middle, and the lace-covered antique table he had seen through the window on his first visit. In the far corner of the house, a hallway led toward the back, steeped in inky blackness.

He hit the hallway quickly, crouching as low as his knees could manage, his heart hammering with the echo of each foot-fall. Perhaps they were both asleep in the bedrooms—Norton had to rest sometime. Or maybe he'd find Norton standing over Gertrude's limp body, savage weapon in hand, sheets soaked in the old woman's blood.

The dark of the hall was more solid than that of the living room, and every padded footstep seemed louder for it as the light disappeared. Taking out the phone would be conspicuous; if Norton awoke and saw light under his doorway, he wouldn't believe Gertrude was using a flashlight to navigate her own home. But he might believe Petrosky's footsteps to be Gertrude's —unless she was already dead. Petrosky held out a hand and felt his way along the wall, three steps, four, conscious of every breath, listening for breath from anyone else. He heard only the wind against the panes of frosty glass.

His fingers found a door casing and he reached for the knob. It turned easily and silently and he pushed it inward, letting the light from the streetlamp drizzle onto his shoes, straining his ears with each incremental movement. Petrosky wasn't sure he wanted to see what was in the room. He definitely didn't want whatever was in the room to see him.

But no one was there—just a twin bed, made up in what looked like black sheets, though the color was hard to determine in the dim light. On the far wall hung a chin-up bar. Three sets of dumbbells beneath it. In the corner sat a weight bench and a barbell holding what had to be hundreds of pounds. Maybe Norton *was* strong enough to have moved Morrison by himself. *My boy.* His breath caught. The guy could be the fucking Hulk and he was still going down.

Nothing else in the room, not even an end table. He crossed to the closet and pulled open the door, bracing himself for the body of Gertrude Hanover to slump from behind it, throat slashed, eyes milky. The closet was empty too—not one shirt. Not one pair of boots.

Norton wasn't living in this room. So where was he hiding?

He's keeping an eye on his victims.

Petrosky turned from the closet, ears prickling at the sound of a car door outside, but when he peered from the window there was no vehicle in the drive out front.

He closed the closet, then the door to the room, blinking in the shadowed hallway once the glow from the room had faded to black. But that passing moment of light had been enough to see the rest of the hallway: two other doors across from one another, both half a dozen steps up the hall.

He stepped toward the door on the opposite side of the hall, hand along the wall until he got to the doorframe. This door was wide open: a bathroom. Sink, toilet, shower. Empty. Across the hall, the thin sliver of light from the opposite door beckoned—

not the yellow of the streetlamp, or the rose glow of Julie's night-light, but the dull red of a flashlight coated in blood; dangerous, harsh. He no longer felt the gentle blush of moon-light lulling him to a peaceful death—this was a bad omen. Not that he believed in omens.

The air inside the room was stale, ripe with something that might have been urine. On the bed … Gertrude, her face painted in crimson like a bloody bridal veil. No … not blood—only shadows from the red night-light.

But she was still.

He approached the bed, his steps indiscernible beneath the rapid pulse of blood in his ears as he bent closer to her. Comforter to her chin. No slash marks on her face or injuries that he could see, her face calm and even and—

He leapt backwards as she grunted, snorted once, and rolled away from him. The ear he could see was empty of the hearing aid she'd worn the day they'd met.

No wonder she hadn't heard him at the front door.

Her breath went silent again, but one fist clutched the blanket to her and then stilled. Alive. And if she was alive, either he was wrong about this being the place, or Norton didn't know Petrosky was on to him yet. Did Norton think he'd gotten away with killing Morrison? Or had he hightailed it to another state?

No … this cocky bastard hadn't gone anywhere—even if he thought they were closing in, Norton didn't have the balls to change pattern, let alone change cities. Worst case, he'd chosen another house nearby. And if he had, Petrosky would find him.

Petrosky hurried back the way he'd come, on high alert for movement around him. Hallway, living room, back into the kitchen. Where was the basement door? It wasn't down the hallway with the bedrooms. Petrosky put his hand on the kitchen wall, peering into the gloom, listening intently for Norton's breath or the thunk of a footstep. Nothing. If Norton was in the basement with his victims, he might not have heard Petrosky through the cement—and probably soundproof—walls.

But it was too late for discretion. Even now Decantor was probably out looking for Petrosky's car, and if he'd called Shannon they'd be on their way here. And Norton had to have a way to watch what was happening on the main floor—he wouldn't leave himself vulnerable to ambush. *Fuck it.* Petrosky flicked on the kitchen light and blinked as his eyes adjusted. At least he'd see the fucker coming.

It was an ordinary kitchen: a stove, refrigerator, white cabinets. Small dinette set on one side. A floor-to-ceiling bookcase stood along the back wall, set with a dozen or so cookbooks, some kind of bowl that looked older than its owner, and several framed photos.

Petrosky walked around the table. The pictures were of Richard—the real Richard—and some other men and women he didn't recognize. A few kids. All with Gertrude front and center. Ordinary family photos.

Had Morrison been wrong? Or had Petrosky misinterpreted the note?

Maybe Norton had a hole dug in the yard somewhere—a bomb shelter or storm cellar. Except there was wet cement on the side of the house, and loosening the old mortar explained the dust on the victims' bodies. Norton had bricked in a window, hadn't he? Even bat-shit-crazy old Gertrude had mentioned his handiwork.

Used to come help me around the house—building things so I wouldn't fall down the stairs ...

But there was no upstairs. From the first floor, the steps could only go down.

The girls were here. Somewhere. Not behind the stove, not hiding behind any of these walls with windows, not beside the back door. Not in the hallway, though there might be a piece of drywall that could be removed. A hidden door ...

He eyed the bookcase. *Has to be.* He put his hands on either side of the shelving and pulled. The stitches in his chest strained painfully, but there was no give in the wooden structure. He tried to slide it to the side, wheezing with exertion, toppling a framed shot of Gertrude and a chubby baby which smashed against the tile. No give on the sides of the case.

That wasn't normal—no standard bookcase was made to withstand being moved, and this one shouldn't even be heavy— it didn't have that many books on it.

He yanked at the cookbooks, the wound on his chest burning, but he ignored the pain. One cookbook, two, three, thunked to the floor, and Petrosky moved faster, hoping against hope that he could find the girls and get them out before the man came home. If Norton was here, listening from below, he'd surely have acted by now, right? Another photo fell and bounced on its wooden frame. And then—

One book in the upper right hand corner, higher than Gertrude would have been able to reach. It didn't slide out of the case … just shifted forward. A click reverberated through the room and Petrosky again put his hands on either side of the case and pulled. One side swung toward him. And behind it—the door, padlocked, a wide metal bar drilled into the casing across the center of the door, secured on the right side of the jamb with a large metal lock. He needed a key to get in, and if he knew this guy, it wasn't going to be an easy pick job. All he had was his Swiss army knife. At least the door handle itself seemed to be free of additional locking mechanisms.

But you know how it is, people get busy with their lives, and the military—well, let's just say he got very private …

Private is right. Anyone would be fucking private if they had captives hidden in the basement like animals.

Petrosky pulled his knife from his pocket, his heart racing far faster than that fucking pacemaker should have let it, and slid the blade under the metal bar. The knife flexed. The bar stayed, hard and rigid.

Petrosky knocked on the jamb. Instead of the echoed thump of a standard wooden frame, this one had the slight ting of metal behind drywall. The fucker had reinforced the frame to make sure no one could break it down. He knocked on the wall next to it—*solid*—then moved over a few inches, knocking until he heard the hollow thunk of open wall. But that would put him nowhere near the stairs, and though adrenaline sang through his veins, emboldening him, the idea of trying to break the wall apart using sheer force was laughable. He'd barely managed to move the bookcase.

Back to the bar. It was a long, horizontal panel of metal, anchored on either side with metal screws—all fastened directly to the jamb, six in each side, twelve in all. He inserted his Swiss army knife into one and turned. The screw held, then gave. *Really?* Norton had based the security of his secret dungeon on the ability of a cop to use a goddamn screwdriver?

Then again, Norton had been trying to keep people *in*. Once the cops found the door, it was already over. Or Norton simply wasn't worried—no one would just wander down there with the door hidden behind the bookcase, and the woman who lived here was unable to tackle stairs at all. *Smug motherfucker.* But Norton hadn't been smart enough.

Petrosky turned the screw as fast as he could. It dropped to his feet with the muted ting of metal on linoleum, but it might have been a gunshot for the way the sound vibrated through his body. He moved on to the next screw. The angle of his shoulders pulled at the stitches in his chest, and the familiar pain came every time he moved, sharp and hot. His chest expanded and squeezed. Another screw dropped. His shoulder was on fire. Julie swam in his vision, her eyes wide and sad: *Why couldn't you help me, Daddy?* Then Morrison was whispering in his ear: *You want me to call someone, Boss? You sure we should be doing this?*

The last screw dropped. He pulled on the metal panel, his arms, his chest, his eyes, everything in agony as he yanked at the bar, heaving, and then ...

It was free. He dropped the bar behind him with a clang sure to wake the dead, blinked sweat from his eyes, and grabbed the door handle. He steeled himself. Then pulled.

There was a whoosh of air and the kind of popping, suction noise you get from opening a sealed jar—the interior of the door was thick with insulating foam. But a sound rose from below: banging, maybe, though weak and rhythmic like someone smacking the floor with a leather belt. Was Norton beating someone? The sound didn't stop. Petrosky pulled out his gun.

48

_____

His legs were unsteady on the steep stairs, made narrower by the dense padding covering the walls on all sides. At the bottom, even the floors were layered with sound-suppressing material—in the light from the doorway above, he could see foam underneath what looked like cork. He stepped down onto the last stair, peering around for ...

The switch on the side wall. He flicked it on.

The light was dim, just barely casting the far wall in a sickly yellow. The room in front of him was a small rectangle, surrounded by reinforced cement walls, probably stuffed with more insulating foam. On the wall beside the switch, one tiny, marble-sized circle reflected the light: a camera. And it smelled like shit. Literal shit.

The banging was louder here, coming from somewhere behind him and to his right—behind the stairs. Petrosky swiveled right, one hand still on the railing, one on his gun.

Oh, fuck.

His vision zeroed in on the girl and all noise stopped. Ten feet from the base of the stairs, Ava Fenderson sat against the wall, staring at him, eyes wide, arms secured to a wooden beam behind her by nails driven through her wrists. Her red hair fanned around her like a firework, half covering a silver heart necklace and trailing toward her bare nipples. Toes gone, just like Walsh's, the nubs of those digits mutilated—disturbing, but healed. A jagged *#1* carved on her belly. And … blood. So much blood. Trickling from her wrists, pouring down the center of her chest in a garish stripe of crimson—bleeding to death through her throat? Had he cut her neck and just left her to die?

Petrosky could get her out the way he'd come—he'd haul her up the stairs … but he had barely loosened the screws without his chest tearing open. He might not be able to get her to safety before Norton returned. But he could try. Where *was* Norton? His gaze darted to the far wall in front of the stairs where the glass block windows had been replaced by jagged mortar, cement blocks, and insulating foam. Blocking light. Blocking hope. Blocking escape.

"Ava," Petrosky whispered, and his voice seemed to be sucked into the walls, away from his ears, disappearing into the foam and cork. "It's going to be okay, honey." He pocketed the gun and rushed toward her, knelt down and—

Her eyes stayed glassy, staring straight ahead at the bottom of the stairs. She hadn't been looking at him. Her head was propped up with some kind of … metal bar?

Petrosky put a finger under her chin—*god, she's cold*—and lifted her face. Her chin stuck a moment, then rose with a wet whisper like a snake through grass, two prongs emerging from *inside her chin*, sharp and horrid and sticky with her blood. *Oh, fuck.* Dead. She was dead. Norton had stabbed her with a serving fork. *That sadistic piece of …* But no, the other end of the fork was not blunt like silverware, simply resting on her breastbone— there were more punctures under her clavicle, two of them, hidden beneath the skin of her chest. And now he could see the collar it was attached to, wrapped around her throat, securing the murderous weapon in place. Holding it in place so as soon as she had fallen asleep, as soon as she had lowered her head … the points had sunk into the flesh of her throat and down into her chest. Killing her.

Now he knew the source of that horrid scent—she'd died sitting in her own excrement.

The hairs on the back of his neck prickled, hot and painful as the wound over his heart. He leapt up, his vision opening, realizing he hadn't even finished looking around, hadn't even bothered to look once he'd seen Ava. Hadn't examined the darkness behind the stairs. But he was looking now.

Something ... some*one. I'm not alone here.*

Norton was there, lurking, waiting in the dark. Petrosky strained his eyes, peering into the thick gloom behind the stairs, expecting Norton to emerge at any moment, billhook held high and ready to smash through his skull. The hammering of Petrosky's heart was fast, horrid, panicked—the soundtrack of hell.

Thunk, thunk, thunk.

His heart. But it wasn't his heart.

The sound came from the corner, called to him with the steady beat of a bass drum—an otherworldly madness. He took one step. Squinted into the blackness at the side of the stairs where no light penetrated. It couldn't be Norton, lying in wait, tapping the base of his weapon on the ground. That cowardly bastard would have slashed Petrosky apart while he was tending to Ava Fenderson.

Thunk, thunk, thunk.

Petrosky crept closer. He didn't want to see, but he pulled out his cell. Clicked the flashlight.

His heart stopped, but the steady drumming did not. Behind the stairwell, lashed to a wooden pole, slumped another girl, banging her head against the beam she was shackled to. The pole... topped with a spike. Stained black with gore.

And the girl ...

"Margot?"

Margot Nace's skin was marred with what might have been dirt or blood or even food—but she had the same hair as her mother, orange and circus clown-y where it wasn't matted down with blood. She was wearing some kind of a ... princess dress. Long, flowing skirt, the bodice embellished with beads, bosom forced upwards like in some horrible Harlequin romance novel. And a *#1* scored into her chest to the right of a silver heart pendant that dangled near her clavicle. Black wires rose behind her like prison bars, though the shadows were too thick to see into the depths of the cell. But he could see the glint of blades hanging in a row on the back wall, and a wooden pole with a wicked looking metal axe on one side, a sharpened, jagged hook opposite. The weapon used to hack apart Salomon. And his partner. The knife used to slit Morrison's throat was surely back there too.

Norton had built himself a medieval dungeon, complete with instruments of torture. He'd even dressed the girl like a medieval princess—royalty doomed to die.

"Margot," he whispered.

Thunk, thunk, thunk went her head on the pole.

Petrosky knelt. He grabbed her face, trying to prevent her from injuring herself further.

Her neck twitched, straining weakly toward the stake.

And above them ... footsteps. *Fuck.*

Margot went completely still. Then she screamed, suddenly, the sound echoing through Petrosky's brain so that he couldn't hear anything else, no footsteps, no heartbeats, no head-splitting thunks. Just as suddenly, she quieted, and metal on metal rang out as her cuffs clanked together, then a dull sound—metal on wood. She strained against the pole. Her feet, still hidden in the folds of the gown, kicked at the earth as she tried to move backward, forward, anywhere but where she was. Then she was screaming again.

Petrosky shoved the phone with the flashlight into his pocket, plunging them into darkness, then swung behind her and began pulling at the cuffs by feel. But they were shackles, made of metal, and the spike was nearly to the ceiling—Norton must have shoved Lisa Walsh down onto it before righting it, stabbing the stake through her innards. Petrosky grabbed Margot under her arms and she flailed, kicked at him, tried to bite him, but he hefted her higher, trying to get her cuffed wrists over the top of the spike. The stitches in his chest went tight, and something popped. He couldn't breathe. His shoulder, his chest, his lungs, everything burned and then—

He staggered back, the girl in his arms hitting the ground beside him, and she scrambled into the corner, free.

He was dying. The pain in his chest radiated through his arms, into his head, and around his neck, pulsing white and electric. He half lurched, half stumbled after the girl toward the back wall, choking and gasping.

Then the basement door closed above them, taking with it the light from the kitchen. The room faded to a dusky landscape, everything fuzzy and alien and awful.

Margot's screams had diminished to a heavy panting where each exhale was a whimper. Footsteps sounded on the stairs. She froze and the whisper of her breath ceased.

Petrosky's chest heaved, spasmed, stilled. How was he going to get Margot out of there? *Looks like you need backup, Boss.* He should have let Decantor come with him. He was a fucking idiot.

"Good evening, Detective." Norton's growly rasp was just as he remembered it, the timber of a monster.

From his position on the back wall beside the staircase, Petrosky could see only the backside of the steps, and the insulation was too thick to reach an arm through the treads, grab Norton's feet, and knock him off-balance.

Margot screamed again.

Hush, goddammit. Petrosky put his hand on her head, trying to get her to lie low to the ground or at least shut the fuck up, but she jerked from him, still screaming. The shoes on the stairs paused. Petrosky pulled his gun. If he missed Norton, he might catch Margot with the ricochet. He needed one good shot before this fucker attacked and took him out.

He crept away from Margot, away from the makeshift jail and closer to the stairs, keeping deep in the shadows. If Norton couldn't see Petrosky, he couldn't slice him up before Petrosky got a shot off. And one bullet was all it took.

Petrosky stepped toward the triangular space under the stairs and slammed his knee into something hard and metal with a sickening crack. He gritted his teeth against the pain and reached down.

Wires, cold and hard, like thin bars. A crate? Or maybe ... *Oh shit.* During Shannon's kidnapping, Norton had kept Evie in a dog cage. Petrosky squatted, peering against the dusk, but he couldn't see inside. But there was a noise, barely audible over Margot's screaming: the squall of an infant. Small. Weak.

No, no, no. Fuck.

Margot stopped screaming. Another step sounded on the stairs. Then a shot, like a crack of thunder.

The bullet ricocheted off the back wall and whizzed by Petrosky's head. He threw himself to the floor in front of the cage, heart hammering more painfully with each beat. Another shot hit the wooden pole with a thwack of splintering wood. Norton's hand was visible now, snaking around the side of the staircase like a ghostly appendage, yellow and hazy in the sallow light. Norton was aiming blindly—he didn't care what he hit. He'd keep shooting until he got lucky.

Norton was expecting Petrosky to have a gun too—expecting him to hide. He wouldn't anticipate Petrosky running toward the bullet.

Petrosky shoved his gun in his pocket and lunged for Norton, ducking under the weapon, and yanking Norton's arm so hard he thought his own wrist might snap. Norton stumbled against the railing, the sound of his body falling down the stairs the most beautiful music Petrosky had ever heard.

Margot shrieked, and when Norton jerked his face toward the sound, Petrosky swung out of the darkness and around the corner of the stairs.

From the floor, Norton raised his gun in slow motion, his blond hair eerily white in the lamplight, the hives standing out at his temples even in the yellow gloom.

Petrosky felt the burn on the right side of his chest before he registered the explosion of gunpowder. He'd been shot. He threw his full body weight onto his knees and landed on Norton's chest. Norton gasped, and the gun tumbled from his hand.

And then Petrosky felt it, a flash like something inside his shoulder had burst, and his air disappeared with the sharp agony of the bullet and what might have been splintered bone. But the gun—Norton's gun was still on the ground near his leg.

Petrosky extended his foot to kick it away and the metal skittered over the floor, the soundproofing turning the noise into the dull, muted smack of a baseball bat on flesh. The yellow light blinked out, then returned. Petrosky's shirt was wet with blood.

Norton shoved upwards. Jesus Christ, he was built like a

WWF wrestler, every muscle rigid under Petrosky's fists as they struggled. Another shove and Petrosky fell against the stairs, the treads digging hard into his spine. His arm was on fire. He clawed at his pocket, grabbing for his gun, just as Norton leapt on top of him and smashed a fist into his eye. Stars blasted through his vision. Petrosky tried again for the weapon but it was pinned under Norton's knee. *Fuck, fuck, fuck.*

A blow landed against his jaw. Petrosky gagged on what could only be a tooth. He jerked his hand from his pocket and grabbed Norton's balls as Norton kneed him in the chest. Pain exploded across his ribs and down his arm, the stitches in his chest torn and aching. He couldn't breathe. Black tugged at the corners of his vision and then he heard Morrison's voice whispering, "It's okay, Boss. It'll be okay. I'm here. Julie's here." Petrosky fought the black. Above him Norton smiled.

Not yet, motherfucker.

With renewed strength, he threw his fists into Norton's jaw and tried to roll off the stairs, but Norton was on him again, kicking, spitting, gnashing his teeth, the two men a tangle of limbs and pain and blood until Petrosky wasn't sure where he ended and Norton began. Then Norton was in his face and back out again, rearing up, gaze darting from the stairs to the floor to Petrosky's pockets. *He's looking for the gun.*

Petrosky jerked at his arms, but they were pinned beneath Norton's knees though he couldn't recall when that had happened. He tried twisting his body—he was stuck. Norton's weight was too much. Then Norton was wrapping his hands around Petrosky's throat, cutting off what little air supply was left, the room wavering, shuddering, darkening.

I'm sorry, Julie. Dizziness wound around him like a blanket—warmer than he'd expected ... cozy. He stared at Norton's face. *This is it.* This was what Morrison had seen. This was the last thing his boy had seen as he bled to death.

I'm coming for you, son.

Norton looked down at him and laughed. Then his head exploded in a shower of bone, brain, and plasma, warm wet pieces splattering against the wall, the stairs, and Petrosky's face. But Petrosky couldn't close his eyes, didn't dare, not even when the mist of brain matter settled over his forehead and made his vision go red.

Norton toppled to the right, his arm twitching. Petrosky sucked hungrily at the air, the gore cloying in the back of his throat, and heaved himself out from under Norton's limp body. He scrambled for the solid floor of the basement, pressing his hand against the bullet hole in his shoulder as he peered into the gloom. With slippery fingers—Norton's blood, or his?—he pulled out his phone and engaged the flashlight app. *You just press this button, Boss.*

Margot blinked in the sudden brightness, the gun still gripped tightly in her hands. She was pointing it at Petrosky's head, the weapon vulgar against her princess ball gown.

"Margot … I …" Petrosky rasped air into his lungs. "The gun."

She looked down at it, brows furrowed, then let it drop to the floor.

"Did you find … ?" Her voice was faint, like the whisper of ghostly breath on the back of your neck. She stepped forward into the garish beam from his phone.

Petrosky pressed his hand hard against his wound, gasping as bright, white agony smashed through his brain. "Who?" He was panting now.

But she said nothing else, just stared at Norton's corpse.

His phone clattered to the floor near his hip. The pain in his shoulder was growing, the stain on his shirt spreading, thick and heavy, across his chest. He was going to die down here. He was going to get exactly what he wanted. In spite of the pain, his breath slowed.

Margot gazed at her still-cuffed wrists as if she had no idea who they belonged to. Then she moved, so fast that Petrosky scuttled back, one arm over his bleeding chest, but she continued past him, over the bottom step, toward Norton's body. For a few moments she stared down at what was left of Norton—his head half gone, his palms to the ceiling as if waiting for someone to give him a hand up. Then she brought her heel down on Norton's testicles, grunting with the force of it, her dress undulating around her as if she were dancing. And again.

Petrosky heaved himself to the wall beside the stairs—five

feet but it felt like miles—and propped his good shoulder against it. He kept his gaze on Margot's dress, billowing each time she kicked, and avoided looking at Ava's corpse. Another girl he'd failed. At least he wouldn't have to notify her parents.

Margot paused in her assault and looked back at him, perhaps waiting for him to tell her to stop.

"Go ahead, we've got time." He had all the time in the world. He let his head fall back against the wall, trying to focus through the bleary dark that was muddying the edges of his vision, while Margot mangled the balls of a man who deserved far worse. "Can you find your way out?" Petrosky asked her.

Margot froze. Met his gaze. Then she ran to him, stumbling, lurching into his lap, grabbing at his pants, fumbling at his shirt like she wasn't sure how to tell him to help her.

Petrosky sighed, blinking hard, the world wavering. He wrapped his good arm around her, and reached his feet toward his cell.

EPILOGUE

"This is the last box." Shannon handed Petrosky the packing tape. "You want to do the honors?"

"Don't mind if I do." He pulled the tape across the cardboard flaps and set the roll on top.

Henry waddled over to the stack of boxes. "Ba!"

"That's right, Henry. Box." Petrosky ruffled his hair. "Are you ready for pizza?"

"Pit-sa!" Henry yelled.

"Pizza!" Evie ran into the bedroom, as if the mere mention of her favorite food had the uncanny ability to extend her hearing across the house.

Petrosky scooped her up with his good arm, and they all walked together to the kitchen. The counter was surprisingly bare without his old coffeepot, which was now at the bottom of the trash container around back. Out with the old, and all that.

The case had wrapped quickly. With Adam Norton dead and the hero cop wounded, the chief hadn't fired Petrosky—though from the look on her face these days, she'd be up his ass permanently. As she should be. He hadn't even killed Norton on his own.

Gertrude Hanover had been shocked when she woke to find her home swarming with cops and a chamber of horrors in her basement. But she'd recovered quickly, offered them Cocoa Puffs, and tried to sweet talk the EMS technician into her bed.

Hanover had refused to believe Norton wasn't her nephew. So far, she'd told them Richard had come by with dinner and had ended up moving in, that he'd met her on the lawn one day when she was getting the mail, and that she'd simply woken up one day and he was there. But no matter what story she told them, the underlying sentiments were the same: she was happy to have him. She hadn't wanted to be alone.

Petrosky had made a few calls to Norton's old employers. The *X-treme Clean* people he'd worked with two years back did have a record of servicing some private residences, and though Gertrude Hanover was not on that list, the woman vaguely recalled hiring them once. If Norton had been the guy who showed up, he'd probably realized she was ill. Taken his time, especially if she had compared him to Richard. Either way, eventually she'd truly believed the prodigal nephew had returned. The doctors who examined her said that her moments of lucidity were far enough apart that had she phoned the police, she might not have been able to remember what was bothering her by the time they picked up the call.

Gertrude's real nephew had informed them he hadn't seen her in years but that he called every Sunday to make sure she was okay. Gertrude had thanked him for his help a few times, but he'd assumed she meant the calls.

She'd meant his company. She was feisty enough—and healthy enough—to refuse all physical assistance. She'd done her own wash. Had groceries delivered. All Norton had to give her was five minutes of eating meals together every month and she'd given him the perfect hiding place. And by doting on him, telling him he deserved all the good in the world, making him pie for fuck's sake, she'd been giving Norton the reinforcement he so desperately craved, building his ego and feeding his delusions without her even knowing it.

Making him more confident. More deadly.

But McCallum had been right. Even without the complication of a partner, Norton had needed someone to bolster him. He'd been a coward right to the end.

Margot Nace had never met Casey Hearn—it was possible Norton hadn't had Casey at all. Just another mystery he'd never know the answer to, like exactly what had drawn Morrison back to Hanover's that night. As for the other necklaces, they might have gone to girls who were less receptive to Norton's advances. Lucky girls like Whitney who took off before he could abduct them.

Baby Stella was out of the hospital and had been placed with a nice family from Bloomfield Hills; a little hoity-toity maybe but they seemed like they'd care for the kid, maybe even adopt her. Not like it could get any worse than where she'd started. The infant in the cage belonged to Margot—just a few months old. Ms. Nace's jaw had dropped when she saw the child, but she picked the boy up and cradled him to her chest the moment they gave her the go-ahead. The last thing Petrosky heard as Ms. Nace led her daughter away was Margot saying, "I'm sorry. I'm so, so sorry."

Shannon filled cups at the kitchen sink and brought them to the table. "I think we drank the last soda."

Petrosky shrugged. "Eh, I hear that stuff's bad for me anyway."

Shannon beamed at him.

Henry banged his fists on the table. "Bad!"

Petrosky slid pizza onto their plates and passed one to Shannon. "That's right, Henry. Bad." He grabbed a plastic knife and cut Henry's pizza into little pieces.

Evie shoved her slice into her mouth, red sauce dribbling down her chin.

"Pit-sa!" Her brother yelled.

"Pizza's coming." Petrosky set the plate in front of Henry, who snatched a handful of cheese. "Tank oooo!"

"You are welcome, sir." Petrosky took a bite of his own pizza, the sauce bland, the crust like cardboard. He shoved another bite into his mouth.

"How are you feeling today?" Shannon asked him.

"You going to ask every single day?"

She smiled. "Yup."

"Figured." He sighed when her gaze did not waver. "Okay,

329

pretty good. The doc says my heart is looking better. I've lost a few pounds. Arm's sore, but ..." He shrugged his good shoulder. The other one would never heal right. A screw was holding it together, but he was more distressed about his tattoo—the bullet had destroyed the skin and reduced Julie's face to a corroded, amorphous shape from an abstract painting. Norton had tried to erase his daughter. But he had failed.

"What about the meetings and stuff?" Shannon was saying.

He hadn't been lately, but he didn't really need to. Or want to. "They're just window dressing," he said. "People who need to reaffirm things over and over. Misery loves company and all that bull"—he glanced at Henry—"stuff."

Evie turned to her mother and leaned close. "He means bullshit."

Shannon raised an eyebrow.

"Hey, I'm trying."

She shook her head. "You have any plans for decorating the new house?"

"I'm an old bachelor. No one who sees it will care, myself included." Petrosky grabbed another slice.

"Oh, come on. Let me help you. I haven't even seen your place yet."

"You've got better things to do," he said around a mouthful of pepperoni.

"Maybe." She smiled. "But Evie and Henry would love to come hang out with Papa Ed. Might as well make myself useful since fabulous home-cooked meals aren't in my repertoire." She gestured to the pizza.

"This is my kind of home-cooking anyway. You know that."

Shannon wiped her hands and grinned at him. "We'd better get going. I have to drop Evie and Henry off at Lillian's by six tomorrow morning. Early case before the judge."

Henry threw his empty plate at her and it hit her in the temple. Crumbs landed in her hair.

Petrosky laughed. "Nice shot, young man. Next time put your wrist into it."

She picked up the plate and walked it to the trash. "So that's where he learned that from."

Petrosky scowled at Henry. "Tattletale."

"Tat! Tat!"

Shannon wiped Henry's face and tossed the napkin into the empty pizza box.

Petrosky stood and gave her a hug. "Thanks for coming over to help me pack. I didn't expect you to do all that. I really just wanted to have some dinner and hang out—one last meal with you guys before the big move next week."

"It was fun. Will we see you at the Decantors' barbecue on Saturday?"

Petrosky shrugged. "I'm still deciding."

"Always deciding. Just make up your mind. And make it up in the affirmative because Evie and Henry and I will be there with bells on." She kissed him on the cheek.

"No promises," he said.

"Fine." She rolled her eyes.

Petrosky pulled Henry from his high chair and hugged him too before handing him off to Shannon. "See you, guys."

"Soon."

"You bet."

Petrosky closed the door behind them and watched her through the window as she buckled the kids into the backseat. He walked through the kitchen to his bedroom, the walls newly bare, the bed stripped, the dresser free of any trace that he'd ever existed.

Whatcha think, Julie? He sank onto the bed, the old springs creaking in protest beneath him, and slid the bottle of Jack out from under the mattress. The cap twisted easily—too easily—and the familiar cracking sound made his mouth water. He tipped the bottle back, relishing the liquid burn as it slid down his throat and into his stomach.

The only thing that had any flavor these days. He reached behind the headboard, pulled out his gun, and set it on the empty nightstand. He kept his eyes on it as he took another deep swallow of the booze.

Should we do it in here, or should we go into your room? Got your poster taken down—protected now so it won't get messy.

He could still picture the boys in the poster, preserved in

their youth—like Julie, like Morrison—every smiling, unlined face caught at its picture-perfect best.

But smiles lie.

He took another swig. A numb peace rolled through his brain like a wave.

Petrosky reached for his gun.

Want to know what happens next?
YOUR NEXT BOOK IS WAITING!
Go to MEGHANOFLYNN.COM for your copy
of *REDEMPTION*, the next book
in the Ash Park series.

Sign up for the newsletter at MEGHANOFLYNN.COM
to get information on new book releases and short stories.
No spam, and you can opt out anytime.

OTHER WORKS BY BESTSELLING AUTHOR
MEGHAN O'FLYNN

———

The Ask Park Series:

Famished

Conviction

Repressed

Hidden

Redemption

"Alien Landscape: A Short Story"

"Crimson Snow: A Short Story"

———

DON'T MISS ANOTHER RELEASE!
SIGN UP FOR THE NEWSLETTER AT
MEGHANOFLYNN.COM

ABOUT THE AUTHOR

Meghan O'Flynn is the bestselling author of the Ash Park series —including *Famished*, *Conviction*, *Repressed*, *Hidden*, and *Redemption*—and has penned a number of short stories including "Alien Landscape" and "Crimson Snow." Her husband now believes her story that she used a machete to hack down the bush out front "for research" (jokes on him), her children think her machete-wielding skills are kinda lame, and her dog fell asleep during the whole bush-hacking ordeal, so striking fear into the hearts of others in person might not be Meghan's thing. You can find out more about that on Meghan's Facebook page along with more on her books.

And if you want the whole package—trailers, special offers, novel updates, the works—sign up for Meghan's newsletter at meghanoflynn.com. Absolutely no spam, ever, because spam sucks. But reviews do not suck, so head over to your favorite book site and let them know what you thought about this novel. Rumor has it that reviews are protective against medieval weapons, too. So there's that.

Connect with Meghan!

meghanoflynn.com
meghan@meghanoflynn.com